BRIDGE BETWEEN STARS

Jennifer Leigh

ISBN: 979-8-9909615-0-0

E-PUB ISBN: 979-8-9909615-1-7

Cover Design by INKBookDesign

CONTENTS

Trigger Warning

W hile *Bridge Between Stars* is a young adult fantasy novel that focuses on self discovery, love, and redemption, there are potential triggers woven into the book. Topics include sexual abuse, child abuse, child loss, miscarriage, violence, torture, and suicidal ideation.

If you are having thoughts of ending your life, please don't and call 988. You are so worth it.

If you suspect child abuse in any form, do not hesitate. Please call 911 or your state's child abuse hotline. Children are worth every second of our time.

To those who are still healing

1

ELORA

I twisted my hands over and over. Scents of stale, day-old coffee and doughnuts permeated the police station. The officer sat in his gray, aged cubicle across from me, leaving little privacy. I did not catch his name while he took my statement. It was the same statement I gave six years ago, but he did not seem to hear me or even take in my presence. Fluorescent lights above me blinked several times, their static annoying every inch of my body. The officer did not appear fit enough to chase down criminals. It was such a stereotype, but I had seen police officers I wouldn't mind arresting me. This one was the stereotypical image of the 5-O.

"Are all your law enforcers so inadequate? Is he distracted?" Peter asked with a hint of amusement.

My Peter Pan, my shadow. He was my best secret, my angel, and sometimes the devil sitting on my shoulder. Truthfully, I did not know who he was. He began speaking in my mind one day, shortly before I graduated from high school. There was no way I could tell anyone—not that anyone would hear me—because they would think I was crazy. I would be okay sitting in a padded room for the rest of my life because my shadow was the only one who truly knew me. But therein was the issue: I couldn't see him, and I desperately wanted him to see me. I desired others to see me as well. It was simple things I wanted, such as someone's face brightening up when they saw me, or someone to text me, *How are you?*

I laughed inwardly while keeping my face straight in front of Officer—it doesn't matter what his name is. He couldn't remember mine when it was on file in front of him.

"Not all, but he definitely fits the bill," I replied to Peter.

A TV mounted in the right corner of the office flickered due to poor reception. *"Reports have just come that Russia and Iran have broken their cease-fire agreement,"* the reporter said. Flashes of mobs and desperate families running in the streets flared on the screen. It distracted me for a moment, watching an inevitable war unfold. They may write today in the history books. This world was always at war. It was only a matter of time until America became involved. Maybe WWIII would finally happen. Street prophets holding their signs, *'The end is near,"* could celebrate. I gave them credit, though, because they were probably right.

My work clothes clung to my sticky skin. It had been ten hours since I put them on that morning. All I wanted to do was give this statement again and go home to take it all off. The officer's chair swiveled and creaked to where I could see his badge. Officer Reuben was his name! He grimaced while reading the file, and I felt what he was thinking. Years ago, I was cleared of being a suspect, but it still seemed surreal that four men would collapse to their deaths around me.

They had chased me on the night of my graduation. All I wanted was to feel like an eighteen-year-old at a party. Not that I really knew any of them. Somehow, I was always an afterthought, someone nobody could fully see. For some reason that night, they'd wanted me. I was pretty sure it was the drugs. I never knew my classmates were such hard hitters, passing around copious amounts of powder and strips for their tongues. Peter kept begging that night to leave, but I drowned out his voice with shots. I never really drank before, but that night I wanted to, like I was making up for lost time.

The next thing I knew, I was running through the woods. Too many times, I stumbled when they came after me. I still had the scars on my legs. Peter's voice screamed through me to keep running. I felt his panic in my blood. But it would not make me go any faster. My black, velvet hot pants rode up on me, and its matching spaghetti string tank gave these men too much access. As I ran,

I guilted myself over for wearing something provocative. I had just wanted to be seen for once. My studded choker tightened around my throbbing throat as I gasped for air. The moment I turned around to see how far I had gotten from them, I tripped over a rock, landing face first. A burning sensation erupted on my face as blood trickled down. I hoped being a bloody mess would make me less desirable. But it did not.

Surrounded. His name was Kev. Dirty Kev. The one who kept records of his home runs on and off the field unbuckled his pants. His friend, Dylan, held down my arms, laughing that he was next. The other two stood to the side, taking pictures, waiting to see every part of me. I screamed for help, and Dylan clamped his hand over my mouth. A silent demand. Inside, I kept screaming for someone to save me. Nobody came. I felt like a sacrifice to their ritual. Darkness surrounded me, and my vision blurred. Kev's body pressed onto me, and then he pulled back, shrieking. Dylan's hand went ice cold, and I saw him drop to the ground like a safe. Kev stood, the color from his face leeched, and then he fell to his knees, choking on something. The other two tried to run, but they dropped just like Dylan and Kev. I did not know what happened, and I had been in too much shock to move.

"So, you see, Officer Reuben, my statement does not differ from the one I gave to this" —I looked around, observing the paint peeling from the walls and the water stains on the ceiling tiles— "fine establishment, six years ago."

He shuffled his belt, and I cringed. "Yes, Miss"—he squinted at the print on the file—"Addison, Elora Addison." His plump lips twisted. "We needed to get another statement before we close this case." He leaned forward, suddenly aware of my presence. "Victims often suffer from memory loss, and it could take years for them to piece together the trauma they experienced."

I blinked. Of course, he was right. I was a social worker at a hospital. I should know that.

Elora, are you okay? Peter whispered. Icy shards pricked me, sending red flags to my wingman.

"Thank you, officer, but I have nothing new to report."

Officer Reuben looked at the name on the file again. "Addison? It's a beautiful street in Philadelphia. You should check it out in the spring when the flowers bud on the trees."

"Indeed."

I grabbed my canvas purse and shuffled out of the station. Addison. I gave myself that name when I was younger. I refused to take any last names from my foster families or any names my case worker had suggested. But after one visit to Addison Street with a potential foster family, I chose that name. They were a beautiful family, though they did not select me as their foster child. I wish they had. It was no better than being the baby dropped off at the fire station. Cliché, I know. My case worker told me my DNA never matched anyone else's in the country. I pretty much dropped out of thin air. I wanted to be more than the lost foster child. Sometimes when I stared at the night sky, I really believed I was more. Then the days would drag on, pulling me into their mundane existence.

"I know something is wrong, Lor." Peter's rich, dark voice rattled me. *"Talk to me."*

"Just a sad reminder," I replied.

Then I broke our connection for a few minutes, blaring whatever screamo music was left on my playlist. Peter always felt my mood shifting. Sometimes it annoyed me, but I invited it anyway. He was my friend, my confidant. My only.

"I would rather hear you sing. You never sing anymore," he said, restoring our connection.

A part of me felt guilty. Reminders of my sad, pathetic life embarrassed me. Yet, he had never made me feel ashamed. After I revved up my car, I came back to Peter. I always did.

"There's nothing good to sing about," I snapped. A vibration buzzed down our thread. *"Sorry, I am just exhausted and want to put everything behind me. Plus, I'm hangry."*

"Hangry?" His laugh smoothed over my skin. *"What is it tonight? Chinese?"*

"You know me too well, Peter Pan."

Since we started mind-speaking, he refused to tell me his real name or where he came from. Maybe I was crazy, but at least he "got" me. Before Peter, I had no friends. Well, sometimes I did, but it was all superficial. Surface type of friends who were cordial but never invited me anywhere or called me. I have been on dates where Peter would "know" if the guy was a complete loser or to go for it.

Spoiler alert, they're all losers.

"I'm getting Chinese. What are you going to eat?"

He cleared his throat. *"I guess some fish and greens."*

"You mean a salad?"

"When you say Chinese food, do you mean sad people food?"

"I hate you." I laughed. *"Chinese food never made anyone sad. Your meal sounds sad. That poor fish had to die to be in your boring meal."*

His deep laugh washed over me again. *"Chinese food sounds so rich. You have to eat lighter if you are going to keep up with your training."*

"I swear I will go back," I said coolly.

Two years after my attack, I began Krav Maga classes a few towns over. I swore never to be a victim again. Every hook punch and elbow strike I perfected felt as if I took my power back. Those classmates might be dead, but their voices, hands, and taunts about what they would do to my body clung to me as if they were alive. I had no clue how they died. In fact, I did not wish it on them. If anything, I would have given them mercy. Peter, on the other hand, believes it was cosmic justice. And that was where we agreed to disagree. It was not the first time I'd seen death. Someone else died who was supposed to be a protector of mine. We foster children only take what is given. We have no choice about who will love us or protect us.

I'd tried asking Peter questions to piece together who he was and where he's from, but I'd always come up short. He knew where I lived, sort of. He knew I lived in New Jersey, right across the river bordering Philadelphia. Once in a while, I went to the goth club by myself in Philly, even though Peter cautioned me not to go alone. I still didn't understand how he could see what I saw, and I had yet to see him. He wouldn't describe himself to me, so had I let my imagination conjure up an image of him—a dark, brooding man with a vicious smile, secrets to tell, and stars in his eyes.

I loved going to punk rock shows as much as I loved getting lost in the heavy bass sounds of the goth club. One night, I dressed in my black and white plaid skirt with studs and fishnet stockings, adding heavy dark makeup. I didn't like precise eye makeup. Black smudges on my eyes and dark eyeliner agreed with me. Pale blonde hair fell to my waist, tipped in electric blue. I had danced the night away at the club, which had shut down since then—definitely due to a health code violation. I had used the bathroom there and was glad I was up to date on my vaccinations. That night, I lost myself in the beat, the smoke from the dry ice, and felt Peter's cool breath on my skin. An invisible hand skimmed down my arms and face. When my breath hitched, Peter's connection went flat. He never confessed it was him. I wished he would do it again.

"I think I'll just get my usual," I said as I pulled up to my apartment building.

"Chow mein and dumplings," Peter scoffed. *"It does not sound pleasing."*

Just by him saying that, I knew he was not American. Jingling my keys outside the door, my breath left me. Violet skies rolled up like a scroll, crossing over bright orange hues and bringing stars into focus. Stars were the most beautiful thing to look upon but a terror when they fell. Peter paused. He was such a mystery. He loved it when I was outside in the sun or the rain, but when it became dusk, he sighed—like it offended him at the last lights canvassing the earth.

I entered my cheap apartment, grateful to be home. It was just a red brick building with a few apartments on the inside and where my neighbors kept to themselves. I kept my apartment plain looking mostly. As a girl, I knew I was supposed to decorate. But as a former foster kid, I had no pictures of family to hang or an urge to make the place permanent. I'd never felt at home wherever I'd been. Plain white walls and bad lighting greeted me, except for a string of lights with interchangeable colors above a simple gray couch to watch TV.

I enjoyed watching fantasy shows and explaining everything to Peter. He got a kick out of it. I had a mental image of him eating popcorn while watching TV through my eyes. Honestly, I found it sweet because he saw things like it was the first time. I always fast-forwarded the love scenes. He never asked why, and sometimes I wondered if it made him uncomfortable or if there was a silent understanding between us. I wouldn't even watch simple kisses or make-out scenes. Dragons, explosions, and political intrigue were my forte.

"Can you turn away? I need to change." I asked him.

He cleared his throat again. *"Of course, my eyes are closed."*

I stripped off my slacks and blouse in my bare bedroom and hung my Presbyterian Hospital badge on the wall. Flannel shorts and a cropped band t-shirt gave me so much relief after a crazy day.

"You have not been to a punk show in a while." I knew he observed my band t-shirt.

"It's kind of hard to rage against authority when you work a nine-to-five," I said, pulling up my hair into a messy bun. *"Plus, I enjoy making money. Capitalism for the win."*

He coughed, and I felt him groan.

"Are you sick again?"

"What? No, I'm much better."

"You had me worried there for a while. I didn't hear from you for a few days, and then you came back and sounded like you were dying." I said, plopping onto the couch.

A phantom smile curled that I could not see but could feel. *"I always bounce back. Don't worry."*

"But I do worry."

Peter's voice quieted. *"So do I."*

I lowered my eyes and crossed my legs on the couch. *"I...uh...I have to order my dinner. Hold on."* Peter listened as I ordered my sad food, likely laughing to himself. *"Delivery guy will be here in twenty minutes."*

I got up to pour myself the unsweetened tea I brewed earlier in the week. An awkward pause between us made me feel anxious. Had I said too much? Of course, I worried. Any good person would worry. I was kidding myself. I worried because I cared. I cared about a shadow, a ghost, someone I'd never met. He knew this, yet he revealed almost nothing. Sometimes I joked with him about who he might be, and I could tell he skirted on the edge of wanting to tell me everything and retreating to where it was safe. Wherever that was.

Minutes passed, and we did not speak. It was a record for us. A warm heat crept up my back, pressing down. It felt whole. Safe. A breath caressed my neck, and I shuddered.

"Peter, is that you?"

It vanished, and Peter's presence grew still. I sighed and looked at the clock. It had been a half hour since I'd ordered the food. *What was taking so long?* I realized I forgot to give them the code to get into my apartment building. I picked up the phone to call to make sure the delivery guy knew how to get in. But before I dialed the number, a knock came.

I nearly lost my breath. A tall, dashing delivery man stood at my door. His eyes were an ice green. His hair a faux hawk dyed the color of red and orange, like a flame. He had a cute button nose that I just wanted to boop. But that would be weird.

"I...I've never seen you before." I could not believe I was stumbling over my words.

His quirky smile and dimples made my heart flutter. "I just got this job to help me in my senior year of college." His deep voice sounded so much like Peter's. Like rich velvet, but with a different tone, more upbeat. It was nice. We stared at each other for a few seconds while I fixated on the curve of his lips, his silver labret ring pierced on the bottom, my mouth drying out.

"Jersey or Philly?" I asked.

"Philly, all the way." His smile made my knees buckle.

"Hold on, I think I have some cash for a tip."

I noticed him peering in through the crack of my bedroom door, but I forgave that. His round chin poked through my front door, slinking back once he heard me coming. I wanted to take a picture of him just in case I never saw him again. *I'm such a weirdo.* I just wanted to look at him after he left and allow the butterflies in my belly to fly out of control.

"So, uh..." I pulled at the top of my messy bun. "Will this be your route from now on?"

He let out a breathy laugh and rubbed his chin. "Will you be ordering more often?"

Oh, he'd flirted with me. I recognized this. "Y-yes," I stuttered, handing him his tip, and he gave me my food.

With a wink of his eye, he angled his head at me. "It was nice to meet you, Elora. I'm Mike. I'll see you again soon."

How did he know my name? Oh yeah, my name was on the receipt. He jogged downstairs in his skinny jeans and studded belt, and I felt so creepy watching him. Peter remained silent.

"What about him?" I asked, trying to break the awkward silence.

A few moments went by, and I thought he was done talking. As soon as I turned on the TV and twisted my chopsticks into the Chow mein, Peter finally answered.

"Not him. Not ever." Then he stopped speaking for the rest of the night.

2

ELORA

I was lost again, in between this nightmare and waking up. Everything felt real. First, I saw a man with a smile much like Mike's underneath a brown cowl. His smile brightened, yet the rest of his face remained hidden. Each time I dreamt of this, I inched closer to remove the hood, but I was immediately pulled somewhere dark where I was cast in a white glow. People shouted in the background, but I couldn't make out the words. I tried to speak, but the metallic tang of blood filled my mouth, choking every word. Something sharp trembled in my hand, coated in blood. I didn't appear frightened or stunned by the blood from my mouth. Stars flickered all around me, the ones I wished on when I was younger. Gold with green and violet flames grew so hot that stars burned out, imploding. My wishes were gone in an instant, and my bloody mouth could not make new ones. Everything became pitch black, and I was utterly alone.

A voice filtered in the darkness, purring, seizing my breath. I froze. This is what genuine fear felt like, the one voice that was a brand upon my heart. *"Shh, pretty flower, you don't want to wake the rest, do you?"* That voice alone shook me to my core, and I screamed.

A dark silhouette of a man glittered like faded stars. Three crescent moons spun on his forehead, only faintly illuminating the blue of his eyes. His dark, warm hand pulled me from the pitch, rescuing me from this hellscape. He then tapped me on the chest, and I lurched out of my dream, gasping for air.

"Lor? Lor? Answer me." Peter must have been trying to shake me out of this nightmare.

Sweat beaded across my forehead, and my throat felt like sandpaper. I gulped down the water sitting on my nightstand and then pulled the covers I'd kicked off back onto the bed.

"I'm here. I'm okay." My voice shook.

"Was it that dream again?" Peter asked, his voice reassuring me I was safe.

"Yes," I choked. There was nothing I wanted to discuss about the dream. Thankfully, he couldn't see those.

"Peter?"

"Lor?"

"I wish you were here." My throat tightened. *"I wish I could feel you hold me."*

I felt him become wary, assessing me, choosing the path of least resistance. Tears trickled down, and I curled up in my blankets, holding myself to keep from falling apart. Who was I kidding? He would never admit he touched me in the club or wrapped his warmth around me in the kitchen. That voice in my nightmare repeated itself over and over. Every time I heard it, it unraveled me. I wished I had run away before everything happened. But I was only thirteen, and I needed a home. I had let it happen, not only for a home but for Emily—wherever she was. I wondered if she knew what I'd done to keep her safe.

A phantom arm caged me in, holding me tight. Safe. Heat bloomed in my chest. I felt his breath, his knuckles grazing my hips. Tears flowed again. I wanted it to be real, to have him here with me, not just a shadow. I leaned into his warmth, savoring his touch. His chest heaved in and out from behind me, slightly trembling. I felt an intense heat coming from where his heart would be. A fire blazed in my chest—the core of my being— as if in response. At that moment, I questioned nothing. Peter was there with me. A sweet, feather-like kiss pressed against my cheek. This was more than I'd ever done with anyone.

"I see you, Elora; I've always seen you," he whispered.

After the incident on graduation night, I'd shut down. Something about the violence my classmates inflicted on me had caused this oily feeling inside. Years later, when I started to see the sun again, I realized it was shame. On the surface, I knew I'd done nothing wrong, but there must have been something disgusting about me to only be wanted for that. During that dark period, Peter and I had grown close. His humor and listening ear helped me feel like I had someone out there who cared for me, helping me laugh away my pain. But there was only so much distance we could close between us.

His hair dangled along my face, breathing uneven. Rational thought eddied from my mind as his fingers tangled in my hair, hovered over my face, his breathing so close. Soft caresses feathered along my jaw. This was real. He was real. And he was the only one I ever really wanted to open up to, to expose every little thing inside that pathetic heart of mine. My lips parted for him. I yielded my pitiful heart, though it had been his for years. His hands felt strong, sure, as he held me close. It was in this place that I felt safer than I had ever been. This was home. I'd never had a real home, but there with him, I belonged.

"Peter." I cried softly.

All the words I'd kept to myself suddenly wanted to crash onto him like a tempest. He had to know how I felt. He could feel everything, but he had not said one word. Maybe I was crazy and reading into it.

Before I said another word, his motions stopped in their tracks.

"I'm sorry, Lor, I can't." He disappeared, leaving a cold space.

I sat upright, pulling the blankets to my chest, wishing for him to return. I wanted him to tell me he'd made a mistake. For the rest of the night, I waited, choking on my sobs until exhaustion took over.

***

It was days since I'd heard from Peter, but I didn't exactly go after him either. Instead, I planned to get my "sad people" food and hopefully invite Mike in. Sure enough, Mike stood in my doorway with Chow mein and dumplings, smiling. I couldn't get enough of watching his icy green eyes gleam as we talked about music. My little round table was just big enough for the two of us to eat but small enough to close our distance. At one point, he gave me the last dumpling using his chopsticks. It was brief, but I forgot about Peter, just living in the moment. Chopsticks slipped from his hands, bits of rice scattering onto the floor. He stood in his black skinny jeans, black and white checkered belt, and chains to get a paper towel. I hardly remembered what I wore until he was looking at my bare knee, wiping up the mess. I opted for torn black leggings and a hot pink shirt that barely reached my waistline.

His eyes traveled from my toes to my face. "Your eyes are incredible. Where did you get contacts to make them look so real?" Mike asked as he threw away the paper towel.

"Well," I bit my lip. "This is the real color of my eyes."

"Lilac. Amazing," he said with a half-smile. His finger grazed my jawline as though he was going to lean forward and kiss me. I'd never really been kissed. Fear lanced through my chest. What if this was all he wanted? What if I was really nothing except a body? Instead, he reached for a fortune cookie. He opened his and chuckled. "Fitting."

"What does it say?" I asked, grabbing one for myself.

"It says, 'You will meet a nice stranger.'" His devilish grin took my breath away.

My cheeks flushed. "Do you want to watch something?"

"Honestly, I don't," he said, running his fingers through his faux hawk. "I've binged enough TV this week."

My eyes focused on the beige linoleum floor in my eat-in kitchen. "I guess you want to go then."

"On the contrary, we can just talk." He motioned his chin toward the couch.

I enjoyed hearing him talk anyway; he sounded similar to… no, I couldn't think of him right then. He'd left. I didn't. I moved our drinks to the side table next to my couch, and Make and I sat pretty close together. It was getting dark, so I turned on my rainbow string lights. Mike rambled about his college classes as purple, pink, and yellow lights shimmered over his face. A proud philosophy major with his sights set on law school. I tried making jokes about him being my personal Aristotle, but he was so impassioned about Voltaire that he missed my humor.

Mike leaned back, his hands resting against his head. "Voltaire was the voice of the French Age of Enlightenment. He criticized slavery, advocated the separation of church and state. America did not even come to that conclusion until much, much later. He was ahead of his time. If only I could amount to someone like him. I remember Les Delices in Switzerland. There were so many plants and herbs that the gardeners found it hard to keep up. But nothing impressed me more than his study." Mike's eyes widened. "I mean, I remember visiting when I studied abroad my sophomore year."

I barked out a laugh. "I was going to say...it sounded like you knew him personally. I'm just a social worker. Overworked and underpaid, as you can see with my simple apartment."

It was then that I became aware of how bare my kitchen was. Old white cabinet doors with handles that had not been replaced since the 1940s, a stove that might as well have been from that era too. No dishwasher, which I did not care about because I barely used dishes.

"Please," he said with an edge of annoyance. "I find social workers key to any growing society. The more we grow, the needs increase." Mike leaned in closer to me. "It might be a thankless job, but you are getting people to where they need to be so they can take the next step."

His warm, honeyed words coated my tired heart. My eyes flicked to the open shades, watching the sun blaze its last rays over the budding tree beside my window. "Some days, I know social work is not where I am supposed to be."

He leaned closer to me, brushing my shoulder with his. "Then why did you study it for six years?"

"I was actually on a fast-track program and finished my bachelor's and master's in four years." I gave a thumbs up, grinning from ear to ear, feeling like a complete idiot.

"Impressive." His breath was close to my ear.

"But I think I chose it because..." I was about to open up to him, something I'd only ever reserved for Peter. But he'd left. He'd ghosted me, but Mike was there, and he sounded interested. "I was a foster child, dealt a lot of bad cards with crappy case workers. I just thought I could do better. So, now I work at Presbyterian Hospital."

His fingers pushed back my hair behind my ear. His voice lowered. "And you have, simply by showing up." He flicked his eyes to the analog clock on the stove across from us. "It's getting late. I have to wake up super early for my TA class."

"TA? Now that's impressive."

Mike chuckled as he held my hand while I walked him to the door. My heart fluttered like a trapped bird in a cage during the awkward moment when we stood in the open doorway. Movies were always like this. He looked at me intently while I waited for him to make a move. I always told myself I would not give in to any man. I would not be a victim again. But Mike's lip ring glinted in the blinking hall lights, and his fingers ran through my hair. Besides Peter, I had not gotten this far. This deep. After all, this was the first time we were alone, yet there was an undeniable heat rising between us. Something felt wild, untamed, and dangerous. But I wanted to explore it, fill the void Peter left behind. Mike had to see how miserable I was underneath, inviting some stranger into my home—a bare home without any trace of a life worth living.

He drew back and let my hair fall to my sides. "I will call you later."

Mike turned the corner to head down the steps. He must have sensed the pointless, shadowed girl. Who needed that baggage? Before I had the chance to close the door and drown myself in self-pity, he rushed around the corner, pulled me by my waist, and crashed his lips onto mine. My whole body lit on fire. It felt ravenous, like he was starving. After a few minutes of relentless kissing, he drew back again, breathless.

"As I said," he said roughly, trailing his fingers down my side. "I will call you later."

I might as well have been a puddle at his feet because even after he left, I stood in the doorway, stunned.

3
ELORA

Two days later and I had not heard from Mike or Peter. Ghosted again. It stung deeply with Peter because we had been close for six years. Every night since he'd left, I had cried myself to sleep, yearning to hear his voice. Yet, Mike was so new, and I could physically see him. I enjoyed hearing his passion and, honestly, how he kissed me. Bypassing all the darkness hidden deep inside me, he lit me aflame. Still, my thoughts circled back to Peter. I needed to get over my pride and check in with him.

After an afternoon meeting to find a nursing home for an elderly man with dementia, I headed back to my desk that other social workers shared. Marla, a middle-aged black woman, who had been doing God's work for too many years, brightened as she saw me. She patted up her hair to keep her thick gray tresses from unfurling. Nobody ever really lit up by my presence, so this had to be a special occasion.

Dark roses, deep red, almost black, sat in a green vase on my desk.

Marla grinned at me widely. Her round brown eyes sparkled underneath her black-rimmed glasses. "Someone must have been very good or very bad."

Marla rested her hand on her belly and chuckled while her perfectly manicured fingers caressed the edges of the rose petals. When she laughed, I swore it was the definitive sound of joy. I have never been given flowers or anything, really. I wasn't sure how to react. A little white card was stuck inside the flowers monogrammed with the letter E in silver ink. Inside the card were two tickets for tonight to see my favorite punk band, Dereliction Friction. *"Thanks for showing up. I'll pick you up at 7."*

My heart warmed, and I knew everyone else saw my blushing face because of their ogling eyes. I tried to hide my flushed cheeks behind the desk. Mike really got me. After spending one evening with him, he knew I favored dark flowers over vibrant ones. He must have pieced it together from my affinity to wear black smudged makeup and, of course, the music that would make my elderly patients faint. There was no way I wanted to question that Mike assumed I had time to see my favorite band. Of course, he knew I'd make time for that; he loved them too. Well played, Mike. Even in that moment of happiness, I drifted back to Peter and finally bit the bullet.

"Peter, why are you avoiding me?"

I felt the static of our connection open before going flat.

"I know you're there; I know you can see everything." Still no answer.

"What did I do wrong? Why did you leave? After six years, Peter...you got too close, and you ran."

I glared at my flowers, wishing he would feel the vacant spot he left behind. *"You see these flowers? Someone gave them to me. ME. What have you done? I left myself wide open, and you left me."*

No answer.

"Fine, Peter. Be that way. Tonight, I will enjoy this date with Mike. His kiss meant something, and he's still here."

"Lor. I said not him, not ever," he snapped. Then the connection went dead.

***

Dressed to kill, I smudged my black makeup, hiked up my lime green skirt with a studded belt hanging on the sides, and donned a ripped-up black t-shirt with suspenders. I left my hair to hang loose over my pale arms. It's a wonder I have red blood underneath my skin. It was also a miracle I never burned under the sun. Save for the few freckles that danced across my cheeks and nose.

I slid on my black boots that went above my calves and heard Mike beeping the horn. He seemed to be in too much of a rush to come to my door. I looked into my apartment remembering all the lonely nights and felt tonight would be the start of something new. When the door clicked shut behind me, I felt one chapter ended and another had begun.

His hair lay more limp tonight rather than spiked up, and he cracked his half smile at me as I got in the car. He was surprisingly dressed, almost like me, wearing green plaid pants with chains and a black shirt. He pressed a kiss to my hand. "It's like we already have a sixth sense with each other."

"It would seem so," I said, leaning in like an idiot. Not him. Not Ever. Just for one night, I needed Peter out of my head so I could live. I pulled back and buckled myself in. No, Peter, not tonight.

We drove across the bridge and made it onto Broad Street amid the traffic on I-95 and Aramingo Ave. It was still dark, being in the beginning of spring. Groups of people hung outside the bar smoking cigarettes, leaving their nine-to-five jobs behind in arrays of Mohawks, studs, and leather. He led me into the dive bar like a gentleman and into the chaos. The band began performing, and people swarmed into the mosh pit. Energy filled me with the need to fight. I let go of his hand and let myself be swallowed in the pit. I didn't mind the bruises or getting hit; it made me feel alive. As many gave, so did I. With every hit I gave, I imagined all my peers who rejected me when I was little, all my classmates in high school who refused to acknowledge my existence. There were other things I hit for, but I tried to remove their faces and focused on my fury.

Guitars thrashed, and the lead singer screamed non-conformist poetry. These were my people. Angry, tired, and yearning. Mike jumped in too. At first, I thought he was coming to protect me, but he jumped to the top of the stage and flung himself onto the crowd, body surfing. Many hands grabbed and pushed me until I was in the front. My fingers traced the edge of the sticky stage, locking eyes with the singer. Sweat dripped from his silken black hair, and he lowered the mic. I did not sing anymore, but I would scream.

"I am me; we are we; we do not bow down to your authority!"

My scream were nails on a chalkboard. He staggered as I screamed his lyrics like a soul in distress. Because that's who I was. Right here, is where I felt freedom from the confines of depression. Was I depressed? I had not thought of it until this moment. I was preoccupied with working and Mike, that I didn't look into myself inwardly. For a split second, I evaluated myself and came to a conclusion. I was depressed. Too long, I treaded a line of being sad and happy and having this gray medium. But at the end of the day, sadness would win. Being heartbroken didn't help. I miss him. I miss his… Mike's feral eyes bore into me briefly before he dove back into the pit. The singer took back the mic, choking on his lyrics, chilled over the echo of my voice. I wanted to disappear. I made myself known for a moment, where people saw me as the ghost I was. Shame burned behind my eyes, and I wanted to drown. As soon as the singer gained composure, he never looked my way again, as if I had already been forgotten.

Red and orange lights swirled above me, and suddenly, an ache consumed me. I was happy to be here, but somehow, I felt alone. Mike was busy diving and moshing. The lead singer bled from smashing his face into the mic, stirring the crowd into a deeper frenzy. Someone elbowed me in the jaw, catching me off guard. I almost expected Peter to whisper to me to get somewhere safe, but he didn't. My jaw flared with searing pain. It hurt so much, but not as much as Peter's absence. Maybe he never saw me.

Drops of blood gathered on my swollen lip. I left Mike to his devices and walked to the bar, pushing through the mob of lost souls. A bartender with unruly red hair greeted me with a stern face. She must have had a rough night, so I made my order simple.

"Two shots of Tequila, please." I turned to the crowd for a second, trying to catch Mike's eye because I needed him to see me.

She flicked her eyes at my jaw. "Ice pack too?"

"Yeah…that would be great." I tried to ignore the pain, but the throbbing intensified now that someone else noticed it.

The bartender slid the shots and lime wedges to me, but I never used the lime; I liked the challenge. To be honest, I barely drank. It felt like one of those nights I needed to numb everything. I chugged them down too quickly, and as soon as I stood up, I felt the effects course through my body. Drops of tequila felt like fire on my lips. She handed me the ice pack, and I found a spot on a ratty old black leather sofa against a brick wall.

"Lor, please stop. You can still leave," Peter begged, his voice coming out of nowhere.

"Screw you. You left," I snapped. Liquid courage kicked in.

"There's so much I can't explain. I'm sorry. I really am."

"Please." I scoffed. *"You can't even tell me your name. You said you saw me, really saw me. And you left me. I really wanted it to be you."* Tears stung my eyes. It could never be him. He was just a voice.

"I... can't tell you my name because..."

"I really don't care anymore."

"Oh, I think you do." He sucked in a breath. *"That was careless of me. I'm sorry."*

"Six years, Peter. Six. I almost told you I love you, and then you ghosted me. But it dawned on me... I can't say I love you to someone when I don't know their name."

"I was afraid of this."

"Afraid of what?!"

He breathed in deeply, *"Be careful with Mike. When you get home tonight, break it off with him, or you will never hear from me again."*

Sobs wrenched free from my body. I didn't want to be told what to do, and I didn't want to lose Peter either. If this was love, then it always leaves, it always disappoints.

"Don't do that to me, don't make me choose."

"I do this because I love you. I am not trying to be some possessive jerk. He is no good."

His words slammed into my chest. I dreamt of hearing them in a better way, not as manipulation. Often, I fantasized about someone saying those words under starry nights, flurries of snow, where the world stopped. Nobody ever said they loved me before, and this just hurt. Peter might love me, but he left me at my most vulnerable, and he's only confessing now because I found someone else.

"Love doesn't leave." This time I cut off the connection when Mike found me drowning in my tears.

"What's wrong?" Mike asked, nursing a bloody nose.

I shook my head, not wanting to explain anything. I wanted to kiss him again and smother the broken pieces of my heart. So, I pulled him onto the couch and sat in his lap, claiming his lips. My own lips screamed in pain, but I didn't care. I wanted the pain, the distraction. He flattered me with flowers, with this date, but I somehow still felt empty. I wanted to believe he really gets me and sees me, but if Peter truly didn't, then who could? He sat next to me for the rest of the night, kissing me, whispering sweet things into my ear. But I couldn't believe a single thing he said. Love is a trap, and I was just biding my time.

4

ELORA

We dated for a month before I began to notice little things that screamed red flags. I ignored them, believing this was all there was. If fate gave this person to me, then I needed to make the best of it regardless of how lonely it felt. Mike disappeared days at a time and then returned to me without an explanation. His texts became cold and off putting. He seemed irritated and on edge every time he was with me, like he was annoyed with a chore he had to get done and over with. Even after I caught him looking at slender blondes with blue eyes on his phone, I stuffed my hurt down, convincing myself I deserved no better.

Mike took me to hole in the wall places for Chinese and Mexican. Each bite he devoured seemed like it was the first time he tasted such decadence. One night, I took him to the state's planetarium in Trenton, and he shifted uncomfortably in his seat. Every spiral of the galaxy illuminated on the screen made him sink deeper into his seat until his backside was inches from the floor. He brushed it off, joking that he was afraid of the dark, but his eyes remained unfocused and his hand trembled in mine. We walked through the rest of the museum in awkward silence. Something heavy hung over him, and I began to think I had done something wrong. However, he stared at a painting of Mont Blanc. Its jagged snowy peaks towered over a quiet town of France. People bustled through the wintry streets, drinking at cafés. Something in him became pained as he burned a hole staring at this painting. It somehow felt personal for him.

As he stood face to face with this painting, I searched the local towns of France on my phone and found that Les Delices could view these peaks from Switzerland. A part of me felt guilty tearing his gaze from this painting, but we had to move on. I shook his shoulder, mumbling my pleas, and his face hardened while turning to me. The corner of his lips twitched, his nostrils flaring. He ran his fingers roughly through my hair, but when he looked deep into my eyes, a look of disgust rippled across his face. Mike pushed himself away from me and stormed out of the exhibit.

After the odd museum visit, Mike was increasingly distant. Enough to keep me at arm's length but not close enough to touch. Was this what I traded Peter's voice for? He began handing Chinese food to me as a delivery boy, not a boyfriend. I didn't understand what happened, and I was too afraid to ask. I was afraid he would say I was damaged goods. It was hard to stomach eating my food while he stared into space, tapping his oddly black tinged finger on my table. Still, I tried to salvage whatever this was and planned to see a battle of the bands show in Philly. Yet again, he brought me Chinese food and pushed it across the table as if he needed to get this date over with.

"Mike," my voice was barely a whisper. "Is this it?"

He jumped from his seat and made an attempt to flee, stopping short of turning the knob. His hair was more disheveled than normal, shadows darkening his face. I set my chopsticks down, my insides turning to ice as I fumbled my way to the door. His hand felt like fire in mine. Flits of amber I had never seen before flashed in his eyes.

"Tell me what's wrong," I pleaded, lacing my fingers with his.

"No," he said coldly, tightening his grip on me.

There were boundaries of his I wanted to cross, but I needed to respect them. If he did not want to talk about it, I had to let it go. Peter hadn't let me in either—and look where that had gotten us. My thoughts spun out of control, believing Mike was breaking up with me or had gotten sick of me. I didn't want to be thrown away so soon. I wanted to savor having someone a little longer. Mike ripped his hand from mine and plopped himself on the couch. The temperature in the room rose to a stifling heat. Sweat beaded across his forehead as he rested his chin on his fists.

I started to speak, and he interrupted me. "I have a lot on my mind. A monster tore my family apart, and now..."

His eyes froze like green chips of ice. A part of me wanted to hold him, but a heaviness landed on my shoulders. Lights flickered as if there were a storm raging, but the bright evening sun streamed across my beige carpets. His jaw clenched, and I tried to hold his hand again. Mike gripped my wrist tightly, his nails digging into my skin. My heart jumped into my throat. Those men were holding me down again.

"Mike, please stop," I begged, tears stinging my eyes. He dug harder as he took his other hand and pressed it on the center of my chest. Flashbacks of Dirty Kev and his crew buzzed under my skin as though Mike was setting those monsters loose from my chains to take what was theirs. "No..." My voice wobbled. I thought he was going to take me right there on the couch, finish what Dirty Kev couldn't. This past month, he never made a move past kissing—which I was glad for because I thought I would never be ready for the rest. I wanted to fight back. All that Krav Maga I learned over the past few years eddied from my mind. "Please don't."

"It's all because of you," he growled.

"What?" His hand pressed deeper into my muscle. "This isn't you. This isn't you."

Mike blinked, his face softening. He gasped as if he were underwater for a while and let go of my wrist. Nail marks circled my wrist, and numbness washed over me. I hated myself, this skin I was trapped in. Mike bracketed my face gently, his words muffled against my forehead. I knew he apologized profusely, but I could not move or hear him. Was this all I was really good for? Men loved to violate me, to inflict violence. The gentlest hands I had ever known were Peter's, and he had left because I made a choice. The wrong choice. I wished Peter had waited for me on the other end, but he was gone. He had screamed for me to run on graduation night. He had assessed every date I went on like he could see through them. But he was no longer here. Finally, Mike left, and I got up, locking the door behind him.

I stood at the door staring at the white paint, adrenaline surging through me. I braced myself as I saw black edges framing the doorway. My breath hitched, colors from my hanging lights blurred, and my body went limp.

"Peter, come back." My voice strangled as my knees hit the floor.

There was a moment in the middle of the night when I stared out of my open windows and let the night sky soak my room that I felt Peter breathing. I did not say a word—I was too afraid he would disappear again. Shadows encased me. Ever the dark girl. Whatever heat had blazed inside my chest weeks ago was gone. Finally, I accepted it. This was my lot. Unseen. Uncared for. Alone. I sucked back in my tears. Nobody would wipe them away, anyway. Heavy bass sounds of a party down the street boomed at all hours, and I usually hated it. That night, however, I needed it under my skin—to feel something other than the sickness that had rehearsed itself over and over again.

Flurries of "forgive me" texts and emojis lit my lock screen. Was that what men did? Rain fire and scatter ashes and then apologize as if what they'd burned could be whole again? I did not have the luxury of knowing if it were any different.

I texted Mike back. *It's fine.*

***

Heat rose in my chest again, so wild and unruly. I felt like I was on fire. I knew I should have seen a doctor. I worked in a hospital, after all. Three weeks had passed since I'd cut off Mike. My co-workers were annoyed at the overabundance of now-dead flowers he had sent me. They had once been a joy of mine, but I let all the flowers die without looking at the cards. Wilted roses, lilies, and paper whites lined the curved desk, yet I hadn't found the energy to throw them away. Shadows gathered under my eyes, and my body became frail. When was the last time I had eaten? It didn't matter. All I wanted to do was go home and crawl under my blankets. I was too tired, sleeping as soon as I came home but restless at night. Still, the heat in my chest rose, burning me from the inside, yet I kept up with meetings and endless documentation. As a social worker, if you didn't document, it never happened. Marla raked her eyes over me and over the flowers.

Her shoulders slumped, and she set aside the many files in her hands. "Are you okay? You don't seem well."

Sweat ran in rivulets down my chest, and my vision blurred. "I-I feel like I'm on fire."

Marla pressed her hand to my forehead, and her eyes widened. "Good lord, child."

She peered around the corner of the desk, yelling for a nurse to bring a thermometer. I felt the cold press on my forehead, and it felt like forever to get my temperature. Marla and the nurse gasped and yelled for the doctor. I think I heard one of them say my temperature was 115 degrees. I knew that was impossible, so it must have been a fever dream. Doctor Carson's pinched face leeched of color looking at the thermometer. His glasses dropped to the tip of his nose as he stuttered instructions. A flurry of panic abounded in muffles and feet running on the ground while I faded in and out. Fear seized my insides. A fire inside consumed me, and nobody understood why. I was alone, screaming inside as darkness crowded the edges of my mind.

"Lor, I'm here. Be strong. Be strong for me," Peter whispered in the darkness, cutting through the chaos.

I reached out to tug on that thread, his voice. It was too late. The connection died. I kept falling as if I slipped off some precipice into the dark unknown. Swoops of gold and green shimmered in the endless night. Orange and red swirled while blue and silver settled at my knees. Still, it was dark, and I was alone. The shimmer was my only solace that I was still alive, that I hadn't passed into the great unknown. Peter's presence filtered in and out of the shadows. He was holding onto me the only way he knew how. Maybe this was love. Despite the flaws and mistakes, he held onto me. Gold and green rushed through my chest, setting me ablaze. I screamed as my body shook with intense heat. Skin flaked off me like ash scattering in the wind, revealing fresh layers of gold and green light racing through my veins. The darkness around me shook, like a veil being torn from the sky. I pushed through that darkness, clawing and pulling, desperate to wake up.

"My violet," a male voice purred. His voice was a color. Gentle and bright like silver. *"Wake."*

I jerked awake, pulling on EKG wires and sticky pads. Behind my heart monitor, Mike curled in a chair, sleeping. Everything I saw felt real. That man's voice was unfamiliar, yet something I had longed to hear. I wanted to sit up and write down everything, but I was too afraid to move in case the feeling from the rush of light or that man's voice would fade like a dream. I tried moving off the bed, but with a catheter in, it was uncomfortable. How long had I been out? Everything was blurry when I tried to remember the last thing that had happened. Looking at Mike, I touched my chest. It was odd he had touched the center of my chest just weeks before. Every guy I've been on dates with, Peter would always say, *he's not worth it*. But with Mike, he had said *not him, not ever*. Strangely, it felt personal, like Peter knew him. As I tugged on the thread, I half expected him to be there waiting for me.

"Peter, are you there?"

"I've been waiting for you to wake." His voice felt like a salve to my wounds.

"I don't know what happened. Did you hear them say my temperature was 115 degrees?"

"Yes, I did."

I shuddered. How was that possible? No human could survive that.

"Listen," Peter's voice turned grave, *"I know he is there with you right now, but you need to leave. I will find a way to get to you. I promise."*

"I can't leave until I am discharged. I don't even know what happened to me. What if I need to see a specialist?"

"Lor, trust me. There's no specialist in your realm who can help you."

Realm. Such an odd choice of words. Why would he call Earth a realm? I always imagined him on the other side of the earth, peering over a balcony thinking of me, but...*realm*? Peter's promise threw me in a tizzy for a man who had manipulated me to leave Mike and then completely ghosted me.

"I want to trust you," I said, weighing each word. *"I felt you with me when I was in the darkness."*

He stilled on the end of his thread. *"I have caused the rift between us, and I am sorry, but please, remember who I have been for the past six years. I have been your best friend. I love you, Lor, and I don't want him to harm you."*

Love.

Peter's connection died. It felt like it burned up as soon as Mike opened his eyes.

"There you are," he smiled, smothering his veneer of darkness.

He wore his black jogging pants and a plain white T-shirt. My breath caught, and I tried ringing the nurse. Panic set in. I felt so stupid for not listening to Peter as Mike inched his way toward me, rubbing his fingers on the metal railing of my bed. Dark shadows followed him. Tendrils of wispy smoke curled over his shoulders. The scent of ash filled my nostrils. My shaky fingers lunged for the call button. Mike flicked his wrist, and my entire body froze.

"They cannot help you. You see, Elora"—he rubbed his finger against the railing again, making a high-pitched sound— "you are very special and dear to so many not of your realm."

Realm. Somehow Peter and Mike were connected, but I could not make sense of it. Then again, I mind-spoke with someone I had never actually met for six years. This could be real.

My body went taut, stretching and pulling, as icy shards pricked over every pore. "Mike. Stop."

"Not until I have your full cooperation." He pressed his hand harder into the air. "It would seem you have already busied yourself with conversations with another man," he said as I sucked in a breath. "Did you really think you are the only one who can mind-speak? He says he can save you, but he cannot. And I will do whatever it takes to conceal you. Do not make me break universal law."

I focused on the rain pelting the windows, the night air drifting from outside. I tapped relentlessly on Peter's thread, but there was nothing. Whimpering in pain, I no longer begged Mike to stop. I just waited for what was to come. My hospital gown left little to imagine as his energy lifted me above the bed. Weightless, powerless, it was exactly where he wanted me. There truly was nothing special about me. I had fallen prey to a jerk with magic powers, groomed to trust him, to want him. Now, I was merely a plaything in his hands.

The hair on my skin rose like fine needle points. A gush of wind knocked Mike into the wall, and I fell back on the bed.

"Run!" Peter screamed.

I tore off the sticky pads, forgetting I had a catheter in me. I had a split second to grab my clothes on the chair, fully realizing Mike had broken into my apartment to get them. I ran with a wheeled catheter down the halls, catching the shocked faces as I sped by. I needed to get far away, but not in a hospital gown. I did not want to be a movie cliché. Instead, I found a nurse I knew and shoved her into a supply closet. Her name was Becca, and she seemed sweet from the little interaction we'd had.

Out of breath and shaking, I pulled her against the shelves, knocking over gauze pads and tongue depressors. I shook the bag half filled with pale urine and motioned to Becca. "Take this out of me."

"Oh my god, what happened? Are you okay?" Her brown eyes flickered under the blinking lights.

"Just do it! He's going to find me."

"I don't understand. Should we call the police and lock down the hospital?" Panic rippled across her soft features, but I just wanted her to rip it out of me already.

"No, maybe, I don't know. I just know if I leave, he won't harm anyone here."

Her hands shook, cutting off the valve to the balloon port and pulling it out. I did not have time to focus on the discomfort. Quickly, I put on my clothes. No shoes, though. Becca assessed me again while jumbling anxious words from her lips. I forgot to thank her as I rushed out of the closet, toward the exit. Moments later, sirens blared. No way did I want to be at the center of an investigation again. I cranked myself at full speed and ran through the automatic doors, dodging an ambulance. No keys, no phone, I ran wherever I could, wherever I could hide. The woods. Why did it always have to be the woods? Fitting, I would take a job where the parking lot met the lining of the woods where those boys had tried to rape me.

I made it where streetlights were not visible anymore and tried to catch my breath.

"Peter, are you there?"

The connection died. I cursed under my breath, my lungs burning. Warmth pooled beneath my feet, becoming aware of the searing pain. I dared to look, and there were deep gashes under both feet, and I stumbled to the ground. There was no way I was going to make it anywhere else. I bit back tears. No use in crying. I pushed back my sweaty hair strands and wiped my eyes. Black makeup streaks the nurses never wiped off me smeared onto my hands. Mike was coming for me. I wondered where he would take me. Likely to some boarded-up basement where nobody would ever hear me scream. Maybe I would just die of infection first.

"Peter, I'm scared."

Still nothing. A cold breeze wrapped around me like a river freezing over. Trees darkened with shadows swirling over them. Fear clung to my throat, choking off my air. Bright light blasted my line of vision. My body fell like a heavyweight hitting the ground. A low, rumbling growl vibrated in all directions. My body froze. Six green eyes aflame stared down at me. Not Mike's green but the evil kind, a shade of green that whispered the promise of wrath. A silhouette of a creature no smaller than a truck stood over me. My bowels turned to water as it flashed its sharp grin at me. It stepped forward, sniffing, snarling, on huge black paws. Jet black fur came into focus. It was like a wolf but with three heads. I willed myself to move, but my feet rendered me useless as I inched away on my backside. It let out a warning snap for me to go no further. Thick drool hung from its dark lips. He would catch me, no matter how fast I could run. If I laid still, maybe it would go away, but I felt its eyes rove over me, calculating, assessing. It wanted something.

You are very special and dear to so many not of your realm.

I would never find out what that meant. I closed my eyes and prayed that it would be quick.

A flash of orange and red pried my eyes open. A thunderous weight hit the ground behind me. I dared to look back. Mike. He kneeled in total superhero landing, snarling at the beast. Veins glowed from beneath his skin of orange and red, but his eyes were no longer green. They were golden, like chips of blazing amber.

I said I needed to conceal you," he growled, keeping his focus on the creature.

The beast reared, and Mike flew over me, slamming into it, blasting undulating light and fire. He hooked his arm behind its knee and knocked it to the ground. Mike's fingers glowed like molten gold as he formed a rope of raging light around the three necks. The creature's face struggled on the ground to breathe, and I almost felt sorry for it, though it tried to sink its teeth into me moments earlier. Small yelps emitted from this ferocious creature, but now, in its sad state, I couldn't see it as more than a puppy.

Mike tugged on the rope. His hair disheveled, his face covered in soot. "This creature failed, but I will not. Do not feel sorry for it. He was sent to kill you by someone else."

Mike took out a gold device from his pocket that looked like a key with a scarlet ribbon tied in the triangular hole. Gears spun like clockwork, forward, backward, until finally it stopped. He held out the key and jiggled it a few times, cursing until he found the spot he needed. Air rippled around us as he opened a doorway of muted light. First, he threw the creature in without losing his breath from the weight of it. It cried out, claws scraping against the earth as Mike closed the door. I thought I was caught in a dream, no, a nightmare. His fiery glare met mine.

"Now we must go. You are no longer safe here." He pulled me to my feet and gripped my shoulders. I stumbled.

My shoulders fought against his strong hands, and I plopped to the ground. "I can't. Mike, please just let me go."

"Let you go?" He marveled at my request as if I understood what was going on. "You just sounded off the beacon in your chest. I can't let you go."

"Beacon?"

"I will either drag you, or you can walk."

"I can't walk."

He surveyed my feet and grimaced. It must have been so annoying for me to get hurt while he chased me. Mike rubbed his lips, those same lips I used to love kissing.

"Dragging, it is."

His hands pulled mine, dragging me to the door. My body was a limp rag. The key moved its gears again like it was changing for a new lock.

"Wait, please, no! Where are you taking me?!" I shrieked, feeling the twigs and dead leaves scrape against my back.

Mike flashed his mischievous smile. "To the land of monsters."

I roared and screamed, and then the door shut.

5

ELORA

Darkness and silvered white light flashed all around me. A force pulled me into a vortex. My insides screamed to stop falling. When we hit the ground, pain sliced through my bones. Mike blindfolded me before I had the chance to gain my bearings. His hands were rough on my face. Long gone was his gentle touch, the sincerity in his eyes. I stopped pleading with him since it was no use. My stomach emptied its contents on the cold soil. I missed my little apartment already, my job, my sense of normalcy. Over and over, I screamed Peter's name internally, and Mike flinched each time.

"Peter does not exist here, so stop screaming his name," he sneered as he hoisted me over his shoulder.

Wherever I was felt damp and dark, like a chilly feeling on your skin that never seemed to warm. His boots clacked on uneven stone while he held me tight. Hooves clicked nearby while wicked little giggles and gruff voices rushed past us. People quieted as if I was a spectacle to behold. Blood dripped down my feet, and my throat was dry. Infection was going to happen sooner than later, and wherever I was hardly felt like a place that offered help.

"A human pet," someone snickered. Hot, rancid breath came close to my face, and I flinched as sharp nails like claws slid down my face. "What a pretty pet. When you tire of her, can you give her to me?"

Mike sighed. "She is mine and mine alone. Go find another wretch to play your games, Sorrel."

More hands touched my face and body as if inspecting me. I shivered against their clammy touch. Some hands felt like frog skin, and others felt as rough as tree bark. I almost fainted, but I could not lose my wits if I wanted to escape. All I needed to do was steal his key and find a door. Even then, I could wind up worse off. Mike's shoulder moved as he extended his hand, and the crowd gasped. Heat pulsed though his body, giving me much needed warmth. For a second, I wanted to believe he did it for me, but I knew he was annoyed with the crowd. He could set them on fire if he wanted to. A moment later, we moved freely, with only whispers trailing us. His heated fingers loosened their grip, and he nudged his head on my hip.

"I know this is strange, but it must be done." His voice softened, "We are almost at the Onyx Keep. I will give you a room to stay in."

"As a prisoner?" My throat cracked.

"No matter what I say, you will believe you are a prisoner." He tightened his fingers again.

"You said I had a beacon. I have no idea what you are talking about."

"I see your Peter explained nothing to you. Did you not find it strange that you could mind-speak all the sudden?" he asked as if I were someone of low intelligence. "Something triggered that thing in your chest to flare. When did you start feeling the fire?"

It was the night when Peter held me. "I don't know."

A low laugh rumbled in his chest. "You are such a terrible liar. That beacon is a star. You are no human. You are immortal."

"You're insane. Of course, I'm human."

"Then why has no blood ever matched yours? Why were you such an anomaly growing up? Why have you been a target of such violence?"

Everything about me felt human. I felt rejection and shame like any other human. How could I be anything else?

"Didn't I just save you from Cerberus?" he asked incredulously. "He was going to claw you to death until he found that star inside you. It is likely the size of a sunflower seed, and he would have taken his time doing it. He hasn't had game like you in eons, and he ached for the thrill."

It made some sense that I was targeted. Humans can detect those who are different, unwanted. Yet, it all still felt like a nightmare, and I would wake up soon. As my legs dangled on his back, I realized that nothing was abstract. Everything was real around me, tangible. I still held out hope that this was all a fever induced nightmare.

"Is this why you were scared at the planetarium?" I asked.

"Yes, I was afraid you'd be triggered. Your star calls to others."

I scowled. Stars were no more than gases in the sky. When I was little, I made wishes on them and hoped they were more than just lights in the sky. But I was no longer a child. "Any moment now, I will wake up from this nightmare and cut you off for good," I said as a prayer.

"Say that now, but wait till I take the blindfold off."

"How do you know Peter?"

"I don't know Peter." His voice turned bitter.

"But you know the voice to whom I am referring."

His jaw clenched by my thigh. "We're here. No more questions. Keep your head down."

There was an air of excitement as gates groaned from opening. More crowds. I stiffened at their touch like I was an artifact. Heat blasted through Mike, radiating from my head to my toes, and they scattered. Mike was someone to be feared. I didn't care what he said about me not being human. I looked human, and my blood was red. He had looked human, too—until he lifted me with a flick of his wrist and put on that light show in the woods. His legs ascended steps that felt like a spiral. My hands scraped against the cold stone walls. I imagined the stone being pure onyx or just plain black rock. The higher we rose, the more heat I felt. Even Mike lost his breath. I assumed I was in the tallest tower. Somewhere easy to hide someone and be forgotten about. It did not matter what he said. I was a prisoner.

A door creaked open, and he did not bother putting me down gently. I made a thud on the floor, my feet burning against the impact. I tore off the blindfold and found myself in a meager room no bigger than a walk-in closet. In one corner was a small bed with a sunken mattress and faded quilt. In the other corner was a wooden desk barely touching the bed with a white basin and pitcher. A small wooden pot poked out from under my bed. No indoor plumbing. Tiny flames hissed and crackled from a fireplace no bigger than the size of my work computer on the other side of the room. I could eat up the rest of the floor in just a few steps. At least there was a window above the side of the bed.

"I have assigned one servant for your quarters."

"More like a quarter," I quipped.

Mike stiffened. "Be grateful! I could have allowed you to be shredded to ribbons. Instead, you have the hospitality of a prince."

"What prince?"

"Me." He slammed the door, locking it. Indeed, I was a prisoner.

I slid over to the basin, hoping there was enough water to drink and wash off my feet, but there was not. It was just a cup full. I had to choose between thirst and cleaning off my wounds. After some thought, I drank because there was not enough water to clean my feet. I shook uncontrollably, refusing the comfort of that bed, which wasn't appealing at all. My phantom finger tugged on the thread between me and Peter, and there was nothing. Peter did not exist here. I was so cold, but I refused the quilt on the bed. Instead, I just held myself, waiting for the inevitable fever, and allowing exhaustion to take over.

Later, I heard the knob wiggle and the door push open. Hooves clicked on the aged wooden floors. I had seen a creature like this before in a book. Soft brown fur covered his legs, fading above his waistline. Pointed, furry ears peeked over the tuft of brown curls on his head. *Faun*. That was the name I remembered. I tried not to shudder. He had the look of kindness in his large tawny eyes, and I didn't want to scare him off. A hint of a smile dimpled his cheeks. He had golden skin, like he had been in the sun, though I saw little light coming through the window. Just a faint glimmer, like it was dusk.

With a slight bow, he showed off his little horns mostly hidden beneath his mound of curls. "Prince Mikhail assigned me to serve you. I am under strict orders to bring you fresh clothes, dispose of your old ones, and provide food and water. He will allow nothing else, my lady."

"No, not my clothes," I said, before realizing what I was wearing. He eyed my tattered hot pants and band tee up and down, clicking his tongue.

"My lady, please do not anger the prince." His soft voice warmed my heart, though it was a warning.

"Fine. Being stuck in here, I will have nothing left of me, anyway."

"My lady, dare not speak such things." He laid down clothes and linen washcloths. He angled his head toward my feet, frowning. "Had I known you were injured, I would have come with bandages." His little hooves clicked closer to me, and he bent down to lift me. For someone who looked so young and slender, he picked me up like a feather.

"This will not do, not at all." His head shook as he assessed my injuries and overall filth.

"I shall bring an extra-large basin and a warming pan, my lady. I will return," he said, shifting to leave.

"What is your name?"

"Luca."

"I'm Elora. Please do not call me 'lady.' I'm just a prisoner here."

"Sorry, my lady, I am forbidden to speak your name." He turned and shut the door, locking it.

I cannot wear my own clothes nor speak my name. It was happening too fast. My identity was slipping from me with nobody here to remind me who I was. Luca must have had great speed because he was back moments later with everything. He laid the warming pan in the fireplace, heating the coals inside. I could tell he wanted to speak but could offer nothing. I bet Mike would have had his head. A few minutes later, he took out the warming pan and put the basin on top. It must have been very hot because the water warmed immediately. Luca bowed before me and lifted my left foot so gently that it was almost a caress. Warm water trickled down my feet, and I hissed in pain. Luca gingerly pulled out bits of stuck grass and gravel from my cuts.

"Please, Luca." I winced again as he blotted my feet. "At least tell me where I am." I sucked in a breath. "Tell me what realm this is."

Luca's brow furrowed. "My lady, you know not where you are? How peculiar." He pressed the heat of the cloth onto my foot, adding pressure to stop the bleeding. "You are in Sidh, the land of eternal dusk."

"Dusk?"

"Correct." He squeezed the cloth into a bowl, brownish-pink blood swirling. "It is a cursed realm, my lady."

"I was told it was the land of the monsters."

Luca let out a soft chuckle. "Have you seen outside?"

"I came blindfolded."

He frowned, pushed himself up, and then stood on the bed. Once again, he lifted me and helped me look outside. The sky was dark violet with a glimmer of light. Thatched houses and what appeared to be huts and hobbles stretched as far as I could see. Tall trees, varying in shades of green and faded orange, shot up from the surrounding hills like forests. Where I was seemed to be the epicenter of Sidh.

He motioned his hand. "Look below."

Creatures of all kinds moved around in the courtyard of the Onyx Keep. I was up too high, no chance of escaping. Fauns and other creatures with longer, goat-like horns caroused around the prince. Prince Mikhail. Prince of idiot girls. Smaller creatures skittered around their feet, but I could not make out what they were. Luca noticed me squinting.

"Goblins, brownies, dryads, sirens, nymphs, but my lady..." I turned, finding his gaze fixed on me. Luca's eyes misted. "Not every creature here is a monster. There is much good hidden in the darkness." With that, he set me down.

He held my hand and pressed my knuckles to his pointed chin. "I will do anything for the prince," he whispered as if it were a secret. "He has already dispatched Kaya and Wren to bring special healing ointments for your feet." Luca turned to leave.

"Please don't go." I tugged on his fur.

He grinned softly. "You need rest, Kaya and Wren will come soon, and you shall be well. Good night, my lady."

As soon as he left, I cried, burying myself in the quilt on the bed this time. This truly was the land of monsters, and Mike, *Mikhail*, was their prince.

6

ELORA

ime was disorienting. The sun never really set, and the moon never fully rose. However, I saw the half-moon phase, though it was not bright enough. Fever set in, and there had been no ointment from whoever Kaya and Wren were. Luca seemed sweet enough, but I had to be careful. If he would do anything for the prince, his kindness might have limits. While I slept, he set out a plate of hard cheeses and fruit and a copper pitcher of water with a matching cup. Condensation streamed down the cup, telling me he came in quietly not too long ago. My appetite was non-existent, but I drank down most of the pitcher. My feverish body did not agree with the iciness of the water. I should have been used to fevers. Too many nights over the course of my life, my temperature rose in my sleep, and when I woke, it was gone.

Scratching noises came from the window. Faint shadows of wings fluttered in the frame. I tried getting up, but I was too weak. Two small voices bickered through the glass until one pried the window open.

"See Kaya, I told you they have not opened it in ages. These old towers are the things of nightmares," a rough male voice said.

"We are the nightmares, Wren. I said, *you* hold the jar, and I will open it. You always try to do everything," a female replied.

Faeries. Two faeries, the size of my TV remote, entered my room. Was this even real? Their pointy ears perked at the sound of my slight breath.

"Look, you woke her up," the male sneered as he rapidly flapped his wings close to my face. "She's the same one Prince Mikhail brought blindfolded." Six deep purple wings with rough black edges stung my face. He wore black slouched boots, a black leather vest, and torn gray breeches. "Tell me your name, miss." His silver hair spiked into sections, and his matching eyes glowed from beneath his irises.

My throat felt like sandpaper despite all the water I had gulped down. "My name?"

They both looked at each other quizzically, bringing me to focus on the female, Kaya. Her six wings shimmered like a rainbow. Her pale skin was the color of moonlight. Black leggings matched her violet corset with a black ribbon long enough to pull up her lavender hair halfway.

"Did the prince say she was hard of hearing?" Wren asked, scratching his head.

"She's been through an ordeal, be nice," Kaya said as she pranced on my forehead. "Oh my, her head is on fire. Luca was right."

Wren's silver eyes flashed. "You still haven't told us your name."

Kaya glared at him with her iridescent, opal eyes. "Pshhh, Wren, you know her name."

"I need to hear it from her mouth."

I dragged the covers up to my eyes. "Luca is not allowed to say my name, so I assume you cannot, either," I muffled.

They both looked at each other, breaking into laughter. "Lucky for you, we don't like rules," said Kaya, winking at Wren.

My brows wrinkled. "But the prince sent you."

"If we put the ointment on you that will save your life, tell us your name. We faeries love bargains," Wren said, twisting the small jar open.

I pulled my feet under the covers. "I don't want you to get hurt. I want nothing bad to happen to you. I've seen what he can do."

"We do not bow, my lady," Kaya said tersely as she scooped this mysterious white ointment into her hands.

"Elora, my name is Elora." I hissed as their tiny hands spread the ointment on. Lavender, honey, and other scents I could not place wafted into the room. "If there is a prince, there must be a king and queen, right?" I asked, as my fingers curled in pain.

Wren sniffed my ankle, grimacing from the stench of infection. "Elora...before I answer that, I will have Kaya change and bathe you, then reapply the ointment. Luca is far too sheepish for that."

My eyes widened that such a small thing could take on an enormous task. "How?"

"We are stronger than you think, Elora." Kaya's sweet voice soothed a bit of my anxiety.

Wren whirred around, brandishing what looked like a dagger the size of a tack, and began digging in the window frame.

"Lift your arms," Kaya directed as she fluttered at my waist. She removed my shirt slowly, flying between both sides.

My face became red when she took unhooked my bra, and I covered myself with my arms. "I can take my clothes off."

"The prince asked us to do anything you needed. And you need to get changed and bathed," Wren said gruffly as he continued to carve the windowsill.

My bra dropped to the ground. "At least let me help," my voice deflated.

Kaya nodded, and I helped shuck my hot pants and underwear off. Completely naked and exposed, Kaya did not flinch. I crossed my legs and continued to cover myself in my arms.

She giggled. "I have seen nakedness before."

The corner of my mouth twitched upward. "Where I am from, we are more modest."

"I see," Kaya said. "Well." She flew to the basin and brought over all my bathing needs. "I will wash your back and hair...you do the rest." Her pale skin shimmered in the dying embers of the fire.

The warm water Luca set out over the heating pan felt amazing. All the filth washed away, revealing clean skin with a subtle shade of gold underneath. My muscles loosened as Kaya ran her strong hands up and down my back. It was nice to be taken care of, even if it was temporary. After I finished bathing, she slid on a black silk top and handed me matching black silk shorts with silver trim on the bottom.

"This is pretty modern." Their eyebrows arched. "I mean, it's something I would wear where I'm from." My fingers ran over the coolness of the material.

"We got it from someone who has been to your realm," said Kaya as she carried away the basin.

Mike, of course. I rolled my eyes at the thought of how stupid I was to let him in. Kaya then reapplied the ointment, its scent relaxing my tired soul.

"Thank you." I pressed a cool cloth to my head, already feeling better. "All of you have been so kind."

Wren's eyes softened, and he fluttered to me as a single tear rolled down my face.

"We will come again." He turned away, flaring his wings. "I almost forgot. There is a king and queen. You will find no greater monsters." Then he flew off with the empty jar in his hands.

Kaya lifted my chin with her tiny pale hand, and her eyes smiled. "Soon, Elora, soon." Her words felt like a promise.

***

Three days passed, and my feet completely healed. At least I could stand on my bed and look out my window. Mike didn't visit me, not that I wanted him to. I missed Peter so much. I wondered if he believed I was dead. I imagined him tapping on our thread relentlessly or maybe he had given up now. But I felt him everywhere when I was in the darkness. He was more than a voice; he was a presence.

Every night, the same scene of hobgoblins, minotaurs, and other mythological creatures that I only ever read about reveled in the courtyard below. If only my hair were as long as the tower, I could cut my hair like Rapunzel and climb down. Luca always removed the sheets before giving me new ones so I couldn't make a rope from them either. I bet Mike had thought of that. Psycho.

Luca tapped on my door, sighing because I did not change out of my black silks. They became filthy, but I did not want to dress in the white silks Mike sent me. Any other girl would dream of these deep-v silks with a gilded belt, but not me. I just wanted to go home, resume my life as normal, and wear my band tees.

"My lady," Luca said, with a hint of worry. "You have barely eaten since you have been here."

"So, what," I snapped. He flinched. "I mean, why does he care if I eat?"

Luca shifted the silver platter of cheeses and glittering fruit off the stool. "Does it matter if he cares? Should you not care for yourself first?"

This time, *I* flinched. Throughout my social work studies in college, self-care was widely preached but hardly practiced. Not once did someone—other than Peter—point out that I did not care for myself. I loved being hit at concerts and shows. The bruises and cuts made me feel alive. It wasn't healthy. Neither was starving myself. But Luca took care of me, day in and day out, without complaint, even when I would not acknowledge him. Unsure if his kindness was bound by duty to Mike, I'd distrusted him. However, I'd also seen something more sincere in his eyes, from the way he'd touched my hand and when he'd lifted me from my bed to test my walking.

"I'm sorry, Luca. You have been so kind to me. I hate the color white on me. If it so pleases him, let your prince send another color. Tell him to send me black. He should know that about me."

His throat bobbed. "No trouble at all, my lady. I will do as you ask...if you eat."

It looked pleasing, but I simply did not want to eat. "Deal." I held out my hand for a shake, but his brows furled, unsure what to do. Instead, he pressed his hand flat to mine and left.

***

The moon hung dimly in the violet, orange-streaked sky. Still half-moon. Maybe soon, it would change phases. I did as Luca asked and ate a few pieces of cheese, a slice of brown bread, and what appeared to be an apple with orange, glittering skin. Admittedly, I felt better. A harsh knock came. After three raps, Mike opened the door forcefully, his icy amber eyes glinting like a pint of stale beer. His slicked-back, flaming hair barely touched the tip of his black collar. Everything about him looked princely, from his tailored black coat to his black breeches. I'll give him credit where credit was due. He did look mighty fine. But since I didn't want a Stockholm situation on my hands, I shook those thoughts of him loose.

"You did not like my choice of silks for you?" he asked roughly. His eyes raked over my body, specifically my feet. "And you barely eat. You are skin and bone."

"Why do you care?" I stood to my feet, facing him like an opponent. "You left me up here to waste away." Shades of blue and yellow whorls shadowed his face. "What happened to you?"

"None of your concern." He twisted away with deep purple silks in his hands, not the black I requested. "You shall accompany me tomorrow for the Maypole festival. I've been instructed to do so."

"By whom?"

Mike let out a heavy breath. "Just wear these silks. The deep vee was wrong for you, anyway. We need to hide your starlight." He turned back to me, gripping my chin with his fingers. "You belong to me." I wrestled in his strong fingers to break free. "Be obedient, and maybe I will give you something to pass the time away in here."

I craned my neck and spat in his face. "I belong to no one."

His hand gingerly wiped his eye, and he chuckled darkly. "You've got spirit. I did like that about you. But you are a mission, and I will not fail." He pointed to the light in my chest that faintly glowed.

"Mission for what?!"

"Wouldn't you like to know?" He drawled.

Heat rose in my body, and I wanted to explode into an inferno. I pushed him so hard that sparks of golden light left my hands. There was no time to process how I had done that as I ran for the door. He fell over the little stool, shock draining his face of color. I didn't make it. Stupid, foolish me. With a flick of his wrist, my body slammed across the room, and I hit the side of my face on the mantle. I went down like a ton of bricks. Burning, searing pain rushed down my face as I met the cold floor. Memories flashed of his smile, his tenacious love for philosophy and law. The way he claimed my lips in my hallway. Where was he? He'd never existed. A girl yearning for love found it in the wrong place, like so many cliché stories. Warmth dribbled down my face, but I hadn't the heart or the will to wipe it away. Everything became so cold, distant.

Mike stood over me, silent, with a hint of sadness flickering in his eyes. "Elora...I" His lips tightened. A sliver of the Mike I used to know surfaced. "I did not intend for that."

He soaked linens in the basin and dabbed my face, his shadowed contours softening. I hissed as the cool cloth pressed my lips. I had not realized the cut trailed from the middle of my forehead down my nose and lip. "I will send some powders for you to cover that up tomorrow." He lifted me into a sitting position.

The air between us stilled. I wished I could see those ice-green eyes again, but they were long gone. Just another glamour to lure me into his trap, this web of hurt. His shoulders drooped as he made his way to the door.

"Was any of it real?" I asked, pressing the cloth to my face.

"Some," he said as if reflecting, "but I would have never gone any further. I may be vile, but I do have some honor left in me."

The door closed and locked tightly. I wished I could die, if this were to be my existence from now on.

Luca came in without knocking after what felt like hours later after my interaction with Mike. He found me curled up on the floor where Mike had left me. Exhaustion must have knocked me out for a while. Luca dropped the plate of food, his face reddened. As soon as I opened my mouth to say something, the pain in my jaw roared.

"Luca," I groaned. "I can't go on like this."

A tear escaped his eye as he knelt before me. "And you won't, my lady. Now I see why he made a big deal about the powders. My lady," He grasped my chin ever so lightly. "Soon, very soon."

His throat bobbed, restraining his own tears. I could see he wanted to tell me so much and how angry he was with his prince, but he was bound by duty. "Please put on your purple silks."

With a slight pull of my hand, he lifted me to my feet. His fingers grazed my back as I walked to the puddle of purple left at the door. I smoothly took off my clothes and grabbed the dress. Luca cleared his throat and turned to face the other wall as I slinked the silks on. The dress covered my chest and flowed down to my feet. No shoes again. Mike had something against giving me shoes. It was probably to keep me running away, though it did not stop me before. I processed what had happened—another act of violence committed against me. Slowly, I picked up the silver tin of power that Luca dropped on the floor and unscrewed the lid.

He sucked in a breath. "No, my lady, you shall not be wearing that today."

7

MIKHAIL

There was not much time before the Maypole festival. I didn't want to face her again. I screwed up royally and let my anger get the best of me. He was going to kill me. I had thought what I was doing was right. If I just concealed her, nobody could take her, use her, or discard her body. He better not kill me, then. I was the one saving her while he sat in his house brooding. After the night I hurt her wrist, I wanted to return here and never see her again. I did not intend to hurt her. In fact, she reminded me of something sweet and pure. I thought I would never see the brightness of joy again. She wasn't my type but a faded reflection of what I used to have.

My mentor, the only father figure I ever had known, strode across my room, his face full of disappointment.

"Greetings, Silas," I said, placing my hands on the fiery mantle.

"Son, I am very disappointed in you." Veins of faded green and brown bark creaked and groaned with age. Sooner than later, he would return to the earth in his favorite place, per dryad tradition.

I winced as Silas caressed my bruised face with his twiggy finger. "I'm disappointed in myself," I said.

"Mikhail. You are abusing her. I cannot stand for it. Have I not taught you well? Is your mother finally winning you over?" His voice of reprimand lanced through my chest.

My eyes focused on the red tapestry rug underneath my feet. "I know. She does not deserve this."

He tugged my shoulders. "Then stop this. Hand her over." His dried leaves shook.

"Never."

"Not to her. *Him*."

I hated his conviction at times, but he was never one to stand in the middle. To Silas, everything was black and white, right or wrong. "If I do that, everything will be destroyed. He's already so weak without the full use of his powers. Imagine when his cymar is there. He will get her killed. Then my mother gets everything she wants."

Silas' thick moss brows knitted together. "Rotting in a tower is your plan? Have you no mercy?"

"I need this realm to believe she is nothing so that no harm will come to her. My mercy is in not killing her in another realm and then burying her body so no one will ever find her star."

Silas' cracked lips grew thin. "You love him too much to do that."

I lowered my head closer to the flames. "Love?"

Memories of Silas teaching me how to count and read flooded my mind. A classroom of one. No friends. No games. Mother would roll over in her grave if she allowed me to play with other kids. Goblins were okay in her eyes, but that didn't happen often. Silas was my only source of companionship, and he never let me down. My father was absent, and Silas assumed his role. Down the road, he began calling me 'son,' and it filled me with identity, purpose. I was somebody's son. Not a tool or a weapon. Silas was the one who taught me how to swing a sword and to read the wisdom of scholars across realms. He was the reason I'd studied under Voltaire, the reason I'd met the most beautiful creature I had ever laid eyes on. His disappointment shook me to the core. I needed to do better, but I couldn't. My mother would suspect me of treason if I truly acted the way he'd taught me.

Silas' creaky voice cut through my thoughts. "Yes, love. Regardless of what you have been told, you are more capable of having and giving it. I see now you don't want his heart to break."

My shoulders shook, silencing the torrent of sadness I felt for my brother and me. "Silas, you see so much good in me. Yet, I must do a lot of bad things for the greater good."

"No, my son, chaos breeds chaos. It is not the natural order of things." His branched arms whisked around me, holding me close to the slow heartbeat in his chest. "This is the truth right here. That you can break everything with mercy and kindness. Son, please heed my advice."

I wanted to melt right there, weep in his arms, smother every curse spoken over me, but I could not. Would not. The world was not made of rainbows and butterflies. I was a monster lurking in dark corners, needing to devour my prey. I shoved him off me, and his russet eyes blinked several times.

"I am not your son." My voice thickened, showing him the door.

He paused, waiting for me to take back my words. When I didn't, he hung his head low and dragged his limp branches with him. When the door clicked shut, I slid down the wall next to the fire. Dread pooled in my stomach, and I keeled over. I'd lied. He was more father to me than anyone, and I'd just broken his heart.

8

ELORA

Luca escorted me from the castle, past the empty courtyard. Yellowed, pink skies stretched above. For a moment, I was grateful to be outside, breathing in the wet air, and finally seeing the castle on the outside. Long, flowing, crimson banners bore the jagged silver crown of Queen Nyx and whipped from the battlements in a sudden gust of wind. Onyx stones shone under the crimson wave. Two drum towers stood on either side with battlements and crenels bearing scars from the past. Marks from arrows along with large, cracked in and cracked areas trailed up the battlements as if a catapult had been launched against it. This castle had seen its fair share of pain. I wanted to ask Luca about it, but panic seized me on the inside, dreading to be seen by these creatures and most of all, Mike. The mark he left me throbbed when I opened my mouth. A part of me wanted to surrender to the pain and just let go, accept my fate.

Luca brought me to grassy plains where creatures caroused with strong drink and mischief. I imagined these plains had given way to battles long ago, leaving those deserved scars on the castle. The festival stretched between the hobbles and thatched houses I had seen from the tower. It opened up to a white wooden dais with two thrones and embellished with crimson rugs and ornate gold trim. To the left, there were shadows encasing some-one. I tried to pay no mind, but my chest felt hot the longer I stared into the withering shadows. Long tables with benches were covered in glittering fruits, and smoked meats lined in front of the dais. Hobgoblins and brownies made a ruckus at the tables, stealing food off plates and giggling while they angered the minotaurs. I was afraid to sit next to a minotaur, fearing they would impale me with their horns. My heart pounded, my skin grew clammy, and somehow, I wanted to go back to my little room and hide. I did not belong here. Everyone gawked at Mike's "pet," surveying every part of me with beastly eyes. Several tiny creatures attempted to see what was underneath my dress before Luca swatted them away.

"I hate brownies," Luca huffed as he sat me at the table.

Something wild stirred in my chest, and heat blazed through my me.

"Luca," I whispered, sweat beading across my forehead. "My star. Someone is going to notice."

"I'm afraid your star cannot be helped," he said, removing his cloak. He gently placed the cloak over me. I pulled it tight to my chest, counting breaths to calm the storm swirling inside.

A gentle, deep violet light caught the corner of my eye. A creature, clothed in the shadows with glittering dark eyes, pulled me into his gaze. His nails clenched the arms of his cushioned chair, starlight scintillating from the center of his chest. I could tell his skin color was blue by his bare feet, the shade of blue that reminded me of pool water. A refreshing blue I wanted to dive into, stay under, and silence everything forever.

Mike spotted me with Luca, and something like rage rolled across his face. He took one ferocious bite from a glistening mutton chop, wiping his mouth quickly. Luca would be punished later because I didn't cover up the bruise. Thinking of it made my gut oily and slick. I darted my eyes to the large maypole hoisted in the center where little ones twirled ribbons while throwing flowers everywhere. The flowers were not as vibrant as on Earth. Dark purples, blues, and crimsons scattered at my feet. Not one white or pink flower in sight.

A shadow enveloped me, causing shivers to run down my spine. From behind, Mike grabbed my wrist, gritting his teeth. His eyes lowered to my bruise, and he released me. With parted lips, he ran his hand down his face as if conflicted. For a moment, I saw the softness in his features that I'd once held dear. *He never existed,*

I had to remind myself repeatedly. I pulled back slightly, and the softness disappeared, his rage returning.

"Insolence. I told you I required obedience, and for that…" He took a black leather leash out and fastened it to my neck. "Come this way, my pet."

Luca's mouth dropped to the ground. His fists clenched. I shook my head at Luca, wanting him to stay away. There was no more fight in me. Mike would do as he pleased. Luca was too sweet and innocent to be marred by him, so I let the punishment fall on me instead. I knew Luca wanted others to gaze upon the prince's cruelty, but did it matter? These creatures looked at me like a plaything.

Every hair stood on my arms as the metal buckle on my leash dug into the hollow of my throat. I knew I didn't deserve this. Luca tried to comfort me, but there was nothing he could say with so many ears. His knuckles brushed mine under the table, and I became aware of his touch. Violet light caught my attention again. My eyes swept over to the dais and the dark creature's long, masculine hands. They dug so hard into the arms of the chair that tiny white feathers released. It was hard to resist not meeting his stare. As monstrous as he appeared, I did not fear him. Even as I hung my head low, I felt that creature's gaze burning a hole in me. Mike dragged me to his table by the leash, his friends laughing at my expense. My neck throbbed from the tightened pull. It was tight enough to exact some pain but not enough to suffocate me. Luca followed after me, his breath quickening.

"Sit. Eat," Mike said roughly. He pointedly looked at his companions, smirking. "Human pets are so unintelligent, they need reminders to take care of themselves."

His laugh cloyed under my skin. I didn't know what hurt more—being treated less than human or being called stupid. If I could handle high school, I could handle this lot, though I was at my wit's end. A female dryad across the table blinked at me with her earthy brown eyes. Most of her skin looked like tree bark, with peeks of mossy green skin speckled on various parts of her body. Two branches spiraled above her long, flowing green hair like a stag. Dark flowers dotted her hair. She was breathtaking.

"Your eyes are my color," she remarked as she tore into a chunk of roasted meat.

"No, my eyes are..." I turned and saw Mike's fiery gaze, shaking his head at me. Talking to others was out of the question too. Further, I sank into myself.

Luca sat next to me in silence. "Prince Mikhail glamoured your eye color," he whispered.

My eyebrows arched. There were too many questions, but I could ask nothing. Mike was already angry I had defied him. Warily, I grabbed what looked to be roasted chicken and some grapes. They were black but tasted sweeter than grapes from my realm. It was all I could do to keep my head down and wish for time to pass quickly. A minotaur with large, curved horns threw food at the silent creature on the dais. The creature remained still, yet his eyes did not move from mine. Others joined the minotaur in pelting him with food.

"Cursed prince!"

"Traitor!"

Prince? Mike never told me he had a brother. I had no clue what this other prince had done, but nobody deserved this inhumane treatment. If he was guilty, he should not be paraded like he was on his way to the guillotine. It reminded me of being in high school and I'd just snagged my first boyfriend. The girl who set us up became jealous and recruited her friends to circle me, throw balls of paper, chanting, *"She's so ugly."* The new boyfriend had withered away because my humiliation had made him think twice about me. I never thought I would feel beautiful again until Peter. My lips parted, wanting to scream for everyone to stop. Luca knew I did, and he restrained me with a gentle hand on my knee, reminding me of my place.

"My lady, he is the cursed prince," he whispered. "Nobody truly knows why he is cursed except for the royal family." My eyes watered with more questions. "I knew him before he was cursed. He was a good man, but when he came back to this realm, all I remember is the light growing dark. It's been like that here ever since."

"The king and queen!" people shouted. One by one, everyone stood to welcome their king and queen. My knees knocked underneath the table as Mikhail tugged the leash for me to get up. "All hail Queen Nyx and King Algol!"

Queen Nyx looked like a moon goddess, resplendent in silver silks, glittering pale skin, and crimson lips. Like a beautiful vampire, her smile beckoned the taste of blood. So slender, her movements lithe. The batting of her dark eyes could make men kneel before her. Her crown of jagged silver fit on top of her raven hair. The king appeared old and frail. His eyes were a vacant shade of gray as if he had seen too much and the light ceased to exist. Disheveled, gray hair curled at the border of his jawline, and his smaller matching crown did not suit him. Rather, it looked as if the crown wore him and not the other way around. By the look of it, Queen Nyx ruled this realm. Though she was beautiful, her eyes flicking over me told me all I needed to know. She was a monster. They walked up the dais smiling at their people and sat on their thrones a ways off from the creature. It was almost as if the price was there just to be a spectacle—which made my stomach turn.

The festivities resumed, and Mike became drunk. That same dryad I spoke to earlier was now his lady for the night. Disgust roiled in me as Mike shamelessly made out with her in front of everyone. He was sure to make eye contact with me as if I would be jealous. Good. She could have him! Fresh fire and burning wood reminded me of Autumn back home. *Home.* I was never going home again. I closed my eyes, remembering every little scent that came with the seasons. I had taken it for granted.

Mike rolled his head back in laughter over something the dryad said, but he stopped cold as he looked upon his brother. Ice raked over Mike's face. He found a head of cabbage on the table and hurled it toward his head. This time, the creature balked, and my heart leapt. An older dryad, a male, closed the distance between the two, shaking his head at Mike. The tables quieted. Disappointment flickered in his old eyes, and he remained between the princes for a minute. The silence spoke volumes.

The queen angled her head at the dryad, narrowing her eyes on him. Unfazed by the sudden silence, he continued to stand between the two brothers, speaking to Mike with his eyes. Mike lowered his hand and dropped the food onto the ground. I had never seen Mike surrender to anything. He always took what he wanted. But this dryad held a certain power over him, and I craved that same authority. If this dryad could stand for what was right, so could I. Everything in me wanted to scream for this dryad to help me but I dared not. Perhaps his only interest was in them, not in some pathetic human pet. He took his leave, dead leaves trailing behind him, and the festival resumed as if nothing had happened.

Luca's legs shook under the table, and he took me by the hand to calm himself. "Sorry, my lady. I just hate—"

A pretty faun with burnished brown hair and jade green eyes approached Luca, smiling, and she handed him a large magenta flower head. The flower looked like an amaryllis. His cheeks flushed, and he let go of my hand.

"My lady, this is the tradition of our maypole. You give flower heads to someone you fancy or someone who needs love. If you will excuse me, I will be right back." He linked arms with the beautiful faun and faded into the distance. I knew he would not be right back. He needed a break from babysitting me.

Mike's laughter in the background slivered down my spine like a snake. I sat back, trying to ignore him while looking at the cursed prince. His shadows looked like a cage. That feeling was too familiar. Maybe we had that in common, and maybe he would never see me again after that day. I needed to blur the lines Mike had been so cruel to draw. At my feet lay a large indigo flower head. I picked it up and rubbed my fingers over the velvet petals, thinking of every consequence of what I was about to do. None of them mattered. If I could do one good thing for someone, I could prove I still had a piece of my heart left intact. Maybe I would have something more to live for. Mike was preoccupied, and there was no better time than now.

I took the flower and walked three white steps up the dais amid the gasps behind me. Ignoring the leash dragging behind me, I treaded on. The air around him felt familiar, inviting. Something about him took my breath away, and I laid the flower head at his feet. My curiosity got the best of me, and I touched his foot lightly. A spark of electricity buzzed through my touch. His breath felt warm even from a distance. Our eyes met. They were as stars in the darkness, a light reaching out for me. My chest heated. It thrilled me and scared me at the same time. Whoever this creature was, I wanted him to break free from his shadows and carry me away from this place. His claws dug into his chair more, leaning back, unsure of my kindness, as if an injured animal receiving affection for the first time. Forgetting the crowd behind me, I stood, trembling in awe. Heat rose in the small space between us, and I dared to reach for his face. These shadows meant nothing to me. I lived as a shadow, and I knew how to brush past them. I found the outline of his square jaw and sharp planes. Strands of silver hair blew past the shadows. He drew in a large breath, his body trembling. Never had I ever been so enchanted before, and I believed I could melt right there before him. All my misery eddied away as if it had never been there. I softly grinned, anticipating gentle warmth to wrap around me. Before I could touch him, though, I felt a yank on my neck, fell backward, and was dragged off the dais. Instant throbbing from the back of my head pounded from the impact.

"Mike! No!" I screamed as I clawed my fingers into the dirt.

"Disobedience," he snarled. "Now, you will walk on all fours back to your chambers."

***

I must have blocked out the sheer humiliation of crawling back to the castle because I didn't remember coming back at all. This was all my fault. I should have never defied him. The waning moon shone just a little brighter as if a fog had lifted. In the end, it was worth it to let someone else know that I had seen them. Too many times, people passed me by—though I was a human disaster—ignoring my pain. My hands had touched the hems of many shirts, begging for help and validation, but it was too much. I was a discomfort to all, so I hid. Peter saw me. He promised he would find me. But he was nowhere and never would be anywhere again.

Mike walked in casually, his face a lethal calm. "What you did is forbidden."

"Humiliating him isn't?" I snapped, curling my knees to my chest on the bed. Mike stood there with his hands on his hips, wanting to say more, but I could see he was at a loss. I railed on. "You once said some of it was real. Is that part of you so easy to shut off that you treat me like an animal? Did you ever think you could love me?"

Mike stepped forward, creaking the floors beneath him. A familiar gaze swept over me. His leather-gloved fingers ran through my hair like he used to do when we kissed, cupping my face with his other hand. I winced from his touch. He nearly forgot about my face being tender. No matter his affection, there was this lingering pain of what he had done to me. He staggered back as if he'd stepped over the line of decency. After assessing me, his eyes became ice cold again. With a growl rumbling in his throat, he turned away and headed for the door. His hand rested on the door frame, contemplating.

"It is easy," he said, his voice lowered. "Love is blood spilled on altars." The door shut, locking me away from the world.

I shimmied out of the dress Mike had so desperately wanted me to wear and put on my pajamas. Luca delivered more nightclothes for me, nothing as luxurious as the black silks, but he left soft linen shirts and pants. He also provided more day clothes, not dresses, thankfully. I realized he was beginning to understand me as I smiled over the trousers, loose shirts, and boots. Finally, some shoes. Since there was nothing to do to pass the time, I sat in my bed gazing outside, watching the moon and stars compete with the setting sun. It was odd how the moon had phases yet never moved from its position in the sky. Stars blinked dimly, but never moved. Perhaps this realm did not rotate around the sun like mine did. Maybe time stood still.

A scratching at my window made me smile. Kaya and Wren came back like they said they would.

"Just hold it there while I open the window," Wren said through the glass. I opened the window for them, and Wren glared at me, his wings fluttering. "I said *I* would open it!"

"I was just trying to help. Why are you—?" I noticed a huge violet flower head turned over. "What is this?"

Kaya's sweet face poked out between the large petals, and she giggled. "It's a message. But you must burn it after you read it."

Wren leaned against the window frame, twiddling his dagger in his hand. It never occurred to me to look at the marks he made on the windowsill the first night. Marks, like an ancient language, were so small that the average person would have missed them.

"They are wards," he said. "Our prince ordered us to use magic to protect you."

My eyes pinched. "Protect me?" I asked, pointing to my bruised face.

Wren's eyes lowered. "What he did was cruel. But we do not serve him. We do not bow."

"We do not bow," Kaya repeated from under the flower.

"It was my wards that kept other dark things from lurking in," said Wren, flapping his way closer to me. "Read your message. It's urgent."

I turned over the flower head, and Kaya flew onto my shoulder. It took both hands for me to hold it. Silver ink shimmered under the pale moonlight, but I could not read what it said. I tossed my legs over the bed, and Wren followed me, sitting on my other shoulder. A part of me wished they could just stay with me after tonight. I knelt by the fireplace and finally saw the message written on four petals.

I see you. My heart jumped. Peter? Peter was here? *Wait for the full moon.* Tears flowed down as I read the next petal. *I made a promise to find you.* Then, the next. *Peter Pan keeps his promises.*

"Who's Peter Pan?" Kaya asked.

"My only," I replied, pressing the flower to my chest. I was about to open the bridge between our minds when Wren flicked my temple.

"No, Elora. You must not mind-speak. The other one can hear you." Wren must have felt a ripple effect from me opening the bridge, and I immediately shut it down. "Three more days. Just wait three more days. We will come for you." He flew to the windowsill, signaling for Kaya to follow.

"Peter works for the other prince?" I asked. "Peter is waiting for me somewhere, isn't he?"

They looked at each other warily, twisting their lips together. Kaya flew to the window. "My lady, the less you know right now, the better. Three days." They dove under the pink sky.

9

ELORA

Dark night shrouded me save for the flickering stars burning hotter with each breath. Once again, I wore white silks, my hair gilded in gold starlight. Something menacing growled from within. Stars swirled around me, picking up the pace gradually until they encompassed me in terrible, blinding light. I collapsed, finding a sharp weapon in my trembling hand, though it was blurred. Anguish crushed me as I heard cries muffled in the background. I plucked a gold star from the tempest and placed it on my tongue. The man in the cowl appeared in front of me, but he staggered back, refusing to reveal himself. I used to be closer to removing his hood in my nightmares. Now, he felt further away.

The star I swallowed lodged itself in the core of my being, invading every fiber. Veins of gold webbed over my skin, burning me alive, raging against the night of my soul. I felt myself falling into an open room with no roof over my head. Shooting stars rained the night sky, lighting up the room. Two bunk beds appeared in my vision. Wrinkled finger paintings of flowers shook off the white walls. This had never been part of the nightmare before. Emily's bed was tightly made and empty, but where I slept was messy, coated in oil. Familiar footsteps echoed, and I ran and ran, trying to find the exit, but my dream would not let me out. Smoke curled around my ankles when I heard the voice again. *"Shh, pretty flower, you don't want to wake the rest, do you?"* Starlight faded, leaving me in complete darkness. The room tilted and pulled everything against the walls to the center. I stopped my bed from crashing into me when I landed on my back and pushed it away with my legs. My heart raced as the floor softened. I sank into the ground like quicksand, grabbing for purchase. *This isn't real*, I told myself over and over as I fell into an abyss. Hands gripped my shoulders, and I fought them off as darkness greeted me. Fists flew in the air until I hit something hard and warm.

"My lady!" Luca shook my shoulders.

With a gasp, I popped my eyes open. "Luca..." I shivered.

"My lady, you were floating." His voice trembled with every word.

I noticed the dropped food on the floor and the shiner I had given him. It was enough to pull me out of my stupor. "Luca, I am so sorry." I sobbed.

He held me to his chest and rocked me back and forth until the trembling became a slight tremor. Everything felt real, like the vision I'd had in the hospital.

"Did you say floating?" I asked once I regained composure.

"Above your bed, as if whatever you were dreaming had a physical hand on you." I felt his chin rest on my head.

I let out a breath. "This nightmare lives inside me even after I wake."

"Sounds like the Hag to me," he surmised, rubbing the chill off my arms. "I should really get up. I don't think Suri would like me holding onto another woman." He winked.

"Suri? The beautiful faun I saw earlier?"

He held my hand, assuring me I was safe. "Yes, I am sorry I stayed away for so long. We played our flutes and made the most perfect melody. It was hard to leave."

I must have been desensitized because I really believed the two of them had gone off to do something else. "That sounds sweet, Luca." I sat up in bed rubbing my arms. "What is the Hag?"

"A spirit who invades dreams and latches onto that person. A parasite feeding off you even when you're awake." Luca's jawline feathered. "She eats joy, my lady. Your despair...is her dessert."

I had only been in Sidh for a week, maybe two, but nothing surprised me anymore. I saw faeries and hobgoblins, so the Hag was easy to believe. However, I'd had this nightmare before Sidh, but nothing as intense as what I had just experienced. Luca picked up the spilled food and set the tray on the mantle.

"I know you serve the other prince, Luca," I said.

He stilled. His eyes turned to icy mud. "My lady, speak of no such things. Ears are everywhere. Spirits are listening. Therefore, your name is not spoken. Names are vows, power."

"But I can say your name," I countered.

"Because I am not tethered to you. The mention of your name would…" He bit his lip, fearing he'd said too much. "I must go. Our meetings will be scarce from now on."

"No, Luca, wait!" I shouted, reaching out my arm. He shut the door anyway. Just two more days. Maybe three. I couldn't tell anymore. Already, I missed him. I hoped Luca would leave with me when it was time.

"My name is Elora Addison. My name is Elora Addison. My name is Elora Addison." I whispered.

Just as I suspected, nothing happened.

The full moon hung above me as I laid in a soft gold gossamer gown Luca procured for me. Normally, it was breeches for me, but since I was meeting Peter face to face for the first time, I wanted to look special. Gold shimmer ran down the free flow of my gown and past my boots. Black boots were not what I'd imagined, but they looked punk rock—which was more "me" than wearing high heels. I braided the front of my hair and tied it back with a violet ribbon I'd pulled from the dress Mike had given me. Wisps of my pale hair fell on my face, hiding the fading bruise.

I opened the window carefully so as not to snag the loose sleeves that drooped below my shoulders. Commotion went on beyond the courtyard. Twin fires blazed from where the maypole took place, but I could see nothing beyond the bobbing of heads. As always, the air was clammy, sticking to my skin. Tonight, the skies appeared blackish, fading into blue, and the brightness of the full moon was increased. My chest warmed and beat so loud in rhythm with the drums below. Pale light flared in my chest, which

I had not yet learned to control. I hoisted my dress and covered the starlight, waiting for my rescue.

Wren arrived at my window with Kaya, his eyes flaring. "It's time, Elora. We will take you down to the ground through the window."

My mouth dropped. "You have to be kidding!"

Kaya not so much as winked at me when she wrapped her little arms around mine. "I told you—we are stronger than we appear."

I looked at Wren as he wrapped his arms around me, nodding. There was no reason not to trust them, so I pulled myself into the window frame. Positioning myself would have been harder if they were not there guiding the way. They pushed and pulled at me until I sat in the window frame, my legs dangling over the edge. I took a deep breath, staring at the wet, glittering ground beneath me. It was so far down that if one of them lost their grip, I was done for.

"Take a deep breath and close your eyes," Wren said.

Like a breath before the dive, I gulped the damp air and closed my eyes. Their wings fluttered a million miles a minute, but they never lost their grip or struggled to hold me. They truly were so much stronger than I'd imagined. Carrying a basin is one thing, but a fully grown adult? It thoroughly impressed me. As I landed on my feet, drums vibrated beneath me, and my chest grew hotter. Little footsteps padded near us, and we took cover behind a broken wagon. Hobgoblins.

"You almost made us late to see the cursed prince. It's the traitor's full moon," one said as they hobbled to the fires. "This crazy queen will have our heads if we do not show."

Wren and Kaya whispered something, but I could not hear them. Something in my gut roiled. I had to see the commotion. Then, I would go with them to meet Peter. If the cursed prince was being humiliated again, I could not let it go. Wren and Kaya shouted my name in loud whispers, trying to pull me back. Kaya pulled on my skirt, ripping some of the fabric. I did not care. Something pulled me, reeled me in. Fire in my blood erupted, and all I could do was breathe to simmer down. I walked through the castle gates, refusing to look back at the Onyx Keep. I would die before going back to that prison. The ground was muddied with tracks of many creatures as they'd stampeded to the grassy plains. I did not realize how long it would take me to get there. Luca had escorted me there before. I must have been in too much of a daze to notice.

Wren and Kaya pleaded with me to come back, but I would not listen. The draw to see the cursed prince overpowered me. Wren fluttered in my face, pulling out his dagger to threaten me. His face froze in shock when he brandished his blade and shoved it back in its sheath. Wren never wanted to hurt me. Kaya cried out for me, but her sweet voice faded as I drew near.

It was a vast crowd. The white dais was left from the Maypole festival. Fires blazed on either side of the dais among the thrones. I almost bumped into a minotaur, the same one who sat at the table with me during the maypole, but I skirted away. There was no plan. I had no idea what I was doing. I just knew I had to be here. Wren and Kaya flew away as if they were too scared to be near this crowd. I hoped they would wait on the edge of the tree lining across the way after this was over.

Huge chains clinked, quieting the crowd. A huge boar-like hu-manoid dressed in leather and bones held a whip as the cursed prince made his way onto the dais in chains. There were no shadows around him this time. My heart stopped. He was the most beautiful thing I had ever seen. His silver hair was shaved on both sides and pulled in little braids down the middle. I wished to see his eyes, but the prince hung his head low. With the tearing of his shirt, the boar exposed hundreds of silvered scars on his blue-muscled back. He made no sound, no fight. Corded muscles rippled down his arms and legs. It was a wonder he did not retaliate.

"The traitor's full moon has arrived, and as decreed, this defector must face thirty lashes!" the boar announced.

Monstrous. To be sentenced to public humiliation on every full moon was cruel. If Luca was right, nobody knew why he was up there. His head perked up as if he smelled something, and he locked eyes with mine. They were midnight blue with a twinkle of starlight in them. For the life of me, I could not stop gazing. I knew it would be easier for him if he hung his head low just to get it over with. His eyes widened, lips parted, wanting to say something. I was so inconveniently pulled by his presence that I'd likely ruined my own rescue. My life seemed so insignificant, yet his gaze alone felt like purpose. I hoisted my skirts to make a run for the dais, but hands gripped my shoulder so hard I knew it would leave a bruise. Mike.

"What are you doing here!?" he screeched. "You can't be here!"

I bared my teeth. "Let me go."

"I think not!" He pulled my wrist to drag me away.

His calloused look, the cut that still burned on my face, erupted such fury. I refused to be anyone's victim anymore. Without hesitation, I swiped the edge of my palm to the base of his neck, and he made a thud to the ground. He grasped his neck, throbbing in pain until I held him by the hair, uppercutting him and knocking him out cold. I smirked at the pathetic man lying in the mud, relishing the power I took back from him. My knuckles screamed in pain, but I loved the feeling. I would no longer be his pet. There was no time to do victory laps as I gazed back at the cursed prince. Static electrified my body, and I heard him. Loud and clear.

"Run, Elora, run!" Peter screamed.

"Not until I find you!"

"That was my promise to keep, not yours. Now run!"

"Peter, please, just tell me where you are."

"Lor, for once, do as I say and ru—" Peter's voice broke as the whip took the first crack at the prince. *"Lor...I love you...run."* Another crack from the whip and his groan slithered down my spine.

My breath left me. Slowly, I turned around and saw him. For the first time, I truly saw him. Peter had been my everything for years, and I would not turn back now, not when I was so close. I drifted closer to the dais, pushing my way through the crowd. My heart ached, looking upon the cursed prince's face, his blood dripping off the edge. It was Peter. My only. So much pain, so much anguish. Slowly, I climbed upon the dais, ignoring the roaring crowd behind me. I almost tripped on my dress; the hem now soaked in his blood. Sweat beaded across his head, running down in rivulets over his lips. The boar screamed at me, but it did not matter because of who I beheld. I bracketed his face, tears flooding my eyes.

"It's really you." I cried. He leaned into the warmth of my hands lightly.

"Please run," he hoarsely whispered. Chains clinked together as he tried to move his arms.

"Never." My voice wobbled.

The boar's screams came to my ears. "Well, if you won't leave, I will whip you too!"

Peter's eyes quivered. "Run, love. I will not have you take my punishment."

I took several breaths and wrapped my arms around his neck. "I said I won't leave you."

Peter's body tensed. He pulled the chains forcefully. The boar reeled back his arm, preparing to strike me. The crowd became frenzied. Hobgoblins ran on both sides, surrounding us. The boar's arm whirred around twice to maximize the pain he was about to give me. Peter's voice growled at the goblins scraping at our feet, and I kicked some away.

"Don't you dare touch her!" His voice snapped like a lightning strike.

"I am going to enjoy this," the boar smiled, raising the whip a final time. The whip came down, cracking at me, but I felt nothing as I disappeared into the darkness, falling somewhere wet and cool.

10

ELORA

A jolt went through me. Pale twilight filtered through the tops of tall dark trees. Leaves rustled in the cool breeze against the circular sky streaked with blackened clouds. Wet moss and leaves mushed against my skin, but the air felt different. Crisp air chased away the clamminess I'd always felt in the tower, allowing my lungs to properly breathe again. I rolled over, nearly tossing myself down the hill we'd landed on. Warm lights from a brick house below twinkled. It sat by a lake teeming with flowers of blacks, deep greens, and crimson twining their way to willow trees. It sat hidden by surrounding hills and mountains. A tall chimney puffed smoke as shadows inside the windows ran around. Peter's arms were draped over me with his eyes closed, though his labored breathing. I leaned against his lean body to see if he was awake. I had no clue how we'd disappeared but glad we did. His skin felt cold to the touch. I tore off pieces of my dress and shimmied my way out of his arms. He bled profusely. That was no ordinary whip. Psycho boar-man had tied on nails to exact the cruelest punishment. Pink and red fleshy ribbons tore through Peter's back. Tears ran down my face as I added pressure, soaking the fabric. It was pointless as I bunched my skirts and pressed more until the entire front of my dress was covered in hot, sticky blood.

"Lor..." he groaned.

It was strange to hear him in person and not across the bridge of our minds.

"My water, get my water," he rasped. A skin of water buttoned to his trousers hung so loosely that it was a miracle we did not lose it.

"Are you hurt?" he asked. I shook my head as my trembling hands unbuttoned the skin from his waist. "Take the first sip anyway."

I did not want to be stubborn or question him. As I took a sip of the sweetest water I had ever tasted, he hurled his guts out. A while back, when he sounded ill, he did not speak to me for days. I wondered if he was a sickly person. While he continued to vomit, I tugged back his braids, grazing the arch of his rounded ears. His nails dug into the wet earth, the pain evident in his face. His black breeches were all that was left of his clothes. He continued on all fours dry heaving, his broad shoulders quivering. He was so human and yet, not.

Peter sat back, trying to regain his composure in a series of ragged breaths. My hands gripped his shoulders softly, and I helped him sit upright so he would not fall over and get dirt in his wounds. His claws gracefully scraped my hand as he took the skin from me, drank some, and poured it down his back. He closed his eyes for a moment like I did when we mind-spoke. His body wavered, and I feared he would keel over. My feeble strength would not be able to move his muscular body if he passed out. Quickly, I positioned myself behind and held him up by his shoulders while I passed the skin back to him. We sat in silence, working the nerve to say something.

"I know you were not expecting someone like me," he said, lowering his head, chugging his water.

"Someone like you?"

He rolled his eyes. "A blue freak of nature. I know you expected someone more appealing."

To be fair, I had never imagined him like this. A blue person is only something you see on TV. But it didn't matter to me. He mattered.

"Peter...all I ever wanted was you. Give me some credit. I knew there was something beautiful underneath those shadows. You're beautiful, even right now, vomiting near my boots."

He let out a painful, broken laugh. I pressed a kiss onto the back of his head, and his hands clenched. "Please, don't do that."

"Why not?"

"Am I still bleeding?"

"Of course, you are, you..." My eyes flicked down his back, and the exposed muscles were nothing more than silvered scars on his back. "How did that...?" I touched my bruise and no longer felt any pain.

"The water. I have a secret lake not far from my house. It was the last of the water where I originally came from. The healing waters of Rinarie." His lips thinned. "It is nothing now."

Sadness clouded his eyes as he pushed himself from his knees and lifted me to stand. I held his hand, interlacing my fingers with his. Peter tore his gaze from me, unable to stomach the sight of me. Before he could utter another word, I wrapped my arms around his rock-hard waist. I waited for him to embrace me, but his arms hung low. Something was different about him, as if me being across the bridge was much more preferable. Maybe now that he had me, it was not as good as he'd imagined.

"Peter, are you not glad to finally see me?"

"No, not like this."

"I get the situation is not ideal, but I'm here, and now we can be together." I cupped his face in my hand. "Peter, please, look at me."

He pushed himself away from me. "Lor, now is not the time. You have no clue what you have done."

Peter took several steps back, rubbing his chin, his eyes darting in every direction but mine. "You are not supposed to be here. Least of all with me."

"That's not true. I choose you. It's always been you."

"You chose *him*," he spat. The words speared through my chest. "My brother who imprisoned and abused you. I told you to stay away."

His bitter words were a weapon, tearing away my hopes and desires. I had always imagined us meeting for the first time, filled with so much laughter and love. Peter unnerved me, unraveling the deep guilt and regret for what I'd done. But he was not right in this instance. He had used his love to manipulate me.

"Screw you." My fists clenched, wanting to hurl them at his perfect face. "I chose him because of your absence. I opened myself wide. I wanted to see you too, bare and exposed, so I could hold you close. Let you know how loved you were, but you would not let me in."

"Let you in?!" His voice echoed across the trees. "What could I have told you? That I was some cursed monster? That the queen of this realm cloaks me in shadows as chains? Maybe that I am useless because of this curse? No, I am not the man you need. No matter how you feel."

"You are no monster, Peter, and I couldn't care less about this curse. Stop locking me out." My eyes stung. The closer he was, the further he drifted away.

"No, that was my brother's job. He locked you out of your realm, your life. You would still be there if I'd never spoken to you."

"And I would be miserable."

"You're not happy now."

"No, but I thought I would be."

"Lor." His voice softened. "You should not have rescued me."

"Why wouldn't I?" My voice shook in disbelief. "When I figured out who you were, I swore to myself I would never leave." A faint, purplish light in his chest pulsed in sync with my star. "Why is it so easy for you to let me go?"

"I had everything planned for tonight. Wren and Kaya would guide you to my house beyond these trees," He took a deep breath. "I made a promise, Lor. Nothing more, nothing less. I beat Mikhail to a pulp for bringing you here and demanded to see you at the Maypole. I just needed to see you, but then you reached for me with that flower head. You do not know how much I wanted to explode and steal you away, but I could not disrupt the order of things. When I saw what my brother had done..." He wiped his face roughly. "It left me no choice but to rescue you and send you back."

I careened toward him, closing the space between us in defiance, as if sizing up my opponent. "I'm not going back."

"Because of what you did by coming to my rescue—which I did *not* want from you—it disrupted the order," he snarled, turning his back to me.

"What order? They were torturing you!" I yelled, hoping he would relent.

He gestured his pressed fingers in my direction. "I am cursed for a reason. The queen quelled my powers. She threatened my friends. I took their powers and hid them inside me so they would not be the target of her vengeance. Now their livelihood is bound by the curse until it is broken. If I use a meager amount of my own, it makes me ill...sometimes it feels like I'm dying. But another part of her curse is a decree for me to be whipped every full moon for thirty lashes. I owe her twenty-eight thanks to you." He placed his hand on a glittering tree. "I will likely face a tribunal for not only having a human pet try to rescue me but the fact I used my power to disappear with you. I never asked you to save me. I don't want your help."

Human pet. Peter's façade slipped away. The man standing before me was a stranger. A stranger who I'd shared countless laughs and tears with. I had bared my soul to him, and this was what I'd received in return.

My lips quivered. "I really am nothing to you." His face slanted, avoiding my teary gaze. I wished for his hands to dry my tears away, to tell me he did not mean it. My teeth bit down on my lip hard enough to smother the sobs in my throat. "You're right. Just send me home."

Rustling leaves filled the cold, silent spaces. I did not want to go back home. I was pretty sure I would be the center of a new investigation, and I would rather die than be in the thick of one again. But I had nowhere to go and nobody to go home to...and that was it. All the loneliness and pain surfaced in a brutal scream that resounded through the forest.

I collapsed to my knees, hating my skin. Years of wanting something pure ripped from my fingers, scraping against my flesh. This unloved skin. The star inside my chest fizzled, and everything became cold. Peter raced to my side, his eyes bulging, his hands shaking as he rubbed my face for warmth. In my realm, they broke curses in faerie tales by true love's first kiss. Except there was no love. It was a scam. A word people peddled around to get what they wanted.

Something like agony tore away at his face as he cradled me on the ground. He was probably whispering sorry like he always did, but I could not hear him through the dark static throbbing in my blood. His nails gently grazed through my hair as he mumbled something over me. Veins in his neck pulsated as if he screamed for help. He pressed my head to his heart, and I felt it pound in my ear like a drum. My hand reached for his hot, soaked face. The light inside him bloomed, warming my glacial skin. He held my hand in his, pressing them to his chest. He angled close to me, touching my forehead with his, so close to my lips.

"Riann, my name is Riann."

Then darkness covered me, and I was nowhere.

Warm, rubbery hands caressed my forehead with a cool cloth, and my eyes fluttered open to a large bedroom. I was lying on a sea of softness in the warmest white blanket. This bed was too large for one person with four tall canopy posts. Across from me, a large fire sizzled and crackled beneath an ornate white mantle. My bloody dress was gone in exchange for a simple white nightgown, something a grandmother would wear.

"She's awake!" a female announced.

My eyes adjusted to the light, and I saw Peter rush to the door-way, dressed in a loose white shirt and gray, knee-high trousers. I leaned into the warmth of the hands rubbing my face with a cool cloth, and I startled myself when I saw her. She reminded me of the woodland dryad Mike made out with, but the woman before me was more ethereal. Pale green skin shone in the light. Splotches of seaweed green scattered down her arms. But what took my breath away were her clothes. She wore a band t-shirt and ripped-up shorts with knee-high goth boots.

Her slender fingers continued to rub my head as I stared at Peter. Mist clouded his eyes, but he did not speak. I was going back to my realm tomorrow and would never hear from him again. The thought of life without him made my stomach clench, and I rolled onto the opposite side, away from his hard gaze.

"There, there," she said. Her turquoise eyes blinked at me and then at him. With a toss of her purple hair, shaved on one side, she angled her head closer to me. "My name is Willa. I am a friend of this guy—Riann—the village idiot."

11

RIANN

My words had caused her star to gutter out. I couldn't believe I'd said something so careless. Nobody else in this godforsaken realm would ever consider saving me, pitying me on that dais. It was amusing for some to watch the whippings without knowing the truth of why I was there in the first place. Too many drank Queen Nyx's poisonous lies and became drunk on savagery. There were still those who remained good, though hidden, waiting for the curse to break. What they didn't understand was that it could never be broken. Not if I could help it. Tribes and clans would die in a generation under her curse. Wombs were the first to be affected, stillborn, miscarriages, and infertility. If I'd had any friends outside that house, I no longer did. Since Nyx had cleverly sown her discord in Sidh, I'd become the "cause" of the curse. People had been truly blinded—I could not have wielded a curse that massive even if I'd wanted to.

The day the curse had happened, my body changed. Peaceful creatures had spiraled into cruel violence. Those meant to heal and cast spells against such evil became vessels of darkness, their lights extinguished. I had created a demarcation line before the blight reached me. However, we were not unscathed. One tribe of the fauns and the faeries each made it.

The earth no longer sprang good fruit, causing subjects to wait for Nyx to bless the crops if she was in the mood for it. She gave just enough for them to be thankful but never enough to be satiated. After everything I'd done to save as many as I could, I was still known as the cursed prince. Then, this angelic creature had tried to save me from tyranny. Though I had known of her existence her whole life, I did not know who she was to me until she'd turned eighteen. Elora became everything to me, and she'd put her life on the line. So why was I angry?

She'd chosen Mikhail over me. Too many times, I opened the connection without her knowing and found them kissing. She didn't know how much pain it caused me, knowing she was giving herself over so easily to him. I tried stopping her, but she was so stubborn. For a month, I could not stop being angry at her and angry at myself for opening my mind so wide for her that Mikhail had slithered his way in. He'd found the mark to hurt me the most. She'd laughed at his jokes, trailed her fingers down his back, kissed him until her lips swelled. But I could not stop listening. At any given moment, Mikhail would turn into the person I knew. All I'd wanted to do was whisk Elora away to London or Ireland, some of the many places she desired to see. I would have been glad to glamour myself forever in her realm just to be with her. But now that she was here...I couldn't stand to be near her. The root of it was something deeper, something I'd ignored since the day I first time I'd cracked open our connection and established that bridge between our minds—I didn't deserve her.

Willa padded her way across the large, bare floor save for the white rug in front of the mantle. My room was much larger than the one Elora rested in. I'd designed it to be the biggest since I knew I would spend eternity in this helter-skelter. My body screamed for a hot bath in the private pool to my right, but I could not move from my dark blue sofa, drinking faerie wine.

"She fell asleep again," Willa said, raking her eyes over me. "I heard everything. After you screamed for me across my mind, you left the bridge open."

I breathed deeply. How fitting someone had witnessed my stupidity. "You weren't supposed to."

Willa rolled her eyes and poured herself a drink from the silver cart next to the sofa. She sat on the arm of the sofa, staring into the crackling fire. I felt the onslaught of words coming, but she remained quiet for some time while I processed everything that had happened. It was enough to make me want to hurl the contents of my stomach again.

"How are you feeling after dusting her here?" she asked.

"Not that bad, actually." Willa's eyes narrowed at me. "Probably would feel worse if there weren't other pressing issues weighing on me." I stared at my glass, contemplating if I should refill it, but I couldn't get roaring drunk. Not that I ever did, but tonight would be a perfect start. Willa stared at me, expecting me to say more. She knew me best. Better than Phil, my best friend. Maybe because she was female. As they often said, females had a higher intuition rate than males.

"Liar." She ran her finger around the rim of the glass. "You're not okay. You keep looking at your hourglass."

I turned my forearm over, clenching my fist. "The queen is furious. More grains of sand reached the bottom after tonight."

After Queen Nyx, my ever-loving stepmother, had cursed me, she branded me with live ink. If I ever made an infraction, or if she simply felt like it, she tapped on the hourglass from wherever she was to enjoy my pain as sand sifted to the bottom. The top was more than half empty. After the last grain of sand fell, I would die. Not that I feared death, but I feared what would happen to those I loved.

Willa shifted onto the couch and crossed her legs. "Makes sense with Elora's arrival. The queen likely detects your stars signaling each other." She watched every tic in my facial expressions. Hiding from her was difficult. "Riann, you know who she is to you." She gulped down her wine and rubbed her lips together. "Are you rejecting her?"

My throat bobbed. Rejection was a harsh word because I would do anything for Elora. The thought of her being alone was killing me when I could just lie next to her.

"I need her to hate me, Willa. When I make a way for her to go back home, it needs to end so she can move on. Hopefully, she will get a handle on controlling her star and live a long, immortal life in her realm."

"Home?" Willa bunched her brows. "She was never home. Her real home is gone. She has nowhere to go, but we can be her home."

I choked on my wine. "I can't do that. The queen will kill her. But before that, she will use her nails to claw out the star while Elora is alive. Her sharpened teeth will tear away at her skin until the star is in her bloodied hands. Then, she will toss her body to the Yaga to feed." I shot her an incredulous look. "Have I painted you a pretty picture?"

"Very pretty," she drawled, pouring another drink. "I think you're scared."

"I am frightened! I would rather Elora live with a broken heart in her realm, but at least she would *live*. And from the looks of it," I lifted my forearm and the hourglass illuminated its black ink in the fire, "I won't be around much longer. She's better off."

I strode to the mantle, drawing close enough to the flames to be within an inch of burning myself as I leaned over. My muscles and mind ached from exhaustion. Still, I could not relax as I tried to knead the knot from the neck. Every bit of tension tightened as I created scenarios in my head of what it would be like if Nyx found Elora. The only thing keeping her there was me.

Willa leaned forward. Her fingers gently rubbed over the silver filigree of her cup. "Tell her everything, then let her choose."

"No, because she will choose me. She needs to find a life without me. Someone who can love her and take care of her." Just a few weeks ago, I'd dreamt of holding Elora and waking up to her every morning. I was doing everything in my power to keep her away.

Willa shrugged her shoulders. "I still believe it's you, and that's the hill I'll die on."

I slammed my empty cup on the mantle. "Can you imagine her accepting a cursed blue freak living with a water nymph, a pyro, a war machine, and a human volcano?"

Wine splashed out of Willa's glass with a swift motion of her hand. "So what?! I love us! And she will too! Who cares that your stepmom and brother are monsters? We have *us*. Me, you, Dolos, Lex, and Phil...we can be her family. Guard her, protect her, plan our escape from this prison. Maybe with her, we have a shot. She has the star of first light burning inside her. Others will use it as a weapon, but we could use it as our refuge."

"Enough! I will not risk it!" I yelled. I tossed my head back as I felt the static rise in me. Mikhail.

"One hour. Tribunal," he said, and the connection died.

"Willa, please look after her. Mikhail just announced my tribunal. One hour." I should have taken that bath. "Don't let Dolos fill her head with his crazy stories."

I cracked a smile, and for a moment, I imagined Elora with us, laughing, creating her own adventures. Trading jokes with Dolos and Willa while Lex broke a smile on his granite skin. Phil would watch warily, with his arms crossed, but once Elora said something clever, his face would light up with joy. My heart warmed, but I could not dwell on it. I couldn't have it all.

Willa leapt from the sofa. "Only one hour!?"

"This is bad for it to be so fast." I straightened myself and put on my fighting leathers with a sword at my side. "If anything happens to me, the battalion of faeries will hold my wards around this land. Not even the queen will get through. Protect Elora. Keep her safe." I wrapped my hand around Willa's, contemplating if I should see Elora before I left. "If I do not return, tell her awful things about me. About all the blood on my hands. I don't want her to miss me. I want her to crave the arms of someone better."

Willa rolled her eyes and clicked her tongue. "Stop your foolish talk. You're coming back."

"Please, Willa." My eyes shone with pleading.

With a huff, she poured herself another drink and swigged it down. Her tolerance for wine astounded me. "Fine. But you're coming back because that's another hill I'll die on."

I slid my hand through the crack of Elora's door, hoping it would not creak. My heart jumped at the sight of her long hair hanging off the edge of the bed. Her button nose and petite frame made my knees weak, but not as much as the faint freckles dotted on her cheeks like stars. How I wanted to kiss each of them the night I had held her. I was stupid to let go. We could have had more time. I wondered what my name would sound like on her lips. But I felt her arms around me and her sweet kiss on my head. I had to let that be enough. She rolled over, cocooning herself in the blankets. With my head held high, I left, leaving her door cracked open so that she would know she was no prisoner. I steeled my resolve as I made my way to the castle, but inside I screamed for more time.

12

RIANN

Shadows cloaked the spires of the dark castle like a gilded cage of what once was. Dark rocky roads greeted me where pixies and sprites used to flutter about. Glittering onyx stones of the castle were a stark reminder of the bleakness that spread like a sickness across Sidh. Ancient stones used to be pearly white, scintillating rainbows during the morning mist. All of this because of my apparent treason, but I'd committed no crime. Dark shorelines graced below the mountains and hills where I'd once basked in the sunshine. Now, it was the thing of nightmares with sirens and sea monsters searching for prey.

My father was betrothed to Nyx, which was odd because that was not our custom in Rinarie. He'd bowed on one knee to Nyx, but his eye drifted to another. Elafina, my mother. Her hair was as dark as the night sky, shimmering with star dust. My father had become so captivated with her, they'd had an affair during a political trip to trade goods across realms. Elafina was a princess in line for the throne. I wanted to believe my father had loved her for the kind, sweet woman she was. After she became pregnant with me, though, he'd left her to live in shame while he married Nyx. My mother having me put a stop to any affection he'd had. She insinuated he'd bribed her to end the pregnancy. Not once did he visit me or acknowledge my existence until he was dying.

No love lost, though. Because of him, no man wanted my mother simply because she did not wait for her bonded one, her cymar. Essentially, she was spoiled goods. I stayed in Rinarie with her for about twelve years until *they* came. The Astryx. The high lords of the realms. They killed off realms at will if they did not pay the soul tax. My mother's family refused to pay the tax for a long time, but eventually, the Astryx came for payment and destroyed our realm. It did not happen overnight. Gradually, the land suffered blight, and more and more people went missing. Then, a brutal shift occurred. Nothing but dust remained on the vacant land. The only reason I'd survived was because of my ability to jump into realms. I tried grabbing my mother, but she screamed as the fates cut her line, and I saw her turn to ash. Phil held one hand while my other carried the remains of my mother.

Mikhail interrupted my thoughts, standing in the arched door-way, nursing a broken nose. He must have just cleaned himself up wearing loose-fitting black cassocks.

"What happened to you?" I asked, not caring.

"Your woman," he sneered.

I chuckled. "Did you really believe she was weak?" We walked down the dark oak halls lined with black candelabras. It became more eerie each time I visited. Even the candles burned a deep crimson flame. "Is this the last time I walk down these halls?" My throat bobbed, thinking of leaving *her* in a place like this.

His jaw tightened, wincing in pain. "Does it matter? At least you won't be bound in that cursed body anymore. You can just float away and become someone's shooting star."

I was not the least bit interested in dying, but I was not afraid either. "Why go after her? At least tell me that before I'm sentenced."

Mikhail's bare arms tensed. "Because I know what she means to you. What she means to others."

I slammed him against the wall, his taut skin brushing my leather bracers. "You know nothing."

Mikhail laughed under his breath. "I know every time she kissed me, she thought of you." A maid dropped her silver serving dish-es, her mouth gaping as she watched me assault the prince. "Let me go, or that servant girl over there will burn for your insolence." He slumped down when I loosened my hands.

I went ahead of him, standing in front of the ornate iron doors. For a moment, I considered the consequences if I plunged a knife into the queen, but I'd seen her ugly string on the spindle before, and I knew she could not die with the power of this curse. I wished I knew how she wielded this much power to find a way to save us all.

Mikhail caught up to me and pushed the doors open slowly. "She tasted like peppermint," he whispered.

Vehement flames coursed through my veins. Elora was mine, and he'd taken her. He'd manipulated her. Kidnapped her. Isolated her. Stripped her identity, and physically harmed her. My knuckles turned white. I would gladly melt his insides slowly so I could enjoy it with a glass of wine in front of his weeping mother. Firelight from the sconces on the marbled pillars spilled across the throne room. Nyx preferred her meetings in the throne room to make us remember her authority.

Queen Nyx's eyes darkened upon seeing me. "Hello, my spindle mage," she said. Her long, pointed, blood-red nails clicked on the center of the ornate black table. "Silas has prepared a special seat for you in case you get out of hand."

The white marble room felt so cold and bleak. Blackish flames tinged with gold flickered from the chandelier above the oval table. Other than those two things, the room itself was bare, save for the crimson swath of heavy curtains in each long window.

Silas, a woodland dryad, creaked his way to me, sliding a chair covered in black chains. They contained elements of a dark star, disabling all powers. I could hardly use my powers, so she must have been afraid of me leaping over the table to slice her throat. She wasn't wrong. Silas' rough bark scraped against my skin as he wound the chains around me. With every loop he tightened around me, his sad eyes fixed on mine, filled with regret. I remembered him coaxing me to play with my brother, though I was much older than him. There were times of happiness between me and Mikhail because of Silas. His wisdom and gentleness planted seeds deep within us. I could only imagine how disappointed Silas must feel about our choices. His hands slightly gripped me as if to say he was sorry for what he had to do. He had to do whatever it took to survive. Surviving the two kings before Nyx, he knew what the realm was like before everything had happened. He must have wanted to change everything by leading us.

More branches withered away each time I saw him. Silas was dying. Like all dryads, they died slowly before collapsing somewhere in the woods and becoming a home to other animals, decomposing over a long period. His long, mossy hair brushed against my knees as he slowly creaked away.

Kain, a russet minotaur with copper eyes, clicked his hooves on the floor. His black scaled armor and short sword at his side did nothing to make up for the pathetic person he was. He tried kidnapping Willa before my wards went up. He sat next to my father, the corpse. Gold robes and ruby rings did nothing to offset his gray skin. My father, the king, died years ago. The king everyone now saw was just a shell of a man to keep up appearances. Nyx filled his dead body with dark magic, and because he never talked anymore, he was called the mute king.

She liked to keep her counsel small. She called the shots anyway, but she also enjoyed the appearance of strength and unity. Mikhail leaned on a pillar, picking at his nails with his dagger. My death sentence must have bored him.

Queen Nyx sighed, folding her pale hands under her pointed chin. "I think you know why you are here." She did not bother waiting for an answer. "Did you know there is a group of people who seek to overthrow me?"

"No, but I imagine your stellar leadership is the reason," I deadpanned.

Her eyes flared. "I have clothed and fed the people. What more do those rustics need?"

"You plunged them into darkness, and you pay the tax by..."

She gave her shoulders a slight shrug. "Such a small price to pay. After all, the Astryx need to feed."

I shifted in my seat to lean closer, baring my teeth. "The people know you snatch innocents in the night and sacrifice them. They know the Astryx feeds on their souls."

A thin smile spread on her face like a relaxed snake. "And how do you know all this?"

"You know who I am." I shook my body in my chains, willing them to break, knowing it was useless. "I tried to cut their strings to save the realms from their wrath."

Nyx's tongue clicked. "Ah, but you couldn't save Rinarie."

My jaw clenched. "That was eight hundred years ago. I was but a boy, not yet skilled in my abilities. Did you really make me come here to reopen the past? If you want to kill me, just do it and be done with it."

"Oh, little Riann," she said coolly. "I do like playing with you, but not as much as I will enjoy what is to come. You see, there is a quiet rebellion happening under my nose. And I think you are a part of it, no matter how much you hide behind your wards."

I shook my head, catching Silas' downcast eyes. "Lies. I have no real power to wield; this is just another fabrication. It's easy to pinpoint it on the traitor."

"No power? You have been mind-speaking to Mikhail's human pet for some time. And last night, you defied the decree. Do not forget; you stole the child from us. We need that weapon against the Astryx. They feed on as many souls as they can, but they will grow tired of eating the same thing over and over again."

I angled my head. Like Mikhail, I was getting bored with this conversation. "Right. As if you care for your people. I know your intentions. You wish to ascend."

Kain vaulted from his seat, brandishing a curved dagger. "You dare speak to your queen this way?!"

I rolled my eyes, pulling on the chains needlessly. "Take a seat, Kain. Nobody cares that you're here." Nyx signaled for him to stand down like an obedient dog. "With that power, anyone could create and destroy worlds, restring the spindle. Our universe could collapse if her star fell into the wrong hands."

"Paranoid delusions," she scoffed.

"As for these spies, this *rebellion*, I have nothing to do with it, so just leave me alone or kill me right now."

"Oh no, I need to see how much that human pet means to you." She gracefully rose from her ornate seat, padded to my chair and grabbed my chin. Sharpened nail tips dug into my skin. "You see, I need to increase morale to stifle this rebel stain. People witnessed a strong, tenacious human protecting the traitor. How much more will they love this human in the labyrinth games?"

My heart sank and my vision blurred. "She's just a pet. Mikhail can help me send her back."

"See how quickly you come to defend her. If I did not know any better, I'd say you loved this creature. But you have three options." She lifted my chin with her talon. "One, she will compete in the labyrinth games. Two, you will let me know the location of the lilac child. Three, I will let you take this human back to her realm, where I will take Mikhail's keys, find her, and rip out her spine. Which do you prefer?"

My body boiled. I would rather die killing this psycho than let her lay a hand on Elora. "One day, I will kill you for this."

My little prince." Her voice simmered with quiet rage. "My blood won't solve a thing." She smiled as she pushed my face to the side.

Cornered. There was no way out for Elora unless she competed. My original plan was to convince Mikhail to use his keys. I had the ability to jump realms and different threads of time, but now I was useless. "Fine! She will take part in the games on the condition that you give us one hundred days. Your crazy son locked her up. She needs time to regain her health and train if you want her to last in the games as long as possible."

Nyx considered my words with her fingers running through her raven hair. Her ornate gold belt held two pieces of plum silk together, barely leaving anything for the imagination. "One hundred days. If she does not show on the hundredth day, I will find a mage to take down your wards and slaughter your friends in front of you along with this human you are so eager to protect." She sat back down and motioned for Silas to remove my chains. "Mikhail will see you out."

"I can walk fine on my own, *your majesty*." They waited for me to bow as I made my dramatic exit, but I refused. She was no queen of mine.

13

ELORA

Underneath the blankets, I felt safe. If I tore them off, light would break in, and I would see a room that was not mine in a world bent on destroying me. But where I came from was no different. I concluded I was never meant to be there, but I didn't belong here either. I felt the urge to pack my things because when Peter returned, he would shove me into my realm and disappear. Yet, I had nothing to pack, nothing to wear. My boots were still covered in his blood and the dirt of the forest. That beautiful gossamer dress was destroyed—the dress I'd wanted him to see me in. I had wanted to take his breath away. Instead, I shut my eyes and waited for the inevitable. But then, I had to pee.

Reluctantly, I moved the covers off me and could not find a bucket. I looked under the enormous bed and inside the oak armoire. When I opened it, clothes from my realm but from different eras and centuries bunched together, letting air breathe into them for the first time in who knew how long. Corsets, tunics, togas, ripped-up jeans, and my least favorite, poodle skirts, burst free from the armoire.

"What is this place?" I whispered.

"I'm a collector of fashion," Willa said, standing in the doorway with a tray of hot eggs and bread.

She wore fishnet stockings, a black leather skirt, and a torn British flag shirt.

I squeezed my legs together. "You've been to my realm?"

Willa placed her hand on her chest. "Been there? Honey, I loved the punk fashion scene," she grinned proudly. "After battling wars, we'd vacation in your realm. My top favorite place to go was NYC in the early eighties. I glamoured myself and looked kind of like you, actually. But I opted for a neon pink hawk. Riann told me you go to punk shows and get yourself hurt."

"Riann...his name is Riann," I said to myself, trying not to say Peter. My knees clenched together, and I was going to burst. "Where is your bucket?"

Willa's brows arched. "Bucket?"

"Yes." I waved my hand. "I need to pee... to relieve myself." I sounded like an idiot, but I didn't know what they called it there.

Realization dawned on Willa's face. "Mikhail made you use a bucket?!" Her full lips twitched. "That's disgusting." She pointed down the hall. "We took some cues from your realm and created indoor plumbing. It's two doors down to your left."

I ran down the hall, my bladder on the verge of exploding. When was the last time I went? I rushed into the ornate silver and blue bathroom. A large white tub angled toward wide-open windows to my right with the silver toilet guarded by a privacy wall to my left. It smelled like apples and sage. After I finished, I washed my hands at a blue sink, fashioned after a scalloped shell. The mirror above revealed a ghastly reflection. I was gaunt, withered. Coming into this realm, I was already thin enough, but now... I appeared starved with shadows rippling down the planes of my face.

Two soft knocks came. "Are you okay in there?"

My head shook no, but I replied, "Yes."

"You need to eat. From the looks of it, you have barely eaten the past two weeks."

Ugh, another Luca—another person looking out for me. Someone I was going to lose anyway. I opened the door and almost hit her in the face.

"Does it matter how much I eat? After today, I'm gone, and nobody will care where I go," I snapped.

Willa's shoulders slumped. "That's not true. I want you here. Riann's told me so much about you. I feel like I am close to you already."

"Just leave me alone," I scowled, walking briskly to my room.

"No."

My eyes widened. Her simple defiance halted my steps. "Are you under orders to be a companion for me? If so, you can just let go of the charade."

"Elora, stop." Willa caught up to me and grabbed me firmly by the shoulder. "You're going to shut your mouth, stop speaking those words over yourself, and you are going to eat. Got it?"

I had no more fight in me, recalling my emaciated figure in the mirror. "Fine." I huffed.

The eggs and bread were still hot when I returned to the room, and I had not realized how hungry I was. Willa smiled each time she brought me more bread. "Good. You need your strength," she said while pouring fruit-infused water in a silver cup.

"So, you kept referring to 'we' when you talked about going to my realm. Who is that?" I asked in between bites.

Willa leaned back on the wingback chaise across from me and tossed her feet on the ottoman. "The misfits. Me, Riann, Dolos, Phil and Lex. We've saved many realms from destruction to restore balance to our universe. But it's exhausting business, so we vacationed in your realm. Riann's favorite time and place to go might surprise you." Her slender fingers wrapped around her goblet as she took a sip.

"Where did he like going?"

"Ancient Ireland when the druids first built Stonehenge. In fact, it was Riann who assisted them with aligning the stones to the stars. Lex helped pull the stones. Can't say it was a vacation for me, though." Willa sighed, fanning herself. "I was bored the whole time, dressed in rough spun clothes and a weathered face."

I dropped my fork. "That sounds amazing and unbelievable. In my realm, it's still a mystery how Stonehenge was built and what it was used for. Some say it was for sacrifices."

Willa choked on her drink. "Oh no, if we knew that had happened, Lex would have toppled those stones with the priests under them. It was used to mark seasons, pinpoint time, like a calendar."

"And who is this Lex?"

She giggled. "He's a war machine. But he's a complete cinnamon roll. Entire armies ran from his presence. He has a large enough sickle to winnow hundreds of soldiers at a time."

I shuddered at the thought of someone having such crazy power to destroy entire armies. Willa noticed I'd stopped eating and smiled. "Don't worry about him, though. He's a softie. Give him a puppy and watch him melt."

"Sounds like you admire him." I stuffed my mouth with more eggs. Willa's face flushed and gazed out the window. "What about Phil?"

"Phil..." Her lips tightened. "The voice of reason. He's no fun, but you need someone on your side who will talk sense. He and Riann are best friends since they both come from Rinarie. He can pour out live lava, burning armies and camps with one fist to the ground. But he seldom uses his power. He enjoys prolonging the fight instead. I think it's entertaining for him."

"And his chosen vacation?"

"Pompeii."

I spit my drink out. "Why?"

"Phil never spent time in the volcano, actually. I think he wanted to warn the people but never did for some reason." Willa took a breath and slowly smiled wide. "Then there's Dolos, our little pyro. His crazy personality is the same on and off the battlefield." Laughter built in her chest. "We saw him skipping on the battlefield over all the carnage while throwing explosives he'd made. He skipped a few times, clicked his fingers, and they detonated. Most of that army was dead. He was making sure none of the bodies hid their leaders."

I gulped the refreshing water. "He sounds insane."

Her shoulders shook as she chuckled. "He's not insane. He's a lady killer. Ever heard of the Nantwich fire in the 1500s?"

"No, I haven't." I settled my hands in my lap, eager to hear more.

"Well, he had an affair with Queen Elizabeth, the Virgin Queen. He said she was a vivacious woman but wouldn't kiss and tell. We all knew what he was doing. Apparently, they were caught doing something, and it startled him so much that he tried to jump into another realm using a device of Riann's while running from her guards." Willa tossed her hair back and pressed her fingers to her lips, restraining her bubbling laughter. "He crashed through the window like a bolt of lightning and landed in Nantwich. But when he landed, an explosive that he had in his pocket set off. He destroyed Riann's device, and we had to find him through wormholes and history books. Good thing he enjoyed being painted. But he never saw Lizzie again."

I was at a loss for words. I wanted to laugh, but I sensed the sadness in her voice. Dolos really cared for the queen, and she'd never married. I wondered if he was the reason.

Willa shrugged and sipped from her goblet. "I think you should take a bath. Please tell me Mikhail at least gave you access to a proper tub?"

I shook my head.

Her lips thinned. "Dillhole."

"Did Mikhail travel with you guys?" I asked.

"Once. We went to Switzerland so he could pay Voltaire a visit, but that was just a guise. He loved a woman there. Marie St. Vernier," she said with a French accent, batting her eyes, "a French woman who studied under Voltaire. The last time he visited, she'd died of the plague that swept through the village. He'd left for too long, trying to find a way to make her immortal. But you cannot create immortality."

"I almost feel bad for him," I said, looking down at the crumbs of my empty tray.

"Don't," she said curtly. "How about that bath?"

Willa must have been super excited about drawing me a bath because I drowned in bubbles. It smelled like lemon and mint. I dunked myself beneath the warm water, scrubbing my hair with the lavender soap bar she'd left beside the tub. Physically, I felt a lot better after eating a proper meal, but mentally, I knew the end was coming and was sick about it. Willa had left clothes from her massive collection on the wooden rack. We seemed to be the same size, and if not, I would just have to grin and bear it. Purple plaid pants with zippers on the legs and a plain black cropped t-shirt. She really got me. Maybe she was not lying when she said she felt close to me because of Riann. None of it mattered, though. He wanted me gone.

With wet, combed hair, I made my way down the hall, following Willa's laughter. I rounded the corner of an ashen oak tree built into the wall and stepped into the bright, sunken room filled with soft blue sofas, chairs, a brick fireplace, and an open kitchen. Staring at me was a hunk of muscle. Lex. His long brown hair was tied up halfway, pulling back his granite-hewn features. He was all muscle and golden skin, like a Greek god. The sun never truly rose, so it was a wonder he remained so perfectly tanned. Even wearing a loose fitted tunic and breeches could not disguise his girth. He looked me up and down and hummed under his breath before turning away.

Dirty blond curls, a pale face, and playful blue eyes danced across the room to meet me. The owner lounged on the sofa with a bowl of grapes in his lap. "Fancy this...you are no human pet. I smell star fire inside you."

"You must be Dolos," I said with a weak smile and walked toward him. I extended my hand to shake his. He looked at my hand warily, and I remembered Luca being weirded out about handshakes.

"What gave it away?" he asked, popping a black grape into his mouth.

"You smelled fire." I giggled, trying to hide how nervous I was around them.

Next, Phil looked me up and down. His rich brown skin glistened over his tight, athletic body. Clad in sleeveless black leather and leather pants, he exuded formidable strength and resolve. Every-one there should have been gladiators because they were built for endurance. "Pleased to meet you," he said. "Riann should be returning soon."

I ran my fingers through my soft, wet tresses. "It is good to meet you, too. But I am afraid my time here is short. I am to leave once he comes back."

Phil's eyes simmered like red pools. "Maybe we can convince him to let you stay. It has been far too long since we've had the pleasure of outside company."

Dolos raised his frosted goblet. "We're sick of you too, bro!" he laughed.

Bro. They really had spent a lot of time in my realm.

"I heard you help people for a living in an infirmary. Are you a physician?" Phil asked, pulling a seat out for me at the kitchen island. The kitchen looked modern with white tiling and gray wooden cabinets, save for a large brazier and an old-fashioned brick oven.

"No, I'm not that special. I help people find the resources they need to live safely on their own."

"Resources?" He rubbed his chin. "Interesting."

Willa poked her head into our conversation. "If it were not for Elora, many people would not have a place to live or somewhere safe to go when they leave the infirmary. It prevents them from getting hurt again. She's a miracle worker."

"Miracle worker," Phil pondered, eating a slice of an apple from his paring knife. "Well, we need some miracles. Maybe we will force Riann into letting you stay."

I shifted around in the swivel chair. If only they knew their friend did not want me there. There was no way I'd force myself into his life when he made it clear I could not be in it.

"Riann's a jerk," Dolos said. "We all heard him on the hill." He angled his head at me as sympathy glistened in his eyes.

Willa's face tugged at him. "Dolos."

With that look, Dolos shut his mouth and retreated to the corner of the sofa.

I wished I could have said I was embarrassed, but I couldn't fit that emotion inside me with everything else going on. "It's alright Willa. I think the entire world heard us last night."

Dolos mumbled something about stars, and Lex growled at him. Dolos appeared to be the hothead, but I liked him. In fact, I liked all of them—even Lex. If only I could get a puppy for him, he would speak to me.

The room quieted. I swiveled around and saw Riann standing in the kitchen doorway.

"See, Riann, I died on that hill," Willa remarked.

He locked eyes with me but didn't say a single word. I waited for him to say we were leaving and this would be it. But he continued to stare as if the world stopped spinning and I was the only thing that existed. Crusts of mud flaked off his arms. He never had a chance to bathe before leaving. My stomach dropped as I felt the weight of everyone else staring at us. I parted my lips to say something, but he huffed and stomped to his room, slamming the door behind him. Glass shattered from small painting that fell. Dolos glared in direction of Riann's room. The tension from Riann's presence was palpable.

Willa and Phil went after him, locking themselves in his room. I needed to move, to do something, before I exploded again. My fingers fidgeted in my lap. Dolos' face softened, and he walked across the room, extending his hand.

"My lady." He bowed his head slightly. "Please accompany me on the couch hitherto, over there." He laughed as he stumbled over old English. "Sorry, it's been a while since I've been to the Renaissance Age."

My voice scraped against my nerves. "I heard you visited England. I would love to hear your stories about it."

Pride swelled in his eyes. "Well, I fed Shakespeare some of his famous lines," he said, clearing his throat. "Did my heart love till now? Forswear it, sight, for I never saw true beauty till this night."

"Romeo and Juliet, unrequited love. Star-crossed lovers," I mused, leaning my head back, understanding the depth of that line.

Dolos' eyes grew distant. "I jumped through time to give him that line, so when my love was old and gray, she would hear it and think of me." He popped a grape into his mouth. "What would you do if you could go any place, any time?"

I had never thought of that. But as voices in Riann's room grew louder with my name tossed around, I wished to prevent my birth.

14

RIANN

A rock and a hard place. Wasn't that the saying from Elora's realm when there were no good choices to choose from? We sat her down and explained why she was staying. She displayed no emotion. Frustration settled in my bones, seeing her face as the picture of calm. She had no clue what these labyrinth games were like. Though she understood she would face challenges, none of which she could handle right now, she remained calm, sipping on guava juice Dolos had made. I wanted to shake her, snap her into reality. Even after telling her that past games had monsters, poisons, mind manipulation and the sorts, she stretched out her legs on the sofa and continued sipping.

"I've seen people stronger than you torn to shreds. Stop acting like it's a walk in the park," I snapped.

Lor glared at me and tossed her hair back. Willa looked at Lex, discussing how to train Elora. Only one hundred days, and day one was already a complete failure. Time was against us, and I couldn't bear a margin of error. I took a deep breath. "You're nothing but skin and bone. From now on, you will eat protein, greens, and fruits every day, no exceptions."

Elora snorted.

"What?!" My thunderous voice made Dolos leave for the kitchen in fear. This wasn't me. Why was I acting like this? I needed to stop, but I couldn't.

Elora pushed herself into the corner of the couch, crossing her arms. "Why go through all this trouble? Just let that psycho kill me," she said nonchalantly.

Silence fell in the room. I felt Dolos' fiery glare on the back of my neck. I was not going about this right at all. The thought of Elora dying was making me unhinged. "What's wrong with you, Lor? We are willing to bet on you, to train you. We want you to survive." I stopped speaking as her glassy eyes met the candlelight flickering in the window.

She ran her hand down the pinned silver curtain. "I'll do it. I'll do it for you and your friends. But don't count on me surviving." Elora smoothed out her shirt as she peeled herself off the couch. "Willa, I never know what constitutes as morning, so just come and get me when you're ready to train."

This could not be the end of the conversation. I wanted more time with her, even if it was discussing terrible things. She walked toward her room in uneven steps.

"Lor! Get back here! I'm not done talking to you!" My large strides ate up the floor beneath me. "Don't close your door on me!" I heard her room door click. "That went well."

With my head lowered, I stalked back to the living room, feeling the weight of everyone's stares rake over me.

"May I offer a suggestion?" Dolos asked from behind the kitchen island while I nodded my pounding head. "Maybe your approach sucks."

I rolled my eyes. "Thanks, Dolos. Your advice is noted."

"No, seriously," he continued, rounding the island. "You are speaking to her like a recruit. She has no fight left, and just now, you gave her even *less* to fight for. She heard you say she has to show up on the one hundredth day to save us, but she couldn't care less about herself. Why do you think she feels that way, Riann?"

I hated it that Dolos was right, but I was in no mood to agree. Instead, I raised my brows in irritation at the man who loved many but could not keep the one he truly loved. Maybe he had some merit, after all. I clenched my teeth. "What do you suggest?"

"Don't treat her like a soldier. Treat her like she's your—"

My hand met his mouth, covering the muffled word he was about to use. "Don't you dare say the word!" It was the one word I wouldn't speak because I feared it would undo me. In fact, another word would undo me—my name. And she has not said it. If only she said it. Just a few hours ago, I had wished for more time just so I could hear her say it, but here I was, barking at her instead.

Dolos ripped my hand off. "I was going to say *lady friend*, but okay. Go get some sleep and stop your brooding," he said and walked out the front door. Through the window, I saw him flipping me off before running to his shed. Or what we liked to call, his house of horrors.

Lex stared at me. His eyes conveyed the message loud and clear. *Stop being an idiot.* But I couldn't stop. She needed to live, and no fluffy goodness would make her fight as hard as she needed. Phil, as always, remained silent, weighing each word. When I walked down the hall and passed her door, I almost knocked. What would I say? What would I do? All the things I wanted to do were out of the question. She needed to focus on her training to go home.

What Willa said about the earthly realm not being her home was true, but at least Elora had survived. Then it hit me. She'd *survived* but never truly *lived*. Lor dreamed of traveling to Ireland and Paris, and how I wished I was not bound in that cursed body because I would have done it for her a thousand times over. Any historical time and place she wanted to go, I would have done it for her. Everything I did was for her. I had been stung by her choosing Mikhail, and I knew I needed to let it go. Lor had been through enough, and I needed to stop adding my petty jealousy to the mix.

I went to the only quiet place to process everything. My pool. Aqua blue tiling and silver trim made me feel I was some place free, without worry. It was large enough to fit everyone, but I think they knew it was my safe place because nobody ever came in. I dunked my head underwater, holding my breath until my lungs burned. This must be how she felt. My chest ached as my starlight flared. A beautiful kaleidoscope of purple and blue light rippled through the water. At this moment, I knew hers shined too. Its warmth and energy left traces I gravitated to. I thought of her face crumpling before me on the dais and how she wanted to take my punishment. Never had I felt more terrified and loved. She had saved me, knowing any moment they could rip her from the stage and be dragged away. My heart synchronized to the pulsation of the starlight shining through me. For a moment, I came to my senses. I needed to make everything right between us. I could be better. I could be who she needed me to be.

"Lor…"

I felt her breathing down our bridge. Darkness wrapped around her, choking on the little spirit she had left inside. Rough terrain of fear and longing scraped against my heart. Everything was easier when it was just us across the bridge. But when I heard her breath, I pulled myself back. She was breathing. Alive. And I intended to keep it that way. She had to hate me to let me go. It was already clear that being near me was a danger to herself. I wished to wipe her memories clean of me so she could properly move on. Maybe from time to time, I could reach in to see if she was happy. No, that would be torture. It was a good thing I didn't have the power to do so. She never answered. Not that I blamed her. I tried to make her hate me, and I had excelled. I ended the connection. Underneath the water, with my lungs on fire, I let out a scream nobody heard.

I woke many hours later, and Elora was gone. Willa had left too. Training had begun. I wanted to meet up with them at the amphitheater ruins to cheer her on. Dolos was gone, too, possibly fulfilling the role I was supposed to play. Thinking about it made me jealous, though I knew Dolos to be a better man than most. I walked into the kitchen, lingering, unsure of what to do. I tied my robe tighter and poured myself hot lemon tea, closing my eyes to the sounds of the songbirds out my window. *There's nothing good to sing about.* Lor's voice reminded me of the soothing, melodic sounds of songbirds chirping in perfect harmony. But she no longer sang. She screamed.

15

ELORA

I had dreamed of walking through ancient Greece, touching each stone, hoping to hear a whisper from the age of heroes. Among the ruins of the amphitheater before me, it felt like I walked the footsteps of gladiators. My mouth dropped at the sheer size. From what I could tell, the semicircle seating had once been pristine white but now was weathered and gray. Grass and weeds sprouted between seats, and some were completely covered in ivy. Such a shame for the ivy to choke on something that was once so beautiful.

I did not expect Willa to dress me in sleeveless fighting leathers. I loved tight clothing, but this was on a whole new level, yet it allowed flexibility to move. At least I was not training in hot pants without shoes.

"First," said Willa, shrugging off her bag, "we run. You need to gain endurance, so every day we train, we run before and after. Got it?"

"Got it." It was strange to train under a rosy dusk sky rather than the sun. I rubbed my arms in the chill.

Dolos sat in a raised box where it appeared an emperor would have sat. He crossed his legs over the ledge, grinning with absolute mischief. "Ladies, don't mind me. I'm just taking in the view," he said, sipping back on a gold goblet.

I wanted to laugh, but I had to get my mind in the game. They needed me to show up to the games, and I would train to set their hearts at ease. I knew what awaited me. If my nightmares and all my experiences were a glimpse into the games, there was little hope for survival. I didn't know the specifics, but I could only imagine someone like me would die in the first minute. I'd seen enough movies to know what I was capable of. Willa took a head start, and I followed suit, running out of breath after thirty seconds. I was so out of shape. I recalled Peter telling me not to eat Chinese food. I could have really gone for Chow mein. Willa snapped her fingers at me.

"Is that all you got?" she asked without a hint of sarcasm. Her violet leathers hugged every curve, stretching over her toned thighs and calves. She was not stick thin like I was, and I wished I could be more voluptuous. If the years of eating Chinese takeout hasn't made me gain weight, nothing would.

"Sorry, the only time I ever ran was when I was in danger." My shoulders drooped, smothering those memories.

She tossed her plum-colored hair, braiding it in swift motion. Since I was a novice, I forgot to pull back my hair before we'd set out. Sweat matted hair to my face. If this was day two of training, I didn't know how to make it to ninety-nine. Just kill me. And let my last meal be chow mein.

Willa reached into her bag and removed a green velvet tie. "Here, it will keep your hair out of your face."

I brightened immediately. "Thank you," I said while struggling to hold my hair in place while tying it.

The corner of Willa's mouth lifted. "Let me help."

Dolos leaned over the ledge. His eyes were playful, piercing, as if he saw something intriguing. "Next time you need help untying anything, Lor, let me know."

"I prefer buttons, Dolos!" I said with a stifled laugh.

He reclined in his seat. "Touché."

Willa chuckled and put her hands on my shoulders. "It's nice. Dolos has a new plaything."

"I need some humor," I said, flipping my ponytail back.

"Listen." Willa's voice turned serious. "If you can only do thirty seconds today, that's fine. But each day, you will increase. Normally, you'd have a day in between to rest, but time is not a luxury. For right now, let's work on building your muscles, then after, we will spar."

My brows arched. "Spar?"

"Swords. You will learn to wield a blade." Pink flush crept up on her cheeks. "Lex will teach you to throw a decent punch and kick."

"I already know some defense moves, hasn't Pet—" I caught myself. I still couldn't let him go. "Hasn't he told you?"

She smacked her forehead. "That's right, I totally forgot. Show me then."

I shook my head. "I don't want to hurt you."

"Girl," she said flatly. "I have snapped necks with these bare hands. Nothing you do will hurt me."

My throat bobbed at the sheer intensity of her eyes, like a furious hurricane. I revved myself up, anxious about hitting her. Her muscles twitched in anticipation. I closed my eyes and thought about Mike. His iciness, the way my face felt when I fell onto the mantle. Without warning, I struck her side with an open hand, palm down. It stunned her, but she came at me, her arms reeled back. I dropped onto my back, pressing my feet against her torso. She leaned into me, attempting to strike. I quickly hooked my leg behind her knee and pulled her down. Before she could move, I mounted her with my fist ready to strike.

Dolos shot from his seat. "No way! Blondie took Willa out!"

I was still on top of her as she lowered my fist from her face. "Indeed, she did!" She offered no rebuke, rather, she seemed proud. "You can get off me now," she giggled. I slid off her, shocked I had almost hurt her for the sake of training. "Now, let's see you spar." She tossed me a sparring sword.

As expected, I was terrible. I got whacked so many times for having my guard down. She shouted instructions to pay attention to her whole body while parrying.

"Hands can lie to the feet where to strike!" she yelled.

Feint right, go left. I learned swordsmanship was about strategy and reading the other person. Those fantasy shows made it look so easy. We sparred for a good hour or two before she made me do push-ups, sit-ups, and other muscle exercises. I couldn't remember how many times I tumbled to the ground over the rocky arena. Finally, we ran a forty-five-second lap, and she made me run up as many steps as I could. I only made it to fifteen.

By the end of our first session, I was bruised and bleeding from scrapes, and it felt good. My body was being put to good use.

Willa shook a familiar skin of water. "Riann gave me his healing water for you," she said, drinking some herself.

I pushed it away. "I don't want it."

She lowered the skin. "Training will go much easier if you do."

"No, I need to feel the pain."

***

Peeling off those leathers gave more relief than taking off my bra at the end of a long day. After bathing, I felt completely sore in every part of my body. Parts I did not know existed screamed in agony. Still, I refused the healing water. In the closet of centuries—as I liked to call Willa's wardrobe—I opted for a soft gold, Grecian dress that crisscrossed at my waist. Crepe fabric kissed my skin, sighing with each movement. It felt right, as if it were meant for me.

Riann sat at the small table by the window in the kitchen, reading an ancient-looking tome. I felt his eyes follow me. The tome rose higher over his obvious stare, completely avoiding me altogether. I had worn this dress so he would see me again. As angry as I was, I still longed for him to look at me the way Peter would have. Yes, I knew he was Peter, but the man I knew had disappeared and been replaced with this guy.

A plate of thinly sliced meat and a vegetable medley of tomatoes and cucumbers awaited me on the kitchen island. Willa pranced into the kitchen, whipping her wavy, unbraided hair. Dolos, Lex, and Phil followed moments after, pushing each other to get their fill first. Why even fight Lex? He could crack their heads like eggs.

Willa breathed in the savory scent. "Riann, this smells so good." She flicked her eyes at me as I sat down. "Riann is our resident chef. Don't let his personality fool you. We don't know what to do with ourselves if he doesn't make anything."

Talking him up was not going to make anything better, especially because I felt his annoyance in every breath. He watched me, assessing my plate and flicking my fork over the food. "It's lamb, kind of like shawarma where you are from." He sighed, his eyes peering over his book.

I picked at it more, losing my appetite. It would be best if I forced myself to eat, but I could not do it. Not with him looking at me, pleased with himself if I ate his food. He snapped his book shut. "Is it not to your liking?"

I shook my head. "I just don't feel hungry."

The chair creaked as I swiveled around, and I padded back to my room. Heavy footsteps followed me down the hall. Before I reached my door, Riann's firm hand gripped my shoulder and twisted me around with the plate in his other hand.

"Eat," he demanded.

I pushed myself out of his grip. "You can't control me."

"You obviously don't care for yourself, so someone has to," he growled, shoving the plate in my face. "Eat."

"No."

"If you do not eat, you will faint."

I bared my teeth at him, wishing I had fangs to strike. "Good!" He blinked, his hands shaking the plate. "Maybe I will fall on something and die. Rid you and every one of this problem!" I cried, turning away, whipping my skirt at him.

His hand gripped me again. "Stop talking about dying and EAT." Incensed, he shoved the plate onto my hands, spilling veggies onto the floor.

I pushed the plate back into his hands. "I said no."

Veins in his neck pulsated. "Why are you so stubborn?!"

"Why do you care!?"

His lips drew back in a snarl. "I just want you to eat!"

I turned, and he shoved that plate into my face again.

"Stop it! I don't want it."

Dolos and Willa murmured his name from the kitchen, but their pleas went ignored.

He slammed the dish on the ground, shattering the plate to pieces. "What is wrong with you!? Why did I ever speak to you those six years ago!?"

We remained in the silence of broken porcelain and ruined lamb, breathing slowly. He rubbed his temples, lowered his shaking head, and reached out his hand. "Lor, forgive me. I did not mean…"

I twisted away from him, tears burning behind my eyes. Before I entered my room, I felt Peter's laugh dance across my skin. A memory. The man standing before me was not Peter. There was no kindness, no mercy. Any love he'd bore me drifted away. I became an inconvenience. *Pet*—Riann—stared at me with wistful, midnight blue eyes, but I could not be moved.

With a chokehold on my throat, I whispered loud enough for him to hear, "I miss Peter." Then, I locked my door.

I lost count of how many times Riann opened and closed the connection. His shadows lingered outside my door for a while before leaving. Did he wait for me to come out and pounce again? Being stuck in my room, I felt the uncomfortable silence in the entire house. Fitting that I would show up and disrupt the harmony they had here. My stomach growled, and my head pounded. I needed to eat, but I refused to eat in front of him. Quiet as a mouse, I crept out of my room and into the kitchen. There was no fridge to raid, but I found some of those glittering apples I'd eaten at the castle.

It was no lie. Riann's food did smell great. I looked high and low in the cabinets for any other food, specifically protein, closing each door softly. Yellowed skies rippled along the kitchen floor. Without candles lit, it was darker than usual. A low hum emitted from behind me. I whipped around, fully expecting Riann with a sharp reprimand, but it was Lex without a shirt, tousled hair, and swollen lips. Clutching an apple tight in my fist, I felt the wind leave me as he towered over my little body, shadowing me like an eclipse.

"Please don't tell him," I begged with a hushed whisper.

His dark brown eyes widened at my request. With another low hum, he looked me over and reached his hand behind me. I thought he was going to push me out of the kitchen for making them uncomfortable earlier. Instead, he opened a hidden door camouflaged with white tiling between the cabinets and granite counter space. Coldness met my skin as he pulled out a plate of leftovers. They had a fridge, but it was small and packed with ice. Lex lit a fire in the oven, heated the meat for me, and tossed in a small ball of readymade dough. Gingerly, he set up my plate when everything was ready. Lex was a gentleman. He did not need words. He was a man of action. His muscles curled, handing me the plate.

"Thank you, Lex, this will be our little secret," I whispered, a faint smile tugging at my lips.

Lex hummed again, patted my head, and escorted me back to my room, linking arms. His arm felt like rocks rolling down a hill from his shoulder.

"Good night, Lex," I whispered in my doorway. Without thinking, I hugged him. I must have really needed it. My arms couldn't reach around his waist, but I didn't care, and he did not flinch as he lightly squeezed me back. He really was a cinnamon roll. Maybe I'd finally found friends. However long it might last.

As I devoured the meal Riann had cooked to perfection, a familiar scraping at the window startled me. I leapt from the sofa. Wisps of fluttering shadows flickered in between the wooden shutters. I pushed up the lock and swung open the opaque window. Kaya fluttered to my face, giving me a warm hug on my cheek. Wren looked less than thrilled to see me as he leaned back on the window frame, glaring at me.

"Elora, I'm so glad you are safe!" Kaya's shimmering skin felt warm against my face.

Looking between them both, I knew I owed then an apology. They'd come to save me, and I'd ghosted them for a complete stranger.

"Wren"—I glanced between them— "Kaya, I am so sorry for what I did. They were hurting him, and I..." I started crying. "I thought I could save him and meet you guys in the forest. I did not know..." I sucked in a breath. "I ruined everything, and you guys were just trying to keep me safe. I owe you both and Luca so much for keeping me sane."

Wren pursed his pale lips. "That's your apology?"

Kaya flew to him and whacked him over the head, releasing a burst of black shadow from her little body. "She's been through enough. Just move on. The skies have been more serene since she arrived. She's an omen."

He hissed and glared at Kaya while rubbing the back of his head. "We risked our lives. If anyone saw two faeries, we would be dead right now."

I held out my palm to him, and he turned his face from me. "I am no omen, just a stupid girl with terrible luck. Please forgive me and never risk your lives for me again."

Wren would not answer.

"C'mon, Wren, she did it for love. She risked her life for the prince, a timely tale of the man being the damsel in distress for once," Kaya said, rounding him.

With a huff, Wren took long strides in my palm. "Think with your head next time and not your heart." I loosely closed my hand around him and pressed him to my chest. Wren's face flushed as I released him, and he fluttered to my shoulder, making himself a seat. Wren yawned, swinging his legs back and forth. "This room looks cozy. Let us stay here for the night. It would be more comfortable than sleeping in the willow tree. Then, I will forgive you."

I chuckled softly, enjoying the warmth of their friendship. "You both can stay here as long as you'd like. I'll get some pillows and make little beds for you. Just don't stab me with your dagger in the middle of the night, okay, Wren?"

"I promise," he said with a sly smile.

As I went to pull the window shut, I saw Riann sitting by the lake. Beside him looked like a horse with a muddied green mane and azure glowing eyes. Riann wrapped his hands around his knees, his head lowered. He reached out to pet this creature, and my heart thumped. A piece of Peter flowed through his hand in the way he was so gentle. The horse nuzzled his wet nose into his hand and snorted. Riann laughed, and I heard Peter.

"Riann's kelpie," Kaya said. "A water horse that only he can summon unless his heart is entwined with another. Then she can ride it too."

My insides burned. "That will never be me. He hates me being here."

I sat them down and told them about labyrinth games and everything that had happened between me and Riann. By the end, Wren shed a tear and hugged my cheek. He was a cinnamon roll too.

"Truth is, I am training to ease their minds. But I do not plan on surviving the games. I know the odds are against me, but at least my life will have meant saving others in the end."

Kaya's glittering gaze lifted to mine. "I know what it's like to want to be loved in return. But you will survive because you have love to give."

Their watery gazes left mine, and we curled up in my bed. Wren snuggled under my chin while Kaya curved into my belly, closing her tiny fists in my nightshirt. I had finally found friends and had less than one hundred days to enjoy them.

16

RIANN

Days later, we were still not on speaking terms. The only difference was that she took her plate into her room, or if I left, she would eat in the kitchen. This existence was miserable, though I was the one at fault for it. With her constant presence, I needed to blow off steam by taking a hike. We treaded up the hill to the east and onto the mountain. Streams bubbled and faelights blinked in between the leaves of the trees. Once we got to the top, we would see the edge of our world.

"How long are we walking for?" asked Phil, sweating in his black leathers. Some warrior.

I threw my skin of water to him as he'd likely drank all of his. Even in the days of our youth, he never conserved his water. "As long as it takes to clear my head."

He wiped the sweat crowning his short brown hair. "We could spar instead of walk, you know."

"No, I don't want to end up killing you," I said, trudging along the rocky terrain.

He swigged down my water. Thankfully, I'd packed extra. "She is just a woman, Riann. Don't let her have this hold on you,"

Lor was in training, and I made sure I'd left before she returned. From what I could see, she was happier when I wasn't around, and I deserved that. Phil was right. She had a hold on me, but I wanted it, craved it.

"She will not last in the games if she is coddled. You're doing the right thing," he said.

"I keep telling myself that, but nothing feels right."

We walked the rest in silence before reaching the top. There were smooth, earthen surfaces to sit on amongst dark blooms and tangled grass. The air thinned and I breathed in deep. I plopped down on the edge, dangling my legs though the salty mist. No amount of walking helped the heaviness I felt. "I miss the battlefield sometimes. It was much easier than this."

Phil's eyes flickered with amusement. "I do miss the excitement of it all. Remember when Dolos was telling inappropriate jokes to the wounded on the field?"

I chuckled. "That was sick. Or remember when an evil enchantress hit on Lex?"

Phil's eyes sparked as he took my skin. "I don't think she will ever drink water again, thanks to Willa."

I leaned back. "Don't cross her," I laughed. "My favorite was when Lex showed up as an army of one, and soldiers on the frontline wet themselves."

Phil spit out the water. "That, my friend, was gold."

We overlooked the great waters below that used to scintillate in sunlight. Mounds of grass remained lush, thanks to the faerie tribes we'd saved. They blessed the earth with their giving, feeding the soil with the richness of their magic. One of my biggest regrets was that I could not save them all. Faun clans still lived on the other side of my wards, and I was afraid they were at risk with this underground rebellion.

"Nyx says the labyrinth games are to win back the morale of the people. I believe she has more sinister plans," I said, threading grass between my fingers. "No matter what happens, she's going to believe we are a part of this rebellion and will stop at nothing until I am dead, and she has ascended."

Phil rubbed the back of his neck, his eyes straining to see beyond the horizon. "I agree. She satiates the people with barely enough provisions, throws grand festivals, but never hears their cries, as if they should be grateful."

"She's willing to pay the price of souls for the tax instead of gathering intelligence and armies to fight against the Astryx." I bit my lip hard, thinking of all the innocents she'd led to the slaughter.

The same innocents I'd fought to protect. And those innocent people had turned on me. Cursed Prince. Traitor.

"Who can really fight off the Astryx? They are the lords, the hands of the realms," Phil said, lying down to stare at the sky.

For a moment, I chewed on his words. "It's been done before."

He turned to his side and propped his head with his hand. "The nameless painting. It was never real. You saw a thread, but..."

"The thread was not complete. It could mean many things. I've heard whispers down the thread. This empress defeated the Astryx, and her realm survived."

"Where is that realm now?" Phil asked coolly.

"I don't know. If I had the spindle..." I trailed off, finding this conversation going nowhere.

The spindle containing the threads of fate were long hidden from Queen Nyx's clutches. When I'd buried it deep in another realm's soil, the last thing I'd seen was an incomplete black thread. It neither frayed nor strained itself, floating upright, pulsating with life. Incomplete threads could mean several things, but I had concluded it could mean one of three. The thread was something that has not yet been written; the thread could have annihilated itself before coming into being; or the thread was an anomaly, one born of mystery, a whisper of ancients.

My heart burned in my chest with the last option. It gave hope for the future that whatever that black thread was, it would find its way around the spindle since I was not there to tie it myself. Useless mage, the spindle mage, to be more exact. When I had the full use of my abilities, I'd opened realms with the rest of the misfits, dismantling armies and empires by cutting threads and creating new ones. We'd battled across the skies, preserving innocent blood as best as we could. Cutting a thread was not simple. Fate was a living, breathing thing. Without the cost of bloodshed, the string could not be cut. So, it was best to kill enemies to fulfill the justification. Brutal, yes, but blood was required by universal law. The black thread haunted me, sometimes writhing in agony, and other times it snapped at me like an asp.

Nothing about the time with Phil soothed me. I wanted to stop myself, but every time I was near Lor, I heard her screaming, her blood spilled, for someone like me. I had stained these my hands with the blood of many, but when I leaned into her warmth the night she'd rescued me, I felt like I was worth something. And I'd thrown it away. No, Phil was right. She couldn't be coddled. I'd never been this conflicted before. I needed to think with my head and not my emotions, but they were tangled together, screaming at me from both sides. Orange skies covered the grass, shifting into dusky blues. Squinting, I strained to see the stars again. Doorways to other realms, galaxies called my name, but I was here, abandoning my call for something far more precious.

***

Phil and I made it to the side door of the kitchen when we heard bass sounds from inside. Dolos hung on the edge of the couch, singing his heart out to the music Elora loved listening to. Willa used the CD player she'd stolen from the nineties and blasted Elora's screamo music. Lex sat on the loveseat, tapping his fingers on the arm. Willa sang into candlesticks, twirling around. But Elora. She screamed, making Phil grimace. He wouldn't get it. He never liked any music outside the typical lute and lyre. Her unbound hair whipped around, soft starlight twinkling above her in a hazy glow. I'd never seen her this unleashed before. The star in her chest burned bright, and so did mine, watching her. A small smile never reached my eyes. Tonight, she opted for Willa's short shorts and a ripped-up tank that said 'anti-authority.' In all the time I had known her, she'd never made a single friend. I saw her try many times, but people turned away without really seeing her. If I were more brutal, I would have dug out their useless eyes for not seeing this priceless one.

Elora tripped over the coffee table, snapping me out of my thoughts. Laughing and stumbling to get up, I thought she was drunk, but I noticed the closet where I kept the wine was closed and untouched. Did she eat? Did she drink enough water? Was she getting enough rest?

"That's enough." My voice alone quieted the room, ever the killjoy.

"C'mon, Riann, we're just having fun," Dolos drawled, slipping off the edge of the couch.

He and Elora laughed together, but she immediately stopped when she looked at me. All her joy faded upon seeing me. She really was better when I was not around. It was my fault, but I had come back home with every intention of making things right. She glared at me, her face darkening. Lex growled in his loveseat as he raked Phil and me over. It would seem our hunk of meat enjoyed her company.

Willa crossed her arms, tapping her fingers on her elbows. "Screw you. We are having fun and living life. She killed it today in training, and we are celebrating her." Willa pointed to the sofa where Dolos fell off. Her black leather straps and studs glistened in the fireplace glow. "If you want, you can sit down and be miserable. Just don't speak."

Dolos snorted out his drink as Elora slowly got up and thumbed through Willa's CD collection. I hated myself for creating the gloomy atmosphere. We used to be loud and proud misfits. She popped out a CD from its case, and immediately, I knew the song. It was slow at first, with acoustic sounds and a soft male voice. Steadily it climbed into a crescendo of love and pain like he was the very definition of it. I sat back and closed my eyes, remembering the first time I'd heard it.

"This song is beautiful," Lor said, twining her fingers in her hair.

"It sounds like something you could sing. Better than this singer," I replied. After hearing her sing a couple of times, there was little I wouldn't do to hear her again. But sadness held her dear voice hostage.

"He sings because he is worth hearing."

The song ended, and I opened my eyes while Lor remained facing the CD player.

"You loved that song," she said softly, holding the CD case close to her chest.

She left her own party and locked herself in her room once again. I found myself drifting toward her door, knocking softly, unsure of what to say. "Can I come in?" I asked, poking my head in.

"You own the place," she quipped as she sat on the plush cream sofa across the bare mantle.

Striding to the sofa, I noticed two little pillows and pieces of fabric on her bed. "Have you been having company at night?"

"My friends," she said, tipping her chin to her chest. "It's nice not to sleep alone."

Her cold eyes gazed into the empty fireplace as if flames flickered, so I took the opportunity to light the fire myself. Struggling with the flint to spark, I cursed, and she put her hand on my shoulder. My breath paused. I did not realize she'd gotten up from the sofa. In fact, she limped. Something she did not show when she was twirling around to the music.

"Here, let me." Her soft voice smoothed over my nerves. Of course, with one try, the flint sparked, and she lit the fire herself.

She limped to the sofa and wrapped herself in a fleece blanket. I reclined on the floor by the fire, not deserving to sit near her. After a long, glassy gaze into the flames as they danced across the floor, she shuddered. "I once asked Mike if any of it was real, and he said, 'Some.' Was any of it real for you?"

Her question pricked at my heart. All of it was real. But I couldn't let my guard down for her sake. "Lor, everything I've done has been for you. Protecting you had a steep cost."

Her breath stilled, and at that moment, I knew I had chosen the wrong words. "Protection? I just feel anger and resentment from you."

"They are not mere words. They are action." I leaned forward. "Do you want a poem? A sonnet?"

"You never answered my question." Her voice was deadly calm, her face as cold as ice. My jawline feathered, wanting to tell her everything and yet tell her nothing. "Mike once told me," she continued, "that love is blood spilled on altars."

I wanted to kill him. "Lor..." I rose to my feet with every intention of cupping her face in my hands and showering her with devotion. "I'm tired. You should get your rest, too." Then I patted her on the head, walking slowly away from her.

"Good night. Make sure you get your rest. I wouldn't want to cost you your sleep," she said bitterly.

My fingernails clawed at her door frame. I'd spoken the truth to her. It did cost me dearly. And if I had to do it all over again, I would.

17

ELORA

The monster of my nightmares entangled me. His cold, brutal hands skimmed down my arms in demand. The more I struggled to break free from his grasp, the more his presence pulled me in. His fingers pushed into my skin, marking his territory as his icy breath traveled down my neck. I hated him, yet I was bonded to him. He craved me, and I longed for punishment. I never understood why I felt the need to be punished in order to feel wanted. His lips hovered over the pulsing vein on my neck. I trembled, begging to break free on the inside. My voice froze, my body so cold and taut I thought I would snap if I struggled anymore. Nobody was here to rescue me. I pleaded and pleaded to wake up. He was dead—this could not be real. Then, his slithering voice skated up my spine.

"Shh, pretty flower, you don't want to wake the rest, do you?" I jolted from my sleep, tossing Wren and Kaya off their little beds, plunged in between wake and dream.

Kaya's face leeched in horror as her hands wrapped around a whitish, silky shadow. "The Hag," she gasped. "Quick! Call for Riann!"

Smoky fingers wrapped around my throat, lifting me from the bed. My arms flailed, the white smoke buoying me. I sensed eyes roaming over my body, lingering on my chest. *"Such a pretty flower."* This being saw into my nightmares, my deepest fears, seizing me under its control. I heard nothing else as Wren jumped on me to push me back down to the mattress. Wren knew it was useless.

He took his dagger, carving marks on the soft part of my belly, though I hardly felt it. His throat strained, screaming at the spirit, but I heard nothing except the static of the Hag purring.

Something bluish silver flashed, and it appeared as a silhouette of a man. It dissipated as Riann ran into the room, holding a sword glowing blue at the hilt. Quick-moving shadows rose to meet their opponent. Riann swung his sword so fast that it blurred in my vision. Shadow fingers wrapped around Riann's throat. His eyes bulged and his skin paled. He struggled, as the smoke flowed through his nostrils, invading him from the inside out. I wiggled my fingers, pain slicing though me as if I were breaking through ice to reach for him. For a moment, time felt suspended. The scene around me slowed. Phil crouched at the door while Dolos stood over me, flickering a moonlit glow. Lex was in a running position coming behind Riann while Willa covered her face from the spirit. Riann's eyes slowly moved toward me and snapped back into focus. His hilt vibrated with light, its filaments burning brighter, and he swung his sword into the spirit. Muffled shrieks fell around me before dropping onto the bed. My window shattered when a final scream tore through the room. Laying in cold sweat, breathing rapidly, I noticed Willa and Lex standing nearby, their faces drawn and pale. Dolos was at my hands, rubbing warmth into them.

"I marked her," Wren said to Riann, sheathing his dagger. "I'm not powerful enough for the Hag, but it should give some protection."

"How did this demon get past my wards!?" Riann shouted to nobody in particular.

He knelt and rubbed my bare legs while Lex threw more wood on the fire. Agony rippled across his face as the warmth of his hands seeped into my skin. He trembled, fighting off the after-effects of the Hag. I felt I was in a dream of a dream, caught somewhere dark and in between. When I was not getting warm quickly enough, Riann pushed Dolos away and scooped me in his arms. He settled me in his lap in front of the fireplace, my cold face against his searing hot chest. His calloused hands scraped lightly across my cheek as he caressed my head. How many battles did it take to make his hand so rough? My breathing evened while he restrained his gaze from me as if he were walking a tightrope, afraid of falling.

His eyes closed, and his lips tightened. "Everyone, please leave. I got this from here," he said, firmly squeezing my shoulder and hip. Footsteps quietly paraded out of the room, and lastly, the flutter of wings faded into the background as the door shut.

"Please," my voice rasped, "look at me."

Drenched in cold sweat, my aching body shook. Bits of joy the Hag had fed on left an icy vacant spot inside me. His throat bobbed as he slowly dipped his chin, his eyes slightly closed. A gleam of tears lined his eyes. Midnight blues twinkled with brighter starlight the harder he resisted those tears. I pressed my clammy hand to his face, and he shivered, leaning into it. He paused. The hand squeezing my shoulder now ran down my arm in a slow, soothing motion. His body tensed. I wanted him to know I was okay, that he was okay.

"I see you," I whispered before blacking out.

Riann curled up in the soft, billowy chair beside my bed while I dressed in my leathers for training. He must have guarded me while I slept. His unbraided hair fell in waves over the side of his face. The edge of his roots revealed tiny markings, silvered runes like the ones Wren put on me. I did not feel them when he carved them, but I felt them now with every move and slide of my leather pants. After what happened, it felt like a wall had broken down between us. His face before me was dark and beautiful, and I knew I wanted to wake up to that forever. If I were indeed immortal as Mike claimed, it would not be long enough. After the turbulence and the nasty words, I was still irrefutably in love with him. I knelt in front of him, running my fingers down the sharp planes of his face. He woke with a fright and grabbed me by the wrist.

"It's just me." I leaned forward, and he loosened his grip on me. "Were you having a bad dream?"

He nodded, putting his hand on his chest, steadying his breath. I wrapped my arms around his waist and rested my head against him. My fingers entangled the back of his loose tunic. This was where I longed to be. A sense of rightness settled in my bones. Though I should be shaken from the Hag, I felt an overwhelming peace just being in his arms. I waited for him to wrap his arms around me, to feel safe again. We could be Peter and Elora again. Thoughts of laughter and him holding me close made my heart warm. I curled my arms tighter, signaling for him to hug me back. Riann's arms slackened.

"I think I shall go now," he said flatly.

My heart deflated. I wanted to plant myself on his lap until he yielded. Perhaps, this had always been one sided. I was such a fool. I thought back to needing to be punished. Riann was my pain for existing. He scooted forward without so much as looking at me and gently peeled back my arms. He left again, stealing his warmth from me.

✳✳✳

Lex came to the arena bare-chested with breeches down to his knees. Willa warned my knuckles would bleed today, but I didn't care. I needed to hit something, and Lex would likely feel my punches as nothing more than a flea bite.

"Blondie, are you feeling alright?" Dolos asked from his VIP seat.

I didn't have the heart to laugh with him or anyone today. So, I just nodded and tipped my proverbial hat to him.

"I'm sorry we have to train today after what happened," said Willa, observing me for any pain or weakness.

"I'm fine," I replied tersely. "Let's just do our run first."

We ran as equals around the arena, dodging fallen rocks and debris. Every day, I grew a little stronger as I hurdled over the rocks that I used to run into. This time, it felt like I was running from something rather than running into an endless void. Willa set up an obstacle course, much like the Olympics, with hurdle bars and posts that looked like shields for me to knock down at each checkpoint. She also set up a pole for me to grab onto and

115

spin myself into a flying kick. Admittedly, that was hard to do, but every day I became a little better.

Being rejected for the hundredth time burned me like a brand. I knew Peter was still in there. I felt it last night. I ran harder, faster than Willa. He'd locked me out. And in the same breath, he held me, guarded me. My lungs burned with every pound of my feet. I pushed back against a post with a shield on it, knocking it to the ground. Rounding the arena, I kicked the dirt from behind me and blazed in a fury of speed. Dolos stood from his seat, shouting something, but I could not make out the words. It sounded like a warning, but I ignored it. Lex stood at the end where the pole stood, pushing on his heels, bracing himself. I knew what I needed to do, and he wouldn't feel a thing. Fire ripped through my blood, a river of undulating flames. I needed to burn. In a flurry of sweat and rage, I hooked my leg around the pole and flung myself off, double-fisted into Lex's chest.

A burst of light came from my hands, and Lex flew back. He crashed into the bottom seating, cracking the rocks beneath him. Dolos hopped from his seat, landing just a few feet from Lex. Poor Lex groaned and hissed in pain. His face dribbled with blood from the top of his head. Willa roared, torn between going to Lex or me. Her voice muffled in static. The edges of the trees and the arena dipped in a haze. My body shook under the strain of this power roiling inside me, and I dropped to my knees. I started screaming sorry to Lex, but my ears were deaf to all the surrounding sounds. Gold-writhing light webbed from my chest to my hands. Willa rounded me, too scared to come any closer.

Getting past her hesitation, she dropped her weapons and met me knee to knee. "I got you, Lor! I got you!" she shouted.

"Lex," I sobbed. "Lex."

"Shh, he will be okay. We have the healing water with us." She pressed her green finger to my trembling lips.

I looked over her shoulder and saw Dolos rubbing Lex's shoulders as he drank the water. For sure, they would hate me now. I didn't know how I'd done it. It was as though I exploded. Nobody spoke a word, processing what had happened. This was it. They were going to leave me. Mike was right from the beginning. I needed to be concealed. My hands loosened to grab my bag as

I prepared to run away. I never wanted to hurt my gentle giant. As I slowly rose to my feet to dash into the forest, Dolos began chuckling.

"Blondie," he tossed back his dirty blonde curls, giving me a wicked grin. "You are the first person in history to ever take down the war machine."

Lex growled at him, but his eyes drifted to me, glittering and proud.

Dolos hopped to his feet, his lips curling upward. "Did you not hear my warning?" he asked, and I shook my head. "You were glowing, burning like the star inside you." He laughed, more so out of disbelief. "You really have no clue who you are, do you?"

I turned to Willa, my body still trembling, her look of concern washing over me. "Why is this happening, Willa?"

Her lips tightened. "How much do you know?"

I told her everything Mikhail told me, and she shook her head in frustration. Perhaps, a part of her became angry that Riann never told me.

"That's it!" she shouted, rising off her knees. "We're camping out! Dolos, did you bring faerie wine?"

"I'm always prepared!" He brushed sand off his white linen pants. He wore gladiator sandals which made me laugh. Dolos would dress like an ancient Greek, carrying wine wherever he went. "Oh, and I have bread and cheese!"

"Let me just tell Riann before he has another meltdown," she said, closing her eyes. After a few seconds, she opened them. "Okay, let's go to the apple tree grove! Free food and an amazing view!"

I grasped her shoulder. "You can mind-speak?"

"Why yes, we've spent so much time together that I did not need to use it on you. That was how Riann summoned me the night you both crashed on the hill." She held out her elbow, and I linked my arm with hers. "Come, let's take a breather."

18

RIANN

The house was cold and empty without them here. I sat in Elora's room, taking in her scent, the traces she left behind. Her pillow smelled like lemon with hints of mint. *She tasted like peppermint.* I could have tasted her so many times, but I'd kept my guard up. And I hated it. Violet skies poured in her broken window—which I'd meant to fix that day—but I was distracted trying to figure out how the Hag had gotten past my wards. Was I weakening? I felt more nauseous and irritable lately, despite not using powers. Nobody knew I constantly felt ill, except for Phil, because I didn't want Elora to believe I was sickly or weak. If she knew, she would tend to my every need, and I didn't deserve it after what I'd put her through.

"How is lover's paradise?" Mikhail slurred his words over the bridge.

"Go away, you're drunk."

"That bad, huh?" His dark laugh slivered up my back.

My lips pressed firmly together. *"What do you want?"*

"I miss her. She was sweet. And you took her." He pouted, shedding a fake tear.

"You can't have your plaything anymore."

"Did you watch us while we tangled our lips together? Did you enjoy it?" His voice purred, and I imagined him licking his lips with pleasure.

Digging my fingers into her soft pillow kept me from throwing things around the room. *"Did you want to talk to me or bait me?"*

"Can't I miss my brother?"

"We are half-brothers."

He shifted around and sighed deeply down the bridge. *"I sent Luca back to his clan. The Arcadian clan, to be exact. The one you could not wrap a ward around."*

A cold sweat broke out across my forehead. *"Why are you telling me this?"*

Wine swirled around in his glass. *"Oh, it would seem he was too formal with my human pet. She left her bridge wide open without realizing it. No worries for you, though. He was honorable enough. Not sure if his beloved would like to hear what I have to tell her."*

"Leave them alone." I growled. *"Or I will make do with my promise soon."*

Mikhail smirked. *"Please, you cannot kill me or cut my thread. Your power is not strong enough. And your curse will never break."*

I cursed at him, wanting to send my shadow to pound him into dust.

Mikhail sighed. *"You will have many visitors in twelve days."* He gulped down his drink. *"Since I can be benevolent, I thought I should tell you."*

"Who?!"

"Never mind that. You should really teach your girl to guard her mind. I can see everything and hear everything." More wine poured into his glass. *"Stellar performance, by the way. She loves you so much, and you continue to destroy her. I could not have done a better job myself."*

Blood boiled beneath my skin. I had spent so much time pushing her away that I hadn't taught Lor how to defend her mind against cravens. I hated that Mikhail was right.

He drank his wine in one swig. *"Did you know she has a heart-shaped freckle right above her backside? That she takes her time trying to find a dress she thinks will impress you?"*

I shut down the bridge, no longer able to stomach his venom. Who were these visitors? Why would he mention Luca and the clans? Luca was his faithful servant for years, though he secretly aligned with me. I never once asked him to do anything for me except to treat Elora well. He could not have betrayed Mikhail. Wait! Luca had dispatched Wren and Kaya at my request when Lor's feet had gotten infected. I wanted to jump out of my skin. Nausea came in waves, and I rolled off the bed, barely making it to the toilet. Would Mikhail destroy Luca and his clan over such a small thing? *Yes.* The answer was yes. He was his mother's henchman, after all.

Phil found me clinging to the porcelain throne, and I explained everything.

"Is Mikhail planning to attack the Arcadian clan? All the faun clans?" Phil asked, handing me a towel.

"I don't know. Something is going on, and I need to warn them all." My voice was strained.

Phil bent low, his face too calm for his own good. "Why would he bother warning you?"

I shrugged my shoulders, loosening my grip from the cold porcelain. "I'm going to the clans. Please make sure Elora stays safe." I groaned as I tried to get up, slipping back down with my arms around the toilet.

"You are too weak!" He held out his hand to lift me.

I pushed it away. "I can handle myself!" I spat into the toilet. "The queen is out for blood for this supposed rebellion. I can't sit by if she is planning on massacring innocents."

His arms crossed and his eyes wary. He sighed. "Send a dispatch instead. I will personally deliver it."

Shaking my head, bile built in my throat, and I vomited again. Phil had watched me fall deathly ill many times before. Nothing about my weakness surprised him. Staring at my insides in the toilet, I nodded my head slightly. He was right. I could do nothing.

Phil left the bathroom so I could puke my guts up again. Dread coursed my veins that innocent fauns were in danger. When the curse had spread, a dark shadow spread like a cancer over the realm. I had tried to outrun it by putting up wards everywhere I could before it consumed me. I'd ridden my kelpie, Lynx, casting my magic. I knew once the curse got me, I could protect no one, much less myself, without wards. Only the Ladon clan and faeries made it past the wards. Unfortunately, too many were left behind under the power of the queen. Wards were like words. Once spoken, they could not be taken back. So, even in my cursed state, the wards glowed their magenta demarcation lines like a wall, separating us from them.

Though my body did not want me to, I scrambled to get up and then headed to my study. Quickly, I scribbled letters to all three clans, warning them to prepare themselves. Writing this would get me into a lot of hot water, but it didn't matter. I was not in the business of staying idle. Phil nodded his head like the soldier he was and ventured beyond my wards. My best friend was so brave. He had no powers to wield except for his strength and skill at weaponry. Guilt washed over me. I held my friends' powers inside to keep them safe from the queen. Sometimes I wondered if they resented me for it. Honor compelled me to never use them. They were not my own. I regarded the faint stars and made a wish Phil would safely return.

19

ELORA

Deep purple apple trees lined the uneven grove, set against the stark orange sky. Blinking lights like fireflies floated between the trees, hovering around us as if looking right at us. The air felt crisp, and the sweet smell of sparkling apples bobbed from their branches. Tall grass sprouted in random areas, making my arms itch with every graze. We found a spot where the grass did not grow so tall, the blades flattened with Lex's footsteps. I sat in front of a gnarly root, the tree behind me knotted and twisted with age. Its span shaded us, giving us the gift of night. Dolos wasted no time pulling out the wine and cheese before building a fire. Neither did I waste any time, chugging the sweet fruity drink they called faerie wine. As expected, Dolos was the life of the party, joking and sharing stories from his time in the earthly realm.

"Dolos!" It was so hard to contain my laughter. "Please tell me you did not poison Lord Robert Dudley."

"Well..." he drawled, rubbing the back of his head. His cheeky grin that could knock women to their knees widened. "You simply had to be there."

"Spill it!" I swigged back on a green bottle.

"I did not poison him," he shrugged. "I simply made him paranoid about it. He was getting too close to my love, and I wanted him to leave. When he used a page or some guard to test his food, I leaned back, watching him unravel piece by piece."

My dancing eyes caught Willa and Lex gazing at each other from across the fire. "Were you both there when he was gallivanting with one of the most famous queens?"

Willa held Lex's huge hand, and he fully enclosed it around hers. The heat between them was undeniable. "We were in the Solarin Realm on our...what you would call our *honeymoon*. Riann was there when we said our vows," said Willa, twirling some of Lex's stray hairs around her finger.

I spun my head, cracking my neck. "You're married?!" My lip curled upward. "And you were with *him*?" I saw it made Willa uncomfortable. She had been friends with Riann for who knows how long before I was even a thought.

"We are cymar. It is deeper than vows and rings." She smiled at Lex, and he warmly tugged her close in his lap.

I leaned forward, basking in the fire's warmth. Dolos hated this fire—it was not big enough for him. For our safety, he relented from using the gray powder he always carried. "Pretend I grew up on earth and never heard of it," I snickered.

Before Willa could get a word out, Dolos cut in, "It's when two halves of souls call out for each other across the distance." He leaned back and propped his legs on a log. "There's no denying its power, especially if both have abilities like Willa and Lex do. They share each other's magic after they"—he cleared his throat—"join." He giggled. So mature.

Willa threw an apple at him. "Oh, stop it, Dolos, we are all adults here! We all knew what you were doing in England. Jig is up!"

A low rumble came behind me, and I realized Lex was laughing. I honestly did not think he could smile or laugh because it would crack his face.

"A gentleman will never kiss and tell," Dolos singsonged while putting two fingers to his lips. "Some realms save themselves for their cymar, namely Rinarie, where Riann is from. So, our blue guy is essentially a pure man with massive restraint." Dolos swigged down more wine. "He's an eight hundred-year-old virgin."

As if I needed the clarification.

He wiped rosy droplets from his lips. "After the joining, two threads on the spindle, Riann's spindle, braid together."

"Riann's spindle?"

Willa held her hand up, motioning for Dolos to let her speak. "Everyone has threads tied to an ancient spindle. Riann has the ability to manipulate threads or cut them. But everything has a price, which is weighed carefully. He's a time mage, Lor. That's why he could jump from realm to realm with us on our crazy vacations." She took a beat, eyeing me for any reaction. "Not only does he have the power of time," Willa continued, "but he is fiercely strong, and his psychic abilities can speak to people across bridges, read their minds, and in other cases, tear their minds apart."

We sat in comfortable silence as I let everything sink in. Peter, ahem, *Riann* had reached across stars to me, like a flare gun signaling on the empty sea. Was I his cymar? Starlight flared from my chest as if in response. If I was his and he was mine, why was he so bent on pushing me away? Did I have the same psychic gift as him, or was it just that he could get into my mind?

Willa smiled, leaning toward me. "Yes, girl, you have the gift. I need to teach you how to put your guard up."

I gripped the wine bottle. "You heard me?"

"Your mind is loud, attracting unwanted visitors. Some thoughts are not your own." She took a long sip from her silver cup. "We three do not have stars. Only you and Riann share that. We are what we like to call *essence*—those born inheriting the power of stars. It was natural Riann took our powers within himself to protect us." She pulled herself back onto Lex's lap, her body so small against his chest, and sighed.

Dolos stoked the fire, grimacing over its small flames. "Riann was the best of us, the one who pulled us together and coined us as the misfits. We owe him a debt of gratitude for the things he has done."

I shook my head, squeezing my eyes. I would have never believed them, but after all I'd seen and experienced, anything was possible. "What is Solarin?"

Willa glanced in between both Lex and Dolos, nodding their heads. "Where you were born."

I dropped my bottle, spilling precious faerie wine. "But I'm from New Jersey, my earthly realm." The impossibility that I came from another realm warred with the truth staring at me. The whole time on earth, I had a living, breathing star inside me. No DNA ever connected me to a family. The way I was drawn to the fantasy genre and the stars since I was very young made more sense to me. Everything felt surreal, yet it settled in my bones—like finding missing puzzle pieces.

She leaned forward, while Lex held her hand. "Honey, you were brought there, but it was never your home."

My body became cold. I'd waited so long to discover the truth of where I was really from because every day my existence felt like I'd dropped from the sky. Warmth seeped into my hand, realizing Dolos held it, squeezing tight.

"Your realm refused to pay the soul tax," Willa continued. "The Astryx imposes a tax on realms to be fed souls to satisfy their hunger. Most realms pay. Even here in Sidh, they pay. Sacrifices are made in rituals to please them, so they relent from their anger." She took a deep breath. "Riann's home, Rinarie, was taken, destroyed by them. Your parents fought to the end. I'm so sorry, Lor."

Often, I laid awake imagining my parents returning to me, whoever they were. There was a point when I did not care why they gave me up. They could have been young teens, druggies, or whatever disqualified someone as a parent. None of it mattered as I passed from one foster home to the next. Burned by cigarettes, starved, and abused, I would have been better with my actual parents. I longed for them to call me back home. My imagination had created a mother with long blonde hair wearing a white sun hat. My father raced through the sand to gather us into his arms. His hair was dark brown with honest blue eyes. But they never came.

"I really am nobody," I said aloud, though I didn't mean to.

"You are the princess of Solarin," Willa declared. "King Sirius and Queen Eos bore one daughter." Hearing their names felt like a piece of home. A swirling warmth filled a space I had long forgotten was there. Willa glanced in between the three of us. "You are the bearer of the first light." She crept closer, slowly letting go of Lex's hand. "A miraculous birth. The only one in recorded history to bear the light of the first star. The star that called life to spring forth, a restoring light source. A star that can make and reshape realms."

A weight fell on me, my chest heavy with undulating power breathing inside. It bore responsibility, accountability, marking me for purpose. My parents had preserved me. My whole life, I had been a shadow aimlessly walking into corners where nobody could see me. Fate would have it that I became the brightest star to have ever existed.

Willa continued, "King Algol heard of your birth, and he and his queen wanted to steal you, kill you. To rip the star from you. If it fell into their hands, they would have weaponized it to overthrow the Astryx and ascend. Sidh's wicked duo convinced the Astryx that Solarin had not paid their tax in eons. So, they came for them with King Algol at the helm, or at least that's what we believe. Too much of the past is shrouded in mystery that Riann does not dare look back on."

Lex stoked the fire, and Dolos leaned his warm head on my shoulder. We sat in silence, eating cheese and fruit. I did not find the silence awkward. It felt welcome and steady as if they gave me a moment to process everything. A girl always stuck in shadowy corners, no more. I was something greater. And somehow, I'd known it all along.

Willa sighed, lowering her head between her knees. "Queen Eos summoned her hunter and begged him to save you. He put you in another realm where they could not reach you. You were but a few weeks old. Your mother refused to go because she would not leave her people. The hunter found the perfect realm and time that was safest for you. The year was 1999, and he dropped you off in front of a fire station with a note that simply said your name."

Dolos shuddered, adding space between us, his head leaving a cold spot on my shoulder. "Our hearts were heavy. We could not save the realm, but it was out of Riann's hands. Fates are living, breathing things, and they can be cruel. We truly loved Solarin, and not a day goes by that we do not think of them."

Tears slid down my face. It was all so much to take in. I truly had no home, no people. All because of a soul tax they refused to pay. A fool's hope to believe I had living parents. Rage and agony coated my insides. I want to be thankful to that hunter for saving me, but what good was I as the last breathing person of Solarin?

"Wait, just wait." I let go of Dolos' hand. "Willa and Lex were in Solarin for your 'honeymoon,' and you were with the queen of England at the same time...how old am I?"

Dolos shrugged. "Time is irrelevant when you are friends with a spindle mage. We make it seem like everything happened so quickly. The curse did not even spread in Sidh until about a hundred years later. But in your earthly realm, it might have been a week in comparison. If I had to calculate, you are at least five hundred years old. But you don't look a day over two hundred."

I barked out a wet laugh. "Gee, thanks." Any amusement snuffed out as I pulled my knees to my chest. "You said it was the safest time for me. The hunter was wrong."

Maybe it was the faerie wine or the fact I'd finally found friends, but my heart wanted to explode with words I dared never to speak. "I was in and out of foster homes." I noted the look of confusion on their faces. "Places for children who have nobody else to care for them. I had a foster mother burn me with cigarettes, starve me." I flexed my forearms, feeling the circles burn me as I confessed. "Over time, I grew a thick skin, convinced myself it would make me a better person. Nobody saw the scars on my skin. Social workers, too burned out to see my pain, visited me, falling for the façade of a healthy home. When I was thirteen, I moved into a new home with this little girl, Emily." I closed my eyes, remembering her warm brown skin and meadow green eyes with long lashes that could make wind if she batted them fast enough. She must have been ten years old. Emily loved painting and posting them on the walls of her bedroom. Her bunk was on the other side of mine. Sometimes, she would giggle in her sleep.

"I noticed his eyes always drifted to her when she was across the room. Or painting. Doing anything. My foster father, Jeff, always came home with his gruff voice and his muddied boots from work. He loved to run his fingers through her hair. Once, I found her hiding in our closet underneath dirty clothes so that she would not feel him touch her. His curiosity got the best of him, and he came into our room at night. He smelled like cigarettes."

Dolos crushed his goblet in his fist.

My voice wobbled. My chest ached with pressure. "I could not bear to watch as he leaned over her bed, so I grabbed his hand and lured him into mine."

I did not want to finish the rest of the story, of how much it hurt, no matter how many times he came for me. I felt dirty, so exposed. I could not bear to look them in the eyes, fearing they would see this damaged person. These three people, who I adored so much, knew my secret shame. The reason I couldn't watch love scenes. The reason I was so unlovable. Jeff was the reason my body betrayed me and I was numb to the idea of being worth something to someone. As a child, I'd learned to accept the love that was given—even when it wasn't real. And then he died. I cried when I'd found him slumped over in his chair, like I was going to miss him. But as I grew older and more aware, I realized I had been a victim and he was a monster. I should have been angry that I did not have justice. Death was his mercy.

My head remained in between my knees, wracked with sobs. I waited for them to walk away one by one. This was too real for anyone to handle. Who would want someone with this much baggage? Friends were great for a laugh, but I knew people always leave whenever darkness surfaces and makes its presence known. That's just how it was. Love leaves. Peter was gone, and Riann...just the thought alone made me weep harder. There were simply not enough tears to appropriately express my pain.

A surge of warmth enveloped me. All three of them put their hands on me, holding me still, pulling me together. "You see, it was *not* the safest time, and I was *not* protected. I was left to the wolves of my realm. All I've ever been is someone who draws in awful people. I don't care that I was born with this star inside me." I pounded my chest, the light inside me guttering. "I'm truly nothing."

Lex's feverish hand lifted my chin. He rubbed his thumb across my face, wiping my tears. A gentle giant before me bent low, meeting me eye to eye.

"Warrior," he said.

As if I did not hear him the first time, he grabbed my chin between his fingers, tears streaming down his muscular face.

"Warrior," he said again.

They wrapped their arms around my sobbing body. Every bit of pain I'd held so tightly was an avalanche coming down. Their warmth and love broke down a wall inside me I didn't know I had. I let my guard down and let them in. They did not balk or run from my past. They simply sat and listened, holding me through it. It was a healing balm to my heart, ravaged by years of loneliness and disregard.

Willa sniffled. "I told you, Lor, we knew so much about you because of Riann. We fell in love with you before we ever met you."

I opened my arms, trying to hold them all, but Lex's size wouldn't let me. They felt me struggle and giggled.

"It's not every day you get to be hugged by a pyro, a walking muscle, and a water wench," said Dolos, between laughing and crying.

Lex looked at me again, his eyes glistening with pride. "We are misfits. We do not bow."

"We do not bow," Willa whispered.

Dolos's voice broke. "We do not bow."

"We are misfits. We do not bow," I said, wiping my eyes.

20

RIANN

My healing water, my only relief, refused to stay down. When my stomach stopped churning, I forced myself outside, anxiously waiting for Phil's return. Leaves from the willow tree breezed across the lake in front of my house as I considered summoning Lynx to ride across my wards to find breaks in its defenses. If there were breaks here, there were certainly breaks around Ladon. My arms shook, holding onto the wooden guardrail. Too afraid to look at my hourglass, splinters dig under my skin from holding on too tightly.

Wren flew solo, fluttering his gray wings toward me. The Willow Faeries were so kind to us because they believed I was special. I assured them over and over that I was useless. Wren believed I could save them from this dreaded curse, but he was also the first faerie to put me in my place. I loved the little guy and his ever-ready hand to stab anything that annoyed him.

He perched on my shoulder, aware of my entire body trembling with aches and pains. "When are you going to tell everyone?" he asked, kneeling down.

I stood tall, letting go of the rail, willing my body to regain composure. "Tell everyone what?"

"That you're dying."

My head hung low. It was true. With every grain of sand, more of me died. "I need to get Lor through the games first, send her home, and then I will die." I said it so matter-of-factly that Wren shuddered.

He snuggled in the crook of my neck and wrapped his tiny arms as much as he could around me—a feeble attempt to warm my icy front. I wanted to live. I wanted to have a family and see my children grow. But now, my only real dream was keeping her alive, for her to let go of me, and for her to find a new dream with someone else. Starlight in my chest pulsed as if in response, but I couldn't obey my star. I needed to ignore its longing.

***

I rode the edges of the demarcation line up and down a million times on Lynx. His seaweed green mane tossed in my face, giving me an agitated glance. Too much time out of the water exhausted him. I strode back slowly, taking one more look over. When I tugged the demarcation line, magenta hues of ancient text and wheels driven by markings appeared before me. Everything appeared untouched, unmarred. Though I was indeed dying, they remained strong. I was not scared of death. I was afraid I would leave my friends alone without their powers returned to them. Queen Nyx would kill them out of spite.

The markings on my head where my hair parted burned like a brand whenever I touched the wards. Wren's tribe leader, Magnus, tattooed them on me after the curse, linking me to the wards. Wren fluttered up and down the line searching for breaks, this time with Kaya. We neared the lake's edge for Lynx to recharge when Kaya found a small, indistinct fissure.

She wiped sweat from her pearly face. Black wisps flared from her wings. "This must be how the Hag entered your home,"

Reality stared me in the face. My death would bring nothing but terror to everyone I loved. A curse rolled off my tongue, and I stormed away, limping. Wren and Kaya had the sense not to come after me as I made my way to the top of the hill where I'd crashed with Elora. I was so angry at the fates for deciding my demise right now, of all times. Angry at the queen and her pathetic son for ruining my life. Furious my father never stood up to her because I was not legitimate in his eyes. I slid my back down an ancient curly oak and stretched my legs on the damp soil. Patches of grass grazed my legs that appeared to curve over my calves as though they were comforting me. Orange skies swept above with a twinge of black. The moon was almost full again, and I didn't believe I could survive another whipping.

Fits of laughter interrupted my dreary thoughts. Below the hill, Lor sat on top of Lex's shoulders, holding a bottle of faerie wine without a care in the world. Dear Lord, she discovered the wine. Thanks, Dolos.

Phil found me as he trudged up the hill, avoiding the joyful party below. "I warned Ladon, and they are making preparations to assist Arcadia and Pine."

My expression hardened. "I sent three dispatches, and you only gave one?"

Phil stepped forward, his nostrils flaring. "Arcadia and Pine are powerless, and there are too many eyes watching. I could not risk being seen."

"But this is who *we* are." I towered over him clenching my fists. "Misfits who protect the innocent no matter the cost."

Phil's heels dug into the ground. "Correct me if I am wrong. Back then, we were formidable. Now we are just useless bags of skin, like flimsy humans. You took our powers from us, Riann. Sorry, but not sorry, it's the truth."

All the pressure and heaviness barreled from my chest to my core. Heat coursed through me, and I saw red. All my shame exploded from its hidden caverns and turned into rage, lancing through my arms. I slammed Phil into an oak tree, shaking the leaves from its branches. Phil laughed as his steel body felt nothing more than a whimper of discomfort.

"Really, Riann?" he laughed darkly. "You just proved my point. You should have been able to pulverize me. You are sick and weak, an easy target." He annunciation each word. "Do you want the same for me?"

My breath let loose, and I softened my grip on Phil's fighting leathers. His words made their mark. I knew it was true, but to hear it from my best friend was something else entirely. "It is to protect you all. You agreed to hand it over after Solarin..." I could not finish the words as my eyes drifted to the house, alive with joy.

"Everything is for her," Phil scowled. "It probably would have been better to let that baby die with everyone else in her realm."

Like a flash of light, I slapped him across his face, leaving a red mark that would surely bruise. I would not apologize or yield to the look of disbelief that I'd struck him. His jawline feathered as he staggered back, and I continued to tower over him.

His eyes glowed fiercely, like a ring of fire. "Fine! I deserve that." Phil did not wait for me to respond as he stumbled away, holding his face and the rest of his dignity.

"Phil, come back to the house and put some ice on it. It's not the first time we've had a fight like this." I kept my tone even so as not to give away feelings of guilt.

"Leave me alone and let me walk it off," he said thickly, descending the opposite side of the hill.

I leaned against the tree, stifling the pain in my chest and my head but also trying to sift through all this rage inside me. Against my body's demand to collapse in exhaustion, I limped down the hill and entered a familiar scene of laughter and light. My head pounded as the bass from the music vibrated the walls. Elora, dressed in a pale yellow Grecian dress, sat in the papasan chair, her hair gilded in starlight. More of her star invaded every fiber of her being, and I was in awe. Word was going to get out. She was the one with first light.

Wren and Kaya downed thimbles of wine on top of the mantle while the rest were playing a drinking game.

"Never have I ever charged into battle hungover," Willa said, looking between the three of them.

Lex and Dolos raised a glass of wine to themselves.

"Lex!" shouted Elora. "I would expect that from Dolos, not from you!"

Nobody noticed my lingering presence in the kitchen.

"Okay, say a statement I could relate to," Lor laughed, tossing her pale hair over her bare shoulder. Finally, she saw me. Her breath caught in her throat, and then she turned her attention back to the hooligan three.

Dolos giggled in between belching and draped himself over the loveseat. "Never have I run out on someone in the middle of a date,"

Elora's eyes lit up and she drank more wine. "I need another cup because I've done that several times," her voice bubbled.

Quietly, I slid into a seat in the kitchen across from her, trying not to disrupt their laughter. Her eyes raked over me, and I hoped she did not see my gnawing pain. My head wanted to explode. It was Elora's turn to make a statement. She leaned back onto the cream cushion, twisting her hands like she always did when she was nervous.

"Never have I ever"—she closed her eyes tight for a second and then popped them open, looking at me— "rejected my cymar." The room fell into an uncomfortable silence as she dragged the faerie wine bottle across the table. Nervously, she filled a cup and handed it to me. "Drink." Her eyes dampened with moisture.

A searing knife stabbed through my skull, twisting and burning. My whole body felt like it was on fire. She was trying to expose me, to gain a confession, in front of my friends. My teeth bared. "You will get nothing from me." *Pound, pound.*

She shoved the drink into my hand. "Say I am your cymar. You reached me beyond galaxies. You said you knew me, that you loved me. Are we not two halves of souls who called for each other?"

"I am not your cymar," I replied, clenching the sides of my seat. I wanted to leave, but the pain anchored me, destabilizing my will to move.

Willa gasped. The weight of the room fell on me. I wished she would stop trying to reel me in when she needed to let me go.

"Liar." She pulled her dress, exposing the center of her chest. "You think it's mere coincidence that our stars flare when we are together?" Our stars glowed for each other, like a silent song.

I waved her off. "It means nothing."

"Nothing?" Elora leaned closer, her sweet breath too near to mine.

"Yes, nothing," I swallowed, lowering my voice. "You can never be my cymar."

Her bow-shaped lips tightened. "That's a lie, and you know it."

My skin felt tight around my body, my blood rushing like a mighty river. This courtroom session hit a nerve, spiraling me into a dark place. She needed to leave. I needed to leave. I was trapped in this surge of pain. Her clawing words confronted the lies I kept telling myself. She needed to be safe and protected. But at what cost? I was no good anyway. She was better off. I plunged myself deeper into a dark door with no windows across my bridge, but her starlight kept shaking me out of it, despite the excruciating pain that radiated through me.

"Why can I not be your cymar?" she asked incredulously, the final arrow to her own heart meeting its target.

Fire formed on my tongue. Words I did not put together formed on my lips. And with an unintentional spill, I blurted, "Because I know your past. What happened to you when you were younger? I will not be another figure in your trauma." I sucked in a breath.

Everyone in the room paused. Fractured. Broken. The haze of shock settled in the room. Dolos, for once, was at a loss for words. Bludgeoned. Tearing. No word could sum up what I'd done to her. Tears clouded Elora's eyes as she slowly crumpled before me. She was strong against me before, but I'd crushed her like a delicate flower. Death crouched at my doors like a welcomed friend. I didn't deserve to live.

"Riann, no," Dolos whispered with a tremble, his head in his hands.

"Lor, I didn't mean..." I reached for her, but she jumped back as if I were a cobra snapping at her. Perhaps I was.

"I'm sorry," I whispered, feeling the futility of my apology. I finally did it. I broke her. All my hard work in getting her to hate me boiled over, and I was not satisfied. In fact, I just realized what I was losing. Thoughts of us together, standing as equals, flooded my mind. I did not allow those thoughts before, but now they wouldn't stop racing.

"I disgust you," her voice wobbled. Her hands splayed across her legs, grabbing the dress fabric as if she hated what she wore. She looked like sunshine in the dress though she was darkening, at odds with the bright starlight in her chest guttering out. This was all my fault. I did not want this for her.

I feebly extended my hand again. "Lor. It's not true." Tears slid down my face.

Fire in her eyes burned beneath the swath of tears that refused to fall. "Keeping me at a distance across our bridge was bearable for you. It was not until you saw me," her voice shook. "I repulsed you. You're so *pure* that you could never have someone like me."

"No." I choked. I got up, dizzying myself, and put my hands on her waist. "You have it all wrong. Please, Lor, believe me." I would get on my knees for her if I could, but if I went to the ground, I would likely not get back up. "This whole time, I have been trapped." Her captive tears flowed down her beautiful face. Black streaks of makeup ran down in streams, beading onto her lips. "That's not what I meant."

"Stop it! Your apologies are worthless!" she shrieked. Her face was as red as the dusky sky. "I'll set you free." She balled the sides of her dress in her hands, tearing at the seams.

She kicked up her feet, running to her chambers. I limped my way to her to beg forgiveness. She slammed the door, locking it. I knocked, and she hurled something heavy at the door.

"Please, Lor," I begged, wishing to take everything back. Clarity hit me like a ton of bricks. We could have been together even if the time was short. I was a fool to believe it would be better this way. If anything, I'd given her less to fight for in the arena.

Slowly, I walked back to the living room, holding onto the wall with my hand to keep myself up. I expected everyone to have left, but they remained, stunned to see the monster I'd become. It was better they stayed. I needed punishment. Lex stood, his body casting an enormous shadow onto the floor. He strode to me, eating up the length of the floor in a few steps. I leaned back on the wall, waiting for something, anything. He clenched his fist.

"Do it," I said, bracing myself for the hit that would destroy my face.

Lex's eyes darkened. He lifted his fist and pounded the wall beside my head, cracking the plaster and splintering wood. "Coward." He growled, turning away.

Dolos grabbed his wine, giving me a look that said, "I want to attach a bomb to you and watch you explode." Wordless, Willa left with Lex, and Kaya fluttered with them, her body sparking black shadows. Before I turned around, Wren pulled out his dagger and pricked me in the chest several times.

"Is this what you want?" he whispered low enough so Dolos could not hear. "Spend your last days destroying her? When my cymar died, my world died with her. Not a moment goes by that I don't wish for one more day with her. You can't even give yourself that." He jabbed the dagger into me one more time. Trickles of blood ran down the muscles of my stomach. "You don't deserve her."

I nearly forgot he'd lost Julie, his cymar, because she was not on this side of the land when the curse took over. Queen Nyx killed faeries, knowing their magic could become a nuisance for her. "I know I don't deserve her."

He dug his dagger into the tip of my nose. "Stop your self-pity and spend the rest of your life making it up to her. At least in the end, she will know you truly loved her."

And I did. I loved her so much. All this time, I'd pushed her away. I needed to prove my love to her before I faded into a shooting star. When I entered my room to plan how I was going to win her back, edges of black appeared before me, and I stumbled. I stretched out my arm, watching a few grains sift in the hourglass. Nyx had impeccable timing. I crawled onto my knees trying to get to my bed but couldn't make it, so I laid on the cold floor.

Darkness crowded around me. My breathing turned slow and heavy as my despair enveloped me.

"Lor, the answer to your question is yes. It was all real. It still is."

21

MIKHAIL

Warm rot and decay hung in the stagnant air. I drifted in and out of consciousness as I struggled to break through the surface. This was not the first or even the second time this had happened. My wonderful mother had drugged me in order to get something out of me. My guards were too strong for her, so this was what she resorted to. She was always suspicious of me, and I supposed she had every right.

"Mother... stop," I moaned, as her black chains tightened around my wrists.

Kain's heavy hot breath hit me, smelling of putrid food. "Just give her what she wants, boy," he snarled.

"Do you ever brush your teeth? You'll kill me with that breath before my mother does." I groaned, kicking him away from me.

Being blindfolded did nothing to disguise where I was. Each time she did this, I ended up in the dungeons. Mother would not risk having servants or Silas seeing her torture me. The last thing I remembered was dining with my mother in her chambers, and suddenly, I'd fallen ill. I realized she'd given me a sedative. Mother of the year. Finally, Kain ripped off the blindfold, revealing the damp, poorly lit dungeons. Torches lined the cold, slimy walls to my right. Slithering insects crawled around my feet. The echo of a prisoner's screams made my heart race as though they called for me. I never put them here. It was either kill or find a way for them to escape. In the end, my mother believed I would shed blood for every enemy she had. Her enemy could be anyone. The beautiful dryad she was jealous of or a faun who played a song she did not like—the list was endless. This was why Riann hated me. To him, I was nothing but a cold-blooded murderer.

A dull ache pounded my face, and I felt warmth drip from my nose. "What did you do to me?!" I roared, trying to push myself out of these enchanted chains.

Her high heels clicked against the uneven surface, casually unveiling herself from the shadows. "What was necessary." Her voice was gentle yet lethal as she rounded my chair. "I know you wish you could burn away these insects. You would hate your mother to walk in such filth."

"Filth you created." I spat blood on her powder blue velvet shoes. "That stain will never come out."

Her crimson lips tightened. The silver silks she wore made her appear darker. "You can make this easy. Tell me what you are hiding."

I rolled my head, bored with the conversation. "I am not hiding anything."

"Hmm." She pushed up her long sleeves and pressed her palms to my temples. "I took more of your brother's grains tonight. He is at death's door. The more you hold back, the more I take."

Coldness seeped into my skin. "Haven't you had your fill? He's going to die, anyway."

She ran her hand inside the lapel of my coat. "He stole from me. It does not seem to anger you that he would disrespect your mother so blatantly."

I shuffled away from her bitter touch. "Maybe you should let it go. Focus on removing the curse for the love of your people." I was never bold with my mother, but the stakes were too high. "Nobody wants this darkness and all the evil that comes with it."

"My son." She pressed her forehead to mine. "You are part of the evil that comes with it. How many times have I asked you to kill on demand, and you did it with pleasure?"

She was wrong about me. I took no pleasure. With each kill, I weighed the grievances heavily. For some, I provided safe passage to other realms. Their fates were tucked so deep in my mind that I could not let her access them. I was no monster. Right?

Her long lips curled. "But you are soft when it comes to Riann, the cause of this curse." She pressed her palms firmly on my temples, electricity tingling, building up to an unquenchable fire. "All he had to do was tell me where the lilac child was, and it would have been lifted."

Static filled my head. "Stop it, mother! Don't do this!"

Throbbing pain coursed through my body, splintering every fiber in me. Each nerve set on ablaze, burning and roiling. There was no part of my body safe from her grasp. Bile reached my throat, bubbling from my mouth.

"I am hiding nothing, I swear!" my voice wobbled as the electricity intensified to the point where I began to convulse.

Hot tears streamed down after accidentally biting down on my tongue. The metallic taste, combined with everything else coming from my mouth, sent my head reeling back. My body went taut as I pushed my heels into the ground to seek some control. Her lips curled again as my eyes rolled to the back of my head.

Mother finally released her hands. "Good," she said, patting down her dress. "I have received a message that this covert rebellion is plotting to kill me."

Honestly, even though she was my mother, life would be easier if they did kill her. The little bit of consciousness I had left had to mean something for her. If she'd pushed me this far, she would have to believe I was telling her the truth.

"Old news," I scoffed, shaking off the large amount of static clinging to me.

"I know it is the fauns." She tapped her polished black nails to her chin. "Just like your servant boy, Luca, whom you mysteriously sent away."

"I sent him away because he was no longer useful. Stupid boy could not clean my garments properly," my voice felt like gravel.

"Is that so?" My mother shrugged and let out a long sigh. "I hope you still feel that way when the sentinels put the heads of every faun on spikes. And I will put Luca's head in a box for you if I suspect you of treachery."

My jawline feathered. "I'm your son. I have been nothing but loyal to you."

"Not in the case of Riann. I know you harbor feelings of attachment to him. Not sure why, though. He hates you. That woman you found in the earthly realm hated you, too, but you still went after her like a lost puppy. That human pet of yours hated you so much that she saved your brother. Seems like everyone you care about never feels the same." Her spindly fingers ran across my shoulders. "But I love you. I love you enough to do this"—her knuckles brushed against my temple, and I flinched— "to keep us safe."

In a sense, she was right. Everyone hated me, and I gave them no cause to think otherwise. But it stung. Never once did I feel love from my mother. My father was...let's just say, him as a walking corpse did little to improve his personality. She used those words to manipulate me. After all, the biggest monsters were the ones who never felt love. I was a knife in the darkness, a blade meant to cut out hearts, not keep them.

22

RIANN

Pale orange light filtered past the slits of my crusted eyes. How long had I been out? Usually, I could tell by the stirrings of the house, but everything was eerily quiet. Somehow, I felt a little better than yesterday, adjusting to the weakness in my bones.

"Lor, are you awake?"

I didn't expect her to answer, but I needed her to hear my voice, to remember I was not the monster I made myself out to be. Every muscle in my body ached as I peeled myself off the floor. Hot water from a quick shower did little to relieve the pain. Healing water on my dark oak dresser sat lukewarm in its skin. I chugged it, willing it to stay down. This time it did, and the effects were immediate. I felt more awake than I had in days, though unsure if I was truly being healed or if it was just a salve that would fade.

I brushed my hair over to one side, rubbing the ward marks on my head before throwing on an apron over my bare chest. When Lor was in her earthly realm, she'd said pancakes were her favorite breakfast. I'd never made them before, and I did not intend for it to get this messy. Flour dropped everywhere on the floor, and some of my secret ingredients to make it the absolute best sifted onto the counter from the sieve. With each plop and sizzle of the pancakes, my chest tightened. She still had not answered. I couldn't even feel her breathe. I padded to her door warily, terrified to see what I had done. Floors creaked by her room, and her door was ajar. Slowly, I opened the door, and she was not there. Strewn papers with sharp black ink marks scattered on the small round table and floor. A turned-over glass with opaque drops teetered off the edge of the table, blotting the ink on the papers below. She must have wanted to write or draw something but was too angry to make anything cohesive. The broken quill on the floor made me shudder, imagining her snapping it.

She must have gone to the arena for an early start on her training today. Guilt washed over me. I never went to cheer her on. Nevertheless, I returned to the kitchen, adding more pancakes onto the skillet. No matter how much I convinced myself she was safe at the arena, a ball of dread dropped in my stomach, and I called down her bridge again.

"Lor, are you in the arena?"

Silence.

"In any case, when you return, devour these pancakes I'm making you, and then we can talk."

Silence.

"I know I messed up. Please let me explain everything, and I promise I won't push you away again."

Silence. Not even a static pick-up, as if she couldn't respond. Panic flared from my chest to my fingertips.

"Willa, where are you?"

Static rumbled. *"Sleeping next to Lex. I don't want to talk to you right now."*

"You're not with Lor?"

"No, after last night, I decided to give her a day's break."

I tore off my apron and ran from the kitchen, shouting Lor's name. Dolos and Phil slinked out of their rooms, heavy-lidded. A beat later, they were shouting for her too. My joints and muscles screamed as I ran around the house shouting her name. Every worst-case scenario played scenes in my head. What if I'd pushed her too far and she'd run away? I wanted so badly to show her I was not a monster. I needed Lor to forgive me for beating her heart to a pulp.

"Something's not right, Willa. We need to find her."

"Already on it. I will go to the arena and see if she's not there blowing off steam," she said as she shuffled in the background, quickly getting dressed.

Less than an hour later, after I scoured the demarcation lines for any signs of Lor, I made my way to the top of the hill to get a better view. This was the spot where we'd fallen after she saved me. I was such a fool. I didn't thank her for her bravery, much less recognize the woman who loved me despite it all. I always told her I saw her, but maybe I didn't. Maybe I'd seen a glimpse of her and convinced myself it was enough. Lor deserved so much more than me. Willa sprinted up the hill in her leathers. The widened look in her eyes told me everything. Lor was not in the arena. My body became stiff under the copse of trees. She no longer felt safe with me, so she'd gone elsewhere. I was no better than Mikhail.

My voice strained, barely keeping myself together. "Her door was cracked this morning. I made her run away, Willa."

She firmly held onto her hilt. "Do you think she ran back to Mikhail?"

Without a beat, I called down his bridge. *"Mikhail, is she with you?"*

After several attempts to kill the connection, he answered. *"After that stunt you pulled, I'm surprised you're asking me. She ran away from you."* He'd seen everything.

Time was fleeting, and he wanted to play games. I swore to kill him for this. *"Just answer the question."*

"I would have opened my bridge so you could watch us entangle with each other again if she were with me. It's hard enough getting anything minty down here."

Ignoring everything he said, I took it as his way of saying she was not with him. *"You better not be lying to me."*

"Brother, you sound like you're going crazy."

I cut off the connection.

Wren and Kaya flew to us with tears in their eyes. They must have been called upon by someone else or perhaps they were watching everything like the sneaky faeries they were.

"We found her, but we can't get to her." Kaya cried molten black tears. "If I go back there, I can never return."

I never knew Kaya's complete story, just bits here and there. She'd betrayed her family a long time ago for the greater good and she's been with the fairies ever since. Of course, she was not always a faerie. She was something much more powerful.

I turned to Wren, who appeared paler than usual. "By the Styx, on the cliff's edge." He drew in a sharp breath. "The Yaga...she's feeding."

I stumbled, bile rising to my throat. "Oh god. No, no, no. Willa, we must get there now. I will transport us."

Willa grasped my shoulder. "You're too weak, Riann. We won't make it. I don't think you can make one trip, let alone two, to get us back."

"Then we will need weapons and extra healing water," I rasped, darting back to the house.

Seconds felt like an eternity. I had not worn my leathers in forever and almost forgot to buckle certain places. When the curse spread, I had laid my weapons down and put them in a locked wooden box, unable to watch them collect dust. As I removed the old linen blanket, the glint of ice blue blinked. Only recently, I'd taken it out to slice through the Hag. It was a blade from Solarin as clear as crystal but as sharp as Rinarien steel. Queen Eos had fashioned my blade with ornate silver metal curling to hug my palm with each strike. Inside the hilt, she'd woven five taut, silver threads encased in crystal, the threads of time. I parried a few times for good measure, and then I slugged down the healing water.

"Dolos!" I bellowed as I left the room. "Prepare the herbs." I fastened my bracers.

His hands tugged at his hair, his mouth tight with displeasure. "You better bring her back."

"If I can't bring her back, I will throw myself in the Styx," I mumbled to myself as I walked out the door. "Ready?" Willa nodded her head, and I felt power surge through me, nearly wiping me out.

The icy sting of the river Styx bit into my bones. We fell onto the edge, right above the Styx, where Wren found her. Gray fog wound around us in ribbons, beckoning us to swim with the rest of them. Whispers made of smoky flesh, much like the Hag, curled around us, speaking delusions of promised peace if we would jump into the black waters below. Many fell for this false peace, allowing their souls to lay adrift in the river, seeking solace and finding none. We got our bearings and stood on the edge of a cliff, peering below at the poor souls deceived by its healing claims. It should have been called the Well of Lies. This river used to be pristine, glistening, with merfolk peeking their curious heads.

I wondered if Gloria, the mermaid I'd befriended long ago, still swam in these waters. She likely turned into a siren.

Dizziness and nausea ramped up fast, but I could not let it win. I swigged down more healing water to stave it off until we returned. Oars creaked below us. Long, black wooden boats with ornate rudders broke through the dark waters below. Dark elves and other creatures of the night roamed the Styx. The Hag rested here before she fed on another person's joy. A pale, grotesque elf in a black cloak slid back his hood from the boat's helm. His dark, wide familiar eyes met mine. I imagined his skin used to be fair but it had become bulging and puckered. Silver hoops pierced along his pointed ears. His people used to be dark healers. One elf's blood was enough to heal an entire army. I remembered calling upon them in times of war in other realms, but they'd looked the other way. They might have possessed great power, but their greed was even greater. *Vejovis.* His name erupted in me as he began to speak.

"Riann of Rinarie." His voice surrounded me in the fog without him opening his mouth. It was not the bridge, but he spoke as if he were the fog. "Have you come to mock us? We were once beautiful healers. Because of your choice, we are reduced to the living dead."

I lost Willa in the fog. Focusing my eyes on any silhouettes, I reached for her.

"You don't understand. I had no choice," I said, cupping misty fog into my palm.

"You know the way to break the curse," Vejovis' voice grated. He moved the rudder closer to the shoreline. "Your flower is wilting. Go. Otherwise, when you come down here. I will make sure the river does not wash away your pain. Tell my daughter to show her disgraced face if you dare make your presence known again."

Suddenly, the fog split in two, and as I ran toward Willa on the icy ground, I heard a crunching, rustling noise. "Willa," I rasped. She stood like a block of ice. Her blanched face slowly turned to me. The Hag's tendrils of torment wrapped around her neck. With a swing of my sword, I sliced through the fleshy smoke. "Willa! Stay with me!"

It took a few shakes for her to blink and realize she was feeding the Hag. Between gasping for air and sobbing, Willa stumbled into my arms. "Riann, I did not see her coming."

"The dark elves want me to find her." I pointed to the clearing, and we made haste. Crunching noises thickened as we raced under a blanket of black velvet. Only there could a fog create an illusion of such darkness. Sometimes I wondered why the queen chose dusk. Though time moved, we were forever disoriented.

Then I saw it. Hovering over my girl. The Yaga. We bent low behind a boulder. She looked like a frail old woman in peasant clothes and walked as if her hips and disjointed legs would give out. Her skin encased a creature so dark that it ate other beings. Wrinkles on her sagging skin and her vacant gray eyes caused many deaths for those taking pity on a poor old woman. Her white hair escaped from beneath her red handkerchief dotted with yellow flowers. Like an animal, she played with her food first before devouring it. Her disgusting talons for nails dug into Elora's side, stunning her and keeping her fresh. Hot blood streamed onto the cold grass. She licked Elora's wounds, tasting her like an appetizer.

"My pretty little flower dancing in the fields of sorrow where we never grow old. Round and round we spin. When it's all over we must play the game again," the Yaga sang like an old children's rhyme.

I was ready to pounce, but I knew if I did anything too fast, she would throw Elora into the Styx. Sweat beaded across my head. "Willa, I will distract the Yaga. You get Elora and move her beyond this place. I will find you to get us out of here."

"What?" Her turquoise eyes blazed. "No. We do this together like we used to. I'm not giving you the chance to stay behind."

"It does not matter. Get her to safety. And if I don't make it, tell her—"

Willa's brows knitted. "Would you shut up? It's the freakin' Yaga. We have taken on scarier monsters without using a drop of power. We're getting out of here; this is," she sucked in a breath, reading me like she always did. "Oh my God, Riann. Are you seriously thinking of giving yourself over the Styx?"

I leaned my head back against the granite. "I don't have much time left. Willa, I'm dying."

She slapped me upside my head. "No, you may not die!"

"I've been sick for a long time. It gets worse with each grain she sifts."

Willa grabbed the leathers on my chest. "We will find a way. Let's go save our girl." She gripped my wrist so hard that her nails dug through my bracers. "You better not throw yourself over because you're wallowing in self-pity, or I swear, I will go down there and kill your soul with my bare hands."

Quickly, I pulled myself together as Willa nocked her bow. "Get her in the eye. It will disable her long enough."

"I haven't done this in years. It feels good to kill bad guys again," she said, stretching her bow, releasing the arrow into Yaga's eye.

The Yaga tumbled down, screaming like a banshee, before becoming still with labored breaths. I rushed to Elora's side, kneeling in her pool of blood. Her lifeless body set me on fire as I scooped her in my arms, holding her close. Red, raw words were scrawled on her arm. *Disgusting, marred, damaged.* The broken quill pen. My carelessness had caused this, and I don't think I could ever forgive myself. Complete tunnel vision took over to protect her. I barely registered Willa's words to get us out of there because I felt nothing. I could not find a beat of power strong enough to send us back. This had been what I was afraid of. The Yaga stirred. She pulled the arrow from her eye, groaning.

"Riann, now!" Willa screamed.

"I'm sorry, Lor, for everything. Please forgive me." I wept over her face, shaking the tip of the skin to her mouth. She was much too weak to swallow. My power was not strong enough to get us from the Yaga quickly enough as she stood. Blood continued to run over my hands with only minutes to remove the poison and stitch her wounds. Elora's star flickered like a light trying to switch on, and so did mine. Light broke through her chest like a web reaching for me. I gasped as the light inside me tangled with hers, winding and fusing.

Willa's lips parted and grabbed onto us. "Riann, her star is giving you the power to leave. Let's go!"

I closed my eyes, and we fell in the front of the house. For the first time in years, I did not feel the pain of using power. Somehow, Elora understood what she needed to do, even while dying. Dolos peeled her from my arms, not bothering to rush her inside. The time was now to save her. No one would have guessed our little pyro was quite the medic. I heard someone screaming Lor's name, but everything around me blurred as I reached for her.

"Lex! Hold him down! He wanted to throw himself into the Styx!" Willa roared.

Lex's heavy hand held my chest down, and I still heard someone screaming her name.

"She's going to be okay," said Lex as Dolos used the detoxicant device, pumping out the venom. Screams grew louder, the haze around me darkened. Then I realized it was me screaming her name.

23

ELORA

A rush of cold filled my lungs, and my eyes sprang open. Soft white blankets and sheets billowed around me. Riann was slumped over on his sofa, which was pulled close to the bed. Snippets of what happened unfolded in my mind as I blinked several times. All I remembered was staring at the fire in my room after trying to write a goodbye letter. Nothing came out but sharp lines and harsh scribbles because even though I was hurting, I couldn't bring myself to do it. Then it had become ice cold, so cold I hardly felt whatever was above me lancing my side. Somehow, I agreed with whatever was happening to me. I wanted to fade away and prolong myself into the dark abyss of silence forever. I pulled up my nightgown and rubbed my side where I was bandaged, hissing in pain. My entire side screamed red with faded black veins crawling from beneath the bandages.

I needed to leave. It was too close to him. Large, three-pronged leaves that smelled like mint flaked off my arms. Flesh-pink words were carved into my arms that I had no memory of scrawling. I traced each word, trying like hell not to believe them. *Disgusting. Marred. Damaged.* I had done nothing like it before, but I may have finally reached my breaking point. Perhaps I needed to punish myself or somehow soothe the pain with more pain.

I lifted my legs over the bed and tried to make a run for it, but I was so weak and lightheaded that I stumbled. Someone had dressed me in a white chemise from the Victorian era. Willa, most likely.

Riann lifted his heavy head. His face withered with exhaustion. "Don't leave." He groaned, reaching his hand across the bed.

Ignoring his plea, I left, but walking in the hall proved difficult. Edges blurred together, but I still reached the front door and staggered to the lake. I got far enough to where I could sit with the water lapping at my feet. Lush, rolling hills filled the horizon in uneven strokes. Violet and yellowed skies clashed, the sun burning brighter than usual. Cold water crested over my toes, waking my senses some before I toppled to the ground and sat in a daze.

What an idiot. How far was I going to go? There was no home. I was not meant for Earth, and Sidh was a hellscape. Solarin was my true home, somewhere long gone. For a split second, I waited for Peter to make a poor joke, but he never came because he'd never truly existed. The hollow ache in my chest thrummed as I wished to never be found.

Soft thuds came from behind. *Riann*. I wanted to hate him, but I never could. Love was not an on-and-off switch. Love could be beautiful, just much as it was terrifying. Riann set down a plate of fluffy pancakes with strawberries and sweet cream with a glass of icy lemon water. We sat there in awkward silence with our arms wrapped around our knees.

"I made those an hour ago. I made some yesterday, too, hoping you would wake. Lex ate most of them," he said with his eyes lowered. He gave no sign he wanted a prize, that he'd cooked my favorite breakfast to perfection. His hands trembled at his knees as he stared at the horizon.

I sat cross-legged and put them in my lap. Without shame, I devoured them. Whatever he did with these were so much better than I could ever get on Earth. Why did he have to be a wonderful cook? Though he did not look at me while I ate, his jaw feathered a muscle, his glassy eyes focusing on the horizon.

Riann blew out a breath. "The Yaga maimed you," he said flatly. "You were minutes from death when we found you." His lips shook and he put his palms to his eyes, but it was no use. The tears came down like a deluge. "I was horrible to you because I needed you to let me go, to make it easier for you to move on. But I think I was making it easier for *me*. I was so afraid of what would happen to you that I lost sight of the beautiful gift given to me. You have never once disgusted me. If anything, I spoke of myself, and you did not deserve that."

My throat bobbed, but I didn't have it in me to cry. Maybe it was from dehydration, or maybe because I'd really cried out every single tear for him.

His body trembled. "Everything was real, Lor. Everything. Your laugh made its way across galaxies and hit me like lightning. I dwelled in darkness under this curse, but you made me alive again."

Though his words pricked my still-beating heart, his harsh words ran rent-free in my mind. I wanted him to pay, yet I did not. Revenge was best as a dish served cold. But I was not built that way.

I sipped on the icy water before speaking, clearing my achy throat. "And you repaid me with rejection."

"I swear, Lor"—he wiped his tears away with his fist—"I thought I was doing it to make you hate me, so you could move on and find someone useful. Someone deserving."

"That's just it. I never thought about those things about you. You did that to yourself."

He nodded weakly. "I know. I will never treat you like that again. I will spend the rest of my life making it up to you."

With a roll of my eyes, I shook off his declarations. He was immortal, and time was irrelevant. Another empty promise, another clanging sound. Moments of torturing silence filled the chasm between us. He dared not to move a muscle as I contemplated what to say. I wanted to be honest. But honesty got me in trouble. The truth hurt, and I wanted him to hurt.

"I wanted the Yaga to finish me off," I said.

Riann hung his head lower, his body shaking.

"I have no place anywhere or with anyone, and I am exhausted from wanting it." I turned my face to him. "And *you*...you say these kind words only after I nearly die." Brimming fire churned in my chest when his eyes did not meet mine. "Have it your way. I will not seek you out. I will hate you if that's what you want."

He picked up his head, wiping the tears from his face. "I deserve that, Lor." Riann turned toward me, and I almost lost my breath.

"But forgive me, I will not let you go that easily. You talk about dying so freely—I know what it means to almost die."

I peered into his puffy midnight eyes, drawing out the sincerity of his words, yet too stubborn to give in. My fingers ached to graze his cheekbones, to slide away those tears while the wheels in my head spun. How many tears had I shed and wiped away myself because of him? Everything he said was what I wanted to hear. But it came with a price. I tried to convince myself it was not love, but I couldn't deny the six years we slowly fell for each other across the bridge, wanting so badly to dismiss the past month. Too many emotions battled in me. I needed to talk about something else and process it later.

"Are you the hunter?" I asked, shifting myself a few inches further from him. The sudden change in the conversation took him aback. "In Solarin, were you the hunter?"

His black brows furrowed. "How did you…"

"I deserve answers," I clipped.

Riann let go of his knees. "Yes."

My lips twisted to the side. "Did you drop me off in New Jersey?"

His head lowered once again. "Yes, when you were but a babe. But I swear I did not know it was your laugh that drew me across realms. You were a beautiful woman when I began mind speaking with you… falling for you. You cannot imagine the shock I felt when I discovered it was you. I saved you as a babe as loyalty to your mother, but loving you came so much later. I still can't believe sometimes that it's you."

I barked a mocking laugh. "You couldn't drop me off somewhere beautiful, like Paris or Ireland?"

He chuckled nervously. "I jumped realm to realm in different places of time, trying to find you a suitable home without war at its gates. It seemed safest. But I could not protect you from all the monsters. After the curse, I was so limited in what I could do. So, I peered in from time to time, and that's how I knew what happened to you." More tears came. "I'm sorry I could not protect you against Jeff, against the four boys. I did what I could for you, but I could prevent nothing. I killed them for you, for anyone else they might have harmed."

There it was. Something like dread and satisfaction filled me. My Peter Pan had killed them. Now I understood his stance on cosmic justice. I used to think I would have mercy. But now that I had people who I cared about in my life, I did not believe my reaction would be the same. Mercy was their quick deaths, knowing Riann would have loved to torture them for what they did to me. Somehow, I always knew it had been him. In a sick sense, Riann had been my guardian angel the entire time. For that, I wanted to embrace him. But I could not.

I scooted over a bit, wincing from the pull at my side. "You knew my parents. What were they like?"

He looked up at the sky. I imagined they were imprinted on the stars, and he could watch them. "I was a young boy when Rinarie was destroyed. For obvious reasons, I refused to stay in Sidh. I left Mikhail behind, which I still feel guilty for. He wanted to go with me, but if he did, his mother would have burned down everything to get him back. Your mother took me in as an orphan." A warm grin spread across his face. "She was friends with my mother, Elafina. My mother had me out of wedlock, which was against our culture. She was shunned, and her bastard boy too." Riann's jaw tightened. "My father never once acknowledged me until he lay there dying."

I tilted my head. "But I saw your father."

"That man is nothing but a shell. He died when the curse took over, and Nyx used her power not to revive him, but to make him into a walking corpse. It's all for show."

I shuddered at the sheer magnitude of her power.

"Anyway," Riann continued, "after weeks of scavenging the streets of Solarin, Queen Eos' maidservant found me. I was brought to the throne room and given new clothes. She paid for the best teachers and saw my gift mature as a time mage, or as some like to say, spindle mage. While all the other boys became men and sowed their royal oats, I kept to the Rinarien tradition of waiting for my cymar. Phil was with me, being the last two survivors of our realm. But he strayed from tradition and was always carousing. I just wanted to hold on to the last bit of my realm.

"Queen Eos saw I was fit, clear-minded, and ready to serve. She sent me on expeditions to find cracks in our defenses, and often there were." His voice broke again. "I killed so many people, Lor. Even before I became a misfit. I wanted to protect the Queen and her people. A woman who became a mother to me. She could have given me the title of jester, and I would have been fine with it, but I became the hunter. She is the one who created my sword and helped forge the spindle of time." Riann rolled his lips, pushing ancient memories to the surface. "She had the power to manipulate time and create devices for time mages such as myself."

I took a deep breath. "Are you the only time mage?"

"No, there's a few of us left," he said sadly. "We're a threat to the Astryx, but not the biggest one of all." He steadied his hands on the ground and shifted to stand on his knees before me. "One of her greatest desires was to have children, but years of barrenness had caused a rift between her and the king. Rumors spread that she took lovers into her bed to get pregnant—which was not true. King Sirius, in all his flaws, knew the rumors were fallacy. They truly loved each other." His lips twitched. "Then, one day, the sun shined brighter. She was pregnant with you. Queen Eos always had a glow to her, but this time, she was radiant. I intensified my hunting to keep her safe. Near the end of her pregnancy, I discovered a breach." A jagged breath left him. "From my father."

Riann clenched his fists into the sand. "That monster and his cloven-hoofed wife convinced the Astryx to strike, or at least, that's what we assumed. You were but a few weeks old. It was just like Rinarie—a slow consumption throwing off the ecosystem and then a brutal shift where all lives were theirs for the taking." His breath released curls of steam from his mouth. "I have never laid eyes on the Astryx. Nobody has. We just know they exist because of the stories passed down. Queen Eos would not leave her people and trusted me to keep you safe. Only you weren't safe with me. I knew of the star inside you, and so did Sidh. They would kill an innocent baby to get your star to become the new order, the new Astryx. So, I hid you in another realm and time." He flattened his palms on his knees. His pointed fingernails dug into his skin, making puncture marks. "This is why I am a traitor.

They made the people believe I betrayed Sidh, but I was saving them." More tears gleamed in his beautiful starlight eyes. "I took the punishment, and I would do it all over again."

This time, I extended my hand to his shoulder. "How do you break the curse?"

"I vow to keep nothing more from you except that. Give me that dignity."

For the first time, I saw the weight he bore on his shoulders. He was a time mage who couldn't control anything because of the curse. I wanted to lean on him and share that burden, but I would not yield. Everything whirred in my mind, and I wanted to fall over and collapse from exhaustion. I wanted to offer something, but I did not feel it was right to allow him to have anything from me. Humor, though. Humor would always be a sliver of light on the darkest days. Here I was, the victim, wanting to cheer Riann up. No, I needed to be angrier. I was a sucker for mercy. However, this time I did not feel merciful. It felt painful as I replayed those words over and over in my head. Even if he did not mean those words, they were rooted in some truth.

Shaking off those thoughts, I cracked a feigned smile. "Seriously, all New Jersey had was the shore and pork roll."

"More sad people food?" He laughed through his residual tears.

"Never made *me* sad," I quipped. The laughter died down, and just for a fleeting moment, I forgot the pain, but it resurfaced as quickly as it left. "Just because we're laughing does not mean I'm not hurt. It does not mean I have forgiven you. You can't take back what you said. I can't unhear those words." I watched his face etched in pain.

"Lor, I know." He instinctively reached his hand for me, and part of me wanted to fall into his arms. "I may never receive your forgiveness, but it will not change how I feel about you."

"Peter—" I cleared my throat. "Sorry, old habit." I refused to say his name. Whatever satisfaction he would get from that, I would not give it to him. "Maybe you should not wait for my forgiveness and work on forgiving yourself."

"Time is not on my side for that, but I will try." He stood to his feet and skipped a rock across the lake. My nose crinkled at what he said, but I felt dizzy. "Come." He noticed me wanting to fall to my side and grabbed me by the hand. "I will take you to your room to rest."

I stumbled over the lumpy sand, and he broke my fall, carrying me back into the house. His heart raced against mine. The warmth I craved from him for so long seeped into my skin, and I wanted to be honest and tell him not to leave as he laid me down on my bed. He gently tucked me in and almost bent low to kiss me, stopping mere inches from my forehead. I set the line, and he would not cross it. After the door clicked shut, I cried. I had more tears for him, after all.

24

RIANN

Twenty years had passed since we'd first gathered as the misfits. Since we'd sat in our circle plotting, scheming, and hoping for the best. After two decades, we'd fallen into a routine of survival, a reduced version of our former selves. I hated that we preserved ourselves sitting around the fire while other realms screamed for help. Most of all, I hated the voice of reason, telling me without our powers, we were ordinary. The truth irritated me, sending me into spirals, because in the end, I could have done more. Once again, we sat in our familiar circle, testing our bonds. Something warm widened in my chest—a feeling of hope, only slightly eclipsed by the dread coming our way. Tonight was about the future of Sidh. A mix of disbelief and anger aired around us as I explained everything Mikhail had shared. Dolos rolled his eyes and tossed his head back.

"I am deadly serious," I said, glaring at Dolos. "They will likely attack the faun clans in ten days."

I had not realized how much I alienated my friends by the way I'd treated Lor. Dolos had cursed me out when I convinced him to come to the emergency meeting, and Willa gave me the silent treatment. Lex growled. The fact I would be whipped soon did not help because I might not survive. But I kept that to myself. They needed to prepare to save innocents, with or without me. Standing on the step to the sunken living room did not give me the authority over my audience I'd hoped for.

Willa rocked back and forth in the rocking chair while Lex kept his hand on her knee from the sofa beside her. "Why would your brother bother giving you a clue they would attack them?" she asked.

"It's a trap," said Dolos, rubbing his pointed chin, "but then again..." He leaned back on the sofa, digging his hands into his hair. "No, never mind. He's a psycho, just like his mother."

"Ladon was warned, but not Arcadia and Pine." Rolling my hands together, I noticed Phil looking down at the tiles in the kitchen. "I will warn them."

"You are a target if you leave the demarcation line," reminded Willa, raising her voice.

"It does not matter. They are our friends, our allies." I looked around the room. Elora's eyes bored into me, her chest rising heavily. "Innocents," I said. "We know what she will do to them. She will turn them over to the Astryx and shove them down their gullets."

Lex rumbled under his breath. His muscles twitched at the thought of innocent fauns being led to the slaughter. I half expected his war shadows to creep from his fingertips. In the past, whenever Lex felt enraged about injustice, his instinct was to slaughter the overlords. A woman in another realm was brought to trial over killing her husband, but only after he had beaten her and bruised her. She used a pan over his head and knocked him hard enough that he'd fallen onto something sharp. Then he hurt her no more. Yet, during the trial, the court was unjust, overlooking the abuse and the need to defend herself. The woman was sentenced by death by hanging. Once she was hung, they flung her body over the gates to make an example of her. In one fell swoop, Lex destroyed the court and every jury member with a snap of his darkened fingertips. He was not simply a war machine just because of his ability to wipe out entire armies. It was because he came to slay the unjust.

Phil shook his head, unable to keep his silence. "What do you want us to do? We are powerless!"

I placed my hand on Phil's shoulder. "We still have strength, and if we come together, the faerie battalions will rise with us. They need to see our unity again." With a deep breath and nausea beginning to roil in my stomach, my jaw tightened. "Willa, can you see if there are any Woodland nymphs or dryads around the demarcation line who would join us?"

Before Willa could answer, Phil abruptly raised his voice. "Wait, you are not only suggesting we go over the demarcation line, but you are also saying we should fight with them?"

Elora's soft voice broke the tension. "We are misfits. We do not bow." She looked between me and our friends.

Phil's nostrils flared and gave her a dismissive wave. "That is who *we* are, Elora. You are not one of us."

Lor sunk back into the cushions of the sofa, absorbing the hit of Phil's insult. I grabbed the lapels of Phil's leathers. "She is preparing for the games fearlessly, which is something I can't say about you. She is one of us. A misfit in training, but one of us."

Dolos' face lit up, shifting in his seat with anticipation. Phil was hard to love, but he was loyal. Lor's eyes bulged, her hands tightening over her knees. I let Phil go, watching him storm out of the house. We'd fought many times before like best friends did. He'd be back, and we'd be happy again. I wanted to run after him. But I couldn't. This was more important than his feelings.

"Fight," said Lex, closing his hand over both of Willa's knees.

"If we plan things out, I could line the battlefield with explosives and give everyone a fighting chance," said Dolos with a devilish grin.

"I expect nothing less from you, friend," I chuckled. For the first time in years, I felt the misfits take their place, without powers, for the sake of our friends. "Lor," I turned to her, and she slowly lifted her face to meet my eyes. "I don't expect you to fight, being so new. You have killed no one or have been in a battle—"

"Just stop there," she interrupted with her hand raised. "I am going into these games fighting for my life and my friends' lives. Ask Willa how quickly I am learning to fight. I am not perfect, but I am useful." She swallowed hard. "My friend Luca is out there. He was one of the few kind people there for me when your brother abused me. I will fight for him. I will fight for who he loves."

I placed my hand on her shoulder, she stiffened, and I imme-diately withdrew. "It would be an honor. As long as you stay by me and Willa. Lex will be too busy crushing skulls in his fist, and

Dolos will be dancing around explosions." She bit her bottom lip, making it very hard for me not to rub my finger across it. "It's dangerous, but do you want to accompany me to Arcadia and Pine tomorrow?"

Her eyes narrowed. "Just me and you?"

I bent my knee to her, meeting her eye to eye. "If we all traveled together, they would notice us. I have to wear a cloak to conceal my skin. Wren can glamour your eyes to whatever color you like. Willa will be busy beyond the line, and Lex is too hard to glamour. Dolos will be in his workshop of horrors." I intentionally left Phil out.

She flipped back her hair and shrugged her shoulders. "Fine," she said with an edge of annoyance, "but allow me to get some extra training today with the sword since I'll be deprived tomorrow." Willa followed her outside with their sparring swords in hand, and they practiced for hours.

I could not lie to myself. This was exactly what I wanted. I'd told Lor I would make it up to her, and I intended to take every opportunity.

***

Watching her eat what I'd cook became one of my favorite things to do. I made garlic chicken with tomato and basil sauce. Her face, illuminating with each bite, did something to me. My mindset mere days before seemed like an eternity ago. However, Lor barely looked at me or acknowledged me. She was hurting. But I could not undo the things I'd done. I could only strive to be better, to be a stronger, more thoughtful man. Though what she deserved was far more than I could ever give.

After dinner, I sat by the lake, watching the violet skies glitter over the gray waters. Lynx emerged from the lake, blinking his vibrant blue eyes at me. He whipped his mossy mane, soaking me. Half of his body remained in the lake, as usual, unless I needed him for a ride.

"Easy boy," I whispered as I pet his muddied face. He snorted at me, pointing his nose to the house. "What do you see?"

I looked back, and Elora stood on the deck that led into the kitchen, wearing a two-piece, white silk pajama set. There was nothing revealing about it, but seeing her in it made my heart skip a beat.

"Oh, her," I said coyly. "Be nice. I'm trying to score some points with her."

Lynx snorted and whipped his head again. Maybe he didn't enjoy sharing the attention, but his eyes remained fixed on her. Curious. Wary.

"She's okay, Lynx," I whispered.

"Just okay?" Elora asked, startling me.

"Don't sneak up on me like that," I said, holding my chest.

She ignored me, and drew near to Lynx, offering her hand. Lynx sniffed her outstretched palm. Kelpies would drag unsuspecting victims into a watery grave, but Lynx and I had an understanding, as did the rest of his kin in the lake. Elora's hands were no longer soft. Calluses appeared on her palms, rough with hard work. It usually took a long time to build those kinds of calluses, but she trained for long periods during the day, only stopping to eat and to party. It wasn't a bad routine. I enjoyed watching her have friends to laugh with, even if it wasn't me. I could only guess how the games weighed on her, much less the inevitable battle to protect the faun clans. Yet, she seemed to take it in stride—as if she were born for this.

She petted Lynx's nose, and he buried himself in her rough hands, sniffing, inhaling her scent.

"What do you smell, boy?" I asked.

"Garlic," Elora grinned. "You put a lot of garlic on that chicken."

"Hey, nobody complained. And now we all smell like garlic together." I smiled at her, but she looked away from me. "His name is Lynx. He won't harm you."

"I know," she simply replied, running her fingers through his mane.

Lynx became more curious about her and walked out of the water. His nose nudged her chest, and he sniffed at her like he could not get enough. "That's enough, Lynx," I said, gently tugging on the back of his neck. He ignored me. "I said that's enough."

"It's okay. If I can go on a slew of bad dates, Lynx still wouldn't be the worst," she laughed softly.

Lynx moved his nose and grunted.

"What do you want to say, Lynx?" she asked, scratching the soft part underneath his mouth.

He reeled back into the water, neighing. It was not the same neigh you would hear from regular horses. It was more like a chant. A calling. Chilling and ancient sounds sang in my blood. Heads of other kelpies emerged from the water, their eyes narrowing on Lor. Swiftly, I put Lor behind me, my arms protecting her.

"Stay back."

I had a good relationship with Lynx and his kin but could not speak for every kelpie. Gold light flared behind me. Her star. My star burned in response. A white kelpie I never saw before emerged, her presence parting the waters, revealing the rocky depths below. I backed into Lor. My hand fisted around my phantom hilt. It was a good time for a sword.

Awe transformed her face. "They mean no harm," she said, rounding me.

Gracefully, she approached the white kelpie. Its eyes were like white opals. Its mane shimmered like rainbow mist. Lor ran her hands down its face in such careful, gentle strokes. She gasped when her hand swept over something hard, jagged. This was no kelpie, or at least it was not one before. Bronze spiral imprints remained on the broken stump of her forehead. She was a unicorn. In all my life, I'd never witnessed such a magnificent creature. And some beast had broken her. I barely heard the fluttering of Wren and Kaya's wings as they perched on my shoulder. They remained silent, as if the world paused.

Humbly, the unicorn bowed before Elora, and then the rest of the kelpies followed. Glass shattered behind me. Dolos and Willa stood on the deck, their mouths gaping, a broken wine glass at their feet. Willa clamped shut Dolos' dribbling mouth.

The unicorn bowed her head. "The Solarin lineage survives." Her voice aired a dulcet and breezy tone.

I couldn't believe I'd heard and seen a unicorn. Such a creature was wrapped in mystery. I darted my eyes over to Lynx, glaring, wondering if this whole time he could have spoken to me.

A visible lump in Lor's throat appeared. "I-I-I'm sorry. You bow to nothing."

Those words felt like needles to my skin.

"Your mother would beg to differ. The light in dark places," the unicorn said, slowly lifting her head. "I am Luna of Caer."

I swallowed hard and looked back at Dolos, who was pale, frozen.

"Wh-Where?" Elora shut her eyes tight, trying to gain composure. "What happened to you?"

Luna shook her mane, freeing her stump from its tangles. "Nyx. She stole me from my homeland long ago and cursed me as a kelpie. Dolos knows who I am. See how pale his face is?" We both looked at Dolos, who still had not closed his mouth no matter how many times Willa closed it. "We are from the same realm, Caer. Don't let him fool you. He's as royal as they come."

"Dolos is royalty?" I asked, flabbergasted.

"I used to call him the prince of unicorns, but he hated that title, didn't you, Dolos?" She chuckled softly under her breath.

"Thanks, Luna!" he yelled, slowly making his way to the lake's edge.

"Nyx knew my horn held special powers and broke it off me with dark magic. Why do you think it was so easy for her to curse an entire realm?"

My heart sank. I had no idea. I had been so preoccupied with keeping Elora safe that I failed to see how Nyx had gained so much power in such little time. Dolos left Caer ages ago but never talked about his life there. My pyro friend had secrets that could maybe save us from this helter-skelter. If he had known the importance of this, I was sure he would have said something. Anytime we'd asked him about his past, he would say something lewd and divert the conversation. Now, I was beginning to understand there were reasons behind it all.

"If we get the horn back, can we end the curse on the land and on...*him*?" asked Elora, pointing at me. She still wouldn't say my name.

"Taking the horn will remove her power," Luna said, tossing her mane to the side. For a moment, I thought she would tell Lor how to break my curse. Luna stared into me as though she were reading me. "His curse is tied to blood magic. I am sorry Elora, for your loss."

I bet Nyx killing my father was how she'd bound me. Demon woman.

"What loss?" Lor's eyes widened.

"You've lost too much. But there is always a light in the deep, deep dark." Luna's soft voice curled under my skin.

Elora rubbed her fingers over the blunt edges of the stump. "Can we reattach the horn once we have it?"

"Everything has a price. The horn desires payment. You've heard the saying before. *Love is blood spilled on altars,*" Luna said, shrinking back into the lake. "You can find the horn in the core of death."

"What does that mean?!" Elora asked.

"I must go. I have spent too much time beyond the waters. Take care, Lor. And Riann," she said as the waters receded. "The answer to your question is yes."

"What question!?" Lor yelled as her neck dipped below the water.

"It was my question," I said, frozen in place. "The horn is inside my father."

We stared at the waters forever, too stunned to move. We'd just seen a unicorn. A unicorn. And Dolos once lived among them.

25

MIKHAIL

Dusk was at its peak. A chill bit the air below the cliffs where I sat on sandy shoreline. Steam curled from my breath, clearing my head little by litter. I wished Mother chose either light or darkness, not this in between, where the weary find no rest. She would not touch the moon for whatever reason. It was my only solace in a realm where there was no birth, no change of seasons. Closing my eyes tight, I remembered snow. Winter ice nipped my lips, the soft thuds of footprints, the glittering stillness offset by the frozen sea. Often, I came here, ignoring the siren's calls. Only here could I quiet my mind and think of her. Wishing for one more touch, one more taste. My Marie. My canvas. I begged Riann to turn back time so I could save her from the plague. But her realm restricted the use of magic, dark or light. I understood why; my mother as the shining example. When magic is performed by the wrong hands, tyranny is the price. I wished to be an exception. But her thread was cut; long forgotten by the ages, except for me. I carried her with me each passing day. Maybe I would have a cymar. But I didn't know how one woman could be greater than her.

Silas' creaking branches interrupted my thoughts. His leaves dragged onto the wet sand, leaving a trail behind him. "My boy, I have not seen you since the Maypole," his voice cracked, slowly sitting beside me. His voice began to decay. I wasted enough time playing the role of the dark prince to keep mother from getting her hands on Lor's star rather than focusing on the only person who truly cared about me.

I skipped a flat pebble across the water. "If you're worried about me being lonely, Grim has been keeping me company as always."

"I worry about that and much deeper things." He pushed back a strand of hair from my face. He stretched out his spindly branches, covering us under his shadow.

I wanted to lose composure. He's been so kind to me all these years, and I didn't deserve one morsel of it.

"I come out here and think of Lena sometimes," Silas said, peering up at the sky. "She was silver and red, the prettiest dryad I ever laid eyes on. Her eyes were like sunlight, her smile like the moon. But I lost her. And my daughter." He dipped his chin, his bark flaking from his dark oak skin. "Childbirth can be so horrific." Not one ounce of self-pity spilled from his lips. "She died shortly before I was tasked to be your teacher. I thought it would be a pleasant distraction. Then I realized though I had lost everything, I gained something."

I shifted around, wanting to put space between us, but I couldn't. He brought a warmth with him I craved, something I had been pushing away for so long. "Why are you telling me this?"

"Your mother's words took root. I know what she says to you. That nobody could ever love you." His branches lowered their guard. "Listen, my boy. You can push me away all you want, disregard every teaching, but I will still love you. Like the father you always needed and the son I never got to have."

My throat constricted, heat stinging my eyes. "I know you do."

I wanted to say it back to him, but shame coated my insides. I would be admitting that I, too, could love someone else, that I was vulnerable. Marie only had that place. I loved my brother, and he hated me. Love is not kind. Love chooses favorites. And I am not one of them.

"Another reason I came down." He stretched his branches again, his lips thinned. "I did what had to be done. I will not sit on the sidelines while more innocents die."

I leaned closer to his shoulder, understanding reached my eyes. He did something for Sidh, something secret. "I would have done the same."

"You shall not have that burden. Other opportunities for you to fight will come. Remember those ancient texts I gave you? The ones I saved from the book burnings?"

After the curse spread, the queen ordered all ancient texts to be burned. Many faeries died trying to save our history as a realm. One faerie, who was not true faerie, saved many texts and hid them with Silas.

My throat bobbed. "Yes."

"You need to read them."

I roughly scrubbed my face. "I don't want to read about witches, brotherhoods, or whatever dark folklore lurks these realms. Is it not enough that I live with this evil inside?"

Silas' leaves rustled as he shook his head. "This is where you are wrong. There is not one drop of evil inside you. This is why she isolated you. To make you like her, but fate had a different path for you."

I wanted to believe his words. But I know the things I've done, the blood that stained my hands. With one look in his eyes, I was compelled. He was so earnest and sincere in every way I wished to be.

Resigned, I lowered my head. "Fine, I will read it for you."

He draped his creaky arm around me, and we gazed upon the quiet sea under violet skies.

26

ELORA

Dolos disappeared into his 'workshop of horrors' which was just a wooden shed about a quarter mile from the house. He was avoiding the elephant in the room. Something about the unicorn pained him so much that his humor leeched from him, and he was, for once, wordless. I needed to rest anyway. When I opened my bedroom door, I found dark violet amaryllises in a clear vase on the side table next to a faded blue Discman. A short, crooked tower of 2000s screamo CDs with headphones dangled off their vintage corners. I grinned, storing this sweetness into my heart. He really knew me. But my smile faded when I unfolded a note in silver writing.

I can't make a mixed CD for you, but there are songs on these that remind me of you.

I couldn't receive it. Riann didn't deserve my thanks, nor could I wrap my head around wanting him, forgiving him, and yet punishing him. Or maybe I was punishing myself. I wanted it to be simple. I loved him. He loved me. He wronged me. I should forgive him, right? He felt unworthy, and I'd waited six years to be deserving of his confession. In the end, maybe he was just a taste of what I thought I deserved before it all came crashing down. After the games, I might be dead, and he would end up finding someone new. Someone pure and bright. A woman full of joy with a wild spirit awakening every dead part of him. I wished I were her.

I put the flowers in the hallway on a windowsill. As for the CDs and the Discman, I left them in the living room where Willa could enjoy the sweet tunes. It was just Riann's guilt speaking, and I was what I was meant to be. Ever the forgotten one. The sooner he understood that I was giving him exactly what he wanted, the more he would stop trying. Those CDs he chose for me were among my favorite bands. He must have spent hours listening to their music.

I was just about to crawl into bed when Riann's persistent knock came. Great. He'd seen his discarded gifts. He stood in linen pants and a loose-fitted shirt, leaning against the door frame. He appeared calm but his tight-lipped quirk failed to fool me. His eyes appeared clouded. Rejecting him brought me no satisfaction. In fact, it ate away at me.

"I've been meaning to talk to you about your bridge connection," he said bluntly, walking in.

"What about it?" I asked, brushing a hair away from my face.

"You leave it wide open. Even after you think to drop the connection, others still hear and see you."

I hugged myself tightly. "See me? How did you find this out?"

He widened his eyes, raking me over inch by inch. There was no need for him to say it. Mikhail had been watching me.

"It's a simple trick called guarding," he said, placing his warm hands on my shoulders. For the first time, I observed his hourglass tattoo in detail. Thick black ink drew the curves of the glass and grains of graphite sand had a life of its own as his muscles twitched. "Most of us leave our minds to wander about the day, but when you have an ability like mine, it comes at a price."

"Seems like everything has a price these days," I scowled, turning from him. "Willa was going to show me that, but obviously, certain events have occurred, and it never happened." It looked as though I'd punched him in the gut. I pinched between my brows. "Just show me."

He leaned against the chair at the table, staring at the broken quill that had been in the same spot since that night. I did not have the heart to touch it—not after. Though the words faded on my arms, they burned underneath. *Disgusting. Marred. Damaged.* We both deserved better.

"Everyone has a door in their mind. Sometimes it's secret, hidden. Others, like me, have several doors confusing intruders. But you...you left a single door wide open. You need to close it." He inched closer to me, closing the space between us.

I tossed back my hair, pulling it up into a messy bun. "How do I close it?" Small ringlets and longer strands of my hair trailed down my neck and shoulders.

Riann bit his bottom lip, clenching the back of the chair. "You," he said, clearing his throat. "You make a mind key. All you have to do is make one in your mind. Some keys look like actual keys. Other keys are memories, words, phrases, whatever it is."

"Sounds easy enough," I said, twirling a ringlet.

"I need to get close to you to make this easier." He walked too cautiously toward me. I rolled my lips as he cupped my face in his hands lightly, my heart skidding sideways. "Close your eyes and tell your mind to take you to your doorway. Once you find it, choose your key and lock those cravens out."

I shuddered from the heat of his touch. "Why do you need to hold my face?"

"For grounding, it's easier so your mind does not wander." His breath met my ear. "Let's begin."

I closed my eyes. At first, I thought it was a joke, but when my breathing rhythm synchronized with his, I felt as though I was floating somewhere. Water. Maybe air. Light as a feather. But it was dark and cold. I felt weightless, buoyed in the unknown. I yelled for Riann, and his name bounced off the hidden walls in my mind. I felt him, though. His breath, his warmth. My mind was as bleak as my reality. There was nothing here. Even with recent memories of making new friends, there was still nothing here to latch onto. Through the tendrils of fog and mist, I found my door. A black door entwined with black roses and violets. Dark light shimmered through the crack, where foreign voices filtered in and out.

"There are voices."

Riann bracketed my face firmly. "They know you are about to lock them out. Don't be afraid. I'm here."

I gripped his forearms as banshee-like shrills screamed on the other side of my door. Heavy darkness swirled around me.

"Pretty flower, pretty flower," a male voice rumbled in.

"I can't do this. I can't," I whispered, tears suddenly running down my cheeks.

"Yes, you can." His nails gently caressed the sides of my head. "Make that key, and it will end."

Voices grew louder. Frantically, I searched for a key. Was there anything to grab onto? Any memory or phrase I could use? I came up short. Everything that was good was also tragic. I thought of Riann, my new friends, but I would have to let them go soon. Too soon. Hissing and cracking noises with the smell of stale lilies pervaded. Death was here. It had followed me my whole life, its scent was a pungent smell I'd grown used to as a child. Their wretched cries to contain me pierced my ears. Bony hands grabbed me and pulled my hair. I screamed inside, grabbing onto Riann's shirt. He was out there but he could not save me in here. This was my battlefield. I was too tired of fighting, exhausted from running. My mind was the arena, and I decided to fight back.

"This is not your home!" I screamed back at them. Only I didn't just scream, I sang it like my life depended on it.

The raspiness of my voice echoed back and forth against every wall, through every bone. They grabbed at me ferociously. One reached for my chest and others covered my mouth, to silence me. My hands wound tighter into Riann's shirt. Then I felt his arms envelope me in their warmth. His star somehow reached for me on the inside like a lighthouse for a ship lost out at sea. I reached for it among the many hands desperate to pull me under.

Riann's voice reached me. "They fear the silence. They fear you. Make them pay for living in your mind for free," his rich velvet voice whispered against my lips.

Fire rushed through me, and my star exploded gold and emerald filaments. Screeching and clicking of bones shook under the light, steam rising from them. Ashes flew around me, and the remaining skeletal hands pulled themselves back into the abyss. An iron wrought door appeared, medieval in its structure. Billowy grass dotted the bottom of the door and bright violets sprouted, twirling in the newfound light. Then it came to me, the only key I could think of. A passing memory of Riann comforting me years ago. He'd barely said anything, yet he'd listened without judgment and did not run from my deluge of tears. It was then my heart thundered for the first time. Somehow, I felt his too.

A brass key materialized in my hand. At the head of the key was one circle and inside were four other circles interlacing each other. I slid the key in and turned it, locking out every single voice. As the door clicked shut, black roses and violets twined around the ornate black knob, tightening the lock. A rush of light flooded my mind and soul. Darkness swirling around me transformed into a golden rotunda of stained-glass windows. Cascading colors of green, gold, red, silver, and blue wound around me like ribbons, enveloping me in their splendor. A small laugh escaped my lips, and I felt Riann's breath like a gentle fog surrounding me. When I opened my eyes, he let me go.

"There," he said, softly grinning. "Sleep well."

My deep, dreamless sleep must have been long overdue because I awoke to Riann sitting across from me with his legs propped up.

"Good morning," he grinned as I rubbed my eyes open. "I made you breakfast a while ago, but the eggs have gone cold. I did not want to wake you."

I stretched my arms and yawned. "How long have you been here?"

He leaned forward. "You don't remember?"

"Remember what?"

"After you locked your door, you collapsed from exhaustion in my arms, so I carried you to bed. I've only been here since I made your first breakfast."

"You didn't need to be," I snapped.

Ignoring my tone, he pulled another plate from behind him of fruits, cheeses, and bread filled with dates and oats. I should not have spoken like that, but I was too prideful to apologize.

His cheek dimpled, with a half-smile. "Here, it's not hot, but it will give you energy for the journey." Riann laid the plate next to my pillow. "Those voices tormented you without you even realizing it. I really hope this is the end of your nightmares, those awful thoughts spinning in your head." His starlit eyes glittered as he stood over me. "Wren already glamoured your eyes blue. Make sure you wear proper foot attire. We will not be taking Lynx. Unfortunately, I am known for riding a kelpie and would stick out."

Instinctively, he brushed my hair from my face and retreated his hand like he'd touched fire. His throat bobbed. "Be ready in an hour." Then he left.

My heart hammered in my chest, and it took all my willpower to convince myself I could not trust him. I stuffed dates and cheese into my mouth while getting dressed in breeches that looked made from a hide and a loose-fitting, white t-shirt. When I finally left my room, I noticed the flowers were no longer on the windowsill. They were scattered on the grass in front of the house as if someone flung them. A sharp pang of guilt pricked me. A part of me wanted to keep hurting him, but another part wanted to yield and forgive him, to remember who he was. There was a larger part of me not ready to reveal things that had nothing to do with him. My heart took a nosedive, knowing I was not completely innocent.

He smiled at me, slinging a large canvas bag over his shoulder. Riann's rough spun cloak had a large cowl, covering most of his face. If it wasn't for the starlight in his eyes, I would not recognize him.

"Ready?" he extended his hand and then pulled away.

I nodded while adjusting my belt and the dagger Dolos had given me. The large water skin I carried was not as heavy as I thought it would be, showing me how much stronger and leaner I'd become. I felt different, like a weight had been removed from my shoulders. Closing that door had given me freedom, and I wanted to thank Riann for showing me the way. But I just looked away, my stomach flopping around, avoiding eye contact.

We pressed on toward the demarcation line without saying a word to each other. Riann stood there for a moment as if having second thoughts. His jaw stiffened and his knuckles turned white from clutching his bag tightly. When was the last time he had passed this line willingly? How painful was it for him to create it, knowing he could not save everyone? I pressed my hand on his back, gently reassuring him. He took a deep breath, leaning into my touch and placed his hand on the line. Scintillating magenta light roved up and down the line like vibrant wheels of fire. He walked through the wards, unprotected and brave.

175

27

RIANN

We strode through winding woods, avoiding the main roads to reach Pine. Arcadia was not too far from Pine but too close to the castle for my liking. The Carnelian Woods had seen better days. Once, the trees were vibrant, like tall peaks of twisting flames reaching for the skies. Now, the bark of the trees flaked off a tinge of faded orange. The leaves were gray, devoid of life. Woodland dryads lurked about in the woods, living quietly to not rouse Nyx. Their kind disposition had remained unchanged since the curse took over, but their ability to communicate with plants had ceased. Strange how the curse stripped us in different ways. I was once a powerful time mage, and now I was useless. Minotaurs were such a proud people, strong in wisdom and might but were reduced to hunger for power, willing to kill anyone in their way.

I thought of Silas, chaining me with those weary eyes. He was exhausted from living behind a mask, caring for Mikhail as if there were any hope for him. He was a good man, and I wished he could live out the rest of his days in peace. I missed him. The way his bark creaked when he smiled wide or roared with laughter. I regretted not taking him and Mikhail with me to Solarin. But the consequences of that choice were unfair and unjust. If I had taken them, maybe things would have been different. Maybe they would be much worse. The forest near the house, where the faeries roamed, was Silas' favorite place on Sidh. I believed it was not just the peace of the forest, but the nostalgia of what Sidh once was that drew him. He had not been there since Mikhail had grown into a man. Mikhail was so lucky that way. He *had* a father figure. I had stern time mages I was never good enough for.

Hours passed since our trek had begun, and my legs steadily became weaker. The uncomfortable silence was killing me. Lor's noticeable distance and averted gaze made me painfully aware I did not have a chance to win her back. I pushed those dreadful thoughts to the side. I needed a break soon because I would surely fall, and then what would she think of me? I also could not take the chance of something happening while I was weak, unable to protect her.

"Let's stop here." I lugged my bag off my shoulder and plopped to the ground.

Instantly, my legs felt relieved. Rummaging through the bag, I took out a blanket and set out dried meats, leafy greens, and Dolos' famous guava juice wrapped in a pack of ice. It was not the romantic picnic I had always envisioned taking her on, but it was what it was. Lor didn't grimace at the simple spread, just simply laid down on the gray blanket and rolled up her pant legs. The canopy of leaves appeared grayer than usual as pale light broke in between the branches. She rubbed the small of her back, softly groaning.

I leaned on a tree, taking in the sight of her. "If you drink the healing water you won't be so sore."

"I'm fine," she said, eyeing the dried meat in my hand. She grabbed some of her own, and her face brightened at the first bite. I'd smoked the meat myself and flavored it, but who's bragging?

"How much longer to Pine?" she asked, her mouth stuffed like a squirrel with acorns.

"Not too much longer," I said, taking a large bite of the herbed meat. "Arcadia is about ten miles from them, so we can get to both of them today and then camp out until we've rested."

Elora rolled her eyes and drew her knees to her chest.

My eyes peeled. "Have I offended you?"

"I know what you're doing," she said coldly, averting her gaze. "You made me come to be alone with you. To somehow make me forget everything and fall in love with you all over again."

Tree bark dug into my back as I pushed into it. "That's not exactly true. I meant what I said. The others could not go with me."

"You could have asked Phil or gone alone."

She chucked the meat onto the blanket. Her hands dug into her knees, making crescent marks from her nails. The hourglass on my arm throbbed. The next time Nyx taps it, I will surely die, but before then, I needed to make sure Elora knew she was loved. But there was no way to tell her that without admitting I was on borrowed time.

I leaned forward, tilting my head. "I just thought it would be a good idea for you to get out and have something else to do besides train and party with our friends."

Her body stiffened. Her eyes became glass. "Maybe it's all that's left for me to do." She dropped her shoulders. "By the way, thank you for last night."

She had absolutely no clue how rare she was. I'd failed her in so many ways, but I would not die until she realized the gift inside her was always meant for her to wield. She picked up the chucked meat, and I gently grabbed her wrist. "Wait." I closed my eyes. "That is not all that is left. You have a burning star inside you that is meant for a purpose."

"I don't have many more days of 'purpose,'" she deadpanned.

Sprouting from the base of the tree, a dark blue flower the size of my hand caught my eye. I pulled it root and stem. Four large, velvet petals grazed my calloused hand as I passed it to her.

She swatted it away. "No flowers! Stop with the gifts!"

"It's not a gift." I remained calm, tearing a petal off. "It is for you to practice."

She looked at me, holding back her anger, her hurt. Starlight shimmered from beneath her shirt, and so did mine. I thought she would be confused, but she nodded in agreement as she roughly took the flower from me.

I angled my head, slightly grinning. "I have watched too many shows and movies with you to know they are all inaccurate with abilities and gifts. They placate audiences by giving the character an ability they gain so suddenly. You have had this star your whole life, stifled because you were the only one of your kind living in the earthly realm." Her head dipped below her knee, and I resisted the urge to comfort her with my touch. "Training for these gifts often seems hopeless, arduous, but that's not the case here."

Lor's head popped up, light flickering around her. "The star bends to your will. Put a leash on it, or don't. You can create peace or create chaos. You can restore, heal, and make." I twirled the flower between my fingers, lifting it between us. "What will you do with this flower now that I've maimed it?"

Lor's lips parted. Her rough hands rubbed the glittering petals as she passed glances at me several times before putting the flower down. "How? The star has a mind of its own. It only burns where you're with me."

My voice thickened. "Simply because it calls for me. But we're not talking about us right now. This is about you. There is a reservoir of deep magic inside you waiting to be accessed. Close your eyes, look past your door, and find the stream."

She lifted the flower again, blinking. Her face softened, like a mask taken off. "Do you need to ground me again?"

I closed the distance ever so slightly, our knees barely touching. "The night we rescued you from the Yaga, our stars connected, giving the boost I needed to whisk us out of there. You did that subconsciously, completely unaware." I lowered my gaze to hers. "You have this under control. You don't need me."

Lor clutched the flower to her chest. "I—" her jawline tensed. "I want you to."

I leaned forward. "Okay," I breathed, bracketing her face delicately. "I'll do that for you." We stood on our knees, her arms trembling. "Hold on to me, Lor."

She dug her hands into the side of my belt, supporting herself. Her eyes shut tight, shuttering here and there. Whatever she saw, her hands tugged tighter on my belt. I had heard that when people finally took control of their abilities, they might see what had been holding them back. Lor was strong, already facing monsters without my help. But I was there, holding her through it. She gasped, and her starlight flared into mine. Suddenly, I saw what she saw.

A familiar scene of teenagers drinking liquor unraveled. The party was similar, but it was not the one she'd gone to on graduation night. This one must have happened before we started speaking. A grungy scene of cheap paneling and posters of half-naked women hung crookedly on the mud brown walls of a basement. Two guys and one girl I did not recognize laughed over spilling their drinks, tumbling on the floor in their stupor. Scanning the room, I found Lor sitting on a high-rise table, staring out the small window. She was younger, thirteen, maybe. Her cheeks were sunken in, her lilac eyes turned down. Frayed overall shorts and a faded orange shirt lanced through my heart. She really had been neglected. Small blades of grass shadowed the bottom edges of the window from the outside. She drew her fingers around each blade as she stared at the bright stars in the night sky.

"Who invited her?" The curly blonde boy pinched his brows as he poured another amber drink. Lor's ear pricked, sighing with her fist resting under her chin. "She's weird."

"I don't know. She seemed like she needed a friend," his red-headed friend said, chugging back the liquor.

"Hey, you!" his blonde friend said, throwing a ball of paper at her. "What's out there? Is the mother ship going to come and take you home?"

Mousy brunette girl laughed and burped. Delightful. "Stop," she said between laughs. "You know those foster kids don't have social skills."

"You guys...that's not fair," the red-headed boy said as he approached Lor. "Take a sip." He tilted the bottle to her mouth. "It'll take the edge off."

"No," Lor said defiantly.

I knew why she didn't leave. She didn't want to go home.

"Come on," he drawled, brushing back her hair. "I brought you here. You could at least act like you're happy to be with us."

Her eyes flashed. "I'm not happy with you guys." She gave the other two a pointed look. "And clearly, nobody's happy I'm here."

He burped inwardly. "What's so amazing about looking out-side?" he asked, putting the bottle down.

Her head turned back to the window. "Maybe I will see some shooting stars. They're beautiful, aren't they?"

The redhead boy's lips curled, and he took back the bottle. "It's just stars. Balls of gas in the sky."

Her eyes dimmed at the thought the stars could be less than she dreamed. "Don't you wish they were more?"

He staggered back, burping again. "You are weird. You should be lucky I invited you here."

A hundred arrows pierced her heart. "I should get going then," she said with a dejected grin, sliding off the table.

"Good!" mousey girl shouted. "Maybe the aliens will come for you on your walk home!"

They had tried to take Lor's dream, her safe place from her. I could see it in her face as she bypassed the cracked concrete on the floor that a rug had been pulled out from under her. Lor's dream could be not become real if nobody else saw her. If only she'd known then how right she was, how she had never been meant to dwell in darkness.

"Lor," I breathed into her ear. "You were right. They *are* more. You are perfect. We are your *muirear*. Your family." I held her tighter, leaving no distance between us. "Find your stream of magic and grab onto it." Her breathing became labored. "Lor, I am here. I am not ashamed of you. I am for you."

Hot tears streamed down her face, and I couldn't help myself as I kissed the tears before they fell. Her breathing steadied. "There it is," she whispered.

I saw the stream, like ribbons of gold light, curling in the darkness. Her pale hand grabbed them, bringing them into unison. Light erupted inside her, so blinding I jumped out of her mind. Her eyes popped open into a watery gaze. With a few quick breaths, we peeled ourselves from each other, caught in a daze. The flower at our knees turned white with its petals restored. Air ripped from my lungs as red light bounced around the woods. No longer were the trees a faded color of what once was. The Carnelian Woods were alive again. I had not seen such rich beauty in years, and I could barely take it all in. Deep red glittering trees on a sea of white flowers. The thing was, Lor did not know what they'd looked like before the curse. Without a doubt, there were some in these woods witnessing the restoration, so I quickly hid her in my cloak.

"How did you know?" I asked, running my hand over her head.

She trembled in awe. "I have no idea. It was like I had seen it before, but I hadn't. Maybe you showed me on the bridge without knowing it."

I palmed my forehead. "There's no way! My doors are locked. I only connected with yours to ground you. I saw those disgusting teens in that ratty basement."

She shook her head, rubbing her thumb on my hand. "Does this mean I can get rid of the curse?"

"No." I pulled myself away, and she flinched at my stony expression. "I mean, I don't know. Magnus might know."

"Magnus?"

"Wren's tribe leader. He's ancient and has seen everything."

"He's Kaya's tribe leader too," she said, trying to correct me.

I turned my head and chuckled a little.

"What?!"

"He is not Kaya's leader. Kaya is not a faerie. She's a dark elf who can shape shift, stuck in her last form."

28

ELORA

My blood sang a new song I never knew I longed to hear. Every broken thing we met on our way to Pine, I restored with my hands. Each broken branch and injured animal became easier to heal each time I bent my will to them. Riann appeared nervous as woodland dryads peeked around from behind the trees, but they never approached us. Their curious eyes darted back and forth before disappearing amongst silvered leaves and rich bark. Finally, we came out of the woods and onto the grassy plains in the open. Riann's face was a lethal calm, turning his head in every direction, pulling me close with every little noise. Tall grass blades grazed my shoulders and Riann's torso. His blue skin glistened under the orange hues of dusk, like a galaxy fading into existence for night creatures like me to gaze upon. Though he was not in his former body, everything else screamed he was himself. His muscular build, broad shoulders, the twitch in his nervous smile. Not even the queen could not take that away.

"We're almost to the line of trees that leads between the mountains. Then we will arrive at Pine," he said, pulling his head further into his cowl.

A river of fire in my body surged with tangible, malleable heat. My core twined and pulled from the licking flames scorching the dead parts of me. I'd never felt more alive. Everything in me wanted to skip through the grass, twirl, and shout for joy, but I honestly didn't want Riann's moodiness to steal the moment.

"Tell me about Rinarie," I said, keeping my voice upbeat. "Tell me about your mother, your childhood before Solarin." My new-found energy had not found a pause button.

Riann's nerves appeared to smooth over as he grinned slightly. "Rinarie is—was—lush. Vibrant colors paled in comparison to Sidh in its former glory. Floating mountain peaks where time mages lived, waterfalls flowing from them into the rivers below. Even on the rainiest of days, the colors of the rainbow scintillated on the bright green grass because it could never become cloudy enough to blot out the sun." He drew in a long breath, tugging the bag on his shoulder. "At night, the stars seemed to lower themselves, making the sky a dazzling brilliant canvas of twinkling lights. I miss the stars." Riann lowered his head. "Sometimes, I forget what my mother looked like. I remember she had my black hair."

I stood on my tiptoes and ran my fingers through his silver strands that flopped over to one side, revealing the markings carved on his scalp. "Your hair was black?"

He rolled his lips and closed his eyes. A flutter of starlight warmed the tiny space between us. Without wanting to, I pulled myself away. He opened his disappointed eyes and pressed forward. "I don't dwell on what I used to look like. My only regret is that you see this"—he gestured over his body—"and not what I used to be. In fact, some days, I can't remember what I used to look like. The only thing that never changed was my eyes."

His starlit eyes were something I could not get enough of, though I refused to show it.

"My mother was kind and had delicate hands," he continued. "I was two years away from becoming of age to join the time mage academia in the floating mountains when she saw promise in me to begin sooner. The highest order assessed me, and they also saw the promise I had with bending the will of the fates and choosing which strings to cut. It was that day they discovered my telepathic ability. They said it was uncanny to have both."

I knocked my fist onto his elbow playfully "You were a big deal then."

Riann stopped for a second, looking at the sky as he always did. "Were."

I realized what I had said as he stepped ahead of me. "I did not mean it like that."

"I know you did not mean it that way. Truth hurts, though." He looked back at me and extended his hand. "Come, we are almost there. These grass plains are not my friend."

Instead of taking his hand, I took the mature approach, pretending not to notice it hanging there. For sure, I thought this would be the moment he finally snapped from my rejection, but he lowered his hand and carried on. Did I want him to snap? Did I want him to suffer? What did I want? When he was not looking, I took the chance to side-eye him, drinking him in. The answer was yes. It was always yes. I wanted him. All of him.

He stiffened. His eyes became predatory, and he swiftly gripped my waist and put his finger to his lips. "We are not alone." His tightened fingers trembled as the grass rustled around us. Like alligators in calm waters, heads surfaced within the sea of grass. Dark, brimming eyes and faces caked with white and red whorls zeroed in on us.

"I know you're here, Sable!" Riann shouted.

A low rumble of laughter sent shivers down my back. Riann held me even tighter.

"Traitor," they hissed, like snakes slithering in the grass.

Slowly, they stood, appearing as tribal people I had seen on TV. Rough, spun clothes covered areas of their dark, rich bodies, leaving little to the imagination. Like their faces, the rest of their bodies were decorated with paint.

"Riann," a woman's voice called. "How's my little spindle mage?"

We turned around and a woman wearing a loincloth with a band wrapped across her chest held a spear. She clicked her tongue. "It has been a long time, traitor." She sauntered through the grass, baring her teeth, revealing bright white fangs tucked in the sides of her mouth. A red and gold ribbon fastened across her forehead, twirling down her lush, wavy black hair that brushed her flaring hips.

Her eyes were like a reptile. She blinked and her slit like pupils dilated. She smiled as though she had captured her prey in the wild. "Who is this pretty thing you have? We heard reports that the prince lost his pet."

I pushed out of his grasp. "I am no one's pet!"

"Oh, she's full of spirit." She licked her lips revealing her forked tongue. "I like that."

Riann pulled me behind him. "Leave her alone. Your quarrel is with me."

She drew closer and ran her pointed finger down Riann's jaw. "It seems you are fond of this pet."

Riann flinched at her touch while grabbing my wrist from behind. "Sable, let us pass. We have come to warn Pine and Arcadia about an attack."

A burly man pushed his way through, wearing dark hides and bone epaulets. His dark eyes fell on me, rolling his lips together. He had similar features to Sable except his hair was cropped short and the sheer size of his muscles could almost rival Lex's. Almost.

Sable's brows pinched together. "Innocent fauns?" She took one look at the man of bones and clicked her tongue. "Carmine! I know what you are thinking, and the answer is no."

"Come on, sis, she is stunning," Carmine said, giving me a smug smile. "I bet I can treat you better than he can."

Riann's breath became heavy. "Please, just let us go."

Sable's face darkened. "Why should I let you go? I've been waiting for you for years." She dug her nails into his arms. "You never came for us. When the curse came, you let it swallow us whole."

"Time was not on my side. I did as much as I could before she used blood magic to take mine away." Another heavy breath rattled off his lips. "Not a day goes by that I don't think of the ones I could not save."

Sable bared her fangs and rammed into him, knocking me onto the ground. "Did you know the curse caused miscarriages?!" Her fangs were so close I thought she was going to rip out his throat. "So very few births since then. Your evil stepmother did something to our wombs because you did not give her what she wanted!"

Carmine raised his hand. "It's not just our people, it was everyone. Sidh will die out in a generation."

Riann put his hand to his chest. "Sable, trust me, if I gave her what she wanted, we'd all be dead right now."

"Trust you? After you abandoned us?!" Sable's face contorted. "We are Draconians! The ones who fought beside you in many wars! You could have at least come back to make us understand instead of letting us believe we were nothing to you!"

As her neck pulsed with rage, a shimmer of greenish scales rippled down her skin.

Defeated, Riann tilted his head, waiting for her to strike. "I did not come back because I was useless to you all, to everyone."

"We loved you. It would have been enough," she said, pushing him to the ground. Her swirling eyes of rage bore into me. "And you... If we give you back to the prince, maybe his mother will release us from the curse."

Tribesmen pointed their spears at me, and my blood ran cold. I raised my hands. "Please, no! He's a monster."

Their desperate eyes flared as the points of their spears nicked my skin.

"Sable! Stop this now!" Riann growled, clutching his chest and stumbling to the ground.

Her face bunched, watching Riann tumble to his knees. "Why are you so weak? You have never once stumbled or have been able to be taken so easily."

His shaky arm reached out. "Please let her go. She is innocent. Like the ones we used to save."

Her teeth seethed right above him. "Why is she so special that the useless spindle mage wants her?"

Riann clamped his mouth shut. Our stars flared in unison, turning their heads in shock. Our shirts did not disguise the bright light breaking through the dark fabric.

Rage slithered from her face. "Never once did I see your star flare, Riann. Who is this woman?"

Still, he kept his mouth shut. Annoyed by his silence, Sable cupped his chin between her fingers. "She's your cymar, isn't she?"

His silence was answer enough. He wouldn't say who I was to him. She pushed his chin away, and he dropped to the ground on his side.

Sable nodded to her tribesmen. "Take them to our camp. Our old friend appears too weak to travel any further."

"Lor," Riann groaned as two tribesmen picked him by the arms, dragging him away.

Tears pricked my eyes, watching him be so helpless. Riann could have revealed everything. It was just a matter of time before the woodland dryads would speak of the Carnelian Woods. Why didn't he?

Sable roughly twisted my arms behind my back and bound me with rope. "Sorry, pretty woman. I can't have you running away, can I?"

She pushed me forward to follow her tribesman. Though my arms ached, I kept my focus on Riann's head drooping below the grass and the soles of his feet dragging through the mud. Something in me broke. His feet. His precious feet. He'd tread for so long on those feet, winning wars, fleeing from enemies, running from me. At that moment, I hated all the petty things we'd done to one another. I just wanted him whole.

29

RIANN

My body was awake, but my eyes remained heavy. I knew I was in the deep woods where the Draconians had fled for safety all those years ago. They lived in huts among thick trees far away from the castle—enough to not be noticed but close enough to keep watch. It felt like the dead of autumn right before winter hit in Lor's earthly realm. We'd gone on "walks" together in her realm. Orange and red leaves clinging to barren trees and Lor's steamy breath had reminded me of when I'd last saw Sable. I'd run. So hard and fast with Willa as the curse had spread. Kain was on our heels. Draconians ran behind us, and before long, I'd heard their anguished cries. They did not keep up as I counter attacked with my demarcation line. Sable, in the distance, cried out as the curse consumed me with rapid speed, and I could no longer help her people. Shame burned a hole through me. What would Lor think of me?

You cannot protect her, but you still have to get up and give everything you've got. Useless mage. You will be dead in days. She will be left to the wolves.

Voices tortured me as I tried to pry my eyes open. They could taunt me all they wanted, but I needed to get Lor out of there. Crackling fire overheated my skin. I hate that I fell ill in front of everyone. Sable wouldn't hurt her, but she could use her to hurt me. Truthfully, I deserved it. I should have been a better friend to the Draconians, to everyone, instead of hiding away being utterly pathetic. Tiny steps trailed my arm. Wren and Kaya must have followed us to their camp.

"Why are you so stubborn?!" Wren never just said hello. He landed on my forehead and used his hands to pull back one eyelid while Kaya softly peeled my other one like she was unraveling treasure. They must have followed us since the beginning, witnessing every little thing.

"Wren, you must not be so hard on him," Kaya said, finally opening my eye to her beautiful, slender face. Her tiny black shadows had been flaring more as if she could no longer hold back her true self.

"He does not have time for niceties, Kaya." Wren finally pulled back my other eye, falling backward into my hair. "Good, your eyes are open. I was about to use my dagger to pry them."

I blinked several times at the canopy above me. Smoke drifted out of the round hole above. It felt like a sauna.

"They put you in here to sweat out your sickness." Kaya's opalescent eyes flickered as she hovered over me. "We both know it's not a sickness that is curable."

I did not have time to think about any of this. "Where is she?" My voice came out hoarse. Kaya put my skin of water to my lips. After clearing my throat, I stood to my feet, wobbling, holding onto the frame of the tent. "Where is she?" I asked again.

They both looked at each other and giggled. Sometimes I hated these two.

Faeries. "Tell me now!"

"Okay, okay." Wren waved his hands dismissively. "She's with her new friends...drinking."

My brows pinched. "What?"

I pulled back the tent flaps, and there she was, dressed in an angular, rough-spun skirt and a band around her chest, dancing among the dead leaves. When Draconians dressed an outsider, it was a sign of welcome. I looked down at my bare chest and black trousers, knowing I was not on the receiving end of that gesture. Someone had braided her hair into tiny ropes with leather and little silver charms that made a noise every time she chugged rich, Draconian red vintage. The same tribesmen who'd pointed spears at her earlier were now cheering her on. Carmine found every opportunity to touch her hand, her shoulder, any place he could.

My skin turned into an inferno. She was mine. *Wait*. She was mine before I'd messed everything up. But I still felt a surge of jealousy.

"Riann," Sable's voice caught me off guard. "How are you feeling?"

She walked beside me, holding a goblet set in bones. I narrowed my eyes at her. "Well enough to leave for Pine."

A smug grin spread on her face. Her fangs pointed devilishly past her lips. "Your cymar seems to have gotten on with my tribesmen so quickly." Sable lifted the goblet to her lips. "You know us Draconians. It does not take us long to become friends...or lovers," she chuckled.

The music pricked at my skin, watching Lor dance sensually from the corner of my eye. She moved like liquid, her body completely possessed by the sound of their drums. I'd seen her dance before, but never this free or bare. "What is that supposed to mean?"

"You've been out for a day. She's already become one of us. You know how we love to live life." Sable slapped me on the back.

Drums and singing voices sped up their tempos. The rhythm changed from a driving beat to something more tribal. Sable's words blurred together as I focused on Carmine manhandling Lor. The way he caressed the slight curve of her hips made me think of bad things. Murderous things. Lor reciprocated his touch as her hand ran down his corded muscular arm. She wanted to be desired, to be touched. Internally, I screamed at myself, watching someone else have the privilege of being close to her. It should be my privilege. What I would give to tear his hands off so he could never touch her again. Just for kicks, I would have Dolos set them on fire and watch the look on Carmine's face as some of his other favorite appendages became ash.

"She has loose lips when she drinks." Sable interrupted my murderous thoughts.

A sudden feeling of guilt sliced me. I hadn't spent enough time with Lor to know that piece of vital information she'd shared. "What did she say?"

One side of Sable's lips curved upward. "It was interesting to hear that her cymar is refusing her. She mentioned in passing that you rejected her." Sable watched my face twitch with a proud look.

Then, her face softened. "I would never kill you, even though you turned out to be a rotten friend. But when I saw you yield yourself to her, it made me want something again."

"And what is that?"

"A family," she said, walking away.

Draconians prided themselves over their children and lineage. Fitting the curse had taken that away. Lor stood on a tree stump doing a trust exercise, and my blood boiled as she fell into Carmine's arms. She shouted something and giggled before getting back on her feet. I had never realized how long her pale hair was as it reached just above the small of her back. Thanks to all her training, her body became more toned yet still had its slender build. It was achingly hard to take my eyes off her. Mikhail said there was a heart-shaped freckle above her backside. Her skirt was so low it would have revealed it, yet I saw nothing. He had said that to get a rise out of me. She was absolutely stunning in anything she wore, and I was an idiot not to enjoy it. Lor climbed onto the stump again, falling into Carmine's arms, seemingly enjoying his large hands roving down her back and across her hips. I careened toward them.

"We must be going!" I shouted, pulling her away from him.

"Stop! I was having fun!" Her fists pounded my arms, and I realized how much stronger she'd become as splotches of dark blue bloomed on my arms.

The music died down, and every eye bore down on me. All the joy she had vanished. "That man had his hands all over you, and you don't seem to care," I snapped.

She reeled her body away, her face red with anger that rivaled the sun. "Why do you care? I can be both disgusting and—what do you call it in this realm? A harlot? Is that right?" Lor shook her wrist free of me and stormed into the tent.

Kaya and Wren fluttered nearby, casting their judgmental glances. Their wings flapped behind me as I chased after her.

I took a deep breath "Lor, we need to leave for Pine."

She crossed her arms. "Nobody told you? Pine is empty. Someone else warned them, along with Arcadia. We wasted a journey."

My brain short-circuited, either at what she'd said or the fact that sweat glistened on her abdomen. "Then let's go home."

Her body went rigid. "I told you I was having a good time here!"

"I am not welcome here," I snarled. "We need to leave."

Lor unfolded her arms and palmed her forehead. "You got jealous that another man enjoyed my company," she emphasized each word. "Or rather that I enjoyed his company!" Truth slammed me in the gut. I hated how she smiled at him.

"I won't deny I hated seeing that." I put my fist to my lips, trying to think rationally. Disgust slid across her face. It was the same look when people discovered I was a useless mage. Standing across from each other, the fire between us, fear poked me in the chest that she would truly see me as worthless.

My arms slackened to their sides. "How come it is so easy for you? Every day is closer to the games. There are those who want you dead, yet you laugh and revel with others as if nothing is happening!" The fire licked its flames in response. "You talked so much about not wanting to live, yet you are skipping in the fields. I can't take it, Lor. I want to know what is going on inside your head!"

She came so close to the fire I thought she would walk in. "I'm scared," her voice quivered. "After finding friends and..." She pierced me with her gaze. I hoped she would say finding me, but the sentence fell dead on her tongue. "I wanted to know what it was like to live. You gave me the key to shutting out my tormentors, and I have never felt so free before. Before I go down to the grave, I want the universe to know I lived. I wished when I was a little girl that the stars would sing for me, that one day I could be a constellation others wove stories about. I was always nothing. But now I am something. And that's worth living for, even if it's a short while." Our hearts beat loudly in Lor's momentary pause. Not even the flames between us could burn away her confession. "I know you were adamant on making me hate you, but my heart was not made like that. It was made for so much more. You've always had my heart. You took every opportunity to make yourself into a monster. But all I see is someone desperate. Desperate for approval and yet not showing one ounce of vulnerability to the one who matters."

Words clogged my throat. How could she give her heart to me after everything I'd done? She knew it was not really me. I wore a mask of indifference to hide myself from her, afraid of everything. I'd lived eight hundred years and so many times, I questioned what love was. Only love could see through the mask and take me as I was. I couldn't hold myself back any longer. How could I, when this piece of heaven stared through me, assessing me, waiting patiently for me?

Her eyes lit up over the fire, a halo of starlight twinkling over her brow. "Do you know what I was told?" she asked. "They wanted to welcome you here. But you rejected me just like you rejected them. They said rejecting one's cymar feels the same as killing one's soul." Tears rolled down her hot cheeks. For the past three days, I had seen too many of her tears that I could no longer bear it. "Does your soul hurt?"

My body went taut, like I could snap and break at any moment. I was so tired of running, tired of hiding. I needed to make things right. Simplicity told me we were two people in love with each other and fate found a way to bring us together. She was my...the word lodged in my throat. Every bit of fear entangled itself on that word, that vow. The world shifted, stilling all the chaos that always screamed for me to pull back. "Every day," I trembled.

"They also told me that," she choked out a sob, "you used to be wound tight, rough around the edges. When you begged them for my protection, you had never laid down your life like that before. Sable could have killed you, and you would have let her just to keep me safe."

"Anyone would have done that for you," I said, rounding the fire, drawing close to her.

Her face softened between the flames. "No, they would not have."

My eyes became hazy as I drifted near. Her sweet breath met mine.

"I have not rejected you, Lor...not really." My fingers trembled as I tucked her hair behind her ears, grazing her braids. She grasped my forearms. Her breath hitched at my slightest touch. I cupped my hot palms around her teary face.

Lor leaned into my touch. "I felt you in the woods, kissing my tears away. But I could tell you did not wish to go any further. You held back. Then, you would not confess in the face of danger that

I am your cymar. Must I remind you of everything else? Tell me. How did you *not* reject me?"

"I gave you my name," I said, hovering my mouth over her ear. "After the whipping, I gave you, my name. Should you have said it then, I would have yielded all that am to you."

Her eyes glistened. She languidly lifted her hands to my chest and pressed my thundering heart. Our stars flared like the light wanted to burst out of our skin. Bands of gold and violet starlight filled the tent in whorls of vibrancy. "This game... I'm tired."

"So am I," I whispered above her quivering lips. "I want to be who you deserve."

The sweet curl of her lips nearly knocked me to my knees. Then the thought came to me. Was she drunk? How much Draconian wine did she drink? I couldn't have our first proper kiss be like this. Was I an idiot, or was I truly honoring her? I wanted her more than reason, but what would she think when she'd sobered up? I couldn't take that rejection from her. Because after I kissed her, there would be no turning back. To most, it was just a kiss. But for me, a Rinarien, it was the beginning of forever. So many times during the past month, I'd heard her call out for Peter in the middle of the night while dreaming. Desperately, I wished for her to call out for me, but I'd given her no reason to—until now.

I must have been lost in my thoughts for too long. Her face crumpled, and she pushed me away. She believed I was rejecting her again, and I couldn't let that happen. I could tell she wanted to curse at me and say so many awful things, but she pulled back her torrent of obscenities. We stood a few feet apart, both of us pulling apart at the seams. Why was this so hard when I dreamed of being with her every night? Was I afraid of losing her, losing this moment? Or was I truly afraid of not being who she needed me to be? Her lips parted, and tears pelted the dirt ground. Flames made the whites of her clenched fists glow. She struggled not to break, not to run away. We're both so tired. My futile attempts to get her to hate me would have never worked. She loved me too much. I wanted it all, even if I only had days to experience what this side of paradise felt like. She bit her lips so hard, I thought she would bleed. Instead, she looked up with her glassy eyes, unclenching her fists and filled with resolve.

"Riann," she whispered.

I staggered back. A surge of fire coursed through my veins, and this time, I was the one choking on my tears. My name. A simple vow.

"Say it again," my voice strangled as I stumbled closer to her.

"Riann." Her voice grew louder. Her eyes widened as I drew near. "Riann, Riann."

My name. My name on her lips obliterated every wall in me. Every step felt like heavy chains falling off me. My cymar. My only. I took too long again, registering the blast of fire that she'd turned to leave the tent. I pulled her by the wrist, twisting her body to mine, and shattered my lips on hers. A low groan emitted from her throat, and I swallowed the sound. Everything about this kiss was raw. Claiming me, claiming her. She was my first and would be my last. Our stars sang in unison. The fire snuffed out, leaving nothing but the glow from our chests glittering on the walls. Stardust particles glowed, floating as if suspended by time and space. It was only us in the world for that moment. My hands trailed the soft skin of her back and her hips. Her fingers deftly left their mark on my sides. As much as I hated breaking the kiss, I pulled away.

She pressed her lips to my shoulder in demand. "Say it. Confess who I am to you."

"Elora." I tilted her head back, gazing upon this gift in my fledgling hands. "You are my cymar. I have known since the day I heard your laughter across realms." The confession felt like a weight lifted, and yet a sudden press of urgency to shield her, love her, consumed me. Strength settled in my bones that I had not felt for a long time. At this rate, I felt like I could take on an army.

More tears ran down her face. But this time, it was joy, and I had made her feel that way. "I love you, Riann."

"Undeserving," I whispered against her lips before kissing her again as though I was starved. After everything I had done, I was most unworthy of her love for me. I almost sank onto the ground to kneel before her. She was to be cherished and cared for, like a knight would do for his princess in those fantasy shows she watched. But that was not who we were. We were to be equals.

I wrenched my lips free from hers. "We cannot go any further. Once we—"

She pulled me close by my nape. "Dolos told me. It's as good as marriage."

"He *would* tell you." We laughed in between sweet kisses. I could not get enough of this. I'd waited hundreds of years for her, for this. Though I would die in a few days, it was worth it.

A sliver of pale light sliced through the tent, washing the starlight away. Kaya and Wren stood at the bottom, giggling. Wren's stern face lit up, and he smiled. This was the first time I'd seen him exude joy that was not wine related, and it warmed my heart. Kaya held out her hand to Wren. "See, I told you they would. Now, pay up."

30

MIKHAIL

Kain's rancid breath curled through my nose as he pinned me against the jagged wall of the empty kitchen. I moved my head as his fist barreled down, hitting the wall instead. Bits of stone and plaster skidded across the room. Stars in my vision, he grunted as he pulled me by the neck and threw me to the ground against a table holding cookware. Pots and pans clashed together as I stumbled to my feet. Kain had caught me. He'd caught me reading the books mother believed were burned to ash. The ancient tomes of witches and their faceless master. Witches who practiced dark magic and fed on the souls they ruled over. The Astryx was a lie! The soul tax never existed. These witches believed in the dark one who would serve their master in fury and storm, a harbinger of death to all realms. I thought I was safe reading them locked away in Lor's old room, but Kain must have followed me. We'd fought all the way down the spiral staircase, landing in the kitchen.

I spit out blood, readying myself to finish this fight. "You've always hated me Kain. Do you really believe she will share an ounce of power with you if I am gone?!"

"You will never yield, will you, boy? Do you think I don't know the lives you secretly spared?" he snarled, clenching his bloodied fists.

"Why haven't you reported me then?"

We stood yards apart, each assessing our next move, breathing hard. It dawned on me he never reported me because I had saved several of his friends. A part of him felt like he owed me his silence, but somehow killing me in the kitchen was okay in his eyes. I grinned at him, bloody teeth and all. "I could easily tell Nyx how I saved your friends, and you kept your silence."

Kain's eyebrows pinched together. "Boy. You know nothing. I serve her alone."

"You serve yourself, traitor," I spat. "I think it's time mother and I had a lovely chat." I turned from him and headed to the double wooden doors.

Kain growled and ran like lightning after me. His footsteps pounded, and before I could defend myself, he was on top of me. His hands were around my neck, muttering curses. His face contorted in rage, veins popping in his arms and neck. Drops of thick sweat pelted me like sulfur to the skin.

Kain's hands wrapped tighter around my neck. "She will not miss you. She is young and can have another one. One of promise."

One of promise. It struck a nerve in me. But I remembered Silas. I was something he'd gained in his world of loss. I was someone important and full of promise for him. On the verge of blacking out, I balled my fists, and they exploded into an inferno. Kain leapt back, his red fur already engulfed in flames. Primal screams echoed the kitchen and surrounding areas. Thankfully, the castle was huge, but it still scared me someone would hear him. His skin blistered as he clawed at himself, seeking relief and finding none. I thrust out my hand.

"I gave you too much mercy, Kain, because you had a family. This is the last of my clemency." I closed my fist, and his neck snapped. He fell to the floor burning away. I added more flames to his body until there was nothing left.

***

Lye wouldn't get rid of the stench. My body ran on full adrenaline as I threw my own clothes into the flames. Minotaur blood was sticky and pungent, but he'd had it coming. Any moment now, my mother was going to find me to warp my mind again. Everything was spinning and so new that if she came, she might be able to read me. Someone had taught Elora how to lock me out. I missed having something nice to look at. I wished I could have caught a glimpse of her just to settle the rattling in my bones. Kain was not easy to kill.

He'd had years of experience killing lowlifes like me, but he did not foresee my telepathic power. It was something I rarely used when keeping people like him at bay—to always have that hidden weapon. I swept Kain's ashes with a broom and poured them into the water drain. Nobody could tell the ash residue was from him and pinpoint his death on me.

"Master, would you like me to call on one of the ladies in waiting?" Grim asked, handing me a towel.

His pointy ears, adorned with black hoops at the tips, twitched in anticipation. Unlike most creatures, goblins loved to serve. I trusted him with my life. The black studded broach I'd given him glittered in the fire's light. Goblins saw jewels as a token of loyalty, and I wished everyone else was as simple as them. Grim's wave of salt and pepper hair reminded me of my brother. Maybe that was another reason I'd kept him around. Still, as he watched me wash off the black stickiness, his ruddy complexion paled.

"No, Grim, I have not had an appetite for them," I groaned, wiping a hot towel across my neck.

"Ever since you lost your pet, you haven't wanted to do much of anything." His hooked nose sniffed me, grimacing. I still smelled like Kain. Good lord. I hated Lor for leaving me. Yet, I'd known the day would come. I wondered if Riann really screwed things up worse than I had with her.

"Some things were worth keeping." I splashed more water and oils onto my face, scrubbing like a madman.

"She was a pretty pet," he mused, tapping his chin. His lips slowly spread into a mischievous grin.

"Indeed."

I missed having conversations with her, honestly. If I'd truly hated Riann, I could have taken her a thousand times over and not lost a single night of sleep because of it. I didn't love the girl, but she jostled a door I'd kept shut since Marie. I missed Marie so much it hurt. Even with having a time mage for a brother, a string could be reattached once it has been cut.

It was the only time in my life I'd felt happiness. She'd smiled at me with those crystal blue eyes past her curtain of golden curls. I'd searched high and low for the gift of immortality to give her but found nothing. When I'd returned for her, she was in the grave because of the plague. Riann was so stupid to have someone immortal and treat her terribly. If I'd had Marie, there was nothing I wouldn't do to keep her safe.

"Grim, you should retire for the time being. I know any minute my mother is going to come for me."

"Master." His bony hand reached for my waist.

I welcomed the touch. It's not like anyone ever truly showed concern for me except Grim and Silas. Maybe the rest of the goblins too. Riann had the faeries; I had the goblins. They may have had crude tastes and enjoyed some cruelty, but they were honest and diligent workers.

Grim's round gray eyes pinned mine. "You should run away from this place. Find another realm to hide in and live a new life."

I sat down on my sofa, staring into the flickering flames. "Grim, my life is here. I can never leave Sidh. Regardless of the cost."

He sighed. "If you stay here for us, it will not matter. We will be food for the Astryx at some point."

"What a miserable existence," I scowled. If he only knew the truth.

But he was right. Eventually, those deemed lesser would find their way into the gullet of those soul sucking witches. If Grim discovered what I'd found out—the reason I killed Kain—there would be an uproar the kingdom was not prepared for.

"But for now, we live," he said, bowing down.

I admired his resolve and wished no harm would ever come to him or his kin. But I was not a hopeful man. Grim padded away, hanging his head low. I tried to shake off his kindness, as I did many times before, but ever since Elora locked me out, I craved goodness. It was like she fed me something that made me feel again, and then she'd run away. I didn't blame her. There were other filthy things hanging around in that head for too long. Things I related to. Down her bridge, crimson roses and violets twirled around an ornate knob, and I was so tempted to knock just to see if she'd answer. Instead, I stood outside her door, peering into the keyhole, but I could not see anything past the petals covering both sides. Well played, Elora.

The flowers reminded me of the ones I'd sent her. Something warmed my blood, touching the velvet petals. I knew she'd love them, and it was the first time she'd ever received anything in her life. At first, I thought it was a charade, a ruse. But giving Elora those things and kissing her made me long for Marie. Each time we collided, I closed my eyes and thought of her. I knew Elora was thinking of Riann, anyway. We'd used each other, and I treated her dreadfully. I knew that now, and I was a hypocrite for hating what Riann had done. Silas was right. I should have just given her to my brother.

An elusive knock rapped at the door. Once again, I built my walls, putting Marie in the forefront. She was my shield. With her face before me, I withstood all the pain my mother put me through. Dressed in nothing but my breeches, I hoped the stench would not reach her as she sauntered into the room. Her deep-cut, black silks sashayed as she wore her dreaded crown just to see me. As if I had forgotten her authority.

"Where have you been lately, son?" she asked. No preambles. She couldn't care less about how I was doing.

Refusing to look her way, I guzzled wine straight from the bottle, preparing myself for the inevitable pain. Her fingers wiggled as she drew closer to me.

"I said"—her eyes became pools of black ink—"where have you been?"

"Nowhere of your concern, Mother." I leaned back, waiting for her to pounce.

"Where is Kain?" she asked, already suspicious of me.

"I have no idea where that oaf is. Maybe you should keep better tabs on your people rather than torturing me," I said, stretching out my legs.

Without hesitation, she lunged forward and squeezed my temples with her cold, dead hands. "Fine, have it your way."

Her talons dug into me, but all I saw was Marie. Beautiful Marie smiling down on this pathetic man.

31

ELORA

Instead of racing back home, we curled up by a tree, lost in the music, the warmth of each other's arms. My skin burned from the passionate kiss we'd shared in the tent. I had kissed before, but this set me ablaze. Basking in the tight pull of Riann's arms around me, under gray and violet skies, there was no place I'd rather be. Sable kept eyeing us, smirking as if she'd accomplished something. I'd told her too much when I drank their wine. Wine here did not taste like wine on Earth. It was sweet, like fruit juice—you didn't even realize you were wasted until it was too late.

Sable knew about my star, my abilities, due to my drunken mouth. She could have ordered the tribesman to knock me unconscious and take me to the queen as a bargaining chip. I may have mentioned the Carnelian Woods, but that was going to happen anyway, with the dryads lurking about. I leaned into Riann's hard chest, burying my head in the crook of his neck. His arms tightened around me, emitting a low groan. Flames ripped through me each time we touched. His heart thundered loudly, and I thought it might explode. I wondered if he felt mine too. My thoughts were interrupted by Sable eagerly approaching us. She crouched down, raking her golden reptilian eyes over me and Riann. Ebony hair swung over her toned shoulders, flowing down the slight curve of her hips. She really had a killer body.

"Pretty woman," she said with a low hiss. "We let your cymar live, so please give us what we want."

Riann's head shot up, and an air of fury rose from him. My hand pressed firmly to his thigh to smother his simmering rage. "What do you mean?" I asked.

His hands wound tightly around my arms. "I have no patience for someone demanding anything of my cymar." His rich, dark voice pebbled my skin.

Sable clicked her forked tongue. "If Elora had not been here today, would you have confessed your devotion to her?"

I felt Riann's body heat like an inferno behind me. "Fate is fate," he responded flatly.

His words left an oily feeling in my stomach. I slide my hand over Riann's. "Sable, what do you need from me?"

His tightened lips softened, and he angled his head toward mine, surrendering his urge to argue further.

"See those over there?" She pointed at two red-splattered tents.

"Since the curse began, we have had no births. Stillborns." Her voice *trembled*. This fierce woman trembled for her people. "These women live in those tents fearing to come outside in case of endangering their pregnancy." She clasped her calloused hand around my shoulder. "Heal their wombs. Break this curse over our people."

Riann took a deep breath and slowly let go of me. Healing trees was one thing, but people? What if I did something wrong? What if I was not capable? Or what if I... Too many what ifs spun around my head. Riann moved in front of me and slid to his knee, crouching next to Sable, and I saw ice melting between old comrades. They glanced at each other, leaving all insults and open wounds behind them. An understanding reached between them. He was as cursed as she. While he wasted away, Sable could have approached the demarcation at any time. For all of his sadness, her anger was in equal measure. Sweet warmth blossomed between them as they feigned smiles that never reached their eyes.

Riann exhaled heavily as though a chain had fallen from his shoulders. His eyes were a deep well of starlight. "Lor, I know you think you are incapable. But here in this realm, we believe in fate. As a former time mage, I know how hard it is to have perfect alignment. But you are here for a reason, and maybe one day, the night sky will paint this moment." He kissed my hand and lingered there. "You are more than enough, more than I deserve. And right now, those precious babes, their mothers, need you."

Sable bowed her head low to me.

"No!" I cried. Both of them were taken aback, their eyes bewildered. "I meant no, Sable, you do not bow."

She tossed back her rich hair and burst out laughing. "Oh my, Riann! Don't let go of this one. She's already a misfit. I can't wait to see what she can do."

I propped my hand on the tree and rose, preparing my mind and will to break anything. Failure was not an option they could afford. The thought of dangling hope in front of them and not being able to heal them rattled me. But I had to try.

I took my cymar by the hand. "Riann, will you please come with me?"

I did not want him to let me go ever again. He could keep me grounded if I needed it. With each step, gold molten veins spread down my body as if in response to my longing. I felt the heat, the anticipation in my bones. In tent one, three women sat around the fire, knitting rough spun clothes. Their dark, expectant eyes flicked up at me, and they slowly stood to their feet. Sable must have already informed them about me. There were no proper words to say. I wanted to heal them and break this cruel curse. I hoped blood magic did not do this, but I thought Sable would have known that. Riann might be the only cursed person with blood magic. Nyx had robbed him of so much. I could only imagine what it was like for these women to live in constant fear. What did their husbands think of them? Were they cared for when they could not bear children?

One woman rubbed her round belly and waddled near me, speaking a language I had never heard before.

"She said you have starfire. Please, pretty lady, have already lost seven," one said, who appeared from behind her.

Seven? Another woman confessed to eleven stillborns and miscarriages. A single tear rolled down my face. She placed her hand on my belly, frowning. "The flowers planted at the base of the trees in the Carnelian Woods are our children. We saw the trees come alive and hoped our children would be there waiting for us."

With bated breath, I touched the woman's belly. Sweet movements of a little one tumbling around to the feel of my hand made my heart leap. There was a limit to this star power, I felt it. I was unable to undo what had already been done. The flower was maimed yet still alive, but I could do nothing in death. Never once did I think of having children, being that I had no mother or father to model what a good parent was. I did not think I could have a husband or a family. Riann stood behind me, and for the first time, I believed it was possible. She placed her hand on my belly as well, and tender warmth pooled in my core. It felt like joy and sorrow wrapped together, complementing each other.

"Hold me," I whispered to Riann.

His warm breath ran over my shoulder as he nestled his head in my neck and wrapped his arms around my waist. He pressed on my belly, entangling his fingers with the woman's. Kaya and Wren fluttered by my ears and perched themselves on Riann's shoulders, earnestly waiting.

"You can do this," he said, grazing his nose near my collarbone.

I closed my eyes, finding the core of my will. Ribbons of gold light surrounded me in the dark place near the rose-violet door. Faint knocking rapped in urgency. Shadows peaked beneath the frame. Warm honey, gold ribbons wound around my hands, so delicate and free. With my other hand, I straightened ribbons of light, pressing my will into them. My will was simply a want, a need. I wanted to heal them. I needed to break this horrid curse. Word would reach the queen about me, but I didn't care. Riann said I could create chaos, too, so it would be in her best interest to back down.

A male voice screamed through the door, *"Flower, pretty flower, open up! I will rip you out root and stem!"*

Another male voice behind the door boomed, but I could not hear his words, only that there was a struggle. I had to focus on these women who needed me. Doubt surged in me, and the light flickered. I could never forgive myself if these women couldn't provide healthy, live births. At this rate, the Draconians, my new friends, would die off in the next thirty-fifty years, or whatever their average lifespan is. With the ribbons at my command, they pulsated with need. I took a deep breath. I was ready. Ready.

Riann's voice cut through the darkness. *"You are enough, my cymar, my only."*

I clung to his voice and opened my eyes to the golden wonder shining in the tent. Light flowed like water in and out of the tent, breaking a shadow that had hovered over the camp for so long that they no longer saw it. People outside the camp began shouting and clapping. The women stood before me glowing, like they were forged into someone new, someone restored. Riann's warmth encased me, and it felt like a catalyst, though I knew he would not hold me forever. Someday, I would have to stand on my own.

"My baby is moving more than he used to!" one woman shouted, tears of joy flowing down her face.

They would not stop touching my hands and my legs. Some knelt and kissed my feet. I was no goddess wanting to be worshiped or revered. Women from the other tent screamed and ran out for the first time since their pregnancy began. Riann guided me out, sensing my discomfort, and crowds stood around us.

Sable pushed her way to the front, her face completely unguarded. "You not only broke this curse and saved us from extinction, but you healed the many ailments in this camp."

Carmine broke through the crowds and removed his bone armor, bending the knee. "Starfire."

"Starfire," another said.

Soon the Draconians shouted *Starfire* on their knees. Even Sable found this moment to be too reverent to continue standing. Most would never know my real name. But they would know Starfire. Riann intensely stared into the distance, and I knew he spoke with Willa. He finally gazed at me, lifting me in his arms. His chiseled face softened under the haze of violet dusk and starlight. I wrapped my arms around his neck, keeping my eyes on him, unable to describe his expression. His arms were never weary of holding me like a prize, like a reward. My fingers slid up and down the column of his neck, where I felt his pulse racing. Then I found a word to describe how he was looking at me. Riann *beheld* me.

The muscles in his jawline feathered. "Starfire, let's go home."

With a gentle push of my starlight into his chest, we dusted, landing on the hill of trees in front of the house, knee to knee. No, not the house. My home.

32

RIANN

Dusting was rather new to Lor. Her rapid breaths thumped against my chest as we landed on the hill across from the house. Oddly, it did not feel like I was at death's door. Maybe she was powerful enough to sustain both of us. Thinking about it made my chest tight. I had nothing to offer her if we consummated our union as cymar. She could give so much of herself, but I had nothing to spare. I wouldn't want to push her away again, but I wondered if the fates were wrong by giving this beautiful gift to someone like me.

Still wrapped in my arms she looked up at me. Desire and longing filled every cavity in my chest. Many emotions pooled behind her eyes. I couldn't help but feel the overwhelming urge to shower her with kisses. Nothing had felt more *right*. Fates be damned. Lor parted her lips and kissed each corner of my mouth, her arms winding around my neck. It was unfair she breathed new life into me with two days left to enjoy it. She and my friends would fight for the fauns without me, which sickened me to my stomach. I'd told Lor to stay by me, and I did not exactly lie. I would always be with her after I blasted the last of my starlight in the sky for some sap to wish on. I wanted to tell her, but I also wanted her to be happy for the rest of our time together.

My fingers twirled in her hair, and she whispered something to me, but I couldn't exactly hear her through the thickened haze. Roving my hands against her bare sides, past the rough spun skirt, I shuddered, thinking about having our union. It would not be right. But the heat was intense. No, not right now. Not on the dirt and moss and where anyone could see us. For Lor, it would be the beginning of marriage. For me, it had begun when we kissed in the tent. Rinariens did not need an officiant, a ceremony, or even rings. Starlight was enough to bind us.

When I'd heard her laugh across realms and galaxies six years ago, that was it for me. But Lor had grown up in the human realm with little understanding of our ways. She understood it at a surface level, but she had not grasped the heart of it. I could tell through her kisses, the hurried need, the way she opened her eyes repeatedly just to see if this was real. I was not offended or taken aback. After all, I was a dying man. Honoring her, to keep her from yielding herself to me, would be pure torture.

Wrapped in each other's arms, unable to let go, she whispered something again.

Finally, I snapped myself out of it. "What did you say?"

"Phil is here," she said, loosening her arms from my neck. Phil was behind us, lurking in the shadows of the trees.

A big sigh tumbled out. "Phil, what are you doing here?" I asked, lifting Lor to her feet.

His blazing red eyes lit up more than usual. "Well, now I see why you chose her to go with you instead of us."

"Phil, it's not like that." I brushed the dirt off my breeches, mildly annoyed at his assumption and that he did not have the decency to turn away while we were kissing. My fingers laced with Lor's. I was done hiding my affections.

Phil strode closer to us in his black leathers, his double swords crossed on his back. "Do not get me wrong, I am not upset." His voice thickened, "Elora, daughter of Sirius and Eos, I humbly sub-mit my apologies to you." He bent the knee, which clearly made Lor uncomfortable. The way he said her name with reverence and that he mentioned my former masters, made me uneasy. "I carelessly spewed harsh words because I was in denial about my failures." His bottom lip quivered as he cast his watery gaze onto me. "I've had some time to think about how jealous I became when Elora came here. Now, I realize she is one of us."

Lor broke out of my arms, the first time I hadn't felt her body's warmth since the tent. "Oh, Phil, of course, I forgive you." She embraced him, and I did not know what to do with myself. I wasn't jealous, but something inside me want to jump out of my skin. She could not be any more perfect. "Please join us for our nightly party with the rest of our family."

Family. The word hit me like a ton of bricks. Willa once said she could be our family, but it felt different hearing it from Lor. Phil grinned from ear to ear, wiping a single tear from his eye. In all the eight hundred years we had known each other, I'd never seen him cry. We'd endured countless missions, coups, and bleak battles. But something about Lor moved him.

"I think that would be a great idea." He choked back a nervous laugh.

It was uncanny to see him like this, but maybe I didn't notice because I had not been that great of a friend. Guilt spread its ugly fingers throughout my entire being. I had been selfish during my time without my abilities because I had believed I was worthless without them. I could have done so much more than hiding in the darkness. Lor linked arms with Phil as I walked closely behind. With a turn of her head flashing her smile at me, she reminded me how beautiful the light was after being in the dark for too long.

Willa greeted us at the door, jumping into Lor's arms and wrapping her legs around her waist. She wagged her finger at me before shuffling Lor inside in a barrage of excitement. "I told you! I told you!"

The stench of something burnt assaulted my senses before crossing over the threshold. I held my hand over my nose, disgusted and absolutely offended something that atrocious was cooking in my kitchen. "What is that smell?!"

Willa skipped to the oven, her braid swishing, and pulled out a burning loaf of goodness-knows-what from the brick oven. She looked so proud of herself. Unfortunately, the scent intensified to the point where I needed to hurl it out of the house. It may have been meat, but it looked like petrified black stone. "You weren't here, so we tried cooking. We wanted to celebrate you both." Her starry eyes widened with pride.

Lor's face lit up. "That is so sweet of you." She gave Willa a peck on her cheek.

Only for Lor could I put up with this blasphemous loaf of evil.

Lex came from the hallway, holding two laurel wreaths of dark waxy leaves. His sculpted face flushed the tiniest bit of pink as he gazed upon Lor. Yet he did not spare me a glance. His anger with me over how I had treated her remained evident, but for her sake, he'd put on a kinder mask.

Oblivious to the tension between us, Lor swept her eyes over the wreaths. "Are these gifts?"

He placed one on her head, gently grazing her jawline and chin. Satin white ribbon curled down her head, past the small of her back. "Love," he said, his voice so deep and warm. Ever since the curse, the only one who truly heard his voice was Willa. After Lor came, he had opened up a little more.

"Love," Lor said, placing the other wreath on my head.

The wreath felt confining. Its twigs and pointed leaves irritated my scalp, but it was more so because this would not last. For either of us. Nausea began to rear its ugly head. I would die a liar. She did not deserve this. But she did not deserve her joy to be stolen either.

Willa put the rock on the table, but I couldn't take it anymore. As always, I would be the jerk and tell her it was inedible and take care of dinner.

"Where Lex is from, they symbolize their union with laurel wreaths," Willa said with the brightest smile, wiping charred bits off her apron.

Such fond memories of their union. Their ceremony took place on the shores of Solarin. Crystal waves had crashed at their feet, and as soon as they knotted their satin ribbons together, they ran into the ocean laughing in the breakers. We were all so much younger then, filled with hope for the future. All hope had died with the curse—until Lor had come crashing into our lives.

Lex's glare did not leave me. When Lor left my side to help Willa, I realized I needed to make things right with before my next whipping. I would not be able to die in peace knowing there was no reconciliation. "Lex, please walk with me," I pleaded, almost as a question, angling my head to the door.

He darted his eyes every which way, trying to fish for a way out. It had never been like this between us, though I had caused this rift. Willa fell silent in the kitchen, pressing her palms on the edge of the counter, facing the cabinets. She threw her head back, obviously waiting for us to leave. Tension thickened. He peeled his eyes at Willa's back and sighed, brushing past me and out the door.

We walked alongside the lake where kelpies curiously poked their heads under tangerine skies. Lex's jaw tensed the longer the silence stretched. I wished he would beat me up and get it out of his system. As large as he was, he could never cast ignorance to someone's brokenness. He knew about being broken too well. The story of what he'd sacrificed for Willa to be with her caused him to be more sensitive toward others.

Tired of waiting for one of us to speak, my throat tightened. "I know you don't forgive what I did. I won't waste time trying to defend myself. But this is about more than just Lor. I have alienated myself from you all. Willa has knocked my door down time and time again, and I thank her for that. I felt useless to you all. I still do. But at least I can be a friend again. No abilities, nothing, just me." I studied the sides of his face, unwavering with indifference. "You were my friends, and I shut you out."

"You were right," I continued. "I am a coward. I know how you fought for Willa in the Shadowlands. And I should have done the same."

Anguish washed over his face at the mention of the terrible memory. Something so awful that even Willa would not speak of it anymore. We were at an impasse. Lex wouldn't speak or look at me with those dark sincere eyes of his. Desperate for some kind of reaction, I tugged at his shoulder. "Will you ever forgive me?" I asked, not exactly wanting a truthful answer.

He froze. His brown trousers that Willa had made for him were snug enough to see his sculpted muscles. She *would* do that. However, she did not make enough shirts for his wide chest and his burly arms, which told me she enjoyed watching him without one. He was menacing to look at. But for her, he was endearing. Silken strands of dark hair fell from his top knot, held together by a chopstick Willa had taken from the earthly realm. Red Chinese letters that I didn't understand glittered at the top, and it suited him. He flicked his gaze at the lake, and his lips tightened.

"Please, Lex, just this once. Talk to me." I gently squeezed his shoulder. He pulled away. "We were friends before. We can talk this out." My voice broke, "Please, look at me."

The muscles in his back twitched as he walked away from me. "We made an oath!" I shouted. That was enough to make him turn around.

I recited our oath, as though I were high and mighty. "We are misfits, bound to protect the innocents, destroy tyrants, to bind ourselves together as one..."

Veins in his throat pulsed, his skin reddening. The air stilled, and I felt my chest tighten. It hit me. He had already considered Lor a part of us long before she had come here. In his eyes, I broke the oath. I humiliated and eviscerated her, untying the bond she had with us. I was a fool not to see it. She was more part of us than I was, yet I'd torn her apart in the name of protection. Oaths were sacred, especially for Lex. Where came from, they were soul binding, whereas for the lot of us, they were more like guidelines. He really was the better one of us.

"Oath breaker," he growled before walking off.

So strange how you do not know how great of a friend you had until they walk away.

33

ELORA

Fear spread its panicking fingers through me. Fighting against Nyx in three days made my chest tight. We were family, or as Riann would say, *muirear*. They laughed together as if there were no onslaught of terror coming. I could not lose them. Not after waiting a lifetime to find them. Riann whipped up a spectacular dinner of lemon fish and capers in place of Willa's burnt disaster. I hated fish in the earthly realm, but it tasted different here. The food satisfied me and never left me tired, unlike my sad people food. Still, I miss chow mein. I was so over-the-moon happy that I'd fallen in love with someone who could cook.

The wreath remained on my head, and it was not going anywhere thanks to Willa's pins that made my scalp scream if I pulled my hair in the slightest. Riann had taken his off, which unsettled me a bit. I thought of what Sable had asked, *"If Elora had not been here today, would you have confessed your devotion to her?"* A part of me felt like she'd churned him to confess, and his jealousy was the nail in his coffin. Riann's wreath sat on the counter like it had been forgotten. After everything I'd been through, I struggled to shake loose the negative thoughts, but I needed to for my own sanity. He was mine, and I was his. That was all that mattered.

Dolos built a large fire for us in the center of several tree stumps outside. Black soot covered his face and arms from all the preparations he had made in his house of horrors. Willa and Lex hung back by the willow tree with his arms wrapped around her as they eyed Dolos. There was always an air of caution with Dolos around fire. He added white powder to the fire, and the flames danced even higher. Lex became startled as the flames pierced the orange sky. All of us had the same thought, worrying that the flames would burn the willow tree. Dolos rolled his eyes.

"I have this down to a science guys, don't worry." He pinned me with his amused eyes. "Hey, blondie! I heard you snagged this brooding male."

Riann shot him a glare while the corners of Dolos' mouth twitched.

"Watch your mouth, prince of unicorns!" I shouted back, grinning.

Dolos nudged Riann's side with a mischievous smile and abruptly tackled him to the ground. Phil shot up from the stump he'd been sitting on and called for bets. "Come on, Riann, take him out! Five coins for Riann! Anyone have five coins?!"

Riann rolled Dolos onto his back, pinning his arm behind. "You want more, pyro!?"

Willa laughed, pulling Lex by the hand. "Fight, fight, fight!"

For me, all humor was lost when all I could think of was Riann being dragged off by the Draconians. The soles of his feet—the pale blue soles that had walked so many realms only to be dragged off so effortlessly. It had carved something deep in me. His feet had dug into lines while bloody cuts trickled from the rocks he was dragged over. And I had just followed in silence.

I shifted around uncomfortably on the stump, wanting to join the family fun but I could not bring myself to do it. After Riann had been dragged off on Pine, I was too busy trying to forget, guzzling that rich Draconian wine. Then, that earth-shattering kiss had happened. I could proudly say I had been sober for that. I had no room to think or breathe seeing Riann like that. It was something I never wanted to see again.

Dolos hooked his leg behind Riann's knee and dug his elbow into his side. Phil rounded them as they went for each other's shoulders. Dirt covered them, and Riann's mouth dribbled with blood as he smiled at his friend. "Come on, Dolos, show me how unicorn princes fight."

Dolos rammed headfirst with a shout into Riann's abdomen, slamming him against the tree. My heart pounded in my chest, swallowing a scream. I knew he was stronger than this. The tree shook so hard I thought it would split. Riann appeared hurt as his head bent low, but then he snapped back up, howling with laughter. Dolos heaved in and out, his shoulders rising and falling.

"You got me," said Riann, freeing himself from Dolos' pin. "It really has been a while." He grabbed Dolos' hand, shaking it in surrender.

Dolos finally laughed and smudged dirt with his thumb on Riann's face. "Glad to see you have something left in you."

They returned to the fire, arm and arm, with bloody smiles, appearing lighter than they had since I met them.

"Wait!" Phil shouted. "In the spirit of training, Lor should spar with one of us."

I parted my lips, not expecting to train right here, right now. Riann held my hand, a question in his eyes. He clearly did not want me to spar.

"I don't know, Phil." Dolos rubbed the back of his head. "She's sparred with Lex, and she's done fantastic. If she can take him, she can take anyone."

"Lex may be a giant, but to her, he's a teddy bear. Let's give her real experience," Phil smirked, nodding at me.

Riann held my hand tighter in silent demand to not let go, but I stepped forward anyway. "Fine, I can do it, but it has to be you."

"You don't have to do this," Riann's grave voice pulsed under my skin.

Too long had he been overprotective. Proving myself seemed to be the only way to calm his worried heart. With a touch of my hot palm to his face, I gave him a look that said everything would be alright.

Phil bowed, his twin blades at his back, welcoming his competition. "Weapons, or no?"

"Weapons," I said, rolling my shoulders. "A battle is coming, and I will not have my hands empty."

He grinned slowly. "Good."

Willa threw me a rapier sword. Phil unsheathed the blade from his belt rather than his back. The group formed a wide circle around us. Phil watched me circumspectly, waiting for me to strike first, like an asp. His red eyes flickered, and I waited for the answer in them. Would he go left and feint right? I didn't trust his fancy footwork, only his eyes. In training, once I stopped looking at Lex's feet and started reading him, I became faster and stronger, more strategic. They said it was unusual I had learned so quickly in such a short time, assuming the star inside pushed me higher and greater.

Like a lion, he pounced. Our steel clanged together, throwing me off balance. I pushed back and struck him from the right, barely scratching his black leathers. Phil snapped his head up, crinkling his nose. He believed this would be easy. Riann held his breath, his throat bobbing, while Dolos fell to one knee, lighting up with pride. We were too close to the fire. If I fell in, I would lose. Lex must have read my mind because he moved closer to the fire, blocking us from the flames.

Phil and I advanced. Moving forward and backward past the circle, closer to the lake. I pivoted away when he swung high. Willa told me when people swung their swords high, they were becoming angry because they were losing. However, I did not see myself winning. Phil was seasoned, and I expected him to run the blade at my throat. He moved swiftly as he spun around me and took a slice to my back, only scratching the surface. In the corner of my eye Riann lunged forward, but Willa held him back. At least Phil was gentle. He could have ripped my muscles open with that hit.

Something burned in me as Riann was restrained by Lex. I wanted to win for him, to prove I could protect myself and that he did not need to fear anymore. I whipped my sword high as a distraction while my legs swept beneath Phil's feet. He flopped to the ground, quickly rebounding. Tiny beads of blood formed on his face.

"Phil, I am so sorry." I staggered back, the tip of my blade to the ground.

He smeared the trickle of blood from his face, his nostrils flaring as he tried to strike me down. "Don't let your guard down!" he roared, each word coming at me full force.

"Phil, really, I'm sorry!" I cried, blocking his blade with mine.

"Will you say that to a soldier coming to kill you?!" He beat down my blade until I was knee-deep in the water.

All I wanted to do was retreat into the shadows where it was dark and wave my white flag of surrender. One look at my friends holding their breaths pulled me from my bleak thoughts. Like a flash, I dove under the water, grabbing his ankles and dragged him under with me. We surfaced, and I hovered over him with my blade. He gasped at the sky and I turned to look. Rookie mistake. Then, his fist met my face. Tears stung my eyes, and my ears rang with Riann screaming, breaking free from Lex.

I pointed my blade at Riann. Blood oozed from my nose, mixed with water, my hair plastered to my face. "Don't you dare."

Phil rose from the water, blinking. He expected me to have Riann come to my rescue, but I would not let him have it. Something inside me snapped. Gold veins ran down my arms, and I willed weapons to form in my hands. I had no idea what the weapons would look like. I just knew I could trust myself, the star inside me. Two ornate, golden scythes of light formed. My whole body felt on fire like the day I'd taken down Lex. Phil dropped his sword and removed the ones from his back. Steel glinted in the light, and he did not appear afraid. I twirled the scythes in my hands a few times before I took my stance. This time, I made the first move. Steel against gold light sparked over the gray waters. I barely saw his face through the inferno. He winced each time a spark burned him. I tried not to hurt him, but the blood running down my nose and down my favorite band shirt made me want to.

"You go too far!" he shouted, his breath becoming heavy.

My scythe wrapped around the base of his sword, tossing it from his hand. If he did not let go, I would have surely cut his hand off. I tightened my grip on the handle. "I thought you wanted it to be real. Did you think I was some weak woman!"

I hooked my leg behind his knee, and he was down again, breathless. The thrusts of his steel became lighter, tired. White satin ribbon from the wreath whipped across my face. With a yank of my scythe, I removed his other sword, and he pounded the ground, gritting his teeth. My scythes wrapped around his neck as I waited for those two glorious words to spill from his lips.

A minute passed, and he spat blood from his mouth. "I yield."

Gold light retracted and filtered back into my body along with the scythes. I pulled him up, and we stared at each other. Disbelief flashing across his face satisfied every bone in my body. Rivulets of water mixed with blood ran down his face. His thin lips tightened. "I curse the day a woman bested me." He choked out his words and wrapped his arms around my shoulders. Coming from him, I considered it a badge of honor.

Dolos' mouth swung open while Willa tried to close it again and again. Lex bypassed Riann and held my chin high with his thumb. His eyes twinkled with delight as he beheld my burning hands. I could tell he wanted to hold me high and parade me around, but he hesitated, drawing a line in the sand. Lex knew his place. He moved out of the way, and Riann was on his knees before me, wrapping his arms around my waist. He did not speak a word, but his face said it all.

Purplish veins of light spread under his skin, surprising him just enough to flinch. Cracking and burning branches swept across his chest and arms, running like rivers into his legs. He slowly rose, gently kissing me, regardless of the blood. Without pulling away, he scooped me in his arms and whisked me into the house. His starlight wrapped around my goose flesh, keeping me warm. At first, I thought he was in the heat of the moment and would take me to his bedroom, but he set me on the counter in the kitchen. Softly, he wiped a cold, wet cloth on my nose, assessing if it was broken. Thankfully, it wasn't. His fingers twirled in my matted hair, and he kissed me again before settling himself between my legs on the counter, embracing me. His starlight dimmed.

"You are incredibly brave." His eyes dampened with moisture. "I was so worried he would get lost in bloodlust." His hands shuffled around the counter crowded with Willa's ingredients and knocked over his wreath. "Will you drink my healing water this time?" He unscrewed his skin.

I breathed in deeply, "Yes." I sipped on the sweetest water I had ever tasted.

The wreath laid on the floor, scattered like yesterday's trash. I touched mine, reminding myself that he was mine and I was his. Over and over. My wreath did not move the entire time I was fighting Phil. Riann stepped back, and his foot crunched on the beautiful leaves without giving it much notice. I wanted the bad thoughts to leave. He was mine, and I was his, I reminded myself yet again. His arms wound around me once more as if he were afraid I would fly away in the wind. I flung my arms around his neck. Wet fingers sent chills down my spine as he rubbed the healing water over my wounds.

"Riann," I whispered, his fingers stilled. "Are you ready?"

A moment felt like an eternity.

"No," he said, and I felt him pull away, not physically, but his heart sprinted far from me. He must have felt my insides turn to ice, and he buried his head under my chin. "I will not have you like this. I like the idea of just being with us a little while longer before we take the plunge."

My brows knotted. "Plunge? Wasn't the kiss itself taking the plunge?"

Riann pressed his face against my chest. "Don't misunderstand. We never got to really spend time with each other outside of the bridge. Please, Lor. I am not pushing you away. I just want it to be right."

I looked at the forgotten wreath on the floor and nodded, ignoring the nagging pain inside me. Perhaps he was using his love for me as a means to send me back to Earth like he'd originally planned. No, he wouldn't do that. I was alarmed that he did not want to fulfill his vow as cymar. But I didn't want to guilt him or make him feel pressured. After waiting eight hundred years, I assumed he wouldn't be able to contain himself. I felt it in every kiss. I wanted no one else. He was the only one that had ever made me feel safe enough to be desired. I slid off the counter, holding the wet cloth to my nose. We walked to my bedroom, and he kissed me goodnight in my doorway. The click of the door behind me never felt so lonely.

34

RIANN

Idiot. She threw herself at you. Tomorrow is the last day you will see her, I told myself in my bedroom mirror. I should have laid down on the sofa across from her to watch her sleep. How dare I give myself to her as a dying man—to have momentary pleasure before my death. I refused to make her feel used and abandoned. Tomorrow, I wanted to spend every waking moment with Lor. And then afterward, she would learn of my demise. This was the worst.

I stayed up all hours, writing letters, jotting down songs reminding me of her. Willa came in a few times during the night, suspecting something off, but all I did was reminisce with her. She was too smart. Willa knew today was the day I returned for the whipping. She detested every time I went, but she could never convince me to stay. After a few sips of wine, Willa informed me the woodland dryads and faeries would assist us with the fauns. Good. I needed some good news. This was crazy. I was not supposed to die like this. Fates were cruel. They dangled my cymar in front of me, only for me to leave her to the wolves. I hated them. I wanted to end them.

Taking a deep breath, I opened Lor's room and found her curled up in white sheets. Her hair glinted in the pale sun, filtering through the new glass window I'd installed. I paced around her bed a few times before deciding to slide in next to her. As soon as my body curled next to hers, she grinned in her sleep. Dark green silks draped over her slender curves. Part of me thought she wore it for me, believing I would change my mind.

"Wake up, beautiful." I pressed a kiss to her temple. "Today is just about us."

Lor's lilac eyes popped open, nestling in my arms. "Did you make me breakfast?"

With everything on my mind, I had forgotten about it, but I loved the expectation as if we'd settled into a routine with each other. "I'm sorry, it slipped my mind today," I said. "How about I make something with you?"

Somehow, we went from making pancakes together to dousing each other with flour. Squealing with laughter, she ran for her life after smashing an egg on my head. Her green silks were a pop of color in the otherwise pale light as she bolted for the lake. A sharp prick inside me told me not to enjoy this, that I did not deserve it after all I had done. But I was laughing and grinning like a madman charging after her and pulling her into the lake with me, defying that poisonous voice inside me. At any moment, a disgruntled kelpie could surface. No matter how much Lor ran her hands through her hair, bits of flour stubbornly caked onto her head. I tangled my hands in her star-spun tresses, rinsing away the flour. Her warm gaze met mine, and she wrapped her arms around my waist, laying her head on my chest. We stayed like that for a while, simmering in the sweet moment. No words were needed. Just our presence. Once we headed home, she took a shower while I cleaned up our mess. As I was swept up the flour, Mikhail screamed down my bridge. Not today, brother. I shut all doors he could access, his voice becoming an incoherent echo.

Lor walked out in a knee-length, gray mesh dress while I wore my usual black trousers and white tunic. Everyone else was awake and getting their tea ready, fending for themselves for breakfast. All eyes fell on Lor as she entered the room. She resembled her mother, and it took me back to my days in Solarin. If only Eos had come with me, if I had convinced her that it was hopeless to stay, Lor would still have a mother. But I didn't have time for bad thoughts, so I grasped her wrist and pulled Lor outside. The sky turned hot pink, making her skin look like an iridescent peach. I pulled her behind a tree—hiding us from prying eyes—rested my arm above her head, and kissed her for a long time.

Her hands firmly pressed against my chest. "Riann, what's gotten into you?"

"I told you I just want to spend time with you," I said, grazing my lips along her jaw.

The corner of her mouth twitched. "As much as I love this make-out session, I think I would rather take a walk and talk for now." She gave me a featherlight kiss on my forehead.

I had no clue what to talk about with all these thoughts spinning in my head. Kissing Lor centered me. But I would do anything she asked. So, we walked off to the crystal green woods about a mile from behind my house.

Petals drifted in the cool breeze, and she giggled trying to catch one. "Are we on a date?"

I beamed at her. "I guess we are. I didn't give a name to it. I just knew I wanted to spend every minute with you today."

***

Towering trees of the forest shimmered a green crystal hue un-der the dusk skies. Rich and dark green colors weaved through the mossy terrain. Large waxy leaves darkened the path, which made the faelights shine brighter. I remembered how it would practically glow at night, and I desperately wanted to show that to Lor. There were many things I wanted to show her. Faeries lived nearby, giving their breath of magic to preserve nature, and it had remained untainted as much as possible from the curse. Lor raised her hand to her mouth. Her eyes widened as the shades of the forest reflected in them.

I angled my head, rubbing the back of my neck, trying to contain myself. "Are you enjoying yourself?"

"Yes," she said, lifting her head with a bright smile. "I never got to spend time with you like this. In fact, there are a lot of things I dreamed of doing with you."

"Oh yeah, like what?" I took her by the hand, leading her into the depths of the forest. Mikhail kept knocking, and I wished I could silence him. Eventually, he would tire himself out.

"Well, we'd go to the Jersey Shore. Swim in the ocean, eat malt vinegar fries, drink lemonade. Cruise the boardwalks and, play carnival games, go on rides. Maybe you'd win me an obnoxiously large stuffed animal." She grabbed my forearm in excitement, just thinking about the possibilities.

Mikhail's pleas were a constant prick under my skin. "What are rides?"

"Machines you can ride, on rails or some other mechanism. My favorite ride was the Gravitron. You're inside this machine that spins you around so fast you can't even move. You just hope and pray nobody throws up during the ride." She leaned on my arm and sighed. "Anyway, that was a silly dream of mine."

"It's not silly. I would love to do that with you."

"I know—" Her focus shifted away from me momentarily, and I knew what the pause meant. She wouldn't leave here without me, and I couldn't leave because of this curse. "Families went there for summer break. Every summer since I could drive, I went alone. At first, I had a fun time just reading a book in the sun, but then the day wound down. Families gathered on the boardwalks, and couples held hands, walking the dark beach together." Her hand tightened around mine. "But you've given me something far more superior."

"I have?" My voice sounded higher than I meant it to.

"Just look around us." She sliced the air with her hand and turned her gaze to the shimmer of the trees. "There's so much beauty here, even under the curse. This queen tried to damage everything but could not undo the spark of hope underneath all this life. I'm so incredibly thankful for you, our friends, and our family." Her bow-shaped lips curved into a soft smile. "I always craved friends and a family, and I have all that through you. All my silly dreams are secondary to that."

I pulled her in, resting my head on hers, my blood rising above Mikhail's incessant yelling. "No, they are not secondary. I want every single one of those dreams to come true for you." She bit her lower lip, closing her eyes for a moment. "I dream one day we can scare everyone with Lex's massive body."

She broke into laughter. "That would be awesome. Poor Lex, I hope he doesn't have a complex."

"On the contrary, it works in his favor once people see how gentle he is."

We walked, talking about her time in New Jersey. I learned that the state would fight over football teams and what the true name of a breakfast meat was. Fascinating. While I was fighting off cruel empires, New Jersey's biggest dilemma was where to get the best coffee and hoagies. How she described hoagies made me think of something new I could create for dinner, but I know it would easily not satisfy her New Jerseyan taste buds. Known for their pride and high taxes, I would want to steer clear of that state, but for her, it was home.

"One time, I went on a date at a diner at two in the morning," she said, shaking her head, holding back her laughter. "I liked him, and he finally drunk texted me to meet him there, where he devoured waffles and eggs. Then, he proceeded to vomit it all up in the bathroom, texted a friend to pick him up, and forgot that I was there. I had to pay for everything."

I chuckled under my breath, not because what the date did was funny, but what I would do to him if I ever met him. He'd have a tough time running without legs. Leaves and twigs crunched beneath our boots. "I hated every single guy you went out with because I was jealous."

"Yeah, I figured. They were all jerks anyway, so I guess I saved the best for last." She nudged her head under my arm. "Sometimes, I went on dates just to make you jealous."

Half my mouth curved upward. "You little so-and-so." She gave an inward laugh, lacing her fingers with mine. "Tell me again about wanting to be a constellation," I said.

"It was just a silly fantasy to escape it all," she shrugged. "Maybe we could make our own constellation and call it home."

I waited for her to laugh, but it never came. "Lor... you are my home."

She rolled her eyes while grinning. "I knew you would say something like that." She hiked up her dress as she walked over a massive curling root. "Did you spend time with Dolos when he was in England trying to impress the queen?"

I snapped branches away from her face. "No, I was in Solarin during that time, waiting for this incredible birth from the queen."

"Oh, that's right, Dolos mentioned that."

"You look a lot like your mother." My knuckles slid down her face, observing her soft cheekbones. "Then, you turn a certain way, and I see your father."

"What were they like?"

"It would shock you how much you are like them. You are stubborn like your father, willing to put yourself in danger. But you're meek like your mother. She had a crazy amount of magic but never used it to put herself above others." My face pressed toward the sky, wishing to slow time down. Mikhail paused his outburst for a few moments, giving me a reprieve, only to start again. I really wanted to hear him out, but to me, this time was more precious than anything else.

She wound the edge of her hair around her finger. "How did they feel about you? Seems like they had a lot of trust in you to put my life in your hands."

"Your parents loved me." I chuckled a bit. "Your mother taught me the importance of patience to wait for all things that were worth it. I suppose she watched my friends giving themselves over to the pleasures of their youth, knowing I strived to be a true Rinarien. Too many women tried to take advantage of me, scorning me for wanting to wait for my cymar. I can't tell you how many times I woke up to the sound of my door being opened by a scantily clad woman baiting me. Some got into my bed and tried to do things I did not want to do."

Lor's hand tightened around mine, and I realized how much I'd talked about things I'd tucked away. "It's sexual assault," she said. Her grave voice burrowed its way under my skin. "I don't care which realm you're in. Just because it happens to a man does not make it right. Women should be held accountable too." Her hand cupped the side of my face, and she put her other hand on my hip to stop me from walking away. "I'm sorry if I pressured you in any way last night. You are no object. I want you to feel safe with me. The way I feel with you."

I lifted her hand and pressed it to my lips. "Undeserving," I whispered. "I've been so caught up these past few eons with being a misfit that I stopped thinking about what had happened. It only resurfaced when those four men..." I paused, realizing we were talking about dreadful things, and I wanted today to be filled with joy. "We shouldn't talk about this anymore."

"Riann, stop," her voice thickened. "You're being weird today." She let my hand go. "You know so much more about me than I do about you. You had the privilege of watching me, and I did not. Let me in. I want to know everything about you, inside out. There are parts that won't be pretty, but I want it." Lor took a long breath and wiped her glistening forehead with her arm.

My mind splintered between wanting to run away from this conversation and scooping her in my arms. I had never confessed what had happened to me before, and somehow, I felt lighter. "I made my decision to wait even before you asked me, and I'm sorry that I disappointed you."

"You didn't disappoint me," she said, her arms slackening to their sides.

"I don't know, Lor." I leaned back, raking my eyes over her with a wicked grin. "That green silk gown you wore was wedding night material."

"I was simply prepared if you changed your mind!" she shrieked.

"Before the day ends, I can give you a constellation," I said.

Her brows knit together, making the cutest little crease on her head. "Thank you, Riann, but even I know that's impossible," she said, peering behind the trees. Faelights sparkled everywhere in a variety of colors against the dark shadowy trail. Pops of gold and pink floated before us with tiny wings fluttering in their halo of light. Tiny giggles whirred by as orbs of blues and silvers danced between the trees.

I wrapped one arm around her waist. "I thought you would want to see this place. It's like those faerie tales you read as a child or even those shows we watched together." She became breathless, and I kissed her cheek. "I may not be able to take you to a fancy restaurant or jump to Paris with you, but I can give you this."

Lor side eyed me with a tender warmth, her face flushed. "Right here with you is enough for me."

"Well, now, who's the romantic?" I smiled from ear to ear.

She reached her hand out, scattering the faelights while I cemented myself in the calm of her warmth. Mikhail's voice was a

distant sound as I soaked in the last few moments of our happiness.

35

MIKHAIL

My mother sat on her throne, clicking her talons. Of course, they were crimson. How many birds did she have to kill to get it that color? Her eyes narrowed upon me, her lips thinning. She heaved in a disappointing breath as I took my place, standing next to her throne of garnet. Onyx and gold webbed in intricate patterns into the rough-hewn stone. The only polished area was the seat and back, cushioned in black velvet. Ever since she'd tortured me last time, she was strangely silent. It spoke louder than anything she could have shouted. She was a cobra waiting to strike. A maid was sent to my room, instructing me to dress for a special occasion. It was no surprise. She had asked me to dress finely in the past for no good reason. I dressed in black-boiled leather and silver filigree, forgoing her blood red colors found on her banners. My cape draped loosely off one shoulder and a crown of short, jagged onyx crystals adorned my head.

Clinking chains and the sound of grunting, edged with pain echoed the halls. What had she done? Silas was shoved into the throne room to the center by dark minotaurs. Bruising bloomed all over his body. Fresh lacerations oozed with thick green blood running in rivulets over the bark that remained on his arms and legs. He shook with pain, but his eyes lingered strength, stealing away my mother's purpose to torment him. I let loose a shaky breath. My insides shook violently seeing him in this state. Wanting to escape my own skin and run to him, to cover him, I noticed he shook his head ever so slightly at me. He refused my help knowing what she would do to me. Time and time again, he somehow intervened to keep my mother away from me as much as possible. Yet, he never spoke ill of her.

Mother lifted the tight corners of her mouth, smirking at me before turning her fiery gaze to Silas. "We have caught you dispatching letters to the fauns, confirming my suspicions of this rebel stain."

He stood silent. There was no way to free him without implication. I read the books he'd saved, fully realizing where he had gone at night when he thought nobody was looking. He sent warnings while distributing goods to the needy. Over and over, I played out the worst-case scenarios, and I wanted to vomit at the outcome of each one. Memories of Marie were far from reach but not the ones of my only father figure. Images of Silas' hands scraping against mine as he taught me to write appeared in my mind. The twinkle in his eye when I mastered every word, every essay, and argued like a scholar. It was only Silas who'd cheered me on. He knew I was lonely and went to great lengths to show me what it was like to have a friend.

"Now, now, little one, you can play with Grim once you are done reciting faerie prophecies. Remember, never to speak a word of this."

He'd taught me love is blood spilled on altars. A high price for love. A crazy faerie prophecy that I did not understand until recently. He'd let me play with Grim because Mother would not allow me near any of the boys from nearby villages. She'd kept me locked away and hidden from the world until I could make myself useful to her.

Silas took a sorrowful glance at me and then back at my mother. "Your majesty, I am but a servant of your people. They are in need of food and supplies. I did what I needed to do to preserve the dignity of the king's legacy." His voice echoed across the walls and white pillars.

She gripped the arms of the throne, her eyes flaring. "You dare speak of the king as if you did not betray my orders. I am queen. My word is law. Only rations are to be given in order to reserve enough food and grain for the year."

Silas squared his shoulders. "With all due respect, my Queen, the land was lush before the horrid curse spread. A generation is gone of children who will never be born."

"You... sympathize with the rebel stain?" her voice seethed.

Silas' leaves stopped shaking for a moment, as if his resolve burned away his pain. He stood taller, his eyes aflame. "Your Majesty, must I acquiesce to the law when people grow weary from hunger? The love of your people has grown cold. I am preventing a rebellion. If your people remain hungry, you are not only inviting it at your gates, but you are also asking for your head to be removed from your body."

Mother leapt from her ornate throne, stretching her boney fingers to strike. I jumped in front of her, swallowing against my constricted throat, prepared to the take the brunt of his punishment. She'd taken away too much, and I couldn't let her have him too.

"Mother, he is old and frail and of not sound mind. Your delusions of a grand rebellion are unfounded. Please allow him the curtesy to retire and live in exile after all he has done for me."

She scowled.

Silas' creaking bark groaned under the pressure of the black chains. I had no idea she would do this. If I'd had an inkling Silas was in danger, I would have found a way out for him, no matter the cost. My mother grew more paranoid by the day, and my head could not take any more of her 'sessions.' Yesterday, she drew some of my fire out and burned my face until I'd given her a piece of information. I may have accidentally told her I speak with some faeries. That was enough to drive her crazy. She knew they had been able to keep their magic and that a dark elf was among them in plain sight.

Dark elves were healers and masters of magic. They were called *dark elves* because of their pale skin and black raven hair—and some of their cultural practices made my stomach turn. Watching my mother unravel after receiving news about the Carnelian Woods and whispers of the Draconians pushing back against her curse made me smile more than I had in years. All her plans were sifting through her fingers. I honestly didn't care too much if I was a target, but not Silas. Not Riann.

Her features darkened, rippling shadows. "Really, my son? Kain is still missing, and I suspect he is in the ground or, better yet, ash."

My jawline tensed.

"Nevertheless," she sneered, sashaying down the dais in her silver silks, "I know Silas warned the fauns of danger, and now he confesses to breaking my law. He may be a scholarly man, but not a smart one." She stepped closer to me and tapped those murderous nails against the pillar, glaring at Silas. "Did you really think you would make a fool of me?"

Silas stood silently.

She smirked and drew her attention back to me. "I will make a spectacle of your brother tonight. He has a precious few grains of sand left." I swallowed hard. "Not only will he die, but I will make him a feast for the Astryx. An open display for those who want to rebel against me—including you."

This had always been her plan. To kill Riann as a traitor slowly so that the people could see her "mercy" and then watch her swiftly execute her version of justice. He owed her twenty-eight lashes, and with how weak he'd become, Riann would surely die. I hated her so much I wished to the dark heavens that someone or something would kill her instantaneously. But she wouldn't die as long as the unicorn horn remained in my father's desiccated flesh.

I clenched my fists. "Leave my brother alone."

"Must I remind you? He doesn't love you. He left you. I know you begged him to take you to Solarin. Marie, was it? She was with other men while waiting for you." She darkly laughed. "I am the only one who loves you. Who protects you. Once you realize—"

"Shut your mouth!" my voice thundered. Every piece of furniture crashed against the walls, splintering wood and shattering glass in the throne room. "I've *been* loved, and what you give is demonizing." Her coal eyes widened in surprise as fire glowed under my skin. "I already know about your coven. Witch of Lamia. Your cruel plans for me, for Sidh. I am not your monster. I am no *promised one*."

Her face became lethal. Veins in her body pulsated and writhed from her head to her toes like living snakes beneath her skin. "Well now, son." Her voice was like nails on a chalkboard. "It seems you know everything." Wisps of shadows clawed their way free from her shoulders. "It was prophesied through your father's seed that the dark one would come. My son, we could rule forever. You shall be the consort of death, ruling and reigning over all realms, and I shall ascend as the queen of the Astryx."

"The Astryx have not been awake for over a thousand years. You are peddling lies, Lamian witch," I hissed.

Silas had saved one book to expose the lies—a sisterhood order of witches who eat the flesh of other beings to stay young. They fed on broken souls, inhaling their pain and dreams like a grand feast. Astryx had never come here. They had never come for Solarin either. It had all been a lie, leading us all like sheep to the slaughter. I took one look at Silas, and he nodded his head.

Mother raised her hands defiantly, drawing fire from me, burning my skin. My arms and shoulders burst into flames.

"Mother!" I choked on the fumes. "Stop!"

I couldn't fight off the searing pain. Scorching, unending agony spread everywhere and all around. My skin bubbled and blistered. The heat sliced into my bones. Then, with a flick of her neck, she tossed me into Silas. Though he screamed, I felt Silas hold my face like he did when I was a child. Bark curled into embers and disappeared into the air. His leaves immediately burned away. He shook, his primal screams gutting me more than the fire. I felt his body give way, his eyes closing in a final surrender. Within moments he was no more.

"No, Silas, no!" The flames deafened my cries.

The only one who had ever been kind to me became ash in my hands, yet Nyx stood there with a triumphant smile. All that love inside him sifted through my fingers. My skin sizzled as she closed her fist to cool down the fire.

"This is what happens to traitors. Let that be a lesson for you. I put the fire in you. It is mine to control. You are the harbinger of death. Accept it." Mother swished her skirt, walked away, and paused. Her face was stone cold as I laid on the marbled floor, fighting to restrain my tears. "Witches of Lamia can bear as many children as they want. But I only wanted you. Don't make me regret it."

Viscous blood and charred flesh covered my body. Every bit of me screamed in agony. I stumbled to my knees, gathering Silas' ashes in my hands. Each moment was raw pain radiating everywhere. I was not used to such pain. If anyone else harmed me, I would be fine, but when it was my own fire, that was another story. The gaping wound in my heart overshadowed that pain. My soul bled out before the ashes of Silas.

My lips quivered as I gathered the last the last of his ashes into a pile. "Silas, I'm sorry, I failed. I'll take you to your favorite place so you can find rest."

Undone. Broken. Regret. A thousand words left unspoken that Silas had deserved to hear. And I was a coward for never saying them. An empty crystal decanter that escaped my wrath caught my eye, and I scooped his ashes into it, trying not to shed a single tear. The salt from my tears would burn my skin, and I couldn't mix them with his ashes. Any excuse I could find not to cry. Home was no longer safe, but I had a role to play, and I needed to see it through.

36

RIANN

"Stay still." Riann chuckled as his hand pressed firmly on the small of my back.

"I'm sorry, but it tickles at first, then it burns." I buried my head in his white feather pillow, hiding my reddened face.

"I said I would give you a constellation, and I meant it," he said, tracing a sharpened bone across my back, between my shoulder blades. "You're lucky I don't have to cut your skin. It's wood ash and dye. The burning is just from the ink settling in."

When he told me he would give me a constellation, I thought it was just a sweet sentiment. I didn't regret my decision. This would be with me forever, like a moment frozen in time.

"You know," he continued, "before the curse, my chest and shoulders were covered in whorls of ink, lined with runes. I had so many wards and runes on me it was impossible to take me down. Well, until..." A sharp line scored my skin, and I gasped. "Magnus gave me special runes on my head after the curse. I have no idea what it says, but I trust him." He dipped the sharpened bone in the little gray pot of black dye. "You will meet him soon."

I raised my head slightly, blinking at the enormous amount of candlelight in the room. "Riann, tomorrow we set up camp. Are you scared?"

His hands paused, and he leaned over me. With warm breath trailing up and down my spine, he pressed a small kiss on the nape of my neck.

"Terrified," he whispered. He inhaled and slowly blew over my tattoo. "Finished." He left the bed.

"Remember to stick with Willa." His voice became steel while fishing for something in his dark oak dresser. A dark blue ribbon fell from the top and he caught it before it hit the floor. His lips tightened, and he let out a soft breath before placing it back on the dresser.

"And you," I said, clutching the sheet to my bare chest, rising to my feet. He shoved a small mirror in my hand, avoiding eye contact.

"I'll always be with you, Lor." His voice thickened as he rounded toward me. "Please, take a look."

A large free-standing mirror stood by the door to his pool, and I faced my back to it, holding the smaller one high enough to see it. The constellation comprised of three small descending peaks with a large one protruding upward, the last two little peaks fell just below the tallest one. Tears filled my eyes, though he could not see as he faced the wall avoiding me. Quickly, I found his white tunic on the floor and threw it on.

"Riann, this is by far…" I couldn't find the right words to say as I gently turned him around. My fingers splayed across his chest, warmth seeping through his black shirt. He was so tall that I had to rise on the tip of my toes to kiss him on the forehead. "Thank you."

Riann's eyes shut tight, tears lining the creases.

"Lor," he said. "This is how many realms were between us when I first heard your laughter." Candlelight flickered across the sharp planes of his face. "Now, people will see your constellation every time you walk in front of them." He tipped my chin with his finger. "Those fools from the earthly realm are beneath you. No matter where you go, everyone will watch you in awe and wonder about the stories you carry. My cymar, my only, your story is just beginning. And I was just the catalyst."

My brows knitted together, "What do you…?"

He hunched his shoulders while running his hands up and down my arms. "It's nothing, really. But I have to say"—his mouth came so close to my ear that his lips almost touched it— "you wearing my shirt does something for me."

My whole body flushed. "Oh, really?"

His eyes starved for something more as he leaned down to kiss me, and I playfully pushed him, making my way to the door.

"Lor, what are you...?" His eyes bulged as I slowly turned the doorknob. "No. Don't do it." He eyed me up and down. "I don't want anyone else seeing you like this."

"I guess you're going to have to chase me down and stop me, then."

Riann let out a breathy laugh. "You wicked creature."

Before he lunged, I flung open the door and sprinted down the hall, pushing Dolos out of my way. He landed on the wall, startled. "Gorgeous legs, blondie! Push me against the wall anytime!"

Riann growled in response as he chased me down. I never knew the hall was so long. After all the time there, I'd explored nothing past the bathroom. Still, I laughed the further I got from him. I finally arrived at two tall white doors with intricate black knobs and hurried in. It took a beat to realize it was Riann's study. Dark wood floors sprawled with bright blue and red tapestry rugs. Two floors of books and scrolls set with spiral staircases on either side and rolling ladders made my knees weak. In between the spiral staircases hung a large oil portrait of a woman, her body scrubbed with age, heralding a sword amongst a red wasteland.

"Lor, I can hear you breathing!" Riann yelled outside the doors, amusement coating his voice.

I bumped into his ornate black desk, and parchments fell, scattering to the floor. Quickly, I hid under the desk, trying hard not to make a sound. My giggling was going to give me away. I wondered why his study was so massive when I'd never seen him go into it. The day we argued over me needing to eat, he was reading something intently and I'd never asked him what it was. We were not exactly on good terms then. Orange light broke through the tall windows, and I caught a few words on a parchment, scribbled in haste.

Lor, I'm sorry. By the time you read this, I will be gone.

My blood foamed. What did he mean? Why would he write this? Was today a ruse to soften me for whatever was to come? Where was he going? He was really going to abandon me after everything we went through?! Too many worst case scenarios swirled inside, and those dark shadowy corners where I used to belong beckoned my name. Once again, Riann was going to leave me. If he did, I would never recover.

His head popped under the desk. "Found you!"

One look at the scattered parchments, and his bubbling joy dissolved. With a sigh, he ran his hand down his face. "I, uh, I can explain this."

Words remained on my tongue as he pulled me from under the desk to my feet. I pushed him away from me and faced the portrait, crossing my arms.

"So, this it? Set me high to bring me low?" I turned around and he just stood there, his shoulders drooping low, heavy with defeat. "After everything Riann?!" My voice boomed across the vastness of the study.

He leaned against his desk, dim light creating shadows under the planes of his face. "Tonight—is the night of the whipping," he said roughly after a long silence. "The queen will not let me survive."

It became clear to me that he wanted to leave behind his goodness when he died. Every mistake he'd made weighed on him. All he felt he could give was perfect memories of us before being butchered. He truly was selfless and more beautiful than I had ever seen. I took slow steps to hold his clammy hands. "So, don't go." I touched his racing heart. "Please, don't go."

"My love." He cupped my cheek. "If I do not, she will come for the others, for you. It was the agreement after the curse."

I slapped his hand away. "Do it for yourself! Stop trying to save everyone! We are just as capable of protecting you as you do for us!"

My tears soaked the front of his tunic. "This is why you were so endearing today, why you won't seal the cymar covenant with me. You're so hellbent on fulfilling the queen's agreement you made under duress instead of fulfilling your oath to me."

Riann swayed as if the truth punched him in the gut. "I meant everything, but I need to abide by the agreement. Us being cymar will not affect my decision."

"Cymar means forever!" I shouted. "It makes sense why you crushed your wreath under your feet. You were placating me the whole time." A hammer in my chest cracked whatever dignity I had left. "After all this time, I really am nothing! A broken thing you thought you could fix with your sweet words!"

Books whizzed by Riann's head as he dodged each one. He didn't tell me to stop or become outraged as he walked toward me, his pained eyes never leaving mine. Parchments flew everywhere, settling onto the floor like snow. Riann wrapped his arms around me, and we both collapsed to the floor, breathing raggedly. Gently, he fisted my hair as if he could not get close enough to me.

"You saved me once, Lor," he whispered into my ear as a prayer. "Do it again."

I pressed my lips to his with a sense of urgency. "You are not leaving ever again. We have tomorrow and many tomorrows after that. Promise me."

His shoulders shook violently. "I promise."

We sat in each other's arms for a long time, soaking in the warmth.

"I was not placating you. I wanted you to have fond memories of us together," he said, breaking the silence, confirming what I suspected.

I lifted my puffy eyes to his twinkling, starlit gaze.

"I wanted you to know how loved you are. I would not take you physically as my cymar knowing how I am a walking dead man. I refused myself that pleasure so you would not feel used or objectified after my death." His hand ran down the length of my hair to the small of my back. "As for the wreath—I was afraid to wear it too long. Afraid because I did not want to let you go."

I picked up a loose parchment of words scribbled in black ink. "How many times did you try to write me a goodbye letter?"

He leaned back on his hands and blew out a big breath. "Too many."

With a contrite look at the letters, he gathered a bulk of them in one swift move and threw them into the empty fireplace across from his desk. After striking the flint several times, a fire blazed, burning away all his apologies, his goodbyes, his regrets.

"The queen will be out for blood," he said, resting his arms on the mantle.

"Let her. We're misfits." I flexed golden threads between my fingers.

His mouth dimpled, giving a half smile. "I've never seen you so angry. I'm just glad you did not go for the painting."

"What's so great about it?"

Riann linked his arm with mine, guiding me closer to the painting of the faceless woman.

"She's a legend, maybe a myth. She ruled a realm that may not even exist and defeated the Astryx. I once saw a black string on my spindle that never attached itself. I always liked to think it was her. Someone who may have never existed yet still breathes a life of her own."

Cracked oil paint underneath the thick protective glass veined through the picture. The woman's slender arms flailed in what looked like a red storm. Billowing clouds were behind her, blowing her white Grecian dress. A sword of many colors impaled the thunderous sky above.

Riann gazed in awe. "I found this painting in Solarin and brought it back here on a short reprieve to visit Mikhail."

My eyes widened, my lips curling upward. "Seems like you have a crush on her." I poked my finger several times in the center of his chest.

"Hey, stop that," he laughed.

With a sigh, I placed my hands on his chest. "We need to rest for tomorrow."

He pulled me closer. "Can we just lie next to each other tonight?"

"Just to sleep," I said more as a question.

"Tonight is just for sleep," he said, though the slight crack in his voice conveyed that he desired more. "We always have tomorrow and the tomorrow after that."

37

RIANN

A sharp cry jolted me awake. Mikhail had left his door wide open, and I saw him at the opening of the Crystal Forest, weeping on his knees. Leaving my warm bed with Lor snuggled in the blankets was something I would never do for him, but this time felt different. Wanting to return quickly, I summoned Lynx and rode under black-streaked skies. Mikhail's face was blistered and swollen with his left eyebrow singed off. His heavy cape covered the rest of him save for his raw fingers peeking through.

A flash of a little boy begging for my attention swept before me. I wanted to hold my little brother. He was broken then. He was broken now. "Oh my god, what happened to you?" My throat felt like sandpaper.

Pus from a blister dribbled down his nose and over his lip. "Nothing that can't be undone with your healing water," his voice was grave as he held a crystal decanter to his chest.

Luckily, I always carried my water and tossed the skin to him. He guzzled it down, sparing no drop. Within moments, his skin became smooth again. He rose on wobbling knees and gingerly placed the decanter full of ash in my hands.

"She killed him with my fire," he said bluntly.

I opened myself up across our bridge, almost consumed by the raging torrent of his despair. My insides throbbed with raw, radiating pain. Agony and regret tore through Mikhail's body. Yet, he stood tall, his hands trembling slightly, holding himself together.

I gasped. "Silas?"

He sliced the air with his hand. "Yes, Silas!!"

My heart sank. All that was left of this honorable man was ashes. Dryads didn't become stars. They became soil, and Nyx had stolen that away from him. She'd taken my brother's truest friend away. Silas was the only stability he'd ever had. I should have been better to Mikhail, but after what he'd done to Lor, he did not deserve my pity or mercy. However, a part of me was forever joined to him, regardless of how I felt. Tonight, though, I needed to let that go for the sake of Silas. He had been good to all and so kind. It made me reevaluate my own heart.

I grasped Mikhail's tense shoulder. "Let us scatter him in the forest as he would have wanted. Tonight, let us be brothers."

A slight grin cracked, and he placed his hand on my shoulder as well. "Tonight."

Something warm and familiar bloomed in my chest. Perhaps, there was a small chance to be real brothers again. What kind of brothers would we be if we just laid aside the past? I wished I was completely the victim, but I was not wholly innocent. Maybe one day, we could be what Nyx never wanted us to be. United. We disappeared into the forest, saying our farewells to our dear friend and confidant. When I returned to Lor, still in a deep sleep, I crawled underneath the blankets and wept.

She remained sleeping, curled in my arms. This was exactly what I wanted to do with her the night I let her go after her nightmare. Coward. I should have stayed. A sharpened edge ripped through me. I couldn't believe I hadn't gone to the whipping and now Silas was dead. After everything I'd done to protect everyone else, I'd made a choice, but I wasn't sure if it was the right one. The hourglass on my arm appeared the same. Nyx could have taken me out the moment I did not fulfill my duty.

Carefully, I peeled myself away from the curvature of Lor's body and tucked her back in. Everything seemed too quiet. Usually, I heard snickering or glasses clinking together at this time of day.

I strode to the kitchen ready to concoct something for breakfast, but then I saw Lex hunched over the outdoor railing with a steaming cup of tea next to him. He liked his tea black. No sweeteners, just pure bitter flavor. He already had his black leathers on, sword and daggers attached to his hip. In our former glory days, he sat up all night drinking and cavorting with us. There had been no use in resting then. But now, since the curse, we needed our rest more than ever.

I missed his voice so much it hurt. The curse itself did not steal Lex's voice. It was the violation of it all. We'd barely glanced at each other since our fight, and it was killing me.

"Were you up the entire night?" I asked, avoiding his glare.

His eyes narrowed into the horizon as if my presence made him want to jump out of his skin and run.

"Your tea is getting cold," I said, sliding the cup closer to him.

His hands tightened over the railing, and he breathed out a long sigh.

"I messed up," I blurted out. Confession felt like a ripping off a bandage. "I want to stop feeling like I am constantly running on coals. For her, for everyone. You were right; I was a coward, a vow breaker."

Though his eyes remained on the horizon, they became glass, trying not to shatter themselves. I felt lighter, exposing the inner workings of my heart. He had been such a good friend over the many years, and I just hid from him, from all of them. Lor was the final straw. From the moment she'd arrived, Lex's eyes became brighter, his steps lighter. It was as though long lost family had been found, and he felt more complete than he had in years. Lex really did love her as a daughter. And I ruined her.

"I could spew a million excuses to you for my behavior. But I just..." The breezy air nipped at my bare chest. "I miss you, and I'm sorry."

His arms slackened to their sides, and he turned his face further away from me. I expected nothing in return. I just needed him to know. I made for the front door when he pulled me under his arm, twisting me around to face him. The hand resting on my shoulder was large enough to crush skulls. As menacing as he appeared, Lex was gentler than any being I'd ever met. His heavy gaze read my soul. He pulled me into the wide girth of his chest like I was a brother. As much as I wanted to crumble into a thousand pieces in this safe place, I restrained myself.

"I don't deserve any of you," I whispered.

Lex blinked and pushed his finger into my chest and then back to his own. He did it again, and after the third time, it clicked. We all deserved each other. I suppose we all did in our sick, twisted way. But that's what family was.

***

Our army encamped beyond the demarcation line. Faeries and Woodland Dryads arrived on the flat land between the rolling hills that separated us from the Queen's epicenter. Pale yellow skies streaked with gray hung above us. None of us knew what to expect. All we had going for us were Mikhail's cryptic messages. Woodland Dryads had no use for tents or armor. They slung their swords and battle axes on their backs and called it a day. Faeries loved to wear steel armor. Wren flew by me like a streak of lightning. Fluttering wings buzzed louder with each step as we drew near. Brilliant lights blinked intermittently as they hovered around, sharpening their weapons and trading old stories with each other.

"Riann, my boy!" The ancient faerie, Magnus, dressed in his priestly robes, landed in my hand. "Does your neck burn anymore?"

Lor's head whipped around at the question but then turned away. "No, it doesn't," I said, rubbing the back of my neck.

Magnus stroked his long white beard. His beady blue eyes raked over me, then at Lor, who was trying to lift Lex's heavy sword next to his makeshift tent. "Wren and Kaya told me you found your cymar."

I lifted him higher to my flushed face. His silvery glow pulsed brighter. "Yes, I've known who she is for some time."

His aged skin wrinkled with a smile that never reached his eyes. "Tell me, boy, why have you not sealed the cymar covenant?" His hands wrapped around my finger, taking in my scent with his nose. "I don't smell her on you."

Heat warmed my cheeks as I saw Lor struggling to pick up the sword. Magnus had never been one for small talk. He got straight to the point. I pressed my lips into a thin line. "I think of all the beings on Sidh, you would be first to know why."

Magnus slumped his shoulders. "You spent so much time cutting strings and manipulating timelines in other realms that you failed to see your own future."

"Nothing good ever comes out of seeing one's own future."

Magnus let out a long sigh. "I suppose not, but some futures are worth fighting for."

His transparent wings buzzed, gathering air to leave.

I curled my fingers, brushing the edges of his wings. "Before you go, I have a question."

His pointed ears pricked up, and I told him about what had occurred in the Carnelian Woods. Lor restored it without ever knowing what it had looked like. Magnus plopped down on my hand. Wheels in his head turned as he closed his eyes, sifting through eons of memories and information. With him being so small, it was a wonder that he could hold so much information.

His rheumy eyes popped open. "Are you sure she is who she says she is?"

"Of course, I do."

"Peculiar." Magnus stroked his beard again. "Has she said anything strange? Something that she would not know or believe?"

I thought back to every conversation we had, but only two things stuck out. "When she held the reins of her power for the first time, I was there. In one of her memories as a child she said there was more to the stars before ever being aware of what was inside her. Then, when we were with the Draconians, she said she wanted to be a constellation, hence, why I tattooed one on her back."

Magnus peered at Lor, trying so hard to swing Lex's sword. She almost hit someone, and Lex took his sword away like taking a toy from a child. She was dressed in black leathers with bracers on. Willa must have smudged black makeup on her eyes to make her more frightening, but she was just a cinnamon roll in goth clothing. My skin pebbled. How can someone so full of light look like the rich night sky?

"Interesting." Magnus tapped his fingers together, studying her from afar. "The fact she has the first light star in her tells me she is much more than who she appears to be." His head snapped up. "Somehow, the fates have entwined you both. So, my advice is, stop running. Leave the door open for her."

Ignoring the last part of his sentiment, I just wanted answers as to who she really was. "You've seen no one else with this star before?"

Magnus pursed his lips. "No, I have not. These eyes have not seen everything. If they had, I'd be dust by now. Fate is fate, my boy. Just like when you were slapped with the traitor's mark."

I rubbed the back of my neck again, feeling for the capital T that Queen Nyx seared into my skin. The mark branded anyone a vagabond, an outcast, something my healing water could not heal. With that mark, I would have received scorn from any realm if I'd had my power restored to jump again. Magnus took pity on me and healed the mark, but from time to time, I still felt it. After all this time, I found myself repeating those words he spoke over me as he carved wards onto my scalp.

"You are no traitor. You are the truth keeper."

I had no idea what the wards said, and he, being ever so cryptic, said I would know in time. Faeries and their prophecies.

"We must get going." I flicked my gaze at Lor. Magnus nodded with a mischievous smile that could rival Wren's and flew to his tribe.

✳✳✳

Lor and Willa sparred with each other and other dryads, killing time. The rest of us and the tribal leaders from each group gathered in the tent, strategizing the best way to defeat whatever was coming at us that would amount to the least loss of life. Not knowing the numbers or how they would flank us made it nearly impossible to plan. Mikhail was not responding across our bridge, which worried me. I had no clue who would be our "visitors" tomorrow. Faeries and dryads yelled at each other, making it a challenge to reach a conclusion. I turned to Phil, pleading in my eyes to intervene because he had taken part in many strategy rooms before.

With a roll of his eyes, annoyed by the bickering in the tent, he stood to his feet.

"Listen," Phil said, demanding all eyes on him, "we may not know what is going to happen, which means to prepare for the worst. The worst thing she can do is to send her sentinels. She will just send a few hundred because their strength will outmatch us. However, they are not invincible." Phil rounded the table and leaned over, creating a battle scene with chess pieces and mini flags. "Sentinels will see this battle as a joke, wanting to get it over with quickly so they can go home."

"It is not a joke!" a faerie shouted. "Fauns are at risk of extinction! She tried to do that to us!"

Phil's eyes flashed their red irises. "Be that as it may, they will see us as a disorganized front and cage us. Flanking on all sides and using shield walls may be the best way to defeat them."

"We have an advantage," I said right before a coughing fit. Hacking until I spit blood into my hand was degrading in front of everyone. My healing water skin was so large it took two hands to manage. I wanted to be prepared for anything.

"We have the cliffs." My voice shook, the metallic taste of blood slid down my throat. "We should use shield walls and rain fire from above. They will attack us on the flatlands, but we can push them into a watery grave."

Phil nodded. "Our other bet is Dolos. He has meticulously worked on powders and oils to set them ablaze. There are trip-wires all around the field, and we have already told you where they are, so none of us dies. They already think we are weak. Let them believe that, so their guard will be down. Let them believe they will make it home in time for dinner."

"Faeries," I cleared my throat. "Work on wards and runes in case the queen arrives to cast her power. I implore you all, please keep Mikhail alive."

Everyone adjourned and went to their respective tribes. In the white field tent, I found Lor resting on our pillows with her sword by her side. Her body was limp with exhaustion. I didn't want to bother her, but it might be the last time I could. When I laid beside her, she opened her eyes, entangling her legs with mine.

"Love, you need to rest." I kissed the top of her head.

She lazily turned toward me and curved her body with mine. "I'm too scared to rest."

"I know, so am I."

"After tomorrow, we'll live forever," she said sleepily.

I choked down whatever cough wanted to come out. Scooting down to meet her face to face, I stared into the whiskey-colored eyes Wren glamoured. "I'll always be with you."

We pressed our lips together, holding each other in the safety of our arms. I'd experienced many eves of battles, and yet this one was the most endearing.

38

ELORA

y teeth pulled the leather thread of my bracers, tightening them. I could have asked Willa or anyone else to do it, but I wanted to be alone. Fear scalded the back of my throat as bile crept up. The brave façade I put on slowly crumbled. I was just a girl from Jersey about to fight in a battle we knew little about. Could I kill someone if they had a knife to my throat? I could never kill those four boys or my foster father. What made me think I could kill someone who wanted to take my life?

Willa drew back the tent flaps with her battle face on. Tight purple braids fell to one side of her face, while daggers and two swords sat on her back. Two white slashes of paint cut over her left eye from her crown to her neck. The epitome of fierce. How funny that Willa could cut men down to size, but she couldn't make a loaf of bread to save her life. She eyed me up and down with a faint curl on her lips.

"This will not do," she said. She reached into a black cinch bag at her waist.

She sat me on the cot and painted my face aggressively. There was no point in being friendly; we were about to go into battle. All preambles and lightheartedness flew out the window, driving every bit of anxiety from my head to my toes. Her hands trembled as she avoided looking into my eyes. Perhaps, there was a part of her that did not want me to fight. I expected Riann to challenge my choice, but maybe there was no fight left in him or he truly believed I could handle it. After Willa was done, she flipped open her pocket mirror, displaying a swath of black paint smeared across my eyes with a splattering of white paint—like stars in the dark sky.

"There, much better," she said with her hands on her hip. "Stay by Riann and me today. Do not fear plunging your blade into another. It's a natural course of justice." She said it nonchalantly as if killing was her second nature, and it was something I would learn to do, like riding a bike. "Oh," she paused while leading me out of the tent, "do not go near Lex or Dolos. They can get kind of crazy."

A bit of shock halted my steps outside. I couldn't imagine my boys being so crazy that I needed to stay away, but Willa's grave tone was enough to take it seriously.

Dryads lined the hills above, nocking their arrows, straining their eyes for visuals of an approaching army. I overheard them say last night, "One horn for sentinels, two horns for sentries. Then blast again, one horn for one hundred men or less, two horns for one hundred or more."

Buzzing faerie wings mingled with the rustling leaves of the dryads. In front was Riann with Phil and Lex. Dolos was off somewhere, ensuring all his trip wires were in working order. Something terrible dropped in my gut as I watched the look on everyone's faces preparing to hurl ourselves into the unknown. If it had not been for Mikhail, they would have ambushed us. There was hope for him yet.

My breath stilled as I came upon Riann in his black leathers, lined with dark violet, snug against his sculpted legs. His hair was in a singular tight braid, trailing down his neck. The blue glint of his hilt glowed. My mother's sword. Carefully crafted threads inside the hilt shimmered under the pale purple sky. She must have really loved him to create this masterpiece. I wondered what she would think of him as my cymar. Would she be overjoyed? Shocked? Dismayed? Maybe he was good enough to protect but not good enough to marry. I chose to believe she would bless our union. Imagining the king, my father, extending his hand on Riann's head made me desire things that could never be. I wished I had known them.

Riann's lips curled into a wicked grin. "You remind me of the shield maidens I met in the earthly realm."

"Willa thought this was absolutely crucial," I chuckled nervously. "Personally, I think it's more like a Greek fury."

The look in Riann's eyes made my mouth dry. I brushed my hand on his, and a tender wave of electricity coursed through me. He felt it, too, as he staggered back. We didn't have time to think of such things. Yet time seemed to pause, and it was just me and him. I'd told him we would have tomorrow, so there had to *be* a tomorrow for the both of us. Tomorrow. The one word I clung to.

Riann cleared his throat, breaking our heated gaze. "Whatever happens today..." he rolled his lips together. "I know you will fight well." He spun around to get back to the front line.

I wanted him to say more, so much more. I felt silly wanting passion right before a battle, but who knew what would happen? We looked to the horizon, waiting for a sign, any sign. I stood between Willa and Riann—with Wren and Kaya perched on his shoulders. All other faeries flew through the rest of our small ranks. Dryads behind and above us, we were still so small compared to what the queen could do. The proverbial clock ticked. Sweat ran down Riann's face in rivulets, his face hardened by the sudden brush of my arm against his. He likely hated that I was putting myself in danger. If only he realized there was no place I'd rather be. My knuckles grazed against his, and his eyes guttered shut for a moment.

"I love you," he whispered.

Then we felt the vibrations beneath our feet.

39

RIANN

Those were not the unified steps of soldiers. Panicked hooves ran in terror.

"Hold!" I cried as fauns crested the horizon. My heel sank into the dampened ground, bracing for what was coming our way.

Shrill screams, the sound of a fierce tempest, boomed. If anyone had ever heard a faun scream, they could never *unhear* it. It was the essence of pain and suffering. Dryads loosened their taut bow strings. Each rank lowered their shields, shouting amongst one another, confusion crossing their faces. Lor's face became pale. She gripped my arm, clenching her fingers around my muscles, ripping me from the panic rising in my blood. Nobody had expected this. We had been ready to fight and protect, but we'd lost the battle before it ever began.

"Dolos!" Lor shouted. "The fauns don't know where—"

Glacial daggers sliced through me. Dolos' wires could trigger explosions meant for our enemy and kill innocents. There was no other choice but to run into the mass of fauns coming at us.

"Flank left side!" I screamed.

Faeries flew like the wind, desperate to move the fauns from the left where traps were laid. Dolos was sure to be panicking, trying to remove the traps, but he was only one man. He could be at risk too, and if an innocent faun... I couldn't entertain the thought. Willa, even without her powers, was a fast runner, outrunning us all on foot.

"Move to the right!" she screamed, her voice becoming hoarse. Every command fell on deaf ears.

Lex used his large, menacing body to scare the fauns from the left, but their adrenaline was too high to register fear. Many were bruised and bloody, some on the brink of death as they fell behind. I couldn't see Phil but heard him yelling futile commands. An explosion erupted. My ears pierced with ringing. I pushed through the panicked crowd, almost taken down by frightened fauns. They drowned in their need to survive while using my body to keep themselves above the surface. A second explosion. Lor was nowhere near me. The scent of death quickened my heart. There was no use in yelling anymore. Dryads flanked the left side. Smoke and fire stifled the air.

"Lor!" My throat felt like it ruptured, and I coughed blood onto the ground.

Ashes fell like snow on my face. Time slowed as I smeared ashes between my fingertips. It could be wood or something else that would burn quickly, but my chest caved in, believing it was some-one's life. I needed to stop thinking about it and get to Lor. She could be getting trampled on. With a swift movement, I lost my balance, slipping onto my knees. The air grew thin between the smoke and being trampled on by hooves. My bones and muscles burned.

"Let me out!" I cried, losing my breath.

Mud filled my mouth and my nose. I reached for anyone but there was too much confusion. Finally, a strong, familiar hand reached for me and pulled me from the stampede. Lex. He hooked his finger in my mouth, causing me to retch. Everything but my organs spewed out. I was breathless, heaving. His clouded eyes made my stomach sink further. This was a lost cause. I didn't have time to gather my thoughts, to reel my stomach back in.

"Like old times," I said dryly with my arm stretched to his shoul-der.

He huffed with a smirk and hurled me onto his shoulders. Dolos and Lor were nowhere to be seen. My stomach twisted, creating worst-case scenarios. Three mysterious figures in dark cloaks on horses looked down from the top of the hill. Their faces darkened. Withered hands peeked ever so slightly from their sleeves. Tendrils of shadows and smoke curled around them. Shadows were death. Necromancy. The ache to have pure control between the layers of realms.

"Riann!!" someone screamed. "Riann!!"

Lex turned. Luca ran straight for us with a huge gash crossing his face and chest, pink and red ribbons of muscles torn from his flesh. He could not survive chaos like this.

"My prince!" he said. "We hid in the caves near the Styx." His chest heaved in and out. "The queen sent foot soldiers after us, but their chase landed us here."

There were no soldiers. Not even poor squires. Just those three figures. There was never meant to be a battle. It was meant to enforce the facade of rebellion. I leaned down as much as I could, adding weight to Lex's neck. "Luca, I need you to listen to me. This is false magic. The queen attacked by using astral projection. There are no soldiers here." I shuddered at the sheer power it must have taken. Nyx likely put her hand on the horn, drawing every bit of power she could.

"Why would she do that?!" He clenched his bloody teeth down so hard he could have shattered them. "My Suri, she's lost."

Tears streamed down as he stared at his bloodied hands. He swayed, and Lex caught him by his shoulders. My heart broke for him. Luca had been so brave keeping Lor as safe as he could within those palace walls. "I am truly sorry, Luca. The queen has been paranoid about a rebellion for some time now. But today, she made it happen. We have become the rebel stain."

Lex pulled in a deep breath and roared like a sonic boom. Fauns fell to their knees, covering their ears. Finally, the chaos simmered down, and the three figures turned their horses and left. Luca stumbled to the ground, fainting. Lex picked him up, cradling him. I slid off Lex's shoulders and whispered wards over Luca in vain while I poured some healing water on his wounds. Then, I shoved my way through the crowd.

"Lor! Dolos!" I screamed over and over.

Nothing. What if she was with him? What if they both...? No, that couldn't be. Lor was smarter than that. But she was too brave. She would have protected him. Phil appeared, his red eyes glaring underneath the smear of mud on his face.

His eyes shook, his chest heaving. "We've been duped."

I gripped his rising shoulders. "I know. We fell right into her hands. But now, I need to find Dolos and Lor."

"Dolos is fine." He wiped across his face with his bracer. "He made it back to the encampment after the fauns triggered the explosions."

"And Lor?!"

Phil bent over, grabbing his knees, his breath returning to him. "I last saw her running to the left side."

My blood ran cold. I bolted, running through anyone in my way. I finally made it to the left side. Debris and plumes of smoke darkened the dusky sky. Dead fauns and dryads scattered at the explosion site. Everything in me turned inside out. A wisp of pale hair peaked from underneath a pile of bodies, and I felt my body leave my flesh. A mix of relief and horror overcame me as I found the hair belonged to a dryad.

"Lor!"

Flames licked the air behind me while fauns scrambled away. I couldn't believe we'd done this. We'd followed Mikhail's cryptic warning, giving Nyx the power to believe we were the rebellion all along. I didn't know what to make of it. All I knew was innocents were dead, and it was all my fault. I ran fast and hard despite blood building in my chest. Willa would have screamed down the bridge if she had found Lor. Was she taken? Was this a ploy to capture her? Given that we'd become the rebel stain, Nyx could back out of the deal and take Lor before her hundred days were up. The very thought made me wobble as I ran. For a moment, I stopped to spit out blood, then whirled myself around trying to find her. My own star shimmered beneath my armor—which meant hers called for me too.

Everything around me blurred. Delicate, strong arms flung themselves around my neck. My ears rang again, my vision weakening. Legs wrapped around my waist, holding me firmly, spreading warmth to my cold body. Focus, Riann, focus. Her voice shouted my name so near, yet so far.

"Riann! Riann! It's me! I'm okay, I'm okay."

Lor. She found me. I tried to steady my breath, but her lips were on mine too quickly. My vision cleared, and I saw her face splattered with mud and blood, so pale. Her eyes had returned to lilac. My arms shook so much, I had to set her down.

"Riann," she whispered, her voice strangled. "I'm okay. Are you hurt?"

"No," my voice was raw. Lor's braided hair had come undone, matted against her face. "I'm so sorry I lost you." I rested my head in the crook of her neck, biting back my tears.

Her hands bracketed my face. "Riann, I can save them."

"I know you can." I leaned my head against hers, savoring the fact she was safe. "Go." I kissed her forehead. "Save them all."

Lor tread to the middle of the field, finding the epicenter and weaving a web of restorative magic. My cymar, my only. I thanked the fates for this moment. This piece of heaven was mine. Even amongst the dead bodies and smoldering flesh, I found peace watching her become who she was destined to be. I didn't notice before that she wore leathers exposing her back to show her constellation. She had already woven across five realms. I could hardly take it in. This fierce beauty, rarest gem in all realms.

Static crinkled in my mind. A man sobbed loudly that I could barely make out who it was. When he took a few deep breaths, I knew it was Mikhail.

"Sorry. I'm so sorry. I'm so sorry, brother." He wept. *"It was not meant to be like this."*

Everything in me seized, and I collapsed. I stretched my forearm. The hourglass was empty. This was it. I rolled to my side, trying to keep Lor in my sight, to be the last thing I saw. But I couldn't find her. Eight hundred years of life passed before me in such a whirlwind that I could hardly register what was happening. But it was her face I clung to, the dreams I had with her. I didn't want to die. Not now. Not when I'd found something to live for. I begged the stars to let me live, but I could not bargain with hungry jaws coming to claim me. Edges blackened. Everything went dark. Death finally came.

40

ELORA

Vines of light spread onto the field through my hands flowed, twining and sprawling, leaving no blade of glass untouched. The ground glowed as my star advanced, branching out, healing each individual. Cuts, bruises, and scrapes were gone as gold threads wound their way through each person. Gold shimmer absorbed into every person, replacing limbs and restoring broken bones. Fine gold dust particles formed missing appendages. Wailing stretched across the plain as loved ones were found whole. What the queen had meant for death, I fought back with life. This star embedded in me brought forth a healing touch, yet deep inside, I was still a little girl needing someone to notice me. If I didn't have this star, would I still be loved the same? Self-deprecating thoughts sliced through my starlight, ebbing away at its vibrancy. I closed my eyes to think of fonder things. Riann. My family. They were enough, yet there was something buried in me that needed more.

Everything became silent, a pause of shock and disbelief. Slowly, all eyes turned on me in the center of it all. Wary glances and parted mouths made me feel like I'd done something wrong. My starlight retreated, flowing into me through my fingertips. Before I could process what had happened, a large circle of fauns and dryads surrounded me. Quickly, they overcrowded me, suffocating, touching me everywhere reverently as if I were a saint or a goddess.

Lex pushed through, ignoring the gasps and sheer terror, and hoisted me by the waist. My heart cracked at the sight of the dead scattered in the field. Hazy smoke partially blocked the horrors. Piles of the dead lined where Dolos' traps were laid, smoldering, filling the air with the scent of burnt flesh and blood. Ashes scattered to the wind, while the anguished cries of mourning met my ears. My star had limits; otherwise, the dead would have been raised. Too many strings were cut with a single shear. Though many lived, I felt a sense of inadequacy. I hated the fact that I could restore yet not feel good enough. No amount of praise would ever heal those wounds. It was me. I had to be the one to break agreements. Break the belief that I was destined for the shadows. Break the belief that I was unseen. Break every little part of me that agreed I was not lovable. Even so, marvelous light shone through the smoke and heaviness, raising the broken ones, breathing new life.

My vision cleared, and the crowd split as Lex trudged through. With tired smiles and bright eyes, I brushed hands with anyone reaching for me. We made it back to the encampment, and he hid me in our tent. Riann wasn't there. Perhaps he tried to get through the crowd. Our pillows still had his face imprinted on them, and as soon as I touched them, all the creases and dents smoothed.

Phil entered the tent. "Lor..." His voice was grim, his skin leeched of color. My heart dropped. "Please come to Dolos' tent."

Willa met me outside weeping. "I'm so sorry, Lor, I'm so sorry!"

"What is going on?!" I asked, fearing the worst.

Dolos left the tent covered in ash, his face completely hardened. Willa grasped me by the shoulders, her head low. "The faeries... they found Riann. He's dead, Lor."

My legs turned to water. Gravity pulled me under and crushed me with every bit of pressure. "He can't be," I gasped. My star rattled and quaked, searching for Riann. He couldn't be dead. He said tomorrow. It wasn't tomorrow yet.

"The Queen...the hourglass...she finally killed him," Willa's voice strangled. "He was dying for so long and did not want to tell you. She slowly killed him."

"He was dying this whole time?!" His letters, his failed rejection attempts, his overt need to have one perfect day with me. The tattoo— Riann knew he could not take those things with him. He'd done it all for me.

Magnus fluttered to me as Kaya perched herself on my shoulder, offering comfort from her tiny embrace around my neck. A life without Riann. I had only ever considered him living without *me*. The tables were turned, and I felt like an utter fool. The pain of losing him cut so deep, I couldn't cry. Something inside went dark.

Magnus wrapped his tiny hands around the tip of my nose. "He's a time mage. His physical body is dead right now, but his mind is still hanging on. He's lived too long for the threads to be cut so quickly."

I lost my breath and staggered back.

"You can save him, but you don't have much time," he said, tightening his grasp.

My throat tightened. "Tell me what to do."

Magnus' beady eyes shimmered. "Go into his mind, dear one. Find the one door he is still behind that's making him hold on. It's in that place you can use your star to heal him."

"He has many doors!" I cried.

Magnus' wings flew against my cheeks with speed. "More are shutting with every moment. You have to go now."

Willa, Lex, and Phil followed me into the tent. Riann's still body did not seem real. So beautiful even in this state. I wanted to throw myself on him and whisper every regret I ever had, but time was running out. Riann needed me. He had always been hellbent on protecting and saving me. He'd used too much power that could have killed him several times over, and I'd never thanked him for that. I had refused to see the love in his actions. Now, I couldn't let him go like this. Not without me.

My lips quivered as I held his temples to ground myself, just like he'd taught me. I pressed a kiss to his cold forehead. "Hold on, Riann. I'm coming."

My eyes opened to dark skies. Occasional lightning sliced through the angry night. Withered trees and stony roads greeted me in his mind. Every door stood alone as if nothing were on the other side. The first door was simple; oak wood with a brass knob and a large fresh crack splintering the middle. Sunlight filled the doorway when I opened it. A young boy with black curls and starlit eyes wore a white and gold tunic. He turned to an older woman with sun-kissed skin and raven hair tied up with a dark blue ribbon, just as he'd described his mother. Her purple shift flowed in the sunlight as she wrapped her arms around his waist. Wisteria hung in the arched terracotta windows. He sat at the simple oak table with a silver frosted pitcher in the middle.

"Did the time mages whip you again?" she asked, brushing back his curls.

He pouted his lips. "I could not set my spindle right again. They said I would be useless."

"If we never suffered, we would never rise, child," she said, appearing to look at me.

Our eyes met, and their skin flaked to dark ash. The window and flowers became grains of sand scattered to the wind. I ran out the door and shut it. That was not the memory he clung to.

The next door was silver-plated with scratches all over, like something tried to claw its way in. Riann was a teenager, his face blurred. He laid in bed watching the stars in a semi dark room. Embers hissed and cracked. He held onto the dark blue ribbon. I understood then. He held his mother's ribbon after all these years. Phil's red eyes and slender body entered the room, trying to drag Riann off the bed by his ankles.

"You can't live like this. They're gone, they're all gone," he said, resting his palms on Riann's calves.

"I couldn't save her," he said, clutching the ribbon, on the verge of crying.

Phil threw his head back. "The strings are cut."

Riann rolled to his side, tears clouding his eyes. I kneeled before him, knowing it was this moment where he believed his life was forfeit as long as everyone else was safe. Before this memory flaked away, I kissed him softly on the forehead. Door after door carried such heaviness that I could not fathom how he'd held himself together for eight hundred years believing he needed to protect everyone. One door showed women sexually assaulting him, forcing themselves on him to the point where he slept sitting up with a dagger in hand. I wanted to strangle them.

A black door covered in violets and twining black roses caught my eye. It was almost identical to the one I had. As dark as the door was, light flooded in when I opened it. I stood in a sunken living room with modern beige furniture and a large smart TV on a white, distressed entertainment center. The pitter-patter of feet ran down the hall and into the kitchen, where I— well, another version of me—washed dishes. She looked through the window, smiling at a man playing catch with a boy with pale ringlets and chubby arms. Another boy, seemingly older, with inky midnight blue hair and vivid blue eyes, swung on his swing looking away. I could only see the back of the man, his black curls bouncing with each catch. A toddler reached for the woman's legs, wrapping his little arms around them.

"Oh, my boy, what have you been up to?" she said in singsong, observing the marker stains of red, silver, and green all over his arms.

When he tried to climb up her legs, she said, "Oh, no, no. Your little sister is sleeping." She turned to the side, revealing a mauve sling clasping a babe firmly.

This version of me looked happy, fulfilled. But this wasn't a memory. This was a dream, a fantasy. Something Riann clung to. I hurled past the kitchen island to the back door to get to Riann, but the door was locked and wouldn't open. Frantically, I pulled at the door, and it felt cemented in. Tears ran down my face.

"Open the door!!" I screamed as though someone would hear me. One more pull. My muscles throbbed. Every inch of my arms turned red. "Open up!!"

I was finally here and couldn't get to him. His time was running out. I fell backward, landing on my backside. Blue legs stretched on the other side of the kitchen island, and I launched myself toward him. Riann's face was planted against the floor, barely moving. It took so much to roll him over. I moved his head into my lap and caressed his beautifully carved face.

"Riann, it's time to wake up." I tapped his cheek numerous times. "You said we would have tomorrow. You need to keep your word." My own words crushed me.

Blood ran through me like a tempest, my hands flared, and I placed them on his chest. His heart still beat. My cymar held on for me. This picture-perfect scene gave him life. Thoughts of home, of a family he desired but did not believe he deserved.

"Live, my love. I am here. Find your way back to me, like you always do."

His skin warmed, and breath slowly filled his lungs. "You found me across realms, and the truth is, I think I had been searching for you all these years." My hands trailed down his forearm over his empty hourglass. With a press of heat, I dissolved the live ink with my hand. He would never be her prisoner again.

"Riann, my cymar, wake." My hair fell like a curtain over his face. "I forgive you for everything. Any debt you feel you owe me, I don't want it. I just want you to be free. I hope you can forgive me for the hidden things I've said and done." Desperate tears pelted his stiff body as if they would wash away the scent of death rising above us.

"Please, wake up," I begged.

Darkness began to close in. "No, Riann! Wake up! Live!"

I moved so quickly that I hardly noticed I was straddling him, caging his body with mine. I crossed my hands together, desperate. "Don't you give up! I need you! You're the one I can't live without!" With that confession, I slammed both hands on his chest, and an inferno of gold and violet light shattered the dream to a million pieces.

Everything went dark for a moment, and I heard panicked voices rising above me. The feel of scratchy fabric covered me. Willa's voice came into focus as she peeled back layers of fabric from my face. I was no longer in his mind because I'd failed. He was gone. My love was gone.

My screams pierced the ears of everyone surrounding me. "Riann... why didn't you fight?!"

Dolos shoved Willa aside and cupped my face in his calloused hands, but I couldn't hear anything. He dragged me from the tent fabric I'd fallen under when I blasted out of Riann's mind. He planted me on my knees next to Riann's bed.

My skin wanted to fall off my bones, staring at his lifeless body. Were they making me stare at him as a punishment for failing?

I didn't think they would ever do that. But death could do scary things to the ones who are left behind. I threw myself on Riann's chest, soaking his cold skin with my tears. A part of my soul ripped away from inside me, leaving a cold, vacant space.

"I'm so sorry," I sobbed, trailing all my tears and runny nose down his sculpted stomach. "You said tomorrow."

The room stilled, waiting for something, anything. But it was too late...

Then, Riann gasped.

41

RIANN

Death never felt so cozy. Soft orange light streamed through the windows, making its way past my heavy eyelids. My arm jerked past my side table, toppling over glasses of water that smelled like ash and mint. Such a strange combination. I grabbed a glass that hadn't spilled and poured some on my face, rubbing my eyes open. Mint gave a slight burn. I was in my room, on my bed, under cotton sheets and my feather-down comforter. Not a single sound. Maybe this was the afterlife of a time mage, an absolute solitude from eons of chaos. My thoughts wrapped around Lor. Even in this after life, I still smelled her scent. Perhaps it was a reward from the fates who'd cut my string. Down the road, she should find someone more deserving, though I hated the thought of it not being me. I inhaled her scent on my pillow, quickening some kind of memory. Something had happened when I died. I couldn't put my finger on it. I'd felt her all around me. Her voice was all I heard when the last spark of light went out.

My whole body screamed as I sat up. I did not think the afterlife would be so draining and painful. It was rather disappointing. Lor would have laughed at the irony of it all—a sound I would never hear again. I hissed and groaned as my back muscles tightened in pain. Before I lifted my legs over, someone ran toward my room. Willa pushed open the door, almost ripping it off its hinges, and jumped on the bed. She flung her arms around my neck, and her tears soaked my warm, sticky skin.

"Never do that to me again!" she sobbed. "Never die on me again, you hear me?!"

I nudged her off me. "I'm not dead?" My voice felt like gravel.

Her brows furrowed. "No! You've been asleep for ten days." Willa screamed for anyone who had ears. Phil, Dolos, and Lex quickly filled the room, their faces a mixture of horror and relief.

"What happened? The queen took the last grain of—" I flexed my arm, finding the hourglass no longer there.

"Lor happened," Dolos said, inching to the edge of the bed. I had not realized I was fully nude under the sheets until he sat beside me, his body pulling at the blanket. "She healed all those fauns and dryads after my traps..." Tears stung his eyes, his shoulders stiffened. "But then you..." Dolos rose from the bed and rounded the table by the window, unable to look me in the eye. "I'm sorry, Riann, for anything I've ever done to hurt you. When I saw your body carried by the faeries, I—"

I tried reaching for him from the bed. "Dolos, you have nothing to be sorry for. You have been a crass yet wise friend, and I would not have you any other way."

Dolos cupped his mouth, keeping his tears silent. Lex strode across the room and wrapped Dolos in his burly arms. His eyes shone while glancing at me. Leaning against the bedpost, Willa lowered her gaze, shuffling her feet. Something in the air changed as they fought to find more words to say. I supposed it was traumatic to find your friend dead and now he was back to life. I couldn't imagine the pain they'd gone through because if I'd ever lost one of them, a part of me would die. Together we were whole. Stoic as ever, Phil stood by the doorway, hand on his hilt. Funny that he became emotional when Lor came back as my cymar, but not when I came back from the dead.

Phil rolled his lips and looked at Willa as if she were going to speak. With a sigh, he slowly paced around my bed. "Lor went inside your mind. She found a door you were still living behind, and she healed you there."

My mouth gaped. She was with me. "Where is she?"

"You need to focus on recovery," Phil said tersely.

"Tell me where she is." My throat scratched, and my head spun, feeling the effects of dehydration.

Willa rushed out of the room and brought me a glass of cold water. The iciness felt like shards of glass going down my throat.

"Tell me where she is!" I tried to leap out of bed, but my back screamed in agony. Defeated, I slammed my head back down on the pillow.

"She's safe," Willa reassured, brushing back my hair. "If you eat some of this bland porridge, I will tell you everything."

She handed me a bowl of mush. No flavor. I died, and they still did not learn how to cook for themselves. After I shoved it down my throat, Willa dismissed everyone from the room.

Lex stopped in the doorway and gave me a look that said, "I'm glad you're alive."

Willa pressed her hands to my calves, squeezing and kneading. "Phil was wrong about dismissing your need to know how she was doing. But he was right about you needing to focus on your recovery. Your muscles have atrophied. You look terrible."

"Gee, thanks. Can you get to Lor?" She shot me a death glare and paused her hands. "Forgive me." I ran my hand down my face.

She continued rolling my muscles like they were dough. "Anyway, after I tell you everything, will you promise to get out of this bed and walk with me?"

"Sure." I groaned at the pressure she put on my legs.

Her dark purple hair brushed my knee as she put all her strength into warming up my muscles. "I will need to help you shower too." She grimaced, cupping her nose. "I've done nothing but wipe you down for the past ten days. It's time to rid this stench. Dolos checked out, and Lex was afraid he'd break you in half. Forget about Phil helping."

"Willa, please," I pleaded. "Tell me."

Willa sighed. "She snapped. Even though you were breathing, she believed you were in a coma and would not come out. Apparently, she had seen this happen in her old realm." Willa's hands reached my outer thighs, making long, pressing strokes to my lower back. "At first, she did not want anyone touching you. She clung to you like you were going to wither away. Dolos used a poultice to knock her out so we could bring you home. But when she woke, she screamed for you." She shuddered. "Her screams were that of a banshee, so raw, primal. She laid on your bed for several days without moving. I never saw her once get up to use the bathroom or drink. Her eyes sank in, her body thinned. We knew you could not wake up to that or let her do that to herself."

She found the right muscle and added an immense amount of pressure and warmth, cracking my bones with it. I groaned into my pillow while my heart dropped to the pit of my stomach.

Willa continued. "I believe seeing your dead body and whatever she saw in your mind traumatized her. She did not have a proper hold on what was real, thanks to sleep deprivation and starving herself. So Dolos created a calming drink. You spilled most of them over." She flicked her eyes to the water that had not been cleaned up. "And he talked her into staying with the faeries at the willows while you recovered. He and Lex delivered her there. As soon as Magnus and Wren saw her, they drew runes on her. She's been resting ever since."

My muscles began to loosen. "How long has she been there?"

"Five days. Dolos sees her every day. She is beneath the willows under watchful eyes. They covered her in laurel leaves and paper-whites." She flipped me on my stomach and rubbed each ache in my back.

"Like a funeral?" I muffled into the pillow.

Willa pounded my back into mush. My skin became itchy as blood finally flowed through my body. "No, idiot! They are blessing her with the green of the earth because of what she did for everyone and what she did for you. They do not have a bed of feathers for her to lie on, but they will shower her with beauty while she sleeps."

"Oh, man..." I dug my forehead further into my pillow.

"What?"

"This is just like the faerie tales in her realm. I need to go kiss her to wake her. She's going to love that," I chuckled softly. "Help me walk to the shower. I will not delay any longer." I propped myself on my elbows, shaking a bit. "Come on, I need to get my girl."

The first few steps were unbearable, but Willa held me through it. At first, I dragged my feet, slumping on her shoulder. After a few minutes, I was limping around, grabbing for the wall to steady myself. I fisted the sheets around my waist because I doubted Willa would want to see *every* part of me. I wouldn't let her wash me as she'd intended. Hot water relaxed my muscles. I braced one hand on the shower, suppressing every urge not to jump out of my skin. Lor saw me die. All this time, I thought my death would lead her to greener pastures, but it didn't. What a fool I was.

In the kitchen, Lex gave me dried meat and raw vegetables. My mind cleared with every bite. Phil's eyes narrowed at me from across the room. He didn't understand. He forsook any prospects of a cymar long ago and knew nothing of his soul being tethered to another. I couldn't sit here and wait while she was out there, waiting. She needed to see me alive. Dolos and Lex offered to go with me, and Willa opted to stay and clean my sheets. I really did have the best friends. The universe took its time with these golden ones. Phil was wary of Lor, but I knew it came from a good place. He'd seen me wait for so long, and a part of him felt guilty for rubbing his dalliances in my face when we were younger. I thought a small piece of him wished he felt something as pure and wholly good as I did when I looked at Lor.

***

During our trek, I was on Lex's back like a little child. Even though I was making inappropriate jokes about having a thick hilt in my pocket, I felt the restraint of his laughter rumbling through those corded muscles. "Can't feel anything," he remarked.

Dolos rattled more inappropriate jokes about the size of his feet. Queen Lizzie must have loved those. Such a strange feeling to be so light. Lor had done something more in my mind, and I wished I could remember. It felt like an anvil had come off my chest. I had not felt that way in forever—except when we first kissed—but this felt different. It did not feel like a small bandage covering a large gaping wound; it was like something had been taken away.

The weeping willows crested the horizon amongst rolling green hills. Violets tangled in the wildflowers of the lush fields. Slow blinking faelights crowded us with soft laughter and a whisper of wings. Their light fell around us like a warm curtain, leading us to the trees. I slid off Lex's back, welcoming every ache and pain as I walked on the soft grass. Dolos leaned into their warmth, closing his eyes. When was the last time he'd felt someone's touch? He missed the unicorn queen, but it would have never worked out between them. It was the curse between mortals and immortals. If you fall in love with one, you watch them die. Mikhail knew better, yet he still tried to find a way to make someone immortal. By doing that, he'd wasted so much time. When he returned, she was gone.

Faelights peeled back, revealing Lor lying in a deep sleep on the ground. Her hair, like spun starlight, spread out on the ground as if floating on water. Wren slept on her belly on a cushion of moss, and Kaya hovered over her, placing paperwhites on her chest.

Kaya's eyes widened with surprise. She dropped the flowers onto the ground, and her sweet little arms flung around my nose. "Riann! You're awake!"

Wren woke, rubbing his eyes, yawning. "Well, I guess you're not dying anymore." He stretched his arms and proceeded to go back to sleep.

Kaya shot him a glare, and the soft glow of her light flashed dark shadows. "Wren!"

"What?" he asked incredulously. "I've lost sleep keeping her calm. The moment she sees him, it's going to undo all my work."

Magnus flew past me and landed on Lor's chest, placing a small garland of chamomile on her. "Now, now, little Kaya, if you are going to be a faerie, be a faerie. Once the curse is broken, you can go back to who you *really* are." His voice dripped with iciness.

Kaya bowed her head, wanting to cry. "Yes, Magnus." She flew off my nose.

"Don't be so hard on her," Dolos scowled, breaking past me.

Magnus gave a dismissive wave. "And as for you, Wren, you've rested long enough."

Wren mumbled curses through his gritted teeth and left his comfortable bed. I inched closer to her, and Wren flew into my face, blocking her view from me. "What are your intentions now?" he asked, grabbing his dagger's hilt.

I gave him half a smile and cupped him in my hands. His eyes became round, meeting my warm gaze. "You have done well protecting her, my friend. But I am her cymar, and I will take it from here."

His taut wings softened, gray light illuminated his body. "With all due respect, prince, she is ours to protect."

I set him down on the grass, nodding. "Indeed."

Lor looked peaceful. The runes drawn on the crown of her head were fading. They must have reapplied the runes each time she woke. As I kneeled before her, I traced my finger against her jaw and down the bridge of her nose. My hand gently tilted her head upward from behind her neck, and her lips parted just enough to feel her breath.

"I'm here, Lor. Wake up," I whispered. I bent my head and softly pressed my lips to hers. A few moments passed, and not so much as a blink. I kissed her again, and still nothing. Then again. And again.

"Um, what are you doing?" asked Wren, scratching the top of his head with the point of his dagger.

This was embarrassing. I gave him a side glance. "Trying to wake her up."

Wren sighed and tipped his head back, "Bro"—I saw he'd picked up slang from Dolos—"even I can't wake her from those runes. You're going to have to wait."

I refused to hang my head low with all the surrounding faeries snickering. I had to keep some dignity. "How long will that take?"

"As you can see, the runes are fading, so give it a few hours," Wren said, putting his bed back on her stomach, curling up like a lazy cat. "When she wakes up, she's all yours, but for now, let me sleep. Both of you exhaust me."

42

ELORA

My body screamed to leave this dreamland prison. Something wild and warm surrounded me, like the sun on the beach. The scent of salt and something like sweet oranges seized my senses. I stood in a plain of tall grass, but when I looked down, the soles of Riann's feet appeared like when he had been dragged away by the Draconians. He would want me to move forward... but he was my cymar. How could I move on? More warmth enveloped me, and the sun shone even brighter. Our family was in the distant field, acting like hooligans in the haze of the rosy sunset. But Riann was not there. We'd almost made it, him and me. My friend through many trials, my love through storms, was gone. A breeze passed through me, and his deep voice soothed me, "I'm here, I'm here."

My hand fanned out from the sudden but gentle pressure wrapping itself around my throat. Between my fingers, I felt something tangible move. Something dug into my palm, leaving crescent shapes. Was his spirit holding my hand? No, he would have become a shooting star. My lips felt as if something pushed against them, warm and inviting.

"Follow my voice, Lor. I'm here. I'm alive. Remember, we have to go to the Jersey Shore, get oversized, stuffed animals and go on rides until we puke. Wake up, Lor," he said.

Could it be? Was he really alive? Could my subconscious desires be leaking into this dream? The crown of my head stung. Runes were fading again which meant Magnus would be right there, ready to draw them on me once more. I knew why they did this. I was slowly killing myself, so they forced me into a deep slumber, using magic to provide sustenance. Dolos practically drugged me to get me here. I had been angry at first, but eventually, I saw he did it for my benefit. Sometimes the greatest of friends made the hardest decisions on your behalf.

Heat bloomed in my chest. Lex, Willa, Dolos, Phil. I loved them so much. My muierar. An overwhelming sense of joy washed over me. Dolos, my wise, witty man of fire and wine. Willa, a loyal, beautiful fashionista. Lex, my gentle giant, who looked upon me as if I were a daughter. Phil, the one who taught me to be a better fighter. I had to wake up. For them.

As my body woke, I gasped as though I were underwater for a long time. Someone's hands interlaced with mine, but I couldn't open my eyes just yet. Someone rubbed a lukewarm, wet cloth down my face instead of shoving me back into my dreams. Two hands cupped my face, and instantly, I knew who it was. My eyes blurred, but I could see him hovering over me, blinking back his tears.

"I'm here." His voice wobbled before collapsing beside me. "Because of you, I'm here."

Faelights flickered brightly above me, shadowing his angular cheekbones and his tousled silver hair. If I touched him, would he wither away? Was this a dream in a dream? Though my hands shook, I ran my finger up his jawline and behind his ear. This felt real, and maybe I shouldn't question it.

Wren's impatient little voice wrenched me from my stupor. "This is really happening, Lor. Your oaf of a boyfriend is alive." He flew off my belly, slicing his hands in the air at the faelights. "She can't see right with all this brightness. Get out of here, you little sky rats!"

Smaller faeries skittered off in tiny fits of giggles. "Is it really you?" I asked, my focus coming in clearer.

"Yes, Lor." He braced the back of my neck and scooped me in his arms, hissing under his breath. "It's time to go home."

It was all so much to process, but I wrapped my weak arms around his neck. Riann pressed his lips to my temple, and we strode home after thanking everyone for their help. Eventually, I walked some, trying to regain my strength. Every time I stumbled, he was there to keep me from falling. His warm gaze met mine. Flashes of his sad memories took a deep root in me. I couldn't undo all that, even with this star in me. His dream of us had kept him alive. There would never be any doubt again about his heart for me. I'd never thought of being a mother because I did not exactly have stellar role models growing up. Yet, I felt a faint stirring to partake in his dream and make it mine, too.

He escorted me to my room at our house. After gently setting me on the edge of my bed, he lit every single candle. His hands brushed against my laurel wreath hanging on a random nail in the wall beside the mantle. Riann flinched and then continued to add wood to the fireplace. "Feel free to take a hot shower or go into the pool. I'll be back shortly," he said, softly plodding across the room to the door.

***

A silver tray of food waited for me in my room. I finally smelled good again. Someone put my favorite lemon mint soap in the tub, and I couldn't stop scrunching my hair near my nose to breathe it in. Riann made a sandwich with thinly sliced meat and cheese inside of a rustic bread roll filled with a tangy white dressing. It oozed throughout the sandwich as I picked it up. Wait. Riann made me a hoagie! He definitely had a knack for cooking foreign food without having a recipe. With my first bite, my stomach screamed for more. Devouring it was not strong enough of a word. This was so much better than the ones I had from the gas station. Condensation ran down the tall glass of lemon iced tea, and it felt like I was back in Jersey. I knew he had hot tea, but I didn't think he'd remember that iced tea was a thing for me. Maybe I should tell him about iced coffee.

Riann knocked and let himself in while I sat on the bed, fully satiated. His black robe swished along the floor.

"Now I know I'm definitely in a dream," I said, patting the space next to me for him to sit down. "You made me a hoagie, and it's the best I've ever had."

Though his robe was tied, his bare chest was visible through a small opening. His signature scent of salt and sweet oranges invaded my space. The couple that smells good together stays together. For a moment, he looked somberly at the wreath and took it off the nail. His face lit up, and he sat beside me, fumbling with it. "That makes me glad. Everyone else loved it, too. Now they have tasted a small piece of Jersey."

An uneasy tension built between us. Before I could say anything, Riann heaved a deep breath.

"I was dying, Lor. For quite some time. Whenever the queen tapped on the hourglass or anytime I used my powers, it stole from me little by little, and I could not..." He ran his hand roughly down his face. "Lor, I was about to die. I could not give all of myself to you and then have it taken away so quickly. You deserve more. That's why I could not go through with sealing the cymar covenant with you. How dare I have a momentary bliss of pleasure before my death? It would have only devastated you more."

I slid my hand over his. He squeezed back.

His breath turned ragged. "I did not want to reject you anymore, not when all these walls I struggled to put up were crumbling down. Then, you said my name. I lost it." He shifted his body toward mine. "We kissed, but I wanted more. I almost did when we were on top of the hill before Phil interrupted us."

I angled my head, my hair brushing against his arm. "And now? How do you see us now?"

Riann placed the wreath on his head. "We need to recover and process everything. Because once the covenant is sealed, it means forever. I hope you understand what that means."

"I know our magic will mingle, bonding us to one another," I said, leaning my tired head on his shoulders.

"It's more than that. A piece of your soul becomes mine, and mine will become yours." His jaw became taut. "So, if you have any doubts going forward, you need to be upfront. I've done many things to cause you to doubt my love and commitment to you. I—"

"Shh." I placed my finger on his lips. "Don't you remember? I forgave you for everything when I saved you."

His eyes widened, and his body tensed. "I have no memory of what you did. What did you see there?"

"Terrifying things." I took him by the chin and graced my lips with his. "But also, things of beauty, things of hope." I did not want to divulge any further, fearing his new lease on life would shatter if I made him rehash his past. Fire hissed and cracked, drawing his attention to its orange flames. His hand gripped the edge of the bed.

Riann gave a tight smile and slapped his knee before getting up. "I think we should call it a night. We need you to focus on recovery to ramp up your training. She will make the games happen no matter what."

With everything that had happened, I'd almost forgotten the reason I stayed here was to be a player in the queen's games. So much of my training must have winked out while I was in my deep sleep. How many days did I have left? I'd lost count. I wished we could ambush the castle, find the horn, and kill the queen. But we were outnumbered and outmatched.

I stretched over the side table and pulled out a worn book Willa snatched had from the 1980s. It was a fantasy novel about wyverns and a team of rag-tags like us with abilities to conquer evil. "One of my silly dreams was that you would read this with me."

His face turned a brighter shade of blue. "It's not silly at all. Wyverns are rare, powerful creatures. Let's see how this book describes them."

He shuffled his body behind mine, pressing me against the firmness of his muscles. He soothed my aches with his heat. With his arms falling to my upper legs, he read page after page.

"Star-crossed lovers dancing along the infinity loop of time and space vowed to fight for each other to the end," he read as if he were reading it for himself.

It was a reminder to keep fighting for what we deserved. I arched my neck, and he bent down for one last kiss before the final chapter. I didn't want the book to end, fearing the worst fate for our main characters. Riann cheated death. That had to count for something. We could have a happy ending if we danced around the fates a little more.

43

MIKHAIL

Land of the monsters. That was what I told Lor. I wasn't lying. I was a monster because the worst one had made me. Nyx prepared to kill me when she discovered where my true allegiance was. In the end, no matter how many iron walls I put up in my mind, it made no difference. Mother knew I'd warned Riann. At least he died with honor. She took everything from me. This grotesque fire she put in me was her insurance that I would never turn against her—or she would burn me alive in its flames. She truly believed I was some chosen one for a mysterious dark lord to become the harbinger of death. It made sense with how I had been raised. She put seeds of hate in me by creating opportunities for me to get hurt.

I tried playing with other children when I was younger, but their parents knew better, making them stay away from me. Mother had poisoned them against me. Isolating me. *Demon child*, those parents called me. I deserved it. I was not exactly kind to those who refused to play with me. It was easier to be everyone's villain so they could not bury me under their insults. But there were three people I could not come to hate at all—and I tried. It was because of them I saw the evil in my mother and began having compassion for those she sent me to kill.

Marie, Silas, Riann. I repeated those names over and over. Three marks against my heart. There was nothing else my mother could take except my life. I dared not to look for Riann's door. In death, all doors shatter, pulverizing into pieces as if they'd never existed.

I didn't want to see that vacant place. I was not ready to accept his death, and nothing I did could stop it. She'd wanted to kill him many years ago, but I convinced her he was better off alive in order to find the lilac girl. My witch of a mother finally got her way.

The temperature dropped to freezing by the Styx. It was the only place I could think of while using my key to run away. Fauns hid here before she sent her soldiers by astral projection to massacre them. I think in the end, she wanted the bodies of the fauns, but when they got the message to run for Riann's land, I believed they would run into a safety net. It was the least I could do. I was so tired of bloodshed. Now that I know she fed off our dead for many years, I wanted to vomit. No soul tax had ever been paid. I tortured this information out of Kain, and he was too dumb to withstand the manipulations I'd sent to his mind. His wife and child were okay. But to him, they were about to be hacked to pieces by Grim and his crew. Goblins can be ferocious.

Fauns left behind stale bread and hard cheese in a scene of chaos, with clothes, bedding, and lanterns scattered every-where. Smears of blood striped the floor. Empty cradles lay by the side. I hoped the babes survived. I couldn't swallow this paltry food, not because it was beneath my standards, but because my heart was in the pit of my stomach. How could I possibly eat while surrounded by such death caused by the same blood coursing in my veins? I refused to light a fire in this freezing cave. Too many eyes. At least it was dark here. I missed the dark where the only light was from the stars puncturing the sky.

Twelve days had passed since Riann died, and the gaping wound inside me that Marie and Silas left behind grew larger. I wished I had been a better brother. A brother deserving of him. He picked on me a lot as a child, but he also shielded me and let me sleep in his room. I never told him how my mother's visits often ended in excruciating pain. She needed to perfect her dark magic in me at night when nobody could witness it. He was the first to spar with me and play ball games the other kids played. I hated that my father refused to play with me. Other fathers taught their sons to fish, fight, and play sports. Only Riann and Silas took the time for that. I never let on that I was being abused. We all had roles to play, but I was done with the act.

I believed concealing Lor would bring an end to my mother's lust for power. If she killed Riann, did that mean she knew the lilac girl was here? I flew into Lor's door, trying to knock it down, but these rose vines entangled around me, pricking me with their thorns. No matter how loud I screamed for her, she did not open. I knew she did not trust me because of the crazy methods I used to keep her and all of Sidh safe. If Riann were here, I would tell him we must get our brains from our father. I missed him so much it hurt. I curled into the side of the cave under a tattered blanket. It smelled like the meadows, a sweet, lofty scent reminding me of blowing dandelion seeds in the air.

Exhaustion overtook me as I screamed less and less for Lor. Suddenly, darkness tugged at the corners of my vision. A shadow came over me. Elongated nails trailed down my neck, and the creature licked its lips with hunger. The Hag. My body paralyzed under the sudden freeze. I couldn't move, much less speak. Chilling laughter stole the air in my lungs as she covered me with her smoky, gray wisps. The Hag had not visited me before. I always figured it was because I had no joy in my life. But I did.

"Oh, my nephew, she's been looking for you." Her cold voice wrapped around my neck.

Marie's locks of golden hair twisted around my fingers as she eased out of our bed. The flash of her dusty blue eyes locked with mine under the flickering candlelight. Even if she grew old, those eyes would never lose their gleam, their mystery. Not wanting to let her go, I wrapped my arms around her slender waist, and she lost the sheet she fisted around her body. A press of her warm lips to mine, I forgot about the world around me. Right there, I was no monster. I was just Mikhail.

44

ELORA

Weeks passed in a blur. Riann busied himself making vats of soup for the displaced fauns while I helped Luca and his betrothed, Suri, with the orphaned children. America's adoption process was way more complicated than here. Finding families for these poor children was too easy. I was a little jealous. Maybe I could have had a happier childhood if a good family opened their arms to me like these fauns did. Dolos wanted to help, but he always ended up doing things that distanced himself. Guilt ate him alive, and that certain fire I always adored in him blew out. Everyone else hauled tents and large items closer to the Crystal Forest where fauns could rebuild. Soon, the field would be empty again.

As for the queen—we decided to lay low for the sake of the fauns. As much as we wanted to strike, the fauns' way of life had been devastated. She'd made fools of us, and we all paid a heavy price. I feared waiting too long would give her an advantage, but our silence could make her more paranoid. The temptation to leave in the night for her castle and rip the horn out of that corpse toyed in my mind. But when I looked at those exhausted faces who needed my help, I could not do it. Riann had been quiet on the issue as though he was brimming with ideas to take her down. With each idea, he cast it aside and spun those wheels again. The truth of it was that the misfits were no match for the queen without their powers.

On top of everything, I resumed training. Willa wasted no time intensifying each activity, leaving my muscles in a knotted mess. Lex built a makeshift maze in the arena and hid, no longer taking pity on me when he found me. He would never hurt me…badly. Couldn't say I didn't walk home without limping and bruises. It was obvious my gentle giant felt awful, but he was doing what nobody else could. Phil showed me I had the skill to fight, but Lex showed me I could get back up and do it all over again. It was about fifty days from games, and with each passing day, I felt my heart drop further into my stomach.

One day, Willa fought me in a lake with water up to our necks. She said the queen could change the elements, so I needed to be ready. My mind needed to be sharp because at other labyrinth games, people went mad due to mind manipulation. Great. It wasn't like I had enough trauma. Out of breath and soaked to the bone, we crossed the shoreline, barely noticing the rough rocks under our bare feet.

"Hey, I thought today we could bathe at the waterfall near the ruins," Willa suggested, stuffing her wet leathers into her bag. A thin, black, torn band shirt clung to her spring green skin.

My skin prickled at the thought of more cold water. "I really want a hot shower."

"Well," she replied, pulling out my favorite lemon soap. "There are ancient hot springs underneath."

I heaved in a deep breath. She had me at hot springs. "Fine, if you insist."

The walk to the waterfall was quick. We passed through an underpass through the small mountain that shadowed the arena. Warm, inviting, mist sprayed us when the waterfall came into view. It was ensconced in semi-circle of mountainous terrain and trees. The waterfall formed a pool leading into a river that streamed further through the mountain. I dipped my toes and found the rocks below the surface were smooth. The top did not reach very high. I imagined swinging off a rope from the top into the warm waters.

Wasting no more time, we went to opposite ends of the pool, fully undressed. I floated on rainbow waters, out of Willa's eye, thinking it was strange Lex did not come. Dolos stopped coming altogether. I felt like a terrible friend because I'd been too busy to speak with him. I knew it ate at him that his explosives killed people. Then, the added trauma of seeing Riann die. We should not be too busy for him. I decided to talk to Dolos that night. I didn't care how busy we were. Being a former social worker, I knew the sad stories of people whose loved ones simply had no time for them.

Afterward, Willa dried herself off and put on a long black skirt with slits up to her thighs, pairing it with a belted leather halter top and knee-high boots.

"Here," she said, tossing her bag to my feet. Water ran down my back as I squeezed my hair dry while holding my towel tight to my chest. A glint of a ruby red silk dress sparkled in the bottom of her bag with a pair of black lace-up flats.

"Um." I ran my fingers over the silk dress. "Why would you pack something like this to walk home in?"

She shrugged, running a comb through her purple tresses. "Every woman needs that one red dress, girl." The smell of honey wafted between us as she opened a container of her homemade hair gel composed of aloes, honey, and sugar.

A bit of fear shot through my chest. I'd never dressed like this before. Nobody had ever given me a reason to. Willa seemed distant as I slid the dress on. It snugly fit around my small curves, flaring at the feet. A breeze hit my bare back and wafted to the plunging neckline of the dress. Thin straps left my constellation exposed. *No matter where you go, everyone will watch you in awe and wonder about the stories you carry.*"

Willa braided my hair into a coronet, weaving in black ribbon. She left ringlets to dance around my jawline. No makeup tonight. Our fresh faces were enough for whatever was happening. It was so obvious something was planned, and I dared not question it, but I needed liquid courage to get brave.

We made it to the hill right before our house came into view. Twinkling lights glittered against the hot pink sky. Lines of lights were strewn from tree to tree, blinking in various blues and white with twirling violet ribbons swaying from the branches. The lake appeared as though the stars reflected onto the water. Kelpies surfaced their heads, mesmerized. Long tables decorated with flowers and ivy lined the front of the largest tree with steaming food. The scent was familiar, and my belly growled. Faeries and fauns gathered around the fire pit, laughing and drinking, while Luca and Suri played their flutes.

As soon as we came down the hill, Lex was the first to see us. He clapped his hands loudly, gathering the attention of everyone there. I staggered back with all eyes falling on me.

"Happy birthday, Elora!" they screamed.

My birthday? Wren flew over with a thimble of wine in his hand with Kaya following close behind. "Drink, my lady," he grinned, handing the thimble to me. "We celebrate you today."

I drank the wine with half a smile, my heart beating fast as everyone gathered around me, wishing me a happy birthday. Kaya brought me a gift of a dark ivy garland. "Dark ivy is supposed to repel evil spirits and mosquitos," she giggled before placing it on my head.

Luca hugged me. "My lady, we have little to offer you as a gift, so I hope you will accept music and mirth."

My face blushed. "Of course! Your music is more than enough."

Finally, I made it to the tables where large steaming bowls fanned a nutty, citrusy fragrance. *No, he didn't.* Noodles spilled over the edges of the bowls, and I was floored. He'd made my sad people food! Somehow, Riann remembered my birthday. Suffice it to say, nobody ever said happy birthday to me except for a card from the dentist telling me my checkup was due. July 15th. How did he know? I racked my brain going over memories. I'd never let on it was my birthday because I preferred Riann not knowing—back when he was just a shadow. Duh. Of course. He was there for my birth.

Lex hooked my arm and gave me a tight hug. "I'm glad you were born," he murmured, his dark eyes twinkling.

I could count the number of words he'd said on one hand, and he never said a full sentence until now. "Thank you, Lex," I said, muffling my voice in the crook of his elbow.

The music picked up its pace, and fauns began dancing. Lex let me go and held out his hand for his cymar, twirling her around the flames. Such a beautiful sight to behold as they never looked at their feet. Trust anchored between them as they gazed into each other's eyes, never missing a beat. Without shame, I piled my sad people food and ate it with delight. Riann had done it again and somehow made it better than what I ate in Jersey. Scanning the crowd, I found no sign of Riann or Dolos. Phil argued with Wren over the best weapons, and Kaya made a makeshift swing from one of the ribbons.

Dolos' blonde curls shimmered across the fire, and his face looked thinner. I made a beeline for him and linked my arms with his, pulling him away from the party. "Dolos, I am so sorry; I've been a terrible friend," I said, walking along the shoreline. "I know you've been sad, and I just want you to know I'm here for you.

"What?" he asked incredulously. "No." He gripped my hands, halting our steps. "First off, you are so hot right now that I saw a shy little boy scurry off. Second, don't make this night about me." His eyes flared for a moment, and he let out a low laugh. Bouncing curls fell over the shadows on his face. "Tonight is about you. For once, Lor, let it be about you." Dolos turned us around and led me back to the party.

"I'm not letting you off that easy, prince of unicorns." I pulled a curl and watched it bounce back into place. "You still have that story to tell me, preferably over faerie wine. Promise?"

"Pinky promise," he said, his feigned smile dimpling. "Happy birthday, blondie." Then he strode off, fading in the distance.

Being caught in the whirlwind of many vying for my attention was overwhelming. Yet, I still felt like the girl tucked away in the shadows, waiting for someone to see me. But that was just it. They didn't see the real me. And that was okay; not everyone would know me beyond skin deep. Magnus flew to my nose, but I could not make out what he was saying. Maybe I discovered I was an introvert and my social capabilities were depleting quickly. Lex and Willa were nowhere to be seen. I could be what they were doing—far away from there. Wren's voice rose, annoyed with Phil as he lost the argument. Kaya swung in the ribbon, completely relaxed with her thimble of wine. I didn't want to sound ungrateful, but I'd never had a birthday party, let alone friends and gifts. It was too much excitement for someone like me. Where was Riann? I didn't care how slamming this dress looked on me. He always knew the right words to keep me from spiraling.

Willa and Lex came to the table, their faces completely flushed, straightening their shirts. They bent down and picked up a three-tiered, purple and blue cake from underneath. I'd never had a birthday cake before either. Riann finally showed up, visibly nervous, and put an assortment of different-sized candles in the cake. Sidh did not celebrate birthdays like this, so it did not shock me when nobody sang happy birthday to me. Not that I cared. That ship sailed a long time ago. Riann's trembling fingers brushed my shoulders. His black breeches matched his deep violet tunic, edged with an intricate gold design.

"Make a wish Lor," he said, meeting my gaze.

I closed my eyes, thinking, thinking. I only had one wish, and I wanted to tell him badly what it was. After I blew my candles out, I opened my eyes, and he was gone. Willa cut the cake in various sizes. I wanted to show her how it was done, but she was so happy and gave rather large pieces to people and then slivers to others. Everyone kept coming back for seconds. But then again, this cake was out of this world. So, Riann could bake too. Of course, he could. I wasn't sure how he colored the fluffy, semi-sweet icing, but it was perfect with lemon zest and strawberry layers. It dawned on me he wanted this to be a surprise and took no credit for it. My heart leaped, and my blood ran hot. Trying to be inconspicuous, I took one of Willa's large pieces on a silver dessert plate and quietly crept away from my party.

45

RIANN

Get yourself together. This is her birthday, and you left. She's your cymar, for crying out loud! You're an eight-hundred-year-old child. My petty internal argument grew dim with each glass of faerie wine. I'd planned on dancing with Lor and giving her my gift, but I was a coward hiding in my room. Someone that beautiful should not exist. If I touched her, she might wither away under my sullied hands. My nerves loosened, and I slumped onto my sofa, staring into the flames. Last night while she slept, I bled violets in boiling water to give the cake icing a rich purple color. As I crushed the petals and their color smeared across my fingers, I recalled when Dolos said every woman should remind me of a flower. Whether they were fragrant, vibrant, or had thorns. Despite Lor's lilac eyes, she was a violet in the winter. Her roots may be shallow, but she was a brightness in the snow peeking through the saturnine canvas, scattering her beauty anywhere the seeds took her.

The door creaked open. There she stood, lithe in her ruby-red dress. A thousand words etched across the soft features of her face. She bit her lower lip and looked back to make sure we were alone. One foot forward and then another back before she made up her mind and closed the door behind. "Riann, why did you leave?" she asked, holding her dress with one hand, a slice of cake in the other.

I didn't want to lie and tell her I was tired, far from it. Her eyes wavered. After everything I'd done, she was unsure of my heart for her. She slid next to me, sharing her warmth. Her fingers interlaced with mine, laying her head on my shoulder.

"Thank you," she murmured, "for throwing me my first birthday party."

I shrugged. "It was nothing. I had a lot of help." Large layers of cake were about to slide off her lap. Before she moved another inch, I set it under the sofa.

"Nobody else would have known about my sad people food or the fact I don't like super sweet icing. Or that my favorite color is violet." A tense pause filled in the spaces between words. "You did all this for me, and you weren't there."

My head hit the wood trim. "I'm sorry, Lor. I hope I didn't ruin your birthday." I was very good at ruining things.

"I just want to know why." The pleading shone in her voice.

Why was I doing this? I should have stayed. I always thought too much and too hard about things and I missed out on what was in front of me.

I shifted her from my shoulder, creating space between us. Pale ringlets touched below her jaw and down her neck, giving me the urge to twirl them in my fingers. Her jawline feathered, and her hands gripped the edge of her seat. Buoying in such loud silence was torture.

Any hope she had deflated. She continued to chip away at my walls, and I gave her nothing. Cymar or no cymar, there may come a time when her patience ran out. I expected her to cry but she nodded her head to herself, perhaps agreeing with the thoughts in her head. Lor did not look at me as she gathered her dress in her hand and rose to her feet.

"Maybe I should go. When you're up for it, eat the cake you made. It's perfect," she said evenly.

I grabbed her hand. "Wait. Don't go."

Lor's gaze met mine, setting me at ease, though the chasm between us remained. She slowly sat down, turning her face toward the flames and already simmering with the expectation of rejection.

I ran my hand roughly down my face. "When you came down the hill in that red dress, I thought to myself, how can someone like me ever deserve you? I thought you would disappear by the mere touch of these hands. All I wanted to do was dance with you, shower every drop of devotion, but I ran instead." My head lowered. "I will never be good enough for you, Lor."

Light from the flames brushed her face, shadowing her button nose and high cheekbones. I didn't know what to expect. She never ran from me, and I didn't foresee her doing that, but I worried I'd worn her down with the mess in my head I just couldn't untangle. It didn't matter how many battles I'd won in the past; I'd never be as brave as Lor. The way she always put her heart on the line and fought for normalcy in a realm that did not want her had put me to shame.

"Then do it now," she said, snapping me out of my self-deprecating thoughts. She stood to her feet. "Dance with me."

I looked around, almost believing for a split second there was someone else in the room she had asked. I wiped my sweaty palms on my pants. "There's no music. The player is in the living room."

Lor shook her head. "Stop overthinking and just dance with me."

She held out her hand in demand. I wrapped my arm around her waist, and we were so close, dangerously close. With my other hand in hers, I moved my feet in a slow rhythm to a song stuck in my head. Her hands clung to my neck, drawing little circles as we moved around the room, the red dress whirring around her feet. Then I heard the most beautiful sound. She sang like a whisper in the wind. I could not comprehend the words, so lost in the sound. *There's nothing good to sing about,* " she'd once said. Today was her birthday, and yet she gave me the sweetest gift and had chosen that moment to lift her voice. I kept her close to me, not wanting to miss a thing. Our stars glimmered in unison, like a gentle tide rolling in. I was going to explode from all this warmth invading me inside out.

The dance ended, and I sat her back down. I turned to pour faerie wine for both of us as her gaze penetrated my back. After handing her a silver cup, we gulped it down lazily, losing track of the time. Lor's party was still going strong outside by the sounds of the lyres and raucous laughter.

"I need to come clean," she said, wiping drops from her lips. Her hand tightened around her cup. "I thought it would be better if I were the victim just to prove I was, in fact, unlovable."

There was so much in that sentence I wanted to refute but the heaviness that built inside her needed to be crushed. I wanted to tell her she was wrong.

She set down her cup. "Please, Riann, let me finish."

My hand folded in hers as she fought to bring me this confession.

Her eyes closed, as she pushed herself off the proverbial cliff. "For my whole life, I was nothing. Just a bit of darkness in the corner nobody cared about. That was until you called for me down that bridge. After everything happened, I rejected you out of spite. I was angry with you. The mature, internal person inside me said to talk with you to smooth things out, but I preferred being a victim and making you suffer. All because I wanted to prove to you that I could not be loved." A tear slid down the birthday girl's face. "For that, I must ask you to forgive me."

I wiped away her tear. "Lor, there is nothing to be forgiven. I deserved it."

She pulled herself away from my touch. "That's just it. You didn't deserve it. You did not deserve to have your realm taken away. Your mother telling you that you must suffer to be stronger. You sure as hell did not deserve those women taking advantage of you or Phil being a terrible friend when you lost everything."

My hand found her face again. "So, that is what you saw. Terrible things."

More tears came. "Riann, when I was in there, I wanted to hold you, to erase all those awful things everyone did to you. All I could do was forgive you and beg you to wake up. I believed my voice, my pleading voice, was not enough when you did not wake." She inhaled a deep breath, fumbling her hand in mine. "You *are* good enough. If there's anything I should have said when I was in there, it is that you *are* enough for me."

I closed the space between us, pulling myself to her side, brushing our knees together. "I felt you there. I couldn't see where I was, but I felt you."

Lor shook her head. "You had no memory to cling to. None. It broke my heart. You've been saving realms all this time, yet there was no memory powerful enough to pull you out." Her voice broke like a dam. "It was a dream. A beautiful dream of us—with children. A lone boy sitting on a swing. One boy full of black curls playing ball with you outside. Another little boy with curious blue eyes like yours clinging to my legs. And a baby girl asleep in my arms, who looked as sweet as can be. That's what kept you alive long enough."

My impossible dream. Children with her without this curse. A family. Something I longed for but could never have. I hung my head, on the brink of crying with her. "And did that scare you?"

"What? No!" She squeezed the bridge of her nose. "I mean. I knew you wanted me, but I had no clue you wanted everything else. I'm messing this up." She palmed her forehead. "No, what I want to say is"—her shoulders slumped, fighting the last bit of words to roll off her tongue—"your dreams are my dreams, Riann. I want it all with you. Whatever the odds."

Frozen on the sofa, I let seconds pass without a breath or so much as a word. I'd spent eons waiting for her, and now she was here. I was so scared of making the wrong move.

"I'm sorry," she said, sniffling, breaking the silence. "I think I spoke too soon. I should get back to the party."

Lor headed for the door, and I was still on the sofa. *Get up, idiot. Don't let her leave. If she leaves after that confession, you will regret it. She poured out her heart to you. If you let her leave, I shall crown you the king of the idiots. Be a man and get up. Get up. Get up!*

She turned the doorknob, and as quick as lightning, I slammed it shut.

"Riann, what are you—?" I interrupted her with a crush of my lips on hers. After her initial surprise, she softened against me, returning my affections with just as much fervor.

"Forever is a long time, Lor," I whispered against her neck. "And right now, I have every intention of tying myself to you." I slid my hand off the door, placing it on her shoulder. "There's the door if you do not wish it."

There was no hesitation, no staggering. She sealed her choice by kissing me again in return. Her hands roved up and down my back, finding the hem of my tunic. Effortlessly, she shucked it off. "I wish it." She pressed her lips on my neck.

My fears and insecurity faded into the distance to claim this moment with Lor. I always knew, deep down, we would end up here, and I could not wait any longer. Though the darkness screamed at me I was not good enough for her, a kernel of hope remained. And she stood by me through it all.

"Wait." I dug into my pocket and took out a knotted gold ring I'd crafted in Dolos' workspace. A rough amethyst nestled in the center of a single knot in the ring, glittering in the flames, like an infinity loop. We were each other's beginning, and each other's end. "I know marriage here is not what you imagined, so I wanted to give this to you." On one knee, I slid the ring on her finger. "I vow to love you forever, to cherish you, devote myself completely to you, and to always find you in the darkest of places."

Her eyes moistened, and she laughed sweetly while lowering herself to meet my gaze. "I wish I had a ring for you. But I, too, vow to love you, to be a steady warmth, and to always find you in the darkest of places."

I pulled myself up, savoring every kiss and touch. Every strap and tie came loose. Though we were both nervous, we smiled as we bared ourselves. Her star-spun hair spread on my pillows, and her eyes raked over me with such love and anticipation. I embraced her and we found little room between us. She ran her delicate fingers behind my ear and pulled me even closer. She gasped with her eyes wide open, wholly unguarded. I could not get close enough to her as I kissed her tenderly, swallowing every little sound she made. Veins of purple and gold starlight glowed beneath our skin, taking the little I had and giving it all to her. In return, her magic absorbed into me, making me feel stronger and more alive than I have in years. Light exploded, and I saw nothing else around us. All I could do was bask in its warmth, in the feel of her arms around me. Flits of dark light I'd never seen before sunk into her. My hands were in hers, and everything felt like a crescendo of a beautiful song building. She said my name, branding me. Our ragged breaths met. The chorus intensified the melody. Each note became higher and faster than the next. Her voice tuned to the rhythm as though she could pluck each chord from the air. The runes on my head burned as her fingers grabbed for purchase. Beautiful music rose from her voice, higher than before. Then, the symphony softened. The song finally met its end. We paused, gazing into each other's eyes. A sense of elation and disbelief overwhelmed me. She was worth the wait. I laid my head on her chest; her heart wildly beat like a drum. She slid down, meeting my teary gaze, and kissed every tear away.

"My cymar, my only," I whispered.

She smiled, glowed even, and pressed her lips to mine before surrendering to sleep. I knew Dolos would crack a joke about me not being an eight hundred-year-old virgin anymore, but I'd discovered his secret. It was not just the act of lying with a woman that drove a man crazy. It was afterward, when she laid in your arms feeling safe and protected. I felt like I could do victory laps as Lor breathed softly, peacefully in my arms.

46

ELORA

Sleep eluded us. No complaints. Losing count of how many times Riann woke me up with his eager kisses was new and exhilarating. He had a tiny smile on his face as he slept so close to me. It was the first time I'd seen him sleep peacefully. The wrinkles on his forehead smoothed out and the cinch between his brows evened. All the weight and sadness he carried lightened, and breath by breath, he came alive again. Carefully, I peeled myself from him, and made my way to the kitchen in one of his white tunics. Surprised to see Dolos standing there with his arms crossed, I blushed. He knew. It was so obvious.

"Long night?" he asked, tapping his fingers on his elbows.

I lit the stove to boil water in the silver kettle for tea and noticed my reflection in the glass pitcher on the counter. My hair was tangled against my flushed skin. The kettle whistled as I threw loose tea leaves in a small sieve. Sweet, floral and orange aroma steamed upward as Dolos continued to stand there, anxiously waiting for details.

Daring to look at him, my face reddened. "Didn't feel long," I singsonged while pouring our tea. Fresh honeycombs from the glass jar looked so pleasing that I grabbed extra to have on its own after adding it to the tea. Hot and inviting, I took a sip.

"Well, that's good to hear," he yawned, stretching his arms overhead. "I thought we were going to have to get him fixed. He started spraying everywhere since you arrived."

I spit my drink out. "Dolos!" I threw a kitchen towel at him.

"Hey! It was a serious problem for the furniture!" he laughed, rounding the kitchen island.

Seriously, though. It was a good one. I howled with laughter and gave him a side hug.

"Do you feel any different?" he asked, taking the towel and wiping the countertop.

With another sip, I processed our time together. Sharing our magic had happened once. Afterward, the starlight ebbed and faded away, and then it was just me and Riann. For too long, I believed I would be an object, something to tire of once it had been used too many times. But with Riann, I never feared that. He saw me. He heard me across the stars. What others had done to me kept me at a cautious distance from feeling anything real. Over time, with Riann's patience and warmth, my heart had fluttered. Something had blossomed in me, reminding me I was alive. We did not have the easiest road to walk and would continue to face challenges. Now that we were so much closer to each other, I believed we could take on anything. I'd never realized until last night, seeing him completely undone, that I was a healing balm for his wounds as much as he was for mine.

"I know he feels different," I said with a sly smile before taking another sip. "I don't feel any different, magically speaking, but I feel...closer. Like I belong to someone."

"Because you do, blondie," he said matter-of-factly. "If Riann feels stronger because of the magic you poured into him, don't be surprised by a frenzy he's in or bloodlust if someone harms you."

"I can never imagine Riann being—"

Dolos cut me off with a fiery glare. "You've never seen him fully fledged in his power. I have."

My lips parted, and my feet wobbled. A twinge of fear edged with excitement pebbled my skin. It should scare me, but it didn't. One more sip. "Dolos, you owe me a conversation."

A flash of anger rippled across his face. "I owe nothing. I just need time to clear my head." He turned away from me and marched out the door.

A part of me wanted to chase after him, yet another part of me wanted to respect his boundaries and let him speak on his own time. I shuffled back to the room with a tray of fruits, tea, and honeycombs. Riann sat upright in bed with the sheet draped over his legs.

A bright smile greeted me. "My, my, this is a first. You brought breakfast to me."

The silver tray clattered against the table. "Don't get used to it." Suddenly, his warm arms were around my waist, startling me. "That was fast," I laughed. "Don't be such an assassin."

Indeed, it was entirely too fast. Rian had never moved like that before; a taste of how he used to be before the curse. The magic given to him during our joining restored something in him, but not completely. We needed to find the horn and figure out how to put it back on Luna. I tried several times to summon her but to no avail.

"You took too long out there. I woke up the moment you left," he murmured, peppering kisses down my shoulder.

"I was speaking with Dolos. Jig is up. He knows about us," I giggled.

"Let him know," he said, pressing his lips to my neck. I inhaled deeply. "Let them all know."

***

Days of passion bled into one another. Weeks even. As soon as I completed training in the mornings, I was with Riann in his room. For fun, I hung a shirt on the outside of his door to let people know not to disturb us. Lex gave a boisterous laugh after jiggling the knob as a joke. After another round, I laid on Riann's chest, his fingers twirling my hair. Our time before the games was fleeting. I felt a surge of confidence after defeating Phil, but now, much more was at stake. I could not bear Riann's devastation if something were to happen to me.

My body felt heavy as I burrowed my head into his chest. "Do you think I will make it...in the games?"

His hand stilled above me. "To be honest, at first, I thought you were done for. But I've seen you become stronger, quicker over the past few months. If you can take down Phil and Lex, I believe you can take down whatever that woman throws at you."

His shot of confidence made my star glow. "She has not come for us since aiding the fauns," I said, drawing circles on his chest.

He ran his hand down his face. "This is a game to her. Testing our defenses. She believes we are some rebel stain. But it is strange she hasn't sent sentries. Like she's waiting for something."

I propped myself up on his chest. "Have you tried to get in her mind?"

"A million times. She has so many walls and locks that it's impossible."

"Have you checked in with Mikhail? He was the one to warn us, after all."

Riann smacked his lips. "My bridge shattered into pieces when I died." We held each other tightly with those last three words. "It takes time to rebuild, and as you can see"—he softly kissed my head—"I've been rather busy."

With a small laugh against his chest, I looked up and found those longing eyes again. "Riann, we should spend time with our friends."

He leaned his head back, sighing heavily. "You're right. I don't want them to think I keep you chained to the bed."

"Oh, Dolos would love to hear that one," I laughed, throwing my legs over the bed. I hadn't dressed in casual clothes since our joining. Usually, I wore my leathers after training and then a whole lot of nothing after. I took his baggy tunic and trousers, belting it as tight as possible. I would've just raided Willa's wardrobe like I always did, but wearing Riann's clothes felt so right.

Everyone was in the living room eating leftovers from a few nights ago. Lately, Riann hardly cooked. I'm sure we were the butt of their jokes. Willa shot up from her seat upon seeing us hand in hand and turned on the music. "Lovebirds are out of their cage!" she squealed, turning the volume all the way up.

Bass riffs and heavy guitars immediately sunk under my skin, and I ran, pushing her, and tearing at her shirt. A two person mosh pit was just as fun as a crowd. Riann watched me in fits of laughter and smiles.

When I'd first arrived, he was so much like a wilted flower needing sunlight, and I was so happy to be that for him. We'd struggled, finally finding our way to each other in the darkness.

Faerie wine misted the room as Dolos cracked open a fresh bottle. I stuck my tongue out, gathering the sweet drops on my tongue. Riann could not help himself and kissed me deeply in front of everyone to show me off. I'd never been one for being the center of attention, but I welcomed this. I was his, and he was mine.

"Bro, let her breathe! It's bad enough I can smell your room from here," said Dolos, drinking straight from the bottle. "I know you love your hard music, blondie, but tonight"—Dolos switched CDs and cranked up the volume—"it's the eighties."

Synthesized beats and lyrics reminding me of freezing hair spray and feathered bangs blaring around us. Even Riann danced a little, cutting loos more than any of us had ever seen. Lex turned red after Willa cracked a joke how sealing the deal made Riann more fun. Dolos pulled out a little strobe light. Colors danced across the room as Phil sat stone-faced, tapping his toes ever so slightly to the beat. I pulled on his arms to our makeshift dance floor, but he wouldn't budge. I guessed having fun was not for everyone.

Riann whispered into my ear, "This, right now, is one of my dreams. All of us together."

I pecked him on the cheek. "Mine too."

Riann was kind enough to bake cookies. Wearing nothing but knee-length breeches and a black apron, he whipped all the ingredients together. I showed him a picture of Snickerdoodles years ago, and he remembered. Sugar and cinnamon wafted into the living room as we played a raucous game of Would You Rather. Of course, Dolos amped up his dirty thoughts, trying to make me and Riann blush. The room filled with so much laughter that even granite-faced Phil smirked.

Lex almost slid off the couch, completely inebriated, slurring his words. He strung together a sentence that came out like: "Been there, done that." Willa blushed and covered her face with a throw pillow, muffling her laughter.

I pranced to the kitchen and hugged Riann from behind while he put on gloves to get the cookies out of the oven. "It's a good thing you're the only one sober. If we were in my old realm, you would be the designated driver," I giggled, pressing the tips of my fingers onto his rock-hard stomach.

"I like having a clear head." He lowered his eyes. "I guess I'm not as exciting as Dolos."

I rounded him and stood just under his chin. With a mischievous grin, I grazed my finger along his jawline. "Are you jealous?"

"Well, he's always been more exciting than me," he said, cracking half a smile.

Standing on my tiptoes, I kissed his neck. "I will always want you."

His eyes were gleeful, and he pushed me against the counter, delivering the most savage kiss. The noise faded in the background, and it was simply him and me for a moment. Abruptly, he pulled away, his body taut. Everything in him darkened. "Someone is at the line," his voice was guttural.

Riann shucked off his apron and swiftly retrieved his sword from his room, brandishing cold steel, alarming everyone. Joy snuffed out, and the music died down. Blue threads vibrated and came to life in the hilt's crystal. It became clear his sword was alive, a living sword, breathing to strike down an enemy. Lex shot to his feet, nodding his head at Riann. All of his drunken stupor winked out as he followed Riann outside. I ran after them.

"Stay," Dolos said, shaking his head.

Phil leaned back in his chair, appearing conflicted about whether he should follow suit.

"He's my cymar. I go where he goes," I snapped at Dolos as he yanked on my arm to keep me from going.

"Lor, trust us. If Riann senses any harm coming to you, it will be something you cannot un-see," Willa said, keeping her voice calm and steady.

I pulled my arm free. "I'll be the judge of that."

Dolos chased after me as I ran for the demarcation line. Hues of magenta flickered at the crest of the hill. Runes and wheels of spells spun up and down the line while three minotaurs in black-scaled armor approached with a scroll in hand. Riann stepped over the line and snatched the scroll from his hand. A deadly rage rippled across his face. His eyes blackened like an abyss, and shadows gathered around him.

"This was not the deal we made. we have thirty more days!" Riann's voice pierced.

Lex side-glanced at me. His eyes widened, telling me I shouldn't be here.

The minotaur with curled horns and black fur stood over Riann, his eyes bloodshot. "Let us look at the human pet. So that our queen may—"

They'd seen me. Their mouths parted, and they stepped forward. Dolos grabbed me by the hem of my shirt. Riann withdrew his sword and became mist as he swung at all three minotaurs. It all happened so quickly. Blood sprayed my face. Their heads rolled down the hill from the sheer force of Riann's sword. I felt like a fist seized my lungs. *This was not the first time you've seen death*, I reminded myself. Shadows of wrath wrapped around Riann. He blinked. There was nothing in his eyes but a void of darkness. It was as if his soul departed. Riann cupped my face with his blood-splattered hands, his chest heaving in and out, reminding me that it was still him in there.

"They wanted to see your eyes. I could not let them go back alive." His voice sounded unnatural, otherworldly. He took several steps ahead of me. "You've been summoned. The games start tomorrow."

I didn't know how long I stood there, watching flies hover over the corpses nobody gave a second thought to dispose of. I had thirty more days. Thirty. The deal was broken, likely because we aided the fauns. But if we had not, too many would have died. I hurled my guts onto the grass. No way was I ready, but I had to be. Or she would come for our friends. I had no clue if she knew Riann lived. I wiped my mouth with shaky hands. Pale, orange light on the ground glowed ominously. Shaken to the core, I could not believe what I had seen Riann do, what he had become. Was this how he was before the curse? Was this what Dolos meant all those weeks ago about his bloodlust?

They wanted to see your eyes.

Queen Nyx suspected I was the lilac child, and she pushed the games to confirm it. I didn't want to do it, but I had no choice but to call down Mikhail's bridge. His door had new fissures on it, but I knocked anyway, only to find it cracked open. I felt him whimper in murky darkness. A familiar cloud of smokey fingers hung over him. Something was wrong. Clattering sounds of chains fell against a stone floor.

"Mike," I whispered. *"Your brother is alive and the queen is coming for me. Help us."*

The clattering stopped, and I heard him gasp as if he were coming up for air. *"I cannot help you."* His voice strangled. *"When you come tomorrow, rain down fire."*

After everything he had done, I felt pity. *"Mike—"*

"I've done all I can for you."

"What have they done to you?!"

"Tell my brother I am sorry. As for you, Lor, I wish I had been kinder." He blasted me out of his door, locking it tight.

I yelled his name several times before giving up and shifting back to the reality of dead minotaurs in front of me. Bile crept up my throat, but I stuffed it down. I straightened myself up, taking several deep breaths. *Rain down fire.* Veins of gold with flits of what looked like dark light ran like a river down my arms. My eyes felt hot, smoldering, as my hands burned like red-hot coals. I looked at the house containing my cymar and my family and made up my mind. No longer would I be someone's victim or let any harm come to those I loved. A scythe appeared in each hand, readying themselves. Tomorrow, I'd play in her games and show the people how weak their queen truly was.

47

RIANN

Fire pulsated my veins. Lor had been threatened, and our cymar bond kicked into high gear. Did I regret killing the messengers? Not one bit. She still remained by the magenta line, stunned, but I had to leave, not sure what else I was capable of. Lex led me to a copse of trees and allowed me to burn off the raging energy inside. He had a cymar and knew what it was like. Lex had done unspeakable things to protect Willa; things that continued to haunt him. He absorbed every punch and kick with such patience. Shadows dissipated, and my vision cleared. Never once had I displayed shadows. Even in my darkest moments, nothing like this had happened to me, and I could not understand why. Time was of the essence, and I simply could not delve into the reason behind it. Either this was awakened by our joining, or something had happened when I came back to life. I hated myself for badly bruising Lex, but he just stood there smirking, like it was nothing but flea bites. By the time we came back to the house, Lor sat on the couch dazed, her face streaked with red.

Wordlessly, I scooped her in my arms and headed to our private bath. Her breath hitched as I set her down and shed her clothes, puddling them at our feet. Her body was taut like a bowstring, though she did not shudder from my touch. When I lowered her into the warm bath and lathered soap on her shoulders, she breathed a sigh of relief. Washing blood off her face was the last thing I imagined us doing today.

"I'm sorry you had to see that today." My voice was scorched as I squeezed more water over her shoulders.

"You did what you had to." She clasped my hand in hers, resting it on her shoulder. "I would have done the same." Lor dunked her head underwater, rinsing off suds. Water ran down in rivulets over her eyes as she blinked at me and pressed her head to mine. "Tomorrow Riann, tomorrow."

I cupped her face in my hands. "I cannot let you go. We had more time."

"If I do not go, our friends will die. She's not just after us," she said, spinning her finger in a circle. "She's after the faeries, the fauns, and she will come for the Draconians. You spent most of your existence protecting the innocent. It's my turn."

I ran my hand from her crown to her nape, giving a wicked smirk. "Am I crazy for wanting to see what wicked things you can do in the arena?"

She giggled while biting her lip.

"Lor, how will I restrain myself if some troll knocks you to your feet or some ghoul comes at you with a sword?" Imagining her being harmed made my star burn, rivers of light coursing through me. I couldn't lose her. Not now, not ever. Though at that moment, I needed to be strong for Lor, to believe in her. Not crumble or falter beneath her touch.

She placed my hand on own her wild heartbeat, undoing any restraint I had. "Trust and believe I will come out, no matter the odds."

We cried in each other's arms, brutally kissing. Even though I had no intention of being intimate with her, we gave in to each other, as though it would be our last time.

✳✳✳

Phil paced around the living room, cupping his hand over his chin. "The arena has defenses we cannot break through. And even if we could, it is surrounded by sentries with innocents in the stadium. We cannot risk those lives."

"I know the castle better than you," I said. "If things go wrong, she needs a way out."

"And what then!?" Phil slammed his hand on the kitchen island. "She runs home where they will come and slaughter us?!"

My lips thinned. With Lor's hand tucked under my leg, squeezing slightly, she gave me peace. "There are exits underneath the arena. If we hide by two of them, she can make it out. We can take down the sentries. If you are on the west end and I am in the east, she has a better chance of escaping."

Phil's face darkened. "We do not know what the layout of the games will be. What if she is engulfed in complete darkness where ghouls rise from the ground? Remember those games from ten years ago? Elora won't be able to see anything!"

Tendrils of gold flared from Lor's hand. "Yes, I will!"

Phil lowered his hands. "I admit you're at an advantage, Lor, but the element of surprise can hurt you, or worse."

"What if I sit in the stands?" suggested Willa. "Riann, your bridge is broken but I can still mind speak with Lor. I have the higher ground where I can see every turn." Lex's eyes widened, and he wound his hand tightly around Willa's. "My love, I will be hidden. Nobody will pay attention to the nosebleeds anyway, and Wren will glamour me." He nuzzled his head in the crook of her neck. "Please do not worry, we need you to go between the east and west ends and crack skulls if needed."

Phil rolled his eyes, pinning his gaze on Dolos. "Plan on being useful?"

Dolos eyes simmered as he swigged down his guava juice. Faerie wine was out of the question for this discussion. He sat in the same seat I had when I agreed to the games. Plush beige pillows billowed around him as if he were sinking into the couch. He ran his finger around the rim of his cup, pursing his lips. He darted a glance at me, his face softening just a little before turning back to Phil.

"If I set off explosives, it will jeopardize rescuing Lor. They will ramp up their defenses, and Nyx will use her bloodthirsty magic in a heartbeat. That being said, if I was given a signal, I could set black powder with fuses far outside the arena to distract Nyx and her monsters while Lor makes a run for it." Dolos tipped back his head, gulping down his drink. "Is that useful enough for you?"

Phil's red eyes flickered like running magma. "This is a suicide mission."

Dolos almost choked on his drink. "What mission hasn't been?!" He slammed his cup down, spilling the contents on the side table. "We fought against the sorcerers in Naavarin. The brute emperor and his undead army in Sashayn. We watched two realms crash into each other because the fates were not happy with our choice to cut off the royal lineages. They saw fit to destroy a whole realm rather than let the people live! But on Zaire and Tanjirun, we fought and dismantled an entire kingdom and their cultural acceptance of keeping slaves. How many slaves did we free? How many masters did we kill? What did it cost us?!"

I gulped. The constant reminder of all the blood we'd shed in the name of freedom. Sometimes it was worth it, and other times I questioned our choices. "Seriously. How many times have we faced impossible odds and came out on top?" I demanded, my voice rising.

Phil surged across the room. "You must be stupid because you keep forgetting we do not have our powers!"

Lor removed her hand, and she gripped the edge of the couch, ready to pounce. "Call him stupid again," she dared.

Phil appeared dumbfounded. She'd beat him at his own game, and he still looked at her as if she did not have the right to speak. I found it strange he shed a tear for her after we returned from the Draconians only to meet her with animosity afterward. His nostrils flared as he fought to say something. Anything. But he knew too well; it would become a brawl between us.

Lor met his glare. "Riann took a massive risk taking your powers. And because of that, you are alive and well enough to complain about how you cannot do anything without them. But tell me again how stupid he was when he put his life on the line for someone who refused to console him when he lost his entire realm."

"Lor, please," I whispered. Everyone darted glances between me and Phil before Lor realized what she'd said.

Her fists remained clenched together. "Nobody calls Riann stupid. He was smart enough to play the game to keep everyone alive at a steep cost."

I caught Lex curling a smile at Lor—like a proud papa—as Phil lowered his head and blew out a breath. "I got carried away, forgive me," he said brusquely. "I will remain on the west end as requested." He pivoted his foot and walked out of the house to cool off, slamming the door behind him.

Dolos dangled half his body off the arm of the couch. "Blondie, if there's anyone that I believe could pull off these games, it's you. Don't let Phil get in your head. He's always been a tightwad." He stretched his arms, yawning. "It's time you all rest. Not me though. My house of horrors is calling my name."

After Dolos left, Lex and Willa quietly went to their room, leaving me and Lor alone in the living room. As each second ticked by, I found myself so grateful to have her in my arms as we stared at the flames in the fireplace. I had been able to slow time down before the curse. I used it to our advantage on the battlefield. There was nothing I wouldn't give to slow it down right then. Fates were cruel, and at best, they could be kind. I believed Lor could overcome anything, but I still feared the worst. Anything could happen in the games. Every dream I had of Lor vaporized. The only dream I could cling to now was her surviving and running back into my arms. Impossibly brave, Lor would do anything to protect us. I'd wronged her so many times, but now, I'd learned to surrender. Letting Lor protect us was my white flag, and as I ran my fingers over her constellation, a twinge of heated rage simmered beneath her skin. I could not deny that I wanted to see her burn.

48

ELORA

Bright sparkling pillars scintillating with flashes of blue under pale pink skies reminded me of the colosseum in Rome. Mischief was afoot as goblins, minotaurs, and nymphs galore filled the seats of the amphitheater. As difficult as it was, Riann let me go a few miles from the entrance before being ushered by a hobgoblin into the holding area. His pockmarked skin and bulging nose cast shadows over his rounded face from the torch he held.

"Grim's the name," he said, eyeing me from head to toe. "Be good for Prince Mikhail, pretty pet." His round eyes twinkled. "I can see why he misses you."

The corridor into the holding area was so dark, I barely made out the rounded archways. Something about this hobgoblin seemed kind, yet disgusting in the most endearing way. There was no way to discover if Grim was trustworthy, but I had nothing to lose.

I placed my hand on the back of his filthy vest and felt rough edges underneath as if there were rocks or diamonds sown into it. "Is the prince okay?"

He shrugged his shoulders, shifting his eyes downward. "No. I have been his faithful servant and friend all these years and have seen the things she has done to him. Leading you in here right now would likely be a death sentence for me, but I had to get to you first before those sentries did. She instructed them to weaken you before you enter the games."

A slice of fear cut through me. "Weaken me?"

"My lady, I am the ears of the castle." Grim pulled on the hem of my leather fighting pants. "Do not fear. My kin have distracted them."

"How so?"

His full, cracked lips arched into an impish smile. "Mischief."

"Does his own mother torture him?"

He tugged at his patchwork pants. "Pretty pet, you must save him. You must save us all. It's her power in him which she uses to beat him to submission." His beady eyes glistened, and he cursed under his breath, shifting his hand in his pocket. "Here." He placed a tiny, mangy scroll in my hand. "The prince sends his regards."

Grim left me to find the rest of my way. Glittering light flickered the closer I came to the end of the corridor. A series of rounded arches and faded red stones bled into one another. Cracked paintings of winged creatures and layers of different landscapes and colors sprawled across the walls. Clutching the scroll tight, I wondered what it said. Was it a map? An apology letter? I really hoped that it was not the latter because apologies sound too much like goodbye—and I was not ready to die. Torches slowly came into focus, glowing on the pillars on both sides, revealing large, ornate wooden doors. A jovial crowd roared above as dust fell onto my shoulders. Quickly, I unraveled the scroll. Some of the ink was smudged as if he'd written it in a hurry and then hid it somewhere dirty so they could not find it.

It was no apology letter, but a warning.

It's a trap.

Thank you for showing up.

I shut my eyes tight and landed on Mikhail's bridge. It cracked and groaned under my weight in a cavern of deep darkness. It felt lonely and hopeless. Mike kept a façade of bravado, but it quickly shattered under the thumb of his mother. Regardless of what he'd done to me, I found a space in my heart to forgive him. If he was indeed a product of his environment it compelled me to have mercy. At the same time, I needed to know if his heart was true. I needed to know if was really for us. His door was straight ahead, but I had no time to run across.

"Mikhail, did you trap us?!"

...

"Answer me."

...

"I will kill you and your mother if you touch any of my family."

Static. *"Lor."* His voice was rough, uneven. *"I am your family."*

My heart wrenched. *"What do you mean?!"*

"Save us."

"What has she done?!"

"More than enough."

"Stop being so cryptic!"

"The Hag, the Yaga, and the queen have their claws in me. They have been playing us all since your arrival. They will soon destroy everyone and everything in Sidh. They know who you are."

Connection dead.

A sharp pang of anxiety ripped through me. Those monsters were the three figures on the hill the day we'd aided the fauns. They knew I was the lilac child and had put me in these games to kill me and steal the star of first light. My family sat on a tinderbox, and they didn't even know it.

"Willa, pull everyone out and run home."

"No way! I'm already seated. What happened?"

"Mikhail. The queen knows who I am. This is all a trap."

She gasped. *"I will not leave you down there."*

"Please," I begged. *"If I can save you guys today, that will matter more to me than my own life."*

"Lor! Imagine Riann's reaction. He will not pull away." Willa paused. *"I will not pull away."*

My sister across realms. If I didn't know any better, I would have said we shared the same heart before finding each other. I never had a friend or family, but Willa had taken me right in, despite the darkness of my soul. Anyone could say they loved me because of my starlight. But when I'd laughed with them and exposed my ugly parts, their affections had settled in my bones. My family was all that mattered to me. And yet, there were thousands in Sidh who cared just as much for their families and want to go home. My star flared, an untamed, unbridled flame.

I stopped begging Willa to leave, trusting everyone to be safe once I made it out on the other side.

My nerves blistered, but my voice remained steady. *"We are misfits. We do not bow."*

The crowd roared for the appearance of their queen. Willa shifted and let out a long breath. *"We are misfits. We do not bow."*

Nyx made the announcement for the games, and cheers erupted throughout the stadium, shaking more dust onto my shoulders. Her slithering voice coiled down my spine. I set my hands on the large wooden doors. Vibrations of cheers rumbled beneath my feet, but I felt something else. Rough plods knocked me to my knees. Too scared to move and yet too impatient to get back to my family, I rose to my feet.

"I see the arena, Lor," Willa said. *"First, it will be a forest of trees, seemingly harmless, but I have seen movement. Get through the forest and you will be in a clearing that appears to be water but test it first."* Willa paused, as though she were squinting to find more in the labyrinth. *"The end is the crystal dais beyond a circular stone formation, where the white flag is."*

The doors creaked open.

"Oh my god, this is really happening. If anything happens to me, please tell Riann I love him, and I wish we had more time. But more importantly, tell him we will always have tomorrow."

"Shut up, dearie. You got this."

49

MIKHAIL

Sitting between the Hag and Yaga in their physical form made me want to wretch. The Yaga appeared elderly, with a hunched back, dressed in silver royal garb. Her crazy sister, the Hag, looked ethereal. Her fine black hair and aqua eyes lured men into her grasp, but she never smiled. If she did, she would reveal her needle-like teeth. Teeth that have torn through flesh and souls over the eons. My loving mother and desiccated father sat in the center of the podium, waving numbly. I wished I could move, but sitting between these two cannibals caused my power to take a deep dive. I was completely useless. My mother was right. She put the power in me; she could take it back. Mikhail, the prince of Sidh. Mikhail, the powerless. If I spoke anymore to Lor, the Hag would snag that bit of hope from me. I couldn't think of *her* anymore. The one always tucked away in my heart. They could just kill me if they robbed me of her. My last shred of joy. My most precious memory of being completely, unselfishly loved.

Riann was out there, putting himself in danger for her, his cymar. I wished I was not jealous, but a pang of want eased into my gut. I stuffed it down quickly to not give away its scent. Across the stadium, I saw the green water nymph, glamoured as a golden-kissed goddess under a hood. Wren's glamours were not lost on me. I could only hope Lor made it out in one piece, but not without burning everything in sight first.

Trees moved below, splitting to make a path. The shine of balding gray scalps appeared under pink skies. Trolls. My mother let out the hungry trolls. Their wide girth equaled to three of Lex. They only understood hunger and could smell Lor from a distance. However, they were blind as could be, which put her at an advantage. If Riann and his ragtag team were smart enough, they would have already taught Lor how to wield her magic. Sometimes, I wished she'd never locked her door on the bridge. At least I could have seen what she was capable of without creating my own conclusions. Wine spilled on the crimson carpet as my mother tossed her hair back, laughing over the incoming trolls, expecting carnage. If Lor did what I suspected she could, I would gladly wrap these black chains around my mother instead and savor her struggle to breathe.

50

ELORA

Two monstrous beings wearing loin cloths charged after me. Bare, wide chests and bulging stomachs glistened with sweat. Their clouded eyes and ragged breath revealed hunger, the desire to hunt. They ran into trees, losing their footing over rocks. Trees rocked and groaned under the pressure. It did not take long to realize they were blind. Grunting and growling, they stumbled, becoming frustrated that their dinner was not easily caught. Sliding fear into my back pocket, I nimbly ran across jutted rocks so as not to make a sound on the soft earth. One barked a primal sound while the other sniffed his nose to pick up on my scent. I hid behind a tree for a moment, catching my breath. When I peeked around, I saw their sunken rib cages. How dare she starve them for her own entertainment! Flash of fury made my star writhe with need. I did not want to make a spectacle of my powers, at least not yet. If I gave it away too early, the queen could stop the games and come down herself.

Sweat rolled down my back as I launched myself into a sprint. My feet hurt from jumping rock to rock. For a moment, I leaned against another tree to catch my breath, but it was useless. Thunderous feet plodded in my direction. My heart thundered. If I was going to do anything, it had to be done under the shadow of trees where nobody could see. My star fell into rhythm with my will, and I opened my hands. Glimmering gold daggers with blades as thin as needles formed above my palms. There were ten in each hand. I hesitated. Harming them felt wrong after seeing how starved they were. A troll snorted his nose past the tree and swatted his hand. A rush of wind almost knocked me to the ground, but the daggers stayed in place. The other troll twisted his back, stomping his feet. Dust from pulverized rocks crept into my nose. *Don't you dare sneeze. Don't you dare.* Golden daggers remained steadfast, but then my nose crinkled, and I let out a sneeze I swore the whole crowd could hear.

Their clouded eyes darted my way, and I didn't have time to think or move. Their hands swept the area closing fists around what they thought was me. *This is self defense*, I convinced myself. My daggers flew into their chests. Nothing happened at first. It was an assassin's wound that nobody could see until it was too late. They stood for a moment, silent, dumbfounded. Brackish blood oozed from their wounds, and the daggers buried deep in them twisted and turned on my command. Their eyes lowered as they looked at each other, their hands clasped to their wide, hairless chests. The ground groaned as they teetered, reaching their hands to grab onto anything. Blood dribbled down one's mouth, and he fell to his knees before landing face first, knocking down the surrounding trees. The other gave a frightful look, collapsing next to him. I took cover from the splintering trunks and snapping branches by casting an invisible shield over me. My first kill. It had been self defense. Me or them. Yet, I felt heavy.

Applause roared like a wave. They cheered me on, and here I was, believing they were here to see me be slaughtered.

Willa released a breath. *"My goodness, dearie, glad to see your training has paid off. Just an FYI. Rumors about you have spread in Sidh."*

"What rumors?" I grunted, crawling over the downed trees.

"I can hear others talk about the golden one. Especially the goblins. We are all rooting for you, girl."

"I wish Riann could see."

"Darling, he can hear."

Though my legs wobbled, the surge of adrenalin propelled me forward. I trudged past the forest clearing and came upon pink sand bordering a lake that stretched as far as I could see. Across was a sand dune rippling through the land before meeting a copse of dark, withered trees. With a long branch, I walked knee-deep into the dark waters, poking around. Icy water sloshed around a gash in my upper leg I didn't know I'd gotten. Everything appeared normal, but I knew better. Something was in there, waiting for me to swim across. I wondered if one of the trees was large enough to throw across—then, I could just walk. But that would mean showing off my magic too soon.

I poked around with the stick in a stabbing motion. *"Can you see anything stirring beneath?"*

"Nothing. It can't be trusted. You and I have seen enough movies."

I let out a dry laugh. *"That's for sure."*

There was absolutely no way to make a raft. Even if I floated on something, it did not mean I would be safe from whatever lurked beneath. If my leathers felt uncomfortable with all this sweat, they were going to feel even worse taking a chance across this proverbial Red Sea. Just then, I heard a whisper in the breeze.

"Daughter of Eos, swim."

My mother's name. The voice was like velvet and starlight, settling in my bones. Something about that warm voice was familiar and yet new. I flexed my fingers, ready to strike, and walked deeper. Waist deep in the water, it was my last chance to turn away from certain doom. I hesitated. Yet, that voice beckoned me. There was no bridge when it spoke, as if the words were born on the wind. My palms coasted the surface of the rippling waters. My breath shuddered. Suddenly, the skies grew dark around me. The audience above did not seem perplexed as though the coming storm was for my eyes alone. The shoreline began to shrink, deepening the water. Inky water curled under my arms and around my neck, pulling me under.

"Lor!" Willa screamed. There was nothing she could do but watch.

My body plummeted into black pitch, and I was running out of air fast. Panic set in. I was no longer the one with star fire anymore. Just a girl, drowning. Flashes of Riann's face whisked by. Every laugh I'd shared with our family felt like honey in my blood. A certain peace overcame me, acceptance of what was to come, then something delicate and scaly brushed against my leg.

"Light the way, Starfire," a male voice whispered beneath the dark waters.

Lips pressed against mine, parting them, breathing briny air into my lungs. "I can smell your cymar all over you," he said, exhaling into me again.

Another one brushed against me. "Give her the bubble shield," a female voice said with annoyance.

With a touch of his soft, jelly-like fingers on my head, I could breathe again.

"I just wanted to taste their magic," he said.

"And?" The female's voice was cross, her form silhouetting in the darkness.

"He's happier now. Not the brooding mess you enjoyed." He cupped my face with his strong, deft fingers. "Starfire, light your hand."

Light broke through the darkness, and I saw fins flap around me. Large fins. *Mermaids.* The little girl inside me screeched with joy. The female's tangerine scales glittered under the light. Dark, mossy hair swirled about her amber eyes, tangled in the large shell necklace sitting around her neck. With everything I had already seen, this was the most surreal. I felt as though I were in a dream.

"You must be the cymar of the man I wanted," she said, tapping her chin. "My name is Gloria, and this blue-finned jerk is Zale."

Bubbles floated upward as I exhaled. "I can't believe you're real. Where I came from, mermaids are myths."

Zale's pale green hair, braided to one side with conch shells, flowed in the current away from his perfectly sculpted face. "We don't have much time. The queen set us here when the curse began. Unseen and invisible. She believed it would cause us to burn with hunger, so when the time was right, we would feed on someone of her choosing."

All this time, she'd starved beautiful creatures for her own pleasure. Nyx planned this all for me. All for the Lilac Child. Yet they did not view me with disdain, or they would have never let me breathe underwater.

Gloria swam several circles around me, eyeing me up and down. "We know who you are. The goblins have a way of communicating with the unseen." Rolls of water waved onto me as she picked up speed. "Give us a little of your power to dust our way back into the sea. Then you can resurface."

"We're prisoners," Zale said. He pulled out one of his blue scales, leaving a tiny trail of blood. "Take this as a token. A mermaid's scale is rare in Sidh and proof we still exist. If the queen's curse is broken, all the sirens of the sea will return to mermaids as they once were."

"Why aren't you sirens?" I asked, rubbing the delicate scale in between my fingers.

Gloria's face darkened, her fins only moving enough to stay afloat. "To make a mockery of us. Riann was my friend long ago, and she knew it. Please tell Riann I am still here, and I have not forgotten my promise to take him to my kingdom."

My eyes widened. "To your kingdom?"

Strands of seaweed peeked through her hair, and she giggled. "Relax! He just wanted to see where the mermaids lived. I knew he had his heart set on someone else. It was the only reason he sat on the shorelines all those years. He was waiting."

My star blossomed into marvelous light. He'd always waited for me. Tiny bubbles raced to the top. I loved mermaids as a child, and I needed to touch her, just once. I extended my hand to her face. She flinched at my abrupt touch, but I could only grin. She returned my smile as I brushed my fingers against the scales lining her jaw, committing this moment to memory. This was real. Everything was real. Grateful for my rescuers, I stirred my star to give them their freedom. Nyx had forgotten the most powerful thing besides hunger was hope.

They looked at me with expectant eyes.

"Please let me have this bubble until I crack the surface."

"Deal," they both said, grabbing onto my shoulders. A pebble of gold light absorbed into each of them, and they misted into bubbles out of the hellscape. I kicked like crazy to the surface, hoping the bubble shield would last long enough. It popped as I forced my hand with the scale through the surface. Gasps with a mix of cheers and shock vibrated the stadium.

"Mermaid scale!" the crowd screamed. These mermaids had not turned to sirens. The glistening scale served as a beacon of hope for the accursed people. Water pulsed with ripples, stretching outward to the shore as the crowd began to rumble into a chant. *"Aurum Unum!"* Over and over again, they cried that phrase, and my star glowed as if responding. The language was foreign to me, but the spirit behind the words were clear. The people wanted me to win.

I swam to the shoreline, quickly healing the cut on my leg. Then, I looked up. The queen's eyes burned, and I couldn't help but salute her with one finger.

51

RIANN

Something roiled in my gut. Balmy wind brushed over the lines of sweat creasing on my forehead. I peeled my eyes to every corner, every passerby. Lex ran between the west end and east countless times. Someone of his size needed to keep moving to stay under the radar. At first, my blood ran cold when I heard the cheers. I thought something bad had happened to Lor until I'd heard the crowd chant *aurum unum*, "gold one," in the ancient tongue of Solarin. The masses recognized the power of old running through her. There may have been some in the stands who saw her mother fighting down there. It would have given me much pleasure to see the look on Nyx's face.

Lex darted back to Phil thirty minutes ago. Our plan was that when Lor made it out, Lex would take her, run, and—as Willa put it—crack skulls if needed. Minotaurs clad in their scaled armor perused the area, sniffing and snorting at the most mundane things. They continued sniffing around the pillars of the amphitheater as if they'd caught something. Dirt from the paved road kicked at my feet when I suddenly felt a brisk, cold snap. My deep brown cowl fell over my nose, and I limped around like an old man, holding the sword at my hip underneath. Thunderous applause heated my blood again, and I wished I could see how Lor was doing. My cymar, my heart was in there. I restrained every fiber of my being from going in myself and tearing the place down to shield her. I had no doubt of Lor's ability, trusting the training she'd

318

undergone. I should have been there cheering her on during those days. There was so much wrong I had yet to right.

Stop, Riann. Don't spiral.

I felt around in my pocket for the fireworks Dolos had given me for our signal. My clammy fingers slicked the threads of the pouch. He'd added black and purple powder to sparkle like Lor. The flint rubbed between my fingers even as I told myself to stop before I accidentally set it off in my pocket. My anxiety was making me feel careless and impulsive. Every part of me wanted to jump out of my skin, but I needed to stay strong for Lor and stick to the plan.

Lex wasn't back. He hadn't been delayed before. My sweat pelted the ground. I began to feel weak and feverish. I couldn't leave the post in case Lor came out. She would want me to run after Lex, but I couldn't leave her. If I walked halfway, I could always run back. I hated being this blind. Lex would hate me for going after him, but Lor would never forgive me if I didn't. *Weigh it. Weigh it.* If I went to the halfway mark, but he wasn't. I need to send out the signal. Lor might not be out yet, but she would know to hurry.

I limped a few steps down the colonnades for appearances. Crimson ivy web wound around each pillar like blood vessels. Fitting for its demon queen. More applause. The golden one lived. A heaviness thickened the surrounding air, puncturing my lungs. Darkness clouded the sides of my vision, and I felt cold chains wrapping around my body. Black chains. I became utterly defenseless. Sounds and colors ceased, and I floated somewhere into the unknown. Nyx had discovered I was alive.

52

ELORA

L^{eft!}

Right!

Right again!

Willa's commands thundered down my bridge. Spikes punctured upward through rocky ground one by one, creating plumes of debris. Bits of rock stung my face, making fine slices in my skin. Undoubtedly, shrapnel forged its way into my muscle. There was no pattern to them or time to heal myself. The second I heard the spike push through might be a second too late if I lost an inch of focus. One jutted out in front of me, almost slicing me upward. I arched my back away from being impaled. Heat rose with each spike I outmaneuvered. Something like chains loosely linked between the dark trees straight ahead. Fine silver threads of metal glinted under the pale, yellow sky. Another spike whooshed up my side, piercing my hip. Searing pain engulfed my senses. I tried to catch my breath while holding back tears. The spike returned to the ground, dragging my blood with it. Nobody could see me in the cloud of debris, this visage of agony. My vision blurred as my hip bled profusely into my hand.

"*Willa,*" my voice shook. *"I'm going to bleed out."*

Her voice was calm and steady, soothing my nerves. *"Just a little more Starfire."*

The clearing was near. Patches of rotted grass and mud swept between the rocks. Twenty more steps to freedom, and I could hang onto those chains to heal myself. Each step felt like knives stabbing upward. Ten more steps as spikes thrusted out faster than before. With all my might, I hurdled over them, landing on my injured side. White hot fire flashed in my eyes. Blood pooled beneath me, and I had to get up or it would be all for nothing. I clenched my jaw and hurled myself up, ignoring the throbbing pain. Before I could test for spikes, I jumped onto the chains, shaking from the adrenaline surge. Red continued to flow down my pant leg and onto the ground below. I was fading fast. My star guttered the tighter I held onto those chains. No healing came. Though my will was strong, something crept beside me. Dark and inky shadows with withered tendrils blanketed the ground below. I felt something malicious lurking. The grim reaper and his hoard came in a different shape. Sorrow. The darkness seeped out the color of the grass, muting all living things. Except for my stone-cold breath. No longer did I hear the audience shouting for me. It was too quiet, as if nothing else existed. I was going to die in these chains. This game was never meant to be survived.

Heat dissipated, and it became desperately cold. I was unable to tell if it was the temperature or my blood loss. Darkness spread across the sky like a canvas, without moonlight or the twinkle of stars. The silver chains gave way, dropping me onto the icy ground and into the shadows. Bile bubbled up my throat. Holding my hip, adding as much pressure as I could, I rose, limping around the smoky gloom. Rattling noises and groans crept around the trees. Their tangled, bare branches clawed their way upward. My hand on my hilt, I shivered violently, losing my balance.

"Willa, something's wrong. My star," I whimpered.

"It's so dark I can't see anything, Lor!"

A few seconds rolled by, and swift movement whooshed behind the trees. Something familiar. More movement raced around me. Each time I extended my hand, my star flickered. Tremors snaked up my body, and I wanted to cry. I felt so alone. These shadows had chased and consumed me all my life. Had they come to claim me at last?

"Willa, I don't think my star works in a place like this." My voice quivered while I leaned my back on a tree with my sword unsheathed.

"Oh, no." The grave sound in her voice hitched my breath. *"Ghouls. Creatures of the living dead. Because they come from the pit, your star cannot react to what is already dead. You have to cut off their heads."*

Pale, ominous gray light slowly filtered through, though it remained mostly dark. Red, ferocious eyes glared, growling and snarling. One by one, like blinking lights, they appeared. I counted fourteen in all. Seven ghouls. Seven heads. Their black talons curled into their fists. Sinister smiles and tongues wagged as if they craved my flesh. Rounded stones that appeared to be graves came into focus. Something dark and metallic glowed beneath my skin while they growled. A whisper of energy wound through my chest, down my arms. A power I had never felt before rumbled the ground beneath me. They blinked, putting one foot in front of the other; finally showing themselves in the dark light pouring from my fingertips.

I no longer felt pain. Power, an unrestrained kind waiting to be unleashed, writhed in me and all around me. The ghouls stood tall on two legs with pale pocked skin, their fangs hanging outside of their grotesque mouths. One cocked his pointy ear to the side, assessing the radiating power flowing from me. Inching closer, they formed a circle around me. They looked at each other, daring one another to touch me first. This was not my star. Something else had overcome me, and I had no idea how to wield it. It was neither warm nor cold. It just was.

This must be what death was. I felt nothing. Numb to it all. Tombstones broke through the barren earth, pushing through rocks and mud. Carved on them was the name of each person I loved, but weathered as if they'd been dead for hundreds of years. Riann's grave, a slick monolith caked with moss, stood in the center and loomed over me. This wasn't real. Alongside it were other gravestones engraved with the names of my family and four blank ones, yet to be written. Nyx could not have created these graves here waiting for them—not unless she had a seer gift. My breath became labored. This was not the end of their story. We would live on, immortal, full of light. We carried future generations within us. Death had no final word. We welcomed death only to produce something even more beautiful. Death was no end; it was a beginning. I grimaced at the graves. These cheap tricks would not break me. The dark light became a tempest around me, seeking command. It snapped and hissed begging for a way to expel itself. Ribbons of energy unfurled, twisting and knotting themselves together.

With one step backward, woozy and fatigued, it was evident I was fading. Though I could not feel the pain, its effects took a toll on me. But I could die so that they would live. With a slow swing of my sword, my blade kissed the dark light, infusing it with energy. The light and I were one. Ghouls crouched low, ready to attack, growling, and hungry for their meal. With one low swing, I spun, with barely a whisper to the raging storm. Sticky blood sprayed as their heads rolled onto the ground. The graves imploded to dust, and pale, yellow light returned, revealing the decapitated ghouls. Trees turned to ash and behind me the silvered chains flailed like threads.

Shock rippled throughout the stadium as my starlight returned. I didn't care anymore. I'd seen enough. My dark energy disappeared when I flexed gold threads between my fingers and felt my pulse stabilize. Shrapnel pulled itself out, disintegrating as it met healing magic. My wound fused itself back together, blanketing me in a steady warmth. Everyone stood to their feet, shouting, *"Aurum unum!"* Giving the crowd what they wanted, I created a circle of fire around me. Peering through the licks of flames, the queen pursed her lips. I'd show her a taste of what I was capable of. I threw a ball of flame onto one of the banners hanging below her seat. The queen's crimson crown of jagged edges burned to ashes so quickly that her minotaur nobles moved in front of her. Mikhail stared dead at me, but even from there, I sensed his inward smile.

Finally, the end. I was covered in grime and blood, making me ache for Riann's pool. With a long inhale, I ran for the circle to reach the crystal dais. Just a little further to go home. My lungs burned, and I still felt some pain in my hip. The crystal dais glimmered under the pale sky. It arched in the center like a throne waiting for me to take. I focused on the white flag, ready to wave it high. The earth rumbled beneath me, and I was knocked underfoot. Fissures formed a circle, cracking and falling, forcing me beneath the earth. I had no solid ground, as everything fell with me. I grasped for purchase, for anything to keep me steady, but it was much too fast. Debris fell like rain, and I only had enough strength to put up a shield of light. Rocks plummeted, breaking to pieces on my shield.

Willa's panic reverberated down my bridge. *Lor! Are you okay?!*

Bones screamed on the rock bed. My vision blurred. Once the worst of the debris was over, I let down the shield. The ringing in my ears dissolved when red-orange heat blasted my face. Swiftly, I picked myself up, limping toward the fiery hot edge. Rivers of magma swirled as I stood on the circular rock formation.

"There's lava here."

"Lava!?" Willa screamed.

I stuffed down my panic, but it was useless. *"This is hell, Willa. If I can't find a way out, I'm going to burn alive down here."*

"Lor, remember who you are. You are the one that burns."

Willa was not only my guide but also my emotional support animal. A brief thought of us by the shore, sipping on piña coladas while our men played football, brought kindling to my tired soul. *Riann.* Something didn't feel right. My tender thoughts disappeared with the feeling of a serrated edge cutting away inside me. Fireworks of black and violet set off above me. Dolos' signal. *No, no, no.* That meant something went wrong, and they were trying to distract the sentries.

"Willa, for my sake, leave me, and check on our family."

"As much as I want to run, I will not abandon you."

Voices. A mixture of high pitched and angry whispers deafened the coursing lava through each channel. The same voices from my dreams spun around me. This was my hell. Fire and brimstone were the easy things to walk through. Those voices though, they could undo me.

"My, my, such a pretty flower. The others were always awake," Jeff's voice cut through me.

My star guttered as he materialized before me, casually closing our distance.

"You let me have you, and it made me want you over and over again, little flower." His fingers tugged at the sweaty strands of my hair.

Pressure built behind my eyes. My arms slackened to their sides, and my legs became jelly. "You're dead. I watched you die."

"My love, I have always been a part of you. I will never leave you." His dark smile caused the same creases on his face I used to count until everything was over. Three creases on both eyes and one crease between his brows. "You were fresh for the picking. The other one was even fresher, but you were so willing."

I blinked several times. "Stop, you're not real. Riann killed you."

"Willa, my foster father is here."

"Mind games. Nothing is real. She wants to break you. And if he is indeed real, I will find a way to kill him myself."

I fully opened my mind so that Willa could see what I was seeing, something I'd never done before. It came so easily for Riann, but I had not done it myself. Willa's small gasp did not escape my ears. *"That man is full of shadows. You are no longer his victim. You are triumphant, beautiful, and loved."*

"That creature." Jeff's lips thinned. "His shadow appeared in my mind, melting me from within. But a man is more than flesh. I have owned many parts of you over the years." His nose swept over my neck, breathing me in. "Your dreams are mine. Your heart is mine. Your soul is mine." The ends of his chestnut hair trickled across my shoulder. "Had I not died, I would have been able to explore you in a more intimate way. But you have angered me, little flower."

It was not true, I kept telling myself. A wave of nausea rippled through me at the scent of his familiar musk and whiskey. I lurched at him, pushing his rock-hard chest away. "Stop calling me that! I belong to me!"

Jeff fell to one knee. "You are mistaken. You belong to the one who killed me. But soon, you will belong to me again."

"What do you mean?"

Jeff darkly chuckled. "You and your friend in the stands should have never left your cymars."

I kneed him in the face and wrapped my hands around his slimy neck. "What happened to them?!"

Thick dribbles of blood snaked from his mouth. "My pretty flower, don't be upset. Anger is not becoming on you." Jeff's hot hands climbed up my arms, bringing me down to him. "Now, where did we leave off before your beloved murdered me?"

Willa's red-hot anger barreled down my bridge. *"Kill him, Lor! Don't let him take you again!"*

Riann, Lex, Phil, Dolos. My family. My cymar. Thoughts of them dying while I was stuck in there brought me closer to Jeff's body. I should have never come to the games. I should have stayed and found another way. Willa on the other end, kept herself together, but her cymar was out there too. Jeff flipped me over, running his hands on my sides like I was his property, pinning me to the ground.

"Lor," Mikhail's voice boomed inside me. *"Don't let him win. If you do, then they all win. My mother, the time mages who beat Riann, the rest of the lot who mistreated you and abused you—including me. Today is the day you burn not only for you but for them. I want to see you win over all of them. Especially me."*

A quiet fire built inside me, burning away every word and curse Jeff and the rest of them had ever laid on me. Only the memories remained, singed by flames, never to torment me again. All those years marred by loneliness and fear of pursuing love became ashes at my feet. Thick, gold bands wrapped themselves around me, throwing Jeff onto his back. I was no longer the pretty flower. I was a flame. Merciless, yet tender. Whole, yet untamed. Feared, yet loved. Riann might have taken this man's life, but I would rid his shadow, his stench forever.

"How is this possible!?" he screamed, pushing against my light.

A sphere of gold light gathered in my hands—writhing, molten light seeking a way to spend its pent-up energy. "I speak for myself and the rest of your victims. You no longer own them. We belong to ourselves."

The whites of his eyes flashed. "Stop it, Elora!"

I released the inferno, burning every inch of him until nothing remained.

The crowd went wild. If they only knew what really happened, they would understand the soft grin, the final chain links falling off my soul.

Two claps came behind me. "Good work, Lor. How about we spar again?"

I spun around and Phil stood before me with Riann's sword. Another mind game? Why him? He was not my weakness. The pulse in his neck quickened. His eyes were a furious, writhing, molten, red.

"Phil's here."

"That makes no sense." Willa paused. *"Why use him?"*

"Doesn't matter. I need you to get out of there. Jeff made it clear they know you are here. Please trust me. Find Dolos. He's beyond the edge of Arcadia."

She paused again. I didn't need her arguing as Phil assessed me, taking in every inch of my torn leathers. *"Fine,"* she huffed. *"Don't let Riann kill me."*

"I assure you I am here," said Phil, smirking, his hand on my cymar's hilt. "You see, Riann took our powers so the queen would not target us. But I found a better deal."

Flashes of Phil being distant to me and often disappearing, took shape. "You were his best friend!" My fingers readied themselves to strike. I'd beaten him once. I could do it again.

Phil clicked his tongue. "Not really, though he liked to the believe the last Rinariens were. The queen slowly killed him with her hourglass and drained my power from him little by little. It was bound in his body through her curse." His arms spread wide over his kingdom of lava.

It was good Riann could not see anything as the betrayal lanced its way through my entire being. "You—you made him sick? Every time you went to cool off, you were reporting to her?!"

He lifted his arms and shrugged. "Well, you could have made it much easier if you had just been finished off by the Yaga as I'd intended. Do you remember that night?"

I tried blocking out that night. Riann's worst moment and my lowest point.

"I came to you to console you," Phil continued. "But you were out of your mind. I gave you water infused with oleander. After you passed out, I carved those words into your arms. I wanted Riann to completely lose it and throw himself in the Styx when he discovered your body. Just so I could get everything back in one shot. Unfortunately, nothing worked out, but the oleander seemed to have wiped your memory."

My scythes glowed, appearing with a graphite edge. "You traitor! Everything was for show!"

"Careful, pet. Last time, I went easy on you," Phil said, whirring Riann's sword. "Now the time has come for them to get their bloody star so I can leave this godforsaken realm."

I set my face, determined to make him regret betraying us. "I have no interest in killing you." Golden rope flew through my hand anchoring itself on my scythe and wrapping around his ankle. Phil thudded to the ground grasping for anything as I dragged him across. "My cymar will do that for me."

He grunted. "He's already dead. Both him and Lex."

My rope loosened. Everything inside me caved in, threatening to implode. "No! That can't be true!" I would know it. My star. His star. I would know if my cymar were cleaved apart from my soul. We were one, and the tearing and rendering of one of us would be unbearable.

Phil did not waste another moment and charged after me. My blood panicked, and suddenly, I forgot to use my powers as I ran. The terrain in the circle was rough and unpredictable with lava plumes rising with ferocity. I tripped over a rock the moment I looked back at him. Phil was a world-class liar, and I had to rise and leave his kingdom of magma. *Get up, Lor. Get up for your family*. Phil landed his feet beside me. His sweat pearled above his brows. His eyes blazed with fury as he raised the point of his blade above me. This couldn't be the end. I'd came too far.

A knotted rope fell to my side, and Grim was above the edge of the precipice, waving. "My lady! One of our friends thought you might need this!"

Phil's lips quivered with rage, set on killing Grim. I swept my leg under Phil. He staggered back. He blocked the inside of me with my hand in front of his neck. My elbow struck his side several times before I hooked his neck into my arm and threw him to the ground.

He coughed up blood and touched the dribble on his lips, disbelief crossing his face. "Oh, so you think you're some Sidh warrior now?"

"No. I'm from Jersey," I said as I grabbed the rope.

Phil writhed on the ground as I made my way to the top. I nodded at Grim, giving him my thanks, and we ran like the wind out of this hellscape and onto the crystal dais. Grim hid behind me as I took the white flag, burning it before the queen's eyes.

53

RIANN

Thunderous roars jolted me from my drugged haze. Flickering light filtered through my heavy eyes. I was beaten half to death, totally immobilized to defend myself. Radiating pain screamed on my right side, where the fireworks and flint ignited after I'd fallen. Every inch of my body cried for relief. My skin of healing water disappeared. Sounds of anguished cries down the hall pricked my ears. My chest caved hearing my dearest friend, Lex, crying out with curses sputtering from his breath. Too fast, much too fast, I rose to my feet. The room spun, but it was not a room. It was a dungeon with small crossbars for windows. Black mold and green algae streaked the damp stone walls. Bits of hay lay strewn across the floor. I wondered how old the hay was because Nyx took no pleasure in keeping her prisoners warm. Black chains clinked together, sapping any strength to attempt an escape. Another scream echoed down the hall.

Then another scream battered through me. My brother, my friend. A piece of my soul was being tortured. "Lex!" I cried. He wailed as I heard a contraption crank its wheels, the leather tightening and snapping, exacting immeasurable pain from his body. "Lex! I'm here! I'm here!"

I thrust my hand through the bars as if he could reach for me. Torches flickered outside of every other cell. Everything blurred as if I were drowning. I staggered back, knocking over a pail of dirty water. The drug needed more time to run through my system. Cold water spread under my feet, and I kneeled, splashing my eyes. Lex panted, bracing himself for another pull of the leather. His voice strained in between wanting to scream and begging them to stop. There was no doubt they incapacitated him with the same chains I wore.

"Stop hurting him!" I begged. "I'm the one she wants! Take me!"

Heavy footfalls echoed nearby, and I leaned back against the furthest wall. Damp, jagged stone pressed into the tender bruises blooming on my back.

A male grunted, tossing himself between his captor to free himself. I rubbed my eyes and saw my brother. "She's going to kill you all! Let me go!"

Soldiers pinned his arms, keeping their legs close to his back to make him walk faster. Another set of black chains trailed from his wrists.

"If you value your lives"—Mikhail spat blood at their feet as he struggled to break free— "you will let me and the rest of the prisoners go. Either way, you will die. My mother will feed on you, or his cymar will burn you all with pleasure. Release us, and you will be pardoned."

They laughed. "Little prince. After tomorrow, we will not have to cater to you anymore. You will die with the rest of the traitors."

The door swung open with a rusty creak, and they threw him in, slamming it shut in his face. "Riann! I see you!" Mikhail pushed his hand through the bars, reaching for mine. Our hands barely touched.

"Mikhail." My hand stretched as far as it could go. "What is happening?"

He backed away and slid down the wall. "Your girl won. Nyx fled. It was all a trap, anyway. The queen knew from the start who she was."

"Who do I have to thank for that?" I snapped.

"Are you serious?" Mikhail sighed, wiping the sweat and dirt from his forehead with his bracer. "I tried hiding her. Nyx was going to find her in the earthly realm after she exploded in the hospital. Do you know how many fundamental laws I broke just to find her?"

I ran my hand down my swollen, bloody face. For a good moment, I looked at my brother and finally saw him. My only flesh and blood.

Mikhail leaned his head on the wall, blowing his breath. "I discovered my mother is of the Lamian Witches, or as Silas called them, the realm eaters. They consume everyone slowly. That's why no babies are born. They can't be stuck here forever feasting on a reproducing population. Her sister, the Hag, torments people in their dreams, while the Yaga feeds on their flesh. The curse on you and Sidh made it easier for them." He pulled his legs to his chest. "This was never about the Astryx or the soul tax. They've been asleep since Rinarie. Maybe even since before Solarin."

I hung both arms through the bars, my head drooping low. Nyx had slaughtered my realm with her sisters. This new piece of information settled in me. I knew it was truth somehow. A quiet fire hissed and cracked in my core. I would have my vengeance, one way or another. "And now she knows you tried to help us. The Fauns, Lor, and stupid me."

Mikhail chuckled darkly. "Hey, I'm pretty stupid. I got caught. Killing her right-hand man set her off."

"You killed Kain?" I laughed a little, wishing I could have seen it.

"Yeah, I did," he said, crossing his legs. "I reeked of him for days."

Both of us laughed. Nothing could bring brothers closer together than killing.

Mikhail's eyes became unfocused, distant. "You would have been proud of Lor. She almost lost it at the end when the mind games came for her. But she held her own."

A bloodied grin reached my eyes. "Thank you, Mikhail."

"For what?"

Recent memories of Lor entangled in bed sheets, fighting me for the bigger side of the blanket, warmed my skin. It sounded odd, but I enjoyed the things that others complained about. She could have the bigger side of the blanket; she could eat my dessert or read chapters without me in whatever book we'd become obsessed with. I didn't care. Nothing mattered as long as I was the one she wanted at the end of the day. Lor had my heart, half of my soul, and she could do with it whatever she wished. "If you'd never brought her here, I would not have faced my fears being with her. What I had with Lor these past few weeks has been a dream. It will never be enough, yet it is enough."

We paused, simmering in thoughts of love. "I hear that, brother. After all, I'm clinging to a dead woman."

Hanging through these bars, almost at the end of myself, guilt washed over me. An old guilt I stuffed away because I was afraid of looking at myself. Maybe I was not the kindest or the bravest for Mikhail. He deserved better.

"I'm sorry, Mikhail." A sob wrenched free from my throat. "I'm so very sorry."

He stood, pushing his body against the iron bars. Our hands tried to reach again. He leaned his forehead on the bars. Tears clung to his eyelashes.

My head pressed against the bar. "I should have fought for you. Taken you from this place. I knew your mother wasn't right in the head, and I left you. You had every right to hate me." I coughed out a wet laugh. "It's ironic that as a time mage, I wish I could turn back the clock for you."

"I never hated you." He loosed a sputtering breath. "You were my peace when I was a child. Even though you called me names sometimes or roughhoused with me"—we both chuckled, wiping our eyes with our arms—"I would never want you to change a single thing. Our paths lead here, and your cymar will come for you. I hated the way I treated her under the guise of protection. I never meant to hurt her. It was an accident. I hope you know that."

My skin erupted in goosebumps. "I know that now."

"I had to play a role and choose my victims wisely. I hated being her monster, her harbinger of death in training." Mikhail paused, his fists clenching around the bars. "I did it for Sidh, for my atonement. But in doing that, I lost you. I lost who I thought I was and I... disappointed Silas."

There was nothing to say. In part, I hated him confessing to me because it sounded like his parting words.

Mikhail loosened his grip on the bars, his face darkening. "You should know that you were betrayed."

My head jerked up. "Who?"

"By me." Dragging my sword with him against the floor, Phil's red eyes swirled intensely.

"No," I whispered, eyeing the blade. "You were my best friend!" Lex screamed again.

"Friends?" Phil glared at me. "You took what is mine, and Nyx gave me a better deal to get them back. But your girl was too hard to kill. Now that you're here, it might not be a problem."

I slammed against the bars, desperate to break through. "Why?! After all this time? The fauns? The curse? Why?"

The last shred of Rinarie was gone. I was the only one left. Nobody after me would remember the Rinariens. I thought Phil would one day settle down and carry on the lineage, and then through our future children, we would be the voice of our people. But no. He'd betrayed their memory. I didn't know whether I wanted to shrink into the dark corner and pretend this moment never happened or jump out of my skin and wrap his neck in my hands.

Phil ran his gloved hand over the bars, grimacing at the sheen of sludge on his fingers. "Nyx is no fool. She knew this whole time who Elora was"—he cut a menacing glance at Mikhail—"who his pet was. But she likes to play games with her meals before she feeds. Especially on Elora." His eyes simmered back to me. "She wanted her powers to run through Elora. She wanted you to become bonded to your cymar. Nothing freshens the meat more than tenderizing it." He dragged the point of my blade closer to me. "The fauns were nothing more than an appetizer for her and her sisters. Your curse trapped everyone here for her pleasure. Do you really think I want to be here for the end?"

I shook the bars violently. "You sick, sadistic, bas—"

He clicked his tongue. "You played your best hand, Riann, and got the girl. But now it's my turn, and I refuse to go out like this. At least I can take my powers with me."

Phil pivoted, his back covered with whorls of purple and black. A fresh cut on his neck bled over his collar. My girl did that. Good.

"Thank you, Mikhail." Phil pulled a mechanical key out of his pocket. "This key will help me on my way," he smirked at me, "after your public execution."

Mikhail flexed his hand, forgetting he couldn't burn him alive in those black chains.

"I call you out, vagabond, traitor to your people!" I bellowed.

"Please," Phil laughed with a sinister smile. "You couldn't brand me if you tried."

Mikhail coughed. "We don't need a brand. Everyone has the knowledge that a girl and a hobgoblin bested you today. That should be enough."

Phil's rage stilled the air around us. His fingers dripped hot magma, burning holes into the damp stone floors. "The only thing keeping you alive is that she wants to make a spectacle of you all. Too bad we could not find the others. But they will come. Then, I can be free of this realm for good."

Muddied in disbelief, I shook my head, processing, recalibrating, editing this man before me—rewriting him in my memories to make sense of who he really was. No longer was he the child that begged me to race him down the shoreline or the boy who refused to share his air-spun sugar treats. He'd embraced my cymar in tears. He'd lived and eaten under my roof while plotting our deaths. Lor could have used her powers at any time to slice him in two. But she'd left him for me. There was nothing more I wanted than to see his pleading eyes beneath my feet before I melted his mind slowly so that I would be the last thing he saw.

"Goodbye then, Phil," I said calmly, walking backward into a dark corner. "Hope your next best friend suits you."

Bristled, he walked off toward Lex's screams. Each anguished plea echoing in the hallway shattered me. A single tear fell. Not for Phil or our lost friendship, but how he'd casually walked past our friend's torture and thought nothing of it. It was just any other day for him. I could have asked more questions, but I feared I already knew the answers to them. Phil had always planned to kill Lor, to kill me. His allegiance was to himself. We were simply a means to an end. I muttered curses under my breath and felt the runes on my head burn. Lor was going to come. And she would rain fire on this whole helter-skelter.

Moments later, Lex was thrown into the dungeon next to me. He laid on his side, barely breathing. His shoulders and legs were popped out of place. The large lacerations on his back being exposed to the mildewy air were a recipe for infection. I slid down the bars, saying his name over and over, but he did not respond. Three shackles tightened against his swollen wrists. His hair matted against his bloodied face. Flickering light rippled across the bruises and ribboned flesh from head to toe. I wanted to cry again. But none came.

54

ELORA

There was no time to mourn, no time to decompress. We'd made it back to the demarcation line, breathless, needing to cry and lose ourselves in the madness of it all. Dolos and Willa hunched over, heaving. Her glamour was gone. Dolos was covered in ash from the explosions, his eyes bloodshot. Our plans went up in smoke, and we'd lost our cymars. Riann's bridge remained broken, but Mikhail's was intact. A flush of darkness streamed in my mind, connecting to his battered door.

"Mike. Are you all safe?"

Static vibrated down the bridge, his voice coming into focus. *"You need to hurry. Our execution is in two days. Lex might not make it until then. They tortured him with nearly an inch of his life."*

I gasped, and Willa went pale, watching my face drip with horror. She knew Lex was in danger, she felt it in her soul. There was no other solution, we needed to fight, and we needed to do it quickly.

"We are going to come. We just need support."

"You have many in your debt. Those willing to fight for you," he said rather quickly.

"Don't you mean with me?"

"No, I meant what I said," he said bluntly. *"We all know you are the one to dismantle this reign, to break the curse."*

Starlight throbbed, mingling with something else; something darker when I was with the ghouls, and it would not yield. *"Riann never told me how to break it."*

Rough voices echoed down the bridge, banging hilts against the bars, finding comic relief in their torture. Mikhail ignored them. *"Because he's a good man. But I am not. What I am about to tell you is not what you need to share with anyone else right now."*

I braced myself for the impact of the one thing Riann said he would never share with me.

"I'm listening."

Mikhail paused while I heard Lex groaning in the background. My chest tightened. *"The unicorn horn is bound to his curse, but she made it with Algol's blood before he died. Nyx killed him by stabbing him in the heart with it. You bound your soul to Riann's, which is also bound to his father's. The curse can be undone if Riann's cymar does the same...to herself."*

He said it so quickly, like ripping off a band-aid. Mikhail took a beat and opened up for me to see through his eyes. Images flickered in the damp darkness of wet stones and crossbars. Riann hunched over behind the bars with his head in his hands. Intense blues and swirling purples blotted his sides.

"I'm so very sorry I had to tell you. I was hoping you never had to find out." Mikhail's voice shook.

I stumbled. Cluttered words and warped syllables danced on my tongue. Death always followed me, so it should be no surprise. Riann once said the fates were cruel, and at best, they were kind. I loved him more than anything. I loved my family above all else. And I could not let this monster take that away. Even if I could not see my family anymore, I knew what was best for everyone. I put away my silly dreams of going back to the earthly realm and splitting boardwalk fries with them. All the books I wanted to read with Riann and the places he wanted to take me. When I'd first come to Sidh, all I'd wanted to do was die. I hated Jeff's voice in my head, Peter's absence, and the violence whispering against my skin. But now—I wanted to live. Live so freely and dangerously that my life weaved a story of its own. It had to end here. With a sharp inhale, I shook off my desires.

"No matter what, I will die."

His chains rattled together. A penitent breath burned my ear. *"Listen, you don't have to die. Just burn this place down and take down Nyx with it. We can live with the curse."*

I shook my head. *"But if it's not undone, the land will live in rot. Sirens will never become mermaids again. Faeries will live as outcasts, and our family will never have freedom."*

"I only told you this so you can find a way around it. I don't want you to die. Why do you think I concealed you? Maybe just a little blood will suffice. Maybe you don't have to sacrifice yourself at all."

A glimmer of hope bubbled in his voice. I knew better. Mikhail may have been many things, but he was no liar. For all the wrong he had done, there was still good in him. He sent Grim to save me, possibly planning it out before the games even occurred. He'd suffered at the hands of his mother, a title she was not qualified to have. Deep inside, I knew Mike's regrets, his shame for how he'd treated me. In his own twisted way, he believed it was the only way to save me, to save Sidh.

"Mike," I stifled a cry. *"I forgive you. And if we get through this, my wish is that you and Riann reconcile."*

"I am undeserving of your forgiveness. Please save Riann and Lex." His eyes moved to the cell next to Riann. Ribbons of torn flesh and pools of blood spread beneath Lex's still body. Everything in me screamed. *"Lex will die,"* Mikhail continued, refocusing on Riann. *"He needs you."*

A rock plummeted in my stomach, rippling in my blood. It felt like I stood outside my skin. I steadied my breath, forcing my knees to stop shaking. Then I collapsed, hitting the ground hard. Dolos and Willa ran over, shouting something I couldn't quite hear. One look at Willa, and I couldn't stand the sight of her becoming a widow. I told myself it was my life for theirs. My life. My life was theirs for the taking—and I would willingly give it. But they couldn't know about my suicide mission. I really didn't want to call it that. Sacrifice was a better word.

"I'm coming," my voice bled into his ears, and I felt soft tendrils of darkness swirl around him. If what he felt right now had a taste, it would be bitter. *"Please tell Riann I love him."*

"No, Lor." Regret marked his voice. *"Tell him you love him yourself when you save our sorry behinds."*

"Mikhail." My heart jumped. I'd never called him by his full name before. *"You deserve more."*

He chuckled softly down my bridge. *"I had what I deserved, and she's gone. Please. For Riann and Lex, come quickly."*

Mikhail closed the bridge in time to see Wren and Kaya flying at the speed of light. Kaya's lavender hair faded into inky black, set against her moonlit skin. She appeared ready to become who she was, shedding off her faerie skin as soon as this curse broke. Her white opal eyes glittered like a blue flame, and something about her was endearing even in this hellish moment. Wren perched himself on my shoulder, battle ready with his dagger and a scythe he made for himself.

"My lady, we made preparations while you were in the games," he said, rubbing the side of his scythe blade.

"We called in some debts for you. For Riann. For Sidh." Kaya's voice was no longer flowery but made of sterner steel. "Look down the hill." She pointed her blade down the hill from the demarcation line.

Dolos and Willa linked my arms and pulled me up. Commotion grew louder with each step. How did we not hear this before? We had been in such a panic that we could not hear this or feel it beneath our feet. We crested the top the of the hill, pink skies brightened more than I had ever seen. Flags and banners sprawled below, nesting in between another hill. A massive army of Sidh's people groups gathered below. Faeries. Draconians. Fauns. Dryads. Their sigils snapped in a cold rush of wind. A twining vine of oak for the Dryads, a flute with horns for the Fauns. A scarlet wyrm curling its tail and flashing their fangs for the Draconians and four pointed stars and wings encircling each other against a violet sky for the Faeries. Once they saw me standing upon the hill, they shouted, "Starfire," over and over, lifting their weapons. I was overcome and anxious over the responsibility this power held. And I would give it all up for each of them.

Sable and Carmine marched up the hill to greet us. "Starfire, our warriors are ready to fight," Sable said, standing in formation.

I planted my hand on her shoulder. "Do not fight to repay a debt. There isn't one to pay."

"Please, woman," Carmine smirked. "I have half a mind to let Riann rot so I could have a chance with you." Sable elbowed him in the gut. "But this way is better. Or so I'm told," his voice throttled.

Sable pushed Carmine behind, rolling her eyes. "We fight for Sidh. This queen has taken too much from us. Your friend Wren has a big mouth. He told us everything from Solarin to how Riann was cursed. Consider us in your cymar's debt." Sable gave a half bow, and Carmine popped a kiss on my hand.

Luca ran all the way up, breathless. His scars from the astral battle screamed red. "My lady, we are not warriors, but we will fight. You healed many of us, giving us hope for a better Sidh."

Dolos, Willa, and I traded glances with each other. Hope anchored in us. We were not alone. The three of us held hands, glancing at the army below, tightening our grip on each other.

"Tomorrow," I said. "Tomorrow, we fight."

55

ELORA

Not again. I hurled my guts next to Dolos' tent. Tonight, I lived; tomorrow, I would die. I repeated it over and over until it didn't scare me anymore. The situation was hopeless. I either stayed alive and watch my family be butchered, or would I die knowing they could create new lives for themselves. Simple. So why did it feel so complicated? I supposed it was because there would be much I could never experience. I would never fulfill Riann's dream of having a family with me. The sound of our baby's first cry in the world. Seeing Dolos at the end of the aisle when he finally found his cymar. Maybe Lex and Willa would have children. Gentle, giant green babes. My heart couldn't take it. My future or theirs. Simple enough. Simple. Simply...horrifying, I wouldn't be there to see it. There was a sliver of hope. Maybe Mikhail was right, and all I would have to do is give a little blood to satisfy the curse. My guts turned inward again. I knew the truth. Nyx had created this curse, so there was no way out because Riann was a good man and would never put his life above mine.

"Blondie, you need some rest," Dolos called from his tent. "Come inside. I owe you a conversation."

Once inside, I saw Dolos' battle gear resting in the corner. Swords and his bow, along with flints and powders, were strewn across the white tented floor. "Sleep in here tonight. I don't think you should be alone," he said, spitting on a whetstone. "Maybe I can take your mind off vomiting."

I tried to feign a smile, but none would come, as I sat on the floor. "You know I love all of you, right?" I inched closer to his side while he rubbed the edge of his blade against the stone.

"I never doubted that." He stopped sharpening. "I knew you were family before you crashed on that hill."

With that, I leaned my head on his shoulder. "So, tell me, what is going on with you?"

"I loved Queen Elizabeth. Fooled myself into thinking she was my cymar." Dolos set his blade down and crossed his legs. "But she was not. Her path was set, and she was going to die. Immortals and mortals can never have each other. It's just too painful." Soft flames from his candles flickered, giving his skin a pinkish glow.

I placed my hand on his warm shoulder. "I understand, Dolos."

"On Caer, unicorns were as common as palfreys. They were such gentle creatures, giving me solace from my otherwise overbearing family. My family wanted me to be something I clearly was not. I refused to be king. I wanted to experience life without the confines of rigid royalty. I wanted to find my cymar, not an obedient wife to make an alliance. So, I left. With Luna's power, I jumped into the realm where I met Riann. Lex and Willa were not even seeing each other intimately yet."

I shifted my feet against the rough fabric of the tent floor. "You knew about the power in her horn."

"Yes." He swallowed hard. "But I swear I did not know she was here, let alone what that mad queen did to her. But I knew how much power Luna held. For that, please forgive me."

I squeezed his hand. "There's nothing to forgive. You could not have foreseen all this."

"That's the thing." Dolos straightened himself up, releasing my hand. "Many think my only power is fire, but it's not. In fact, I don't enjoy playing with fire as much as I let on."

My eyes widened.

"I'm a dreamcatcher, Lor."

A beat went by, and three crescent moons glowed upon his forehead. Their shimmering, pearly colors spun slowly in a circular motion, changing from waxing and waning phases. "I can enter dreams and carve them into use. Or I can give hope to someone. I can even make dreams happen if I should choose. I can take away nightmares. By the way, you're welcome."

I was stunned. Floored. "Wait, what?!"

His folded hands trembled. "Riann knew, so he requested I take away your nightmares. Combined with you locking that door in your mind and me taking the nightmares away, you could see the light again."

My brows pinched. "Why do you have your powers? What does all this have to do with the day with the fauns?"

"Riann is the only person—was the only person—who knew. Secretly, I think he let me keep them because he was struggling." Dolos blew out a quick breath. "I entered someone's dreams in your realm. My cymar. She does not know she's immortal. I don't have the psychic bridge like you guys, so I communicated in dreams. Which I guess is another type of psychic ability, but at least you all are aware it's real. My cymar did not think I was real until recently."

I cupped my mouth, slowly digesting all that Dolos confessed.

"After what happened to those fauns, my failure," he continued, his voice on the edge of breaking, "I did not feel worthy enough of her. I stopped visiting her dreams. But the night after your party, she visited mine. She seems to have this ability to absorb power. Which explains how she is immortal."

"Who is she?"

Dolos slapped his knee. "Names are powerful, blondie. You know this. I dare not speak her name until I see her face to face. And you are the only one who has given me hope I will see her one day."

I shook my head. "How long have you been in her dreams?"

He leaned back his head and brushed back his loose blonde curls. "Way before you arrived." We paused, and he wrapped his arm around my shoulder. "Too many died that day, and each of them weighs on my conscience. I can barely take it, let alone dragging someone with my emotional baggage."

"It was not your fault."

"It is. I tried so hard to enter Nyx's dreams. She is a fortress." He let out a broken laugh. "Who was I kidding? Even Riann couldn't break her shortly before the curse. The magic was so thick that day that it was suffocating. Everyone ran for themselves. Too many faeries died on the spot as if she'd rained down poison." His veins snaked from his arms to his neck, pulsing beneath his reddened skin. "I want to kill her. I want justice for it all. Maybe then, I can be worthy enough for my cymar."

"You already are," I whispered.

"This is why I hated how Riann acted before," Dolos' voice darkened. "It was not him. He was outside of himself. When he did all those things to you, I hated him. I think that's part of why I sparred with him that day. I wanted to hurt him for it. But then I saw how hard he went after you to make things right." He angled his head close to mine. "He never told you this, but the night the Hag attacked you, he held you in his arms for hours after you passed out. Brushing your hair back and gazing at you like you were the grandest painting to have ever existed. Because to him, you were. Every recipe he made has been something he saw you eat or talk about. Do you know what we mostly ate before you came along?"

I giggled through tears and a runny nose. "Oh, dear lord. Fish and greens, right?"

Dolos rolled his eyes and slid down. "Yes," he groaned. "Riann was always a great cook, but he lacked variety."

"You know," I drawled, "you could learn to cook for yourself."

He lifted his hands and shrugged. "What's the point of that when you have a chef in your house?"

We broke into laughter, momentarily forgetting about the dread coming our way.

"I feel like I could fail too." I pulled my knees together. "If I fail my cymar, please save him Dolos." My eyes misted.

"We misfits stick together. At least most of us do," His jaw tensed, and I knew he thought of Phil. "You will not fail tomorrow. We simply won't allow it. This is the first time we've ever had to save Riann from a demon witch queen," he smirked. "It's one for the books."

"We are misfits, we do not bow," I said, strengthening my resolve.

Dolos rolled onto his stomach, propping himself with his elbows. "Hey, blondie. If we're ever around other people together, can I tell them you're my sister?"

"It would be an honor. You can call me that, and I will tell others you are the prince of unicorns."

He smiled widely. "Deal."

56

MIKHAIL

Thank you, Mother. I quite enjoyed your soldiers beating me senseless while wrapped in chains. I loved it even more when they took turns on my brother and his dying friend. I thought a lot about how you kept me from other kids my age and how you threw me to the goblins. By the way, thanks for that. They are more loyal and keener on killing you than I am. Call me the prince of goblins, if you will. By the way, I think you threw me in with them so I would never see how other kids were treated by their parents. I would have realized the stark difference in how you raised me and eventually turned against you.

Mother, I have **always** *been against you. It was the eight-year-old boy inside me feared what you would do to me.*

Marie was my only solace, my peace in this otherwise chaotic realm. And though she is above the stars now, I still feel her warmth, her strength wash over me. You thought I jumped realms with Riann to sow my royal oats, but I did it to find peace. She became the voice in my head when you abused me, neglected me. Voltaire said, "Love is a canvas." We painted on that canvas with such vibrancy to the point I let her go to find a way for her to become immortal. You tried so hard to take that from me, but you can't. It's a song in my blood. You tried taking away my brother, and you took away Silas. Anyone who had the smallest amount of affection for me, you had to destroy. Take my life, if you please, but you will never take the joy I had of being loved and loving in return.

I wish I had parchment and a quill to write all these thoughts down. Instead, I scraped them on the dungeon wall, hoping you would read them. Maybe you will win the Mother of the Year award after my execution.

Love always,

Who am I kidding? You don't know love.

Mikhail

Voices of soldiers crept down the damp hall. Faint green light filtered through the barred windows. Our doors creaked open. Riann twitched at the sound. Sharp nails dug into my skin. They dragged us into the open air onto the battlement. Lex groaned with the last bit of life in him. He was a bloody pulp and though he had never been fond of me, I didn't wish for Willa to become a widow. Gleaming black stone beneath us stretched on, and I'd hoped to see something more colorful before I died. The foul stench of debauchery wafting from the courtyards made me wretch. Bodily fluids and stale beer were the last thing I wanted to smell before my soul departed this body. Riann's breath became ragged as he was pulled aggressively alongside me. His eye was completely swollen shut. Yellow drainage seeped from the lacerations sliced over his face and chest. Shivers completely wracked his body while sweat ran in rivulets down his head. He was not much longer for this world either.

"Brother, I hope we meet in the next life," I whispered, trying to meet him shoulder to shoulder before a hungover minotaur pulled me from him. The chains tightened around my wrists and neck.

Riann nodded at me slowly, a faint acknowledgment and a promise we would meet again. Crenels came into view and mother stood in the center. Swathed in garments of silver and white, a large group of minotaurs surrounded in scaled armor. Father's crown sat upon her head as he stood next to her, void of emotion. This was it. I hoped she would take me first. I didn't want to watch Riann die. The skies were pale green, the color of seasickness. What I would have given to see a sky the color of cornflower, like Marie's eyes. Marie rested her hand on my shoulder, her hair tickling my jawline as she pressed a soft kiss to my temple. I wound my arms around her waist refusing to let go. Even at my very end, my heart was always hers. Dearest Marie. Please meet me above the stars.

The castle vibrated. Loose stones fell from their place, clattering against the battlement. Mother's eyes widened. Her minotaurs took several steps back. Something sulfuric mixed with ether blew in the breeze. A sense of urgency carried the scent. Lex clenched his chains weakly, his hair rising from the static. The sky broke with light rain, something I had not seen since the curse. Pops of electricity scattered around us. Minotaurs flinched and ducked each time an electric current brushed them. The queen's mouth dropped open. She covered it with one hand to hide her obvious shock. This was no sweet healer coming. Nyx underestimated the star of creation and chaos. Elora came to wield both.

Sparks of gold erupted in the sky like fireworks. Flutes resounded shrill cries. Footsteps marched. Drums. Shouting. My mother believed the rebels were powerless after witnessing what had happened during the fauns' plight. She had not expected their anger or their music as they charged the front line with Elora, Dolos, and Willa in the center. The Rebel Stain arrived and took their rightful place. A mix of relief and regret flooded me as I glanced at my brother's face, breaking into a slight grin. Elora came. Our salvation. She came for us. For Sidh.

She came to die.

57

ELORA

ountless minotaurs in black scaled armor filed from the castle gates, their hooves vibrating the soft earth. Above us, my family remained chained with enchanted stone on the battlement. They never stood a chance to fight back. Dolos and Willa stood on either side, steadying their hands. We appeared utterly alone with fauns at our back. Nyx, the Yaga, and the Hag came into view between the crenels. The Yaga licked her lips, inhaling the stench of coming death. I stifled a groan, biting back every urge to cast fire upon them. My family were on the verge of death and likely welcomed it. Torn skin and flayed muscles ribboned from their torsos to their backs. Blooming bruises left no part of their flesh untouched. Mikhail appeared beaten and filthy, but he was more alive than the others. I remembered the lives Riann took for me. In my limited sense, I had wanted them to live, to show mercy. But now, being on the other side of the coin, I want nothing more than to rip their souls from their bloodied corpses and burn them all. Impatience gnawed at me. Every bit of mercy ebbed away, replaced by surging dark rage. The same fury I'd felt in the graveyard. The Hag smiled, revealing her yellowed pointy teeth. Today would be a feast for her, but we would flood this place. Army behind me. Weapons on our side, shields in place. We were ready.

Nyx glared below, lifting her hand in a tight fist. Her thin scarlet lips gave a mocking grin. Dewlike threads of soft gold moistened the ground as they dripped from my hot fingers. Everything in me pooled into fury and desire, an inferno of longing and destruction. She'd stolen what was mine. No matter what it took, I was prepared to sully these hands for those I loved. The field fell silent, many eyes of my enemy before me. They set their shoulders at ease, appearing to be relieved it was just us three and some fauns. Nyx's fist opened and the minotaurs marched forward.

"Did you really think I could not feel your magic crawling to your men, lilac child?!" The queen's voice pricked me like a thousand needles. "I thought you wanted to pay your last respects to your cymar." She waved for Riann, and a minotaur pushed him to the front. Riann stood, barely able to hold himself up. A minotaur brandished his sword beside him, its dreadful blade glinting under the pale green sky. "The Troubler of Sidh shall go first. Unless *you* want to bargain."

Riann shook his head as if to say, *"Let me go."* His eyes widened, anchoring his gaze into mine. Time slowed down. Seconds felt like hours.

Draconian drums pounded their battle cry. There would be no parlay today. Faeries and dryads flanked on both sides, confusing the minotaurs as they began to realize they were surrounded. Humid air swept their fur back, the scales of their armor clattering. Each eye dilated as they were left with a choice for fight or flight.

"Really? Is this all you have?" Nyx mocked, fixing her crooked crown. She had not killed Riann, which meant his life was still worth something until she had me. This was all a game. A sick cycle of rampant abuse of power until she got what she wanted. What if she stole my star? In what ways would she make it obey her will? Realms would be destroyed. Innocent lives snuffed out like candles in a storm.

Dolos shouted something, but I could not comprehend it. His leather armor molded around his muscles so intricately, reminding me of a Greek god. Willa, in all her glory dressed as a fury, gripped her sword. Fluttering wings amplified around us. Nyx's eyes bulged in surprise. Faeries came in droves, runes shining from their hands. Kaya, wrapped in darkness, flew onto my shoulder. Peals of lightning flashed in her tiny shadows. Wren perched on my other shoulder in total superhero stance, dagger out, covered in whorls of runes.

Nyx's hands slackened to their sides, her scarlet nails clutching her silver robes. Faeries were her blind spot. The ones she would never count on face to face. It was long believed they preserved themselves out of survival, but they'd orchestrated this for years. Magnus flew above me, arcing his graphite runes above the army like a halo. Sharp lines and edges came together and swiftly sunk into the ground. Her minotaur army murmured amongst themselves, their confident poise now shaken. Overwhelmed by the surge of power building around them, the queen's army staggered back, wobbling like they had drunk every ounce of faerie wine in Sidh. Nyx had not bothered to use astral projection this time, believing this would be an easy win. I laughed inwardly. This was going to be a slaughter.

The queen stepped back, the color leached from her already pale skin, revealing black veins underneath. "Swing your sword, soldier!"

A whoosh of silver light streamed upwards to the battlement, faster than I could blink.

The blade reached an inch of Riann's neck when it stopped midair, struggling against the light. Wren, glowing gray, his sharpened wings flapped in the soldier's face, and fixed his daggers onto the blade's edge.

"Don't touch my best friend," he growled as he lit the sword with magic. The blade fissured and broke into pieces.

Wren ripped open his pouch and blew gold dust on them, a concoction I'd made hours prior. Lex rose, his eyes turning obsidian, his chains fractured just enough to pull himself free. Wren flew off, worried he would be in the path of Lex's rage. Wounds sealed themselves together and a breath of fresh life went through him. He pulled Riann away from his executioner and crushed his head like an egg with a single fist. Thick blood covered his hands, and he slung it at Nyx, splattering her with his kill. Mikhail ran behind him. Nyx's sentries fell back at the sheer strength of Lex pulling them closer with his chains to meet their end. They made several thuds to the ground before retreating.

"Come back and fight for your queen, you cowards!" she screamed from the battlement, her voice painted with terror.

Though they regained their vitality, Riann and Mikhail remained in the enchanted chains. The Hag appeared behind Lex and entangled him in smoky tendrils, whispering into his ear. His eyes became a void of nothingness. Riann tumbled in front of Lex, shielding him from the Hag but it was too late. Lex's shoulders slumped. The Hag smiled and he nodded as if being commanded. One forceful pull and Mikhail and Riann were face down on the ground.

"Lex, it's us! Whatever she showed you isn't real!" Mikhail screamed.

Lex dragged them in their chains back into the dark entrance of the castle. Riann lunged for him to wake. "Think of Willa! Willa is out there!!"

Her name echoed far enough for Willa to hear. She stood proud, believing her cymar would fight the spell he was under. Loose hair strands stood upright from behind her ears. A surge of electricity built around us. Heat wiggled in our vision; the torrent skies darkened. Shadows gathered in my hands, pooling, writhing, waiting for command. All that had been taken from me—without choice—had led me here. But this was my moment, was my choice. Pain screamed its way through my body, and my veins pulsated like fire within me. Streams of graphite silver and dark blue ran under my skin, meeting the shadows growing in my hands. No longer did the gold strands meet me. Scents of ether flowed. I turned to face Willa, and she gasped.

She trembled with her hand partially covering her mouth. "Lor, are you still you?"

Sparks of electricity wound around my fingers. My eyes became a storm, a violent tempest. Gravel coated my throat. "I've always been me."

Instead of scythes, two lightning bolts, like white fire, formed in my hands and I held them high for all armies to see. Shock and awe rippled through the masses. Riann once told me I could create and destroy with this star inside me. Today, I was not meant to heal and restore. Destruction became me.

"Blondie's on fire!" Dolos cackled. His blonde curls frayed, strands reaching for the sky.

Battle was beginning, and he was somehow gleeful, excited for carnage. He whipped around his bow and readied an arrow. With one swift pull he shot the arrow into the distance in the east away from the castle. Moments later droves of hobgoblins ran from the courtyard, Grim raising a torch at the helm. Families and their crying children were desperate to find shelter. Though they worked in the castle tirelessly, like Grim, they'd witnessed atrocities and held no power to free themselves from Nyx's grasp. Dolos' arrow was the signal, and this was the time to run as if their lives depended on it. I knew little of them, but I knew they'd helped me avoid being beaten by the sentries before the games.

Dolos smirked and nodded at me before he ran off to play with fire. Most hobgoblins hastened to the forest, but others stationed themselves at various locations around the castle. Grim, breathless, met up with Dolos on the right flank side. Less than a minute later, explosions erupted. Right drum tower. Down. Crumbling. Black, slick stones fell onto the queen's army, sending the rest in a panic. Debris rolled like a tidal wave. We covered our faces and waited for the air to clear. Hobgoblins wrapped Dolos' long fuses into the long night around the tower. Minotaurs would not suspect them as they had served under the prince and the queen for so long.

Grim stood on Dolos' side, wearing his patchwork clothes, holding the detonator in his hand. His wry smile made Dolos laugh. "I've always wanted to do that. I hated that tower," said Grim, handing back the detonator.

Dolos chuckled, marveling over the damage and frenzied mob of minotaur sentries. "Why is that?" he asked, wiping ash from his forehead.

Grim squinted at his kin, jeering at the queen. "It's where she took the prince many times to hurt him."

With a swift move of Nyx's hand, a black shadow fell among the goblins. They fell to the ground, choking on the air. Poison. She was going to wipe them out. They foamed at the mouths, their bloodshot eyes bulging from their sockets. Grim screamed, tearing his clothes. He could have a brother, a son, down there. For the one who rescued me from Phil, I would do anything. The brackish stench of death swallowed me. The lightning retreated inward, and my gold threads pushed its way through my fingertips. My will knew what I needed to do before my mind could fully process what I'd seen. I took my eyes off the battlement and surged my power forward. Every bit of Nyx's shadow dissipated, and waves of gold light fell upon the goblins. The air cleared, and Grim made a run for his people. They appeared bewildered, as if they did not believe they were still alive.

When I looked back up, nobody was on the battlement. *Stay alive*, I told myself. Just long enough. I raised my fist in the air, the lightning bolt returning. Electricity wrapped itself around my arm. No mercy, no mercy. Truthfully, I was merciful. I could have chosen to abandon and forsake each life on Sidh. What they would eventually find out after the battle was that my body was theirs to have. Any enemy who robbed them of their joy, their livelihood, I would incinerate. But afterward, I would be their sacrifice. I tossed a lightning bolt into the heart of Nyx's army. Primal screams ripped through the battlefield. Stifling, burning flesh swam around us in hazy smoke. A shield flew up in front of us marked with gray runes, rotating spells like wheels. Half the queen's army was dead, buzzing with electricity in their corpses. My army behind me shouted, beating their shields, *"Sidus Irae, Sidus Irae!!"*

Willa approached me slowly, warily. "Today, you are a star of wrath. Tomorrow, you will be Lor again."

I raised my fist in the air, opening my palm. "I already told you, I've always been me."

Then my army advanced for the rest of them.

58

RIANN

Panic was the only word to describe the scene of chaos once we were back inside. Lex dragged us in our chains into the throne room. Nyx and her sisters huddled together, their voices screeching like banshees. Nyx slapped the Yaga after she suggested leaving the realm to find another. Nyx's pride kept her heels in the dirt. We couldn't let her leave anyway. Other realms would be at stake if she left, and who was to say she wouldn't return for revenge? Dust fell from the ceilings as they fractured. *Boom! Boom!* Lex came to his senses as the Hag's power wore off during the power struggle with her sisters. They were wise to tighten Lex's chains much to my dismay. War cries flooded my ears. The true people of Sidh were fighting off this regime while we remained hostages.

Lor was clever for not bargaining. It would have been useless. We strained our eyes past the shattered windows. Flashes of gold lit up the darkened sky. Years of oppression crumbled inside the castle walls as light flooded in from Lor's star. Lex grinned with each explosion as raw magic sank its teeth into us, renewing parts we thought were long dead. *Boom! Boom! Boom!*

"I never thought she would be capable of so much, brother. I am genuinely afraid of her." Mikhail chuckled, running his mangled hand down his face.

I smiled back at him. He should be afraid. So should Phil, who charged toward us, his face molten with rage. Sweat beaded across his forehead, red eyes bulging so hard, I prayed they would fall from their sockets. What I would give to get out of these chains and destroy him for not only his betrayal, but for trying to kill Lor.

I scoffed as he closed the distance between us. "Looks like your plans did not go the way you intended."

Phil tightened his grip around the hilt of my sword.

Mikhail cracked a bloody, swollen smile. "If you're about to touch my brother, it would be wise not to. They've blasted the castle gates wide open and any minute this place will be flooded."

Phil's face whipped toward me. "I should have put more oleander in her drink the night the Hag took her. Nothing would have pleased me more than for you to find her rotting body by the Styx," he ground out.

I angled my head, tasting the victory drawing near. "But here we are." Patience tested my fury. The moment the chains fell off, he was mine. *Boom!* Phil stumbled and landed face first onto the fractured marble floor. "Any more lies to spin?" I asked while he struggled to pick himself back up.

Blood from his nose splattered on the ground, and he grunted. Nyx ran inside, hoisting up her bloodied skirt. Only the Hag was present, which did not shock me. She had been about to kill her own son. Murdering her sister seemed like a downgrade.

59

ELORA

Gold and white flames rushed through my body on the slick battlefield. One moment, I was the star of first light, the next I became Lady Wrath. A gray minotaur caught me from behind, raising his blade to my throat. A black streak flew onto me. A pair of gold sparkling eyes of shadows and starlight hovered over me. Kaya. She was no longer a vibrant, colorful faerie but a dark creature releasing pent up magic in her bones. The minotaur staggered, his eyes becoming a black void, his lips peeled back. He did not take a final breath as if death was so sudden. Before I could thank her, she flew off to her next victim.

My eyes remained on everything, everywhere at once. No sentry passed me without a hook on their horn and a rounded blade to their throat. Coated with blood, I resisted the protest of my muscles pulling and tearing with each kill. Our army advanced closer to the castle gates. Sable and Carmine fought on the field like an elegant dance. The swing of their swords, a rhythm to music. Years of oppression and a generation almost lost was their furious melody. Willa moved like she was wind and water, agile yet brutal. Every now and then she would make eye contact with me, pointing her blade with an approving smile. Bloodlust fueled Dolos, completely at war with the wisecracking, sweet man I came to know. He had no bouts with shredding it on the battlefield. There was no competition. His body count was too high.

Most fauns did not fight, save for a few brave ones like Luca. They were on standby for the injured since I could not stop fighting to save everyone. Luca stayed by my side, his jagged short sword plunging into anyone charging my blind spot, though he missed the gray minotaur. Strewn across the wet field lay bodies of minotaurs and my army, mangled, their eyes devoid of life. A sharp edge of guilt shot through me because I could have saved them from dying. But it was nearly impossible in the chaos. If I was willing to sacrifice myself, others must felt the same way. May their memory be a blessing. Dolos clotheslined two minotaurs barreling for me and shoved small explosives in their pockets. He ran toward me and pushed me down covering my body. Pieces of minotaur thudded to the ground. Red mist painted the sky. He said nothing as he smiled above me, his face so close to mine. As the mist cleared, he gently gave me a "good sport" slap to the face and pulled me up. Before I could thank him, he ran off, skipping across the field shooting his arrows.

Something inside me paused at the devastating scene, moving everything in slow motion. I focused on Luca's curls. He kept his sweet countenance while covered in filth, and I could not stand idly by while battle washed away his innocence. He'd survived too much. I imagined that he and Suri would marry and begin their family, build their dreams together. But it was only possible if I completely broke the curse. Nobody else on this battlefield had the power to dream outside of it.

In the center of chaos, I cupped my hands around his face. Those beautiful brown eyes, wide and delirious, stared into mine. His body shook with adrenaline, his precious hands that held his flute to play beautiful songs, were now stained with blood. He was sullied, corrupted.

"Please Luca, it's time for you to leave the field. I can no longer risk your life."

His eyes were glassy. "My lady, we are about to breach the gates."

I pulled him by his nape and his lips shook. "Suri needs you. Do not worry about me. You have been nothing but loyal and kind to me since the moment we met. Remember that well."

His brows knitted together, stuck between loyalty and his future.

"Luca, *live*. As cymar to your prince, I command it," I said, tipping up his chin with the tip of my dagger.

His eyes were a mix of relief and sorrow. "As you wish, my lady." He tightened his arms around my waist and took one last look at me before disappearing into the horizon where his people gathered.

Carmine shouted across the field that they breached the gates. I inhaled sharply. The battlefield was the easy part. If the fates were kind, I would see my cymar one last time.

***

Dolos and Willa walked beside me as we entered the castle, shoulders forward. We ran on adrenaline, making me crave a soft bed to plop on after everything was over. I nearly forgot I would have no rest in the end. I would simply no longer exist. Sable and Carmine were at our heel, finding and destroying anything lurking in the shadows. Gurgled noises and the sounds of bodies of thudding gave me some relief. My arm hairs stood up. Ice whipped around us, and Sable fell to her knees. The Hag. Her familiar breath of cold. Sable had never experienced the kind of dread the Hag's frosty shadows carried.

This was my chance. I glanced at Dolos, the dreamcatcher. He could not destroy her smoke form before, but here she stood in the flesh. Her ethereal eyes darkened, her veins twisted like black vines winding from her hands to her crown. Tresses that were normally lush and pale dried and withered. Crescent moons spun above Dolos' eyes, but when he opened them, I stared into an inky abyss of faint starlight and flame. A thing of nightmares.

Willa gasped, tightening her hand on her hilt. "Dolos! Who are you?!"

Understanding reached her eyes as he grinned, rippling pale blue magic through his veins. Tendrils of energy pulsed from his fingertips the moment he saw the Hag's decayed face. Her true form. She brandished her needle teeth prepared to strike, but it was too late. The moons wrapped around her, spinning like a cyclone. Dolos stood, appearing taller, while his eyes remained shut.

He pulled the Hag into a dream state. Her eyes rolled back. Dolos lifted her cold body from the floor without so much as jutting his chin. A satisfied grin broke on his face. Her bones cracked under the pressure, her screams were inward and hallow. Her hands and feet broke outward, and her skin sank in, becoming pallid. Dolos squeezed his fist, and she gasped for air, desperate to cry out for help.

I planted a hand on his shoulder. "The Hag is yours, brother." I gave Willa a pointed look, trying so hard not convey a farewell. "Willa, steady him, love."

Her arms stiffened. "Where are you going?!"

"Don't worry about me. I'll be right back," I lied. It tasted bitter on my tongue with how easily it came out.

Each turn was a different corridor with similar rooms. Every time I burst open a door, the room was empty or there were servants hiding, quivering. All I wanted was to find Riann, but I couldn't do that yet.

Please, Fates, let me look upon him once more before you claim me.

Illuminating my path from within intricate sconces, crimson candlelight glistened off black onyx stones in the walls. They beckoned me forward. Perhaps after I departed, Riann would take the crown and rule Sidh. Maybe he and Mikhail would fight over it. Whatever they decided to do, I hoped they would let the light in. Once again, I reminded myself that my life was worth all of Sidh. I'd gotten to experience more than most in the short time I'd had lived in the realm. If only I could tell Riann that I only truly started *living* after he'd first spoken to me. Clicking hooves interrupted my thoughts. Minotaurs filed down the next corridor parallel to me. The king was likely there. Nyx would not leave him unprotected. I rounded a corner, quickly counting them. Twenty-eight minotaurs stood in groups of four.

They became still at the sight of me.

Lightning danced between my fingers. "Move or die where you stand."

There weapons wobbled. They side-glanced each other, assessing which was more dangerous—leaving the king or taking me on. The scent of their burning kin wafted into the castle, reminding them of their fate. One by one, weapons fell to the ground.

Clank. Clank. Clank. They slid against the wall, backing away from me before making a run for it. An oak door with a black latch came into view. When I opened it, the king stood in the center of his simple room. A room fit for a servant. Nothing but a small bed and a small side table. I reminded myself he was not real. I was not killing their father. Just his corpse. Such a pitiful sight. He was not a noble father to Riann or Mikhail, but something about his presence made me feel sad for him. His empty eyes gazed into the flames whipping upward from his mantle. He made no indication he noticed me in the room.

My voice softened, pacing around him. "You must be tired of carrying such a heavy burden."

His wrinkled red robes and disheveled gray curls glinted in the firelight. Dark shadows curled beneath him and onto the floor in gentle waves. It stopped a few feet from me, staring at me with its primordial darkness. It was sentient, ancient. My star shuddered and drew back. The shadows snapped and caught me at my feet. I thudded to the ground, landing on my shoulder. I cried out as sharp pain lanced through my side. He was not in control. Algol stared ahead, no hint of emotion. A husk. Shadows dragged me across the floor. My body pulled in several directions, hitting each wall. My head hit the leg of the bed, and my ears rang. Phantom claws dug into me. Maniacal laughter whipped in each direction, echoing across the room. I gasped and shuddered, trying to break free. Tendrils of black wrapped themselves around my wrists and ankles, spreading my arms and legs apart. Keeping quiet about my mission turned out not to be such a good idea. Nobody could hear me cry for help. Suffocating darkness choked every part of me.

A dark male voice erupted. "The ruination of realms has come."

Sulfuric breath and jagged teeth nipped at my neck. My veins popped from straining too hard. Blistering pain stabbed my body into a thousand places. The unseen enemy continued to cackle and bite down on my flesh, feasting on my fear. Everything would be for nothing if I died here.

I cried. "Riann, I am sorry."

Cemented to the ground at Algol's feet, his head slowly dipped to meet my gaze. His clear eyes glazed over. One blink. Two blinks.

His sleeve slinked down his arm as he slowly raised his hand upward. Algol never left my eyes, while I writhed in utter pain. Dark laughter danced over my body from this shadow being. Algol's hand swiftly reached inside his own body, without a sound, and pulled the horn out. Dropping it into my hand, its power amplified mine, surging through my body. Sharp edges of different shades of silver and gold burst forth, swallowing the shadows whole. The horn's broken spiral was bronze, shimmering all colors in the light. A mere brush of the tip sliced into my palm.

Algol's body dropped to the floor. A piece of him was still in there. He'd lived all these years, by a thread. Nyx kept him alive, which led me to believe she was not powerful enough to raise the dead. And that meant she was easily overthrown. She had created a world of fear with a spark of dark magic and the horn. She believed she was unstoppable. Without it, however, Nyx would fall. Algol looked at me, regret forming lines around his face. Though the world outside needed me, I could not let him die alone. As hard as I tried, I blocked out all the noise and sat beside him. He could not move his head or speak, but the slight clenching of his boney hand wrapped around mine. All the torture he'd experienced caught up in real time. His hand withered in mine, his breathing short and shallow. His eyes shook. If he could have cried, he would have.

"Riann will know one day that you gave your life for us and saved his cymar," I said, unsure how Riann would discover his father becoming an unsung hero.

"Algol, I wished things were different, but your sons… though they act like they hate each other, I truly see a deep affection. Whatever you did or didn't do, they turned out to be great men." I took a deep breath, my lips quivering, "I wish I would have known what it is like to have your grandchildren, for them to play in the castle, while Riann and Mikhail argue over something stupid. I think we would roll our eyes at each other and break up their little fight." I smiled, tears falling into my mouth. "But Fates are not kind, are they?"

I wiped my face with my arm and found the decaying creases of his face relaxing. He found a kernel of peace. I brushed back his brittle hair behind his ear. "Riann and Mikhail will forgive you. Be at peace, King Algol."

Algol took a deep breath, letting his soul depart from his body, giving himself away at the sound of his sons' names. Rapidly, his body decayed inside his robes. His bones became dust, and withered flesh turned into a fine powder. For good measure, I thanked him by setting his robe on fire. No time for a proper funeral, but at least nobody could ever take him again. His ashes skirted around the room, covering my boots. I wished I could live to tell Riann that his father had saved me. In the end, perhaps his father would be known as the savior of this day, and not me.

60

MIKHAIL

Everything happened too fast. Dolos and Willa set us free from our chains, except for Riann who was at the furthest part of the room. I never knew Dolos was a dream catcher until he pulled me into a dream to break the black star links off me. My chains fell off in real time when he threw me out of my dream state. Nyx strode in like she was still queen, hoisting her skirts over the rubble and debris. The castle was under siege, and she believed her crown, my father's crown, held weight. I said something flippant to her, and the next thing I knew, we were pinned to the wall before they could reach Riann. Her dark magic held us there, though I felt it was becoming unstable with every wobble and twitch of her face. We were too high up. Blood rushed to my feet. I would hate to drop from this height. She cruelly turned Sable and Carmine upside down as punishment for their healed wombs. Lex reached for Willa, but the black magic seized our bodies, pulling us onto the wall. Cemented in the center of a crimson circle before the dais, Riann was like a sacrifice offering. I'd never seen the arches of the castle this close before. Someone had inscribed on the rafters, *King of Rot, Prince of Spring*. The words were likely older than Riann. Sidh had its fair share of rotten kings over the eons and today we stood against its ruthless queen. I would carve next to it: *Queen of Cravens, Starlight and Flame*.

Archways cracked and splintered, gold light flooding them, shaking their foundations. Phil shielded his eyes like the weakling that he was and fell into fetal position as the entrance exploded.

Falling rock and debris nicked my face. A silhouette took shape in the smoke. Lor appeared, waving bands of gold infinity circles, pushing back against the dark magic. I hoped it would just take a little of her blood, and then all would be restored. A lump lodged in my throat. My foolish hope could kill her. Nyx's attention waned from us while running across the throne room and onto the dais. We dropped to the floor. My bones screamed and I saw white in my vision. Lor fixed her eyes on Riann while we tried to gain our bearings. Carmine shouted that he'd broken his leg. Lor had no time to heal. She came to destroy.

My mother pulled every shadow in the throne room, gathering them into her hands. A harsh wind blew and for the first time in ages, complete darkness blanketed the skies. The room quaked, knocking everyone but Nyx to their feet. "You think you can overpower me!? There is something in me you cannot defeat, lilac child!" her guttural voice echoed.

Crimson energy erupted from Nyx's fingers, blasting Lor across the room. Lor flailed above as the wind caught her, buoying her. Riann outstretched his arms, screaming her name, but he couldn't move. A cacophony of red and gold threads flashed above us in violent fury. Nyx hurled Lor's bludgeoned body from one wall to the next. A normal person would have died by now. Terror sliced through me. Nyx smiled with each wave of her hand. We inched forward and took steps back into the maelstrom. Lor caught her hand on the mile-long curtain, anchoring herself to the ground. Limping, she was pale and breathing heavily. Then, I saw it in her hand, completely covered in her blood. I was wrong. So wrong. I sentenced her to death.

"Whatever you bound yourself to is mine! You stand alone!" Lor screamed, raising the horn.

Horror washed down the queen's face. Nyx fell back onto her throne, kicking back as if there were somewhere to go.

"Lor! Get these chains off! I will finish her myself!" Riann bellowed, the wind muffling his voice.

Her eyes glistened, as if saying goodbye. She glowed from within, sorrow and longing rippling down her face. A goddess of light and love before us, my heart began to crack. She considered me *family*. After all I had done, the abuse I inflicted, she forgave me and bestowed upon me the mercy of her presence. I should have never taken things into my own sullied hands. I should have never told her the ultimate price for breaking the curse. I had hoped and dreamed my mother was not as powerful as it seemed, but with the horn, she was. Then, the goddess of light shifted into darkness and furious starlight.

Lor extended her hand, holding Riann in place, while walking up the dais, overcoming the wind. Her eyes became dark like pitch, a tempest roaring from beneath her irises. Before, she only wielded the star of first light, but this was different. Something dark and formidable writhed all around her. Shadows slid from the walls meeting her with every step as if they bowed to her. Rain poured into the throne room through the blasted ceiling. Lightning wound around Lor from head to toe like a pet snake, ready to strike. Riann weakened under the pressure of Lor's magic. She never intended for Riann to leave that circle. My stomach pooled with dread.

"Lor!" I screamed, slipping on the water. But she did not look back.

Nyx's hands slackened to her sides. Her eyes bulged, mouth gaping. The power she once wielded largely diminished in Lor's presence. We fell back again—except for Lor. She rose upon the top of the dais, swathed in dark energy.

Don't, Lor!" I screamed again. "We can find another way!"

Riann snapped his head at me.

Dolos and Willa realized what was happening, and they scrambled to their feet, searching for purchase, but the wind pulled them back. I was not sure who controlled the wind anymore. Dolos almost made It to Rlann before the wind dragged him against the wall. Riann wriggled, using every muscle in his body to set himself free, but her will was stronger.

"Lor! We can live with the curse, just please..." he begged, every ounce of dignity bleeding from him. "Don't do this!" She refused to turn around, her shoulders shaking. "We have tomorrow, right!? We always have tomorrow!"

Fresh tears streamed down her face as she turned her back to the queen. She squeezed her eyes tight, trembling. Her beautiful eyes swept over all of us, a farewell she could barely muster. The rain, the lightning ceased with a nod of her head.

"I love you," her voice rasped, holding in the anguish we felt in the air.

She raised the horn. Nyx's blood curdling scream deafened our ears. Lor plunged the horn into her heart too fast, much too fast, as if she would stop herself if she didn't do it quickly. She staggered. Her surprised eyes transfixed on Riann, whispering *sorry* over and over. Riann stiffened. Threads of light dimmed from her veins. Then, she collapsed. Crashed. Like a star. Lor's precious essence of life spread down the steps of the dais. Her chest no longer moved, and her eyes became devoid of life. All was silent except for her wrist hitting the floor. Silas was right. Love is blood spilled on altars.

Riann ripped his blue flesh off, revealing bronzed skin covered in whorls of runes of intricate design. Cannons of magic splintered through his bones, finding their rightful owners. Fiery orange, blue and black streams filled Dolos, Willa, and Lex. They took it in with a deep breath. Their skin glowed from within, filling them with new life. Bits of clotted blood and flesh clung to Riann as he misted to the throne. Nyx tried to plead her case with blubbering words, but in a matter of seconds, her entire spine was on the floor. I almost threw up. I wanted to be sad for her; after all, she was my mother, but I just couldn't. Anything we had ever shared stopped at DNA. In a blink of an eye, Riann held Lor, cradling her body.

"What about tomorrow, Lor?" he wept and roared again. Grief over a cymar was turbulent. Violent. I could not comprehend it. I was supposed to have died that day. Riann should have killed me for what I'd done.

I rose to my feet. The loss burned the back of my throat. "Brother," my breath rattled, "I only told her the truth because I hoped just a little of her blood would do."

Pain etched across his face. His fingers gripped her lifeless arms tightly. "You led her to the slaughter. I waited eight hundred years for her. I couldn't care less about my powers. I had her. She was enough."

Lex glared at me, then placed his huge hand on my shoulder, squeezing, giving a silent threat. He then roared with Riann. Dolos and Willa followed.

Father's crown lay on its side by Riann's feet. "I don't want it," he snarled, his voice echoing through the crumbling throne room. He kicked it at me, sending it tumbling to my feet.

"Brother, please…my intention was for her to live." Tears slid down my face.

"Was any of it real?"

"Some of it."

How I wished to go back and tell Lor she'd restored my hope to love again. In the end, she did not do this solely to save her family. For a tiny blip in time, she'd felt loved and knew what it would be like for others to lose their families. She did it for them and for the ones without family. Pain pricked my core, replaying our last conversation. Lor had forgiven me, considering me as family, even after all I had done. She and Riann could have lived comfortably under a stale curse while others suffered. But no. She gave her life without hesitation. Fates were cruel. Lor used to want to die because she believed she would never be loved. Now that she was loved by many, she had died for them. Ironic. The realization ripped open a wound in my heart I hoped would fester as a daily reminder of Lor's sacrifice and my brother's loss.

Phil pulled himself up from the rubble, attempting to flee. Riann bared his teeth watching the coward run and burned the letter T into the back of his neck with a flick of his wrist. Riann growled. "Vagabond traitor, you shall always be. That is far worse than death for you. I have destroyed your powers." Riann angled his head toward his blade. "Leave my sword."

Phil's eyes guttered. A red river no longer swirled in them but a pale faded color as if Riann had leeched the life from him. Riann's sword clanged on the floor, the blue threads pulsing to life in the hilt. Phil left in haste, and I promised myself that I would see to his long, painful death if he ever stepped into this kingdom again.

Dolos did not care to lift his head. He looked upon Lor as a brother, and I hated it. I wished I had chosen differently to be worthy like him. He muttered over and over, "Sister, sister."

Sunlight spilled into the throne room for the first time since the curse. A light breeze wafted through the broken windows, and something sweet and floral floated in the air. A slight charge of electricity buzzed my ears. Wren and Kaya flew in, astonished by the sight. Their wings quaked, and they fell to the floor at Riann's feet. Wren wept loudly, cursing the runes he carved into her for failing to protect her. It seemed I was the only one who noticed the change in the throne room. Wave after wave of electricity made my hair stand up. I looked at Lex's burly arm, and his hair also stood up.

Lor's body dematerialized in Riann's arms. Leathers were left behind. No trace of her. Riann dug into her leathers, panicking.

"Where is she?! Where's my cymar!?" His broken voice wrenched.

Searching for her, a deluge of tears overflowed, spilling behind his parted lips. He found the laurel and gardenia wreath she'd hidden in her backpack and the ring he'd given her. Fates. I hated the Fates. Riann had waited eight hundred years for this happiness, only for Lor to be taken from him ruthlessly. As if struck by lightning, Riann fell like a ton of bricks.

61

ELORA

F alling. Falling. An endless dark abyss awaited me after I sank the horn into my chest. Searing, burning pain, seemed to last forever. I beheld Riann's face, completely overcome with indescribable pain. His crying, pleading voice faded as my whole world went black. Hair whipped my face like shards of glass, and I wanted to scream. Light, airy fabric curved against my body, which was impossible. I'd died wearing—a thunderous realization ripped through me. I'd died. And this was death. *Let me go back. Please.* I needed to know if my sacrifice meant something, to know if Riann and the rest of my family were okay and Sidh was safe. Agony lanced through my chest, but I couldn't cry from the sheer velocity of falling deeper. *I beg you. Whoever holds the chains of death on me right now, I will go easily. Just let me know that everyone is okay. Please.*

Crash! My back landed into a few feet of water, hitting the bottom of a smooth rock, yet it did not hurt. I didn't know how I'd been able to do this to myself while looking into Riann's frightened eyes and watching him struggle to break free. Had I done the right thing? I was no person of consequence in the earthly realm, but I had become loved, someone to mourn over. It was tortuous to be trapped in quiet darkness while they grieved over me. I would rather have their memories wiped clean of me so they could live in peace.

A sharpened edge of blueish silvery light broke through the darkness. Then another light of gold and green accompanied by red-orange hues surrounded me in a circle of whispers. Glittering stars swirled in a violent tempest, materializing into three women veiled in their colors. The gold one extended her pale hand, and slowly I rose. All the water disappeared, and I was wearing an elegant white gossamer gown. My wound continued to pulse, blood soaking the right side of my dress.

"You have done what nobody else could do." Her voice simmered. Golden hair peeked from behind her silk veil.

My shoulders shook as I stepped forward. The light they held felt familiar and distant, like a faded memory. I stumbled closer to them, prompting Red to put her arms out to keep our distance. My throat felt like sandpaper. "Who are you?"

"We have many names, but the one your cymar refers to us is of hate," the blue one said, a voice like calm waters. "We have aided him many times without his knowledge. Even in bringing you to him."

"Fates," I grumbled. "Do you not think it is rather cruel to give him his chief desire, only to take it away so quickly?"

"We did not take what you easily gave!" the red one shouted, raising her first just high enough to see her cracked face. "We are still for him, for you, child of first light."

I moved past Red's arms, and they appeared to grow larger. "Is he well? Is everything okay? Did I do the right thing?"

Gold shuffled her elongated sleeves, baring cracked arms veined with a green light thrumming through her. All three appeared as fractured porcelain dolls. "We are not in the business of telling the future if it means interfering with the things to come."

"You can't do that!" I screamed, echoing in the vastness. "I gave everything. I died for this! I beg you, please!" My knees gave out, pulling me to the ground, and an endless echo of the thud traveled.

Blue patted my head. "Child of first light. You are among the living. There is too much life inside you. We cannot allow your death. Neither will he who empowers us."

I leapt forward, grabbing the hem of Blue's dress. "Take me back then!"

Blue came down to my level, caressing her hand across my waist, her hands like a gentle stream. "You might see your family again by choosing to walk through this door." Blue pointed at a rectangular shape in the darkness, edged with red light.

"Really?" My throat bobbed. Hope reached my eyes. I could go home. It was all I wanted. *Home.*

Gold tipped my chin with her warm, graceful finger. "You are the child of first light. A beacon. A maker and destroyer. A healer and a monster. He chose rightly to give you this star because of your heart. Your cymar was destined to give you all that he had. You've awakened realms, and now you shall take your place behind this door."

Nothing she said registered. My thoughts alone revolved around Riann and my family. "You said I *might* see my family again, that implies they are okay, right?"

"Let's just say we have a way of saying things without saying them," Gold said, her emerald, green light webbing down her arms.

"What are your names?"

Red put herself between Gold and me. "Names are powerful. You know this. We are nameless. No creature can invoke us." Her voice was molten and fiery, burning into me like a brand. She held out her hand, pulling me up with a command.

As I nervously walked toward the dark door, I looked back, watching them hold hands.

"Do not be afraid, Elora Addison. Every decision, every experience, every bit of suffering has brought you here. Now, shine," Blue reassured me.

With a gentle push, the door cracked open. Brutal red light flooded to the point I could not see what was in front of me. I shielded my eyes, desperate to back away. This was not where I wanted to go. This was not it. They'd lied. My heart fell into panic. Riann wasn't here. Harsh wind pulled me closer inside, not taking no for an answer. I grabbed the door frame, my nails digging into the wood as I screamed, begging to go home. The wood splintered in the frame. The intensity of the force pulled me in further. My legs swept from beneath me as I held on with the last bit of strength. My power meant nothing in this void of space and time. Whatever they wanted was meant to happen. Fates stood behind me, unperturbed by my anguished pleas.

“No, don’t make me go in!” I begged, wind and tears stinging my face.

“Be gone, child,” Gold said with a flick of her wrist.

The door pushed me in, and it shut. Forever.

62

RIANN

Sitting by the lake waiting for this unicorn to show up and take back the horn tested my patience. It did not help that I'd picked a fight with Lex on our way home after Willa tried to talk me down. All I said was to throw me into the Styx, forgetting it no longer existed. Dark elves must have already gone back to their original homes where they could practice necromancy and scare the living daylights out of people. Kaya refused to go back right away. She'd become her true form, a princess of the night. Her long, inky black hair crowned her slender pale face, and her golden eyes flashed at me from the corner of the house several times before I finally gave up looking behind.

I didn't know how to live, but I also didn't know how to die. Too many times, death had crouched its foul presence at my feet and never succeeded. One would have thought I had more to live for, but life without Lor was no life at all. The heavy concern of my friends pressed on my back. I felt it from the house. They were worried, but I couldn't help but scowl at their overbearing consideration of me. After all, they were grieving too. Lor's blood still stained my hands. I was afraid of removing it because it would mean wiping the essence of her existence away forever.

My original skin was now intact. Runes and whorls of black ink trailed from my shoulders down my arms like they'd never disappeared. Black curls hung above my brows, itching my forehead. My sharpened nails became curved, manicured. Lor had dealt with so many scratches from me but never complained. She would never know what I truly looked like. My chest caved in, and I lost my will to breathe. I missed her. I missed her smell, her skin, her laughter, and how she lit up when she ate. I missed it all. And it consumed me.

I put the horn in a few inches of water, and seconds later, every kelpie, including Lynx, popped their heads above the surface. Lynx lay beside me, nuzzling his head onto my lap. I wanted to pet him, but I was in no mood to give any part of me right now—no matter how small. I had been content to live under the curse if it meant being with her. But Lor would have never wanted that. Even with the queen dead, Sidh needed the restoration to guard itself against more enemies—because once you snuffed out one, another would always spring up.

Waters parted, making way for this illustrious unicorn. Luna trotted her way to me and kneeled. For a beat, she stayed on her knees before settling the rest of her body. "As I told her, I was sorry for her loss," Luna said, bowing her head.

My teeth clenched. "You knew her choice. You knew she'd die."

"Sweet Riann, she did what was necessary."

"Stop it! Death is hardly ever necessary!!" I wretched the horn away from her. Her calm eyes lowered as if she had lost something too.

Luna extended her leg, touching me. "Riann, how well do you know your cymar? How well did she know herself?"

My blood boiled at the most absurd question. "I know her better than most."

"Right, you know her heart. Her triggers, her likes, her dis-likes. You know all the ways to give her butterflies." Luna lifted her head. "Magnus warned you. Riann, you do not know her."

I leaned forward. "What are you talking about?"

"Who is she, Riann?" Luna asked.

"I thought you were supposed to answer that."

Luna chuckled, eyeing her horn. "You've waited so long, and you don't know who your cymar truly is? The cosmos must really have fun with you."

I shot to my feet, horn in hand like a dagger. "Do you want this or not!?"

"Please put the horn on my head, and I will help you," her voice was somber yet irritated.

At first, I hesitated, but Lor's blood had paid for this, and I could not let it be in vain. The horn fused to Luna's stump, and a fresh wave of breezy rainbows scattered over the waters.

"Thank you, I shall return promptly to Caer;" her eyes darted behind me. "We miss you, Dolos!" I caught Dolos "cleaning" the side of the house as he waved back to Luna in embarrassment. "I love embarrassing him," she laughed. Luna straightened herself up, in a perfect stance. She flipped her mane to the side, gesturing for me to get up.

"Who is she?" Luna asked again.

"She's the unfortunate girl who crossed her path with me," I said, half-believing those words.

Her voice became stern. "Once again, who is she?"

"She is the one who carries the star of first light."

"Nice answer, but no. You have won battles in so many realms, changed the time continuum, snapped the threads of those who could no longer live, and you can't figure out the simplest thing. Is Lor one of adoration, one frozen in time? Does she not enchant you in that way? She's been under your nose your whole life."

I wanted to punch this unicorn.

"This conversation is tiring me, and home is calling," Luna yawned. She backed into the water and began to fade. "She lives, son of Rinarie." Then, she disappeared.

Impossible. I'd held Lor's body. Nothing made sense. I grabbed the biggest rock and hurled it into the lake, forgetting my restored strength. It hit the mountain, miles down the lake, making a rumbling noise from the crack I made. My mind melted. It had been so long without all my magic that I needed to re-acclimate my mind and my body to it. I used to be quicker on my feet. *Come on. Think. Think!*

Luna was cruel enough to say something without saying it—just like the Fates. The black string came to mind. The thread that had reached for the spindle but would never attach itself. An anomaly. One I could not figure out before the curse. Frozen in time? What did it mean? I crouched on the ground, trying to breathe, filling my hands with small, washed-up rocks, pulverizing them to dust.

Does she not enchant me? Of course, she enchanted me, but I truly had not known her until she was much older. It was impossible Lor had been under my nose my whole life. My eight hundred years of living, filled with war, time continuums and...Then something snapped. It couldn't be. Impossible. I'd watched the day of her birth. But time. Time was irrelevant.

I sprinted inside, bumping into every little thing, pushing anyone out of my way. My study felt further away even as I turned the brass knob. Time changed everything. The truth glared at me, and I let out a punishing scream. Lor was the anomaly, the whisper of ancients. My own spindle tried to tell me before I buried it far away from Sidh. I truly did not know her, but I swore to myself that if I found her, I would promise to discover her every day. Dolos, Lex, and Willa ran after me, and one by one, we fell to our knees. Sunlight bathed the room, making the paint colors bounce with vibrancy. This couldn't be. Swathed in white and adorned with her scythes, her lilac eyes pierced me from the painting on the wall. My lips parted, but no words came out. None of us could speak. A red waste stood behind her, her hands filled with light. Silver, four-pointed stars encircled her like an infinity loop. A beginning and an end. The empress. My painting came to life. The one I'd admired and adored and only half believed she ever existed. She who destroyed the Astryx was my cymar, my only. She always was and always had been.

And I needed to find her.

ACKNOWLEDGEMENTS

It took me two years to write this book, but the conception had been birthed long before. When I was little, I loved watching fantasy movies at my grandparents' house. Some I should not have been watching at such a young age, but it produced a hunger in me to dream for the impossible. When I watched *Willow, Labyrinth,* or *Never-Ending Story*, it stirred a deep place in me to come up with stories of princesses and elves. However, my writing dwindled down for many years, and I was so tired of stories running rampant in my brain. After COVID hit and we were all on lockdowns I began to write again in a small two-bedroom apartment with no desk or fancy Book Tok aesthetics. Finding my writer's voice was difficult, but thanks to my husband, who left me alone for hours to write, I was able to. He took our son out on the town just so I could write in peace. He read one of the first drafts overnight and even shed some tears—which really encouraged me, though I kept pestering him for finite details of his opinions. Thank you to my cheerleading squad: Mom, Tracy, Audrey, Paulina, and Ellen. Love you guys!! Thank you, God for your incredible patience with me, my one constant in every season. Thank you to my extended family who supported me through this process. To all the women out there who read this and relate to the material, I am with you and for you.

ABOUT THE AUTHOR

Raised by faeries and sirens when she was little, this author found a way to live on land, fly, and swim while sending sailors to their deaths. Whether she was fighting pirates or hunting orcs with her own fellowship, she found the time to drift away from this world to imagine lands far off and write about them. In those imaginary places, she envisioned a world where women were free of chains that bound them.

Alas, when she awakens from these dreams and is not writing, Jennifer Leigh is enjoying Mexican food and watching the latest fantasy series, anime, reading a good book, and spending time with her family